HUNTING AND HERBALISM

BOOK THREE

HUNTING AND HERBALISM

BOOK THREE

Leif Roder

aka Synonymoose

Podium

Cover design by Jason Nathaniel Artuz

ISBN: 978-1-0394-7501-4

Published in 2025 by Podium Publishing
www.podiumentertainment.com

Podium

HUNTING AND HERBALISM

BOOK THREE

CHAPTER ONE

Saviour

Zalia

Zalia quietly crept through the woods, bow in hand and Boreal by her side. She had left the desert behind some two days ago and encountered the first of the demons that roamed Endaria. They were similar to the winged ones she had fought back in Cormaine yet smaller, much smaller.

They had been easy to kill, only Tin and Iron ranked, with the strength of her Healing Presence aura enough to counter their own weak corrupting auras, rendering them helpless. Unfortunately, killing them had brought attention from something not so easy to kill.

A Silver ranked winged demon much like the one that had . . . that had killed Delphi. Seeing it had brought that memory back from the vault where she kept it stored.

They had fled, vanishing into a patch of woods. There, Zalia and Boreal had the home ground advantage. There, they had been able to lose their enemy, disappearing further into the kingdom.

Things were bad, but . . . not as bad as she expected. The little news she had received from the woman, Sazcha, in the desert had made it seem like everything was on fire, destroyed by demons and humans warring.

There was some of that, patches of land withered and dead, towns with chunks missing from their centres where an explosion had gone off. Or worse yet, towns where a group of the roaming demons had appeared and slaughtered everyone. Signs of battles having taken place, entire swaths of land trampled, burnt, and broken.

It was at one such ritual site that she first discovered land corrupt. What was once perhaps a beautiful, bubbling brook was now the scene of a dried-up riverbed, withered trees, and soundless, still, noxious air. The stark comparison of the corrupt land, which formed an almost visible border between life and death, served to increase how bad the corruption looked, but to Zalia it was nothing compared to Cormaine. Her healing aura swept over the patch of land, trees shifting and cracking, their twisted shapes returning to ones of health and vigor. Dead, grey grass grew green again, sprouting upwards as flowers shot from between once dead blades. The toxic air was blown away in a fresh breeze smelling of earth and green growth. The land was alive once more, thrumming with the energy of life. It felt . . . right.

She continued onwards, doing what she could, using her healing to wipe away the patches of corrupted land, burying the dead where she was able if their numbers weren't too great.

Despite all the bad she found, there were still large chunks of land unaffected by the battles being fought. Green forests, endless plains, rushing rivers, and still lakes. She had missed all of it so, so much. The sky above was blue and the air fresh. Her time in Cormaine had made her forget these things, but the beauty of the world brought joy back to her mind.

Too bad it was overshadowed by the sights she saw and that . . . memory.

She was focusing on making her way to the north. By her best guess she was in the southeast of Endaria, which was a shame since she wanted to get northwest. Fortunately, she could first travel north and see if the rebellion was still camped up where she had last seen them.

She highly doubted that. Last she had spoken to them, they had plans to launch an assault on the centre of Endaria, the capital and home of the king. Still, it was as good a destination for now as any. Until she found some other trace of life, that was.

So far, all of the towns she had come across had been empty, devoid of life. Whether they had been unoccupied due to the occupants fleeing, or the death of the entire population, empty they were. She was still on the outskirts of the kingdom, though, so she had hopes that some bigger towns would have survived.

"Ready to keep moving?" Zalia whispered to Boreal.

They were currently sitting in the boughs of a large tree, hidden amongst the higher up branches and leaves. She'd decided that flying wasn't worth the risk of drawing the attention of another Silver ranked demon, or worse. They were quick enough on foot that it wouldn't make a huge difference.

Boreal looked up from where she rested, head on paws, tail dangling down.

"*Sleep?*" Boreal asked, blinking her eyes slowly.

"Not here, we have to keep moving," Zalia said.

Boreal breathed out a slow breath.

"You don't even have to sleep more than once a week or so," Zalia added.

Boreal looked at her as if to say, "Not having to doesn't stop wanting to."

Zalia lithely stepped over and poked Boreal in the nose. Boreal promptly covered her face with a paw.

"Come on, let's go. If you want to, you can sleep a whole day when we find some semblance of a resistance to this whole demon invasion," Zalia promised, knowing full well Boreal would be too excited to sleep when they saw the others again.

It worked though, and Boreal finally got up.

They travelled for a few hours before finally finding the first signs of human life. It looked to be a group of refugees, maybe two dozen, with four guards in armour that looked a little worse for wear.

She quickly moved back and stepped out onto the game path they were travelling down single file.

"Hey there!" she called out, somewhat quietly.

The lead guard froze and looked around, searching for the voice, whilst the few behind him looked at him in confusion, like they hadn't heard her.

"Who's out there?" the first guard called.

In a manner quite unlike meeting Sazcha, they couldn't see her despite being maybe ten metres down the narrow track. Maybe they had no perception abilities?

Remembering some of her early testing with passives, she willed the Stealth passive to stop.

It still took a second before the first guard's eyes caught on her, and she quickly removed her helmet, just in case.

"Stop right there. You with the 'king' or the rebellion?" he called out, disdain entering his voice at the word "king."

He now had his beaten-down wooden heater shield held up, hand on his side sword. The soldiers behind him were similarly on guard, with the civilians beginning to murmur.

"The rebellion. I've spoken with General Faian and General Ballast, if you know them. You?" Zalia asked, though she hardly needed to.

"Aye, the rebellion. What are you doing out here by yourself?" he asked, more relaxed, but still somewhat on guard.

"Trying to find the army, I've been out of Endaria on a little bit of a mission for quite some time. Since the day the glowing beams hit the sky, really," Zalia explained.

The first guard was Bronze rank, and she could tell by the way he stood, despite the worn-down armour, that he was an experienced soldier.

"Well, you're close, they're four days' walk north and west. If you'd like to come back down south so we can deliver this group of refugees, you can come back with us north. Groups are better than alone these days," the guard suggested.

"I'll be alright, I need to get what I know to the generals, might help with the war," Zalia explained. "Uh, and I saw one of the Silver ranked flying ones some two hours back, might be worth taking a detour around east ways."

"Thanks, and that we will, a little lost time is better than losing all of it," he said.

"Good luck on your journey—what's your name? So I can tell the generals you're alive," Zalia asked

"Hendrik, and you?" he asked.

"Zalia," she said.

"Good luck on your journey, Z—" He cut off, staring at her. "Not the Zalia that died stopping the ritual from working?"

"Well, I'm not dead and the ritual still worked, but yes, that Zalia. Why?" she asked in confusion.

Then, to her surprise, he knelt.

"Thank you for the sacrifice you made," he said solemnly, like he was speaking an oath.

"What?" Zalia asked, even further confused. She eyed the kneeling man wearily. "Please stand up."

Hearing the conversation, some of the townspeople behind the guard were muttering to each other and giving her looks ranging from confusion to admiration.

The guard stood up at her request.

"It's an honour to meet you, though I don't understand how you're alive."

"I don't understand why you think I was dead, or even why you know who I am," Zalia said.

The guard was starting to look a little confused as well.

"Well, we've all heard the story. You, Lady Indis, and Ember went to the top of the tower at Endelbyrn, and when the kingdom-wide ritual took place, you sacrificed yourself to cause a chain reaction that shut down the whole thing. Some of the demons got through, and other ritual sites exploded from some type of feedback, yet it was stopped. All thanks to you. Except, you're not dead," he explained, a frown forming on his face.

"You know of Indis and Ember? Are they alive? What of Zen and Larel, they were on that tower too, are they alright?" Zalia asked, a frown also forming on her face. It seemed there was some sort of misunderstanding.

"They are alive and well, last I heard. Lady Indis has become a great leader, but Ember we haven't seen in a while. She has a tendency to run about on her own anyway. I'm not sure who Zen or Larel are, but I heard the story from Lady Indis's mouth herself. I'm sure she would have mentioned if there was someone else on the tower that day," the guard replied.

"I'm sure she would have," Zalia said coldly. Indis would have some explaining to do when Zalia found her.

There was a moment of silence as the two of them regarded each other before Zalia put her helmet back on.

"Best get going again. Safe travels Hendrik," she said, waving an idle hand. "Come, Boreal!"

Boreal emerged from the tree line, causing quite a few of the people listening to jump in surprise.

Zalia allowed her Stealth passive to take effect once more, and the two of them stepped back into the woods, moving around the group of refugees.

"Safe travels to you, too!" the guard called out, followed by a muttered, "Like a forest spirit or something."

Zalia thought about the odd conversation as she walked. The way the man had knelt and spoken made it seem like he thought of her as some sort of war hero or something. She wasn't really surprised that Indis and the others had thought she was dead. In all fairness, there were quite a few moments where she would have died, but had been saved by luck or the fact that her powers were strongly based around survival.

The part of the conversation that confused her the most was the guard saying he had heard the story from Indis herself. Did he know Indis?

Well, she would get an explanation when she found *Lady* Indis either way.

The guard had said there was a camp four days' walk north and west, which would put them closer to the capital than they had previously been, but definitely not as close as they should have been if all had gone to plan. Unless the plan had changed. Or the plan they had told her hadn't really been the plan in the first place.

It made sense to her that would be the case. The chances of her group being able to lie with any success to the Hidden was a ridiculous notion to her now. That was an opinion she held only because of the absolute failure their attempt had yielded. She felt like she had learned a lot in the time she had spent in this new world. A lot of things about dealing with people that she hadn't previously needed in her old life.

The whirlwind of stress and emotion that had been her life previous to Cormaine had been the cause of not a small number of bad decisions. Going forward, she just needed to learn from those decisions.

It was two more days of travel, healing corrupted lands, and killing small groups of demons when necessary. Two more days before she came across the next living person.

She and Boreal were travelling across the plains, keeping to the long grass and low bushes as cover. They had just come from another town that had been empty, though this one had shown no signs of combat or damage. It had simply been empty, evacuated perhaps.

A scream resounded from the trees to their right. It was shrill, high-pitched. Both Zalia and Boreal froze, staring towards the origin of the sound until its source came into view. It was a child, a young girl, running out of the tree line.

They didn't move at first, watching as the girl ran through the long grass across where their path would have led.

Then they saw what the girl was running from. It was a new type of demon than the ones they had seen before. It had four legs, and much like Boreal, it blended into the woods and surroundings like it was born into them. Its jaw split much further than looked natural, and its head and body were sleek, yet covered with a . . . slimy substance.

The creature was stalking the child, almost toying with her in a manner not unlike a cat with a mouse.

Neither Zalia nor Boreal said anything as they moved as one. Boreal ran out to the right, vanishing into the grass as Zalia ran straight towards the demon. She used her teleport to gain as much distance as she could before releasing two arrows in quick succession.

The arrows took it by surprise, both nailing into its torso just behind the front shoulder. Its head jerked to the side, spotting Zalia as a deep growl resounded. Rather than running at her, it slunk back into the woods and vanished.

Zalia stopped, carefully watching the tree line as the child kept running.

"*Run to your left, child,*" Zalia said into the girl's mind.

Luckily, the child did as she was told, running closer towards Zalia as she crept carefully forward.

"*Do you see it?*" Zalia asked Boreal.

Her question was promptly answered as the demon came flying out from the tree line, followed soon after by Boreal in her armour. The two thrashed and clawed at each other in a ball of metal and flesh as they rolled through the plains.

They smashed through the long grass near the fleeing child, and Zalia ran forward to help. The demon was Bronze ranked, an even match for Boreal, though the heirloom armour she wore gave a distinct advantage. While the demon bore deep wounds, Boreal was fairly unharmed, only her armour bearing any damage.

Closer now, Zalia could feel the aura of corruption and countered it with her own, pushing her Healing Presence into Boreal to keep her safe.

The child finally reached her, and she pushed the girl behind herself, trying to find a good shot as the other two brawled. Boreal finally disengaged and Zalia shot the demon in the back leg, crippling it. The wounded demon limped back, but was frozen to the floor by ice summoned by Boreal.

That spelled the end for the creature as Boreal pounced, slamming the demon to the ground, her jaws grappling onto its head. A crunch and an unearthly sound resounded before all was silent.

The silence was broken only by the crying child behind her.

"You're alright, you're safe now," Zalia said, quickly turning and taking her into a hug.

The girl tried to say something but failed through the sobs.

"Where are your parents?" Zalia asked gently, holding the girl by the shoulders.

The only response was the girl's eyes locking onto the body of the demon behind her.

"Oh, you poor child," Zalia said, hugging her once more.

CHAPTER TWO

Camp

Zalia

Zalia picked up the child and moved away from the dead demon until the long grass covered it up. She put her down and kneeled.

"Where did you come from, is your town nearby?" she asked the kid.

The child shook her head.

"Did you leave home to try to find somewhere safer?" Zalia asked.

The girl gave a little nod, her hands rubbing at her eyes as she continued to cry.

Zalia stood, looking around. They couldn't stay here for long; the sound the demon had made when it died was much too loud to not have brought some attention. First she needed to go check something.

"Boreal, come protect her for a moment please," Zalia sent.

A few moments later, Boreal pushed through the grass, her armour stored away. The girl jerked away at seeing Boreal, but Zalia caught her by the shoulder again.

"Don't worry, it's ok. This is Boreal. She's very friendly, and a real puffball when you get to know her. She's going to protect you for just a little bit while I have a quick look around, alright?" Zalia explained. "Do you have a name?"

Boreal sat down a few steps away.

"Aylie," the girl said in a small whisper.

"Alright, Aylie, would you like to give Boreal a hug?" Zalia asked. "She's very fluffy."

Aylie gave a small nod, so Zalia walked up to Boreal with her and put the girl's hand on Boreal's side. Boreal began quietly purring to help.

"See? Nothing to worry about. She will protect you while I'm gone for just a moment, ok?" Zalia said.

Aylie pushed herself into the fluffy side of Boreal, giving her a hug.

Zalia stepped away and made her way to the tree line where Aylie and the demon had first come from. It took only a few minutes of searching to find what she had been hoping not to find. Further into the trees, there were bodies. Well, what might have once been bodies.

There were maybe five, though it could have been one more or less. It was hard to tell.

It looked like the demon had taken its time tearing the people apart one by one—a nauseating sight. She didn't look to even bury these people; the time needed to figure out which piece belonged to whom was too time-consuming and gruesome a task to undertake. Instead, she used a quick Flame-root ritual and controlled it to burn the remains to ashes, making sure to heal any damage she accidentally did to the surrounding plants.

They had been what Zalia assumed was the family of the child, now all dead. She left the ashes behind, leaving it to the effects of rain and time to bury them now.

Making her way back to Boreal and Aylie, Zalia managed to get the girl onto Boreal, and the three of them continued the journey. A war camp was no place for a child, but there wasn't really much else Zalia knew to do. Perhaps a new family could be found for her, or she could be taken down south with a group like the one she had run into two days past. There were options, just none of them were something a child should have to go through.

Zalia left her armour off, stored away in her glove, but easily accessible through Druid Grove's storage ability. The appearance of the armour and the incorporeality it gave her lent a somewhat inhuman look. Something real and human was perhaps what Aylie needed right now.

Wildlife was scarce as they travelled, either having fled or been killed off by the various demons now roaming Endaria. That said, the wildlife wasn't entirely defenceless itself. Along their travels, Zalia found a few bodies of demons that had been left to rot, their meat not something that any creature seemed to want to eat, Boreal included. From inspecting a few of the bodies, Zalia found a few types of injuries that she recognised. One was entirely withered, with no drop of water remaining in its body, probably as a result of a run-in with one of the huge centipede creatures Zalia had encountered once. Others had differing claw marks, bite wounds, and other similar injuries as a result of some particularly dangerous wildlife.

That said, the number of demon bodies she found was far fewer than the number of dead animals she found.

Over the course of the next two days of travel, she could feel a familiar sensation building. An odd sense of danger. It struck her, the realisation of what exactly it was, late on the second day. It was the corruption—the aura of it, at least—so weak as to be initially unrecognisable, yet growing stronger the further she travelled.

As Zalia, Boreal, and Aylie crested the top of a hill, they were able to see down the other side across a huge plain. Close to them was something of a fortress. It was a huge compound surrounded by tall, crenellated stone walls. Carved into those stone walls were various glowing runes emitting an almost palpable power. A shimmering, translucent light of some sort stretched up from the walls, forming a dome over the bustling camp within.

The camp was an extremely well-organised affair of stone buildings, open areas, and canvas pavilions. Zalia knew that this was the camp of the rebellion, or one of them, at least, due to the flags flapping in the wind. Dark green and brown, a crossed sword and staff with a crown broken in half underneath.

Far, far into the distance, she could see the capital of Endaria. She wasn't sure if the city had a name, as everyone simply called it "the capital," and even maps had it labelled as such. It made the organised camp of the rebellion look small and weak.

Its walls were higher, made of a stone that shimmered with power. Though she couldn't see from here, she knew there would be the flags of the king hung on the walls.

The source of the corruption she felt, which was a different feeling than the spots of corrupted land she had been healing nearby, was most definitely the capital. She could tell that because of the red haze that hung over the city. Seeing that brought her dread, her memories of Cormaine flashing through her mind. She was terrified of what it meant for the people who had lived there. She knew firsthand what that aura could do.

First, though, she had to go down to the fortified camp.

The trio went down the other side of the hill, travelling with ease down the grassy slope. It was only another half hour of walking before they arrived at the gates. Zalia knew they had been spotted, with all plant life having been removed from around the walls to allow for visibility.

The camp was a significantly more intimidating sight than the previous one had been. That one had only had wood log walls and was much smaller than the one before her now. This one was four or five times bigger, and most likely held a large number of soldiers and refugees.

"Stop there for inspection!" a voice called down as they stepped up to the large gates.

The trio stopped and weren't kept waiting long as the gate opened and two people walked out. One was a knight in full plate—something oddly familiar about the figure—and the other was a short, nervous-looking man.

As they approached, Zalia checked them with Aura Observation.

Knight Alara - Silver rank.
? - Silver rank.

Alara? Zalia thought.

It took her just a moment to realise what that meant. This was Alara, the knight she had met when she first came to Endaria. The one that had fought for the king. She had only been Bronze rank back then but had obviously managed to reach the next milestone. Had she defected?

It looked like Alara had tried using her own Aura Observation on Zalia because her hand went to her sword.

"Zalia, long time," Alara said, coming to a stop in front of her.

"You were fighting for the king last I saw you," Zalia said, ignoring the greeting.

"Things changed," Alara replied.

"That they have," Zalia admitted.

Zalia gently lifted Aylie down from Boreal.

"What does inspection entail exactly?" Zalia asked.

"We need to determine if you're an enemy or not," Alara said.

"Well, you know I don't fight for the king, that's for sure," Zalia pointed out.

"Yes, but they have a . . . method of disguising themselves as us. And you're meant to be dead," Alara explained.

"I've heard," Zalia said.

Alara turned to the nervous man beside her who still hadn't spoken. "All seem good?" she asked.

"Y . . . yes, definitely not one of *them*," the man said.

"Them?" Zalia asked.

"And who is this?" Alara asked, ignoring the question. "I don't remember you having a child last we spoke."

"This is Aylie, I found her being hunted by one of the demon creatures. Her family is . . . well, they didn't make it," Zalia explained. "And this is Boreal. She has been my companion for a while, though she is much larger now than she used to be."

Aylie was staring up at Alara with round eyes. She hadn't spoken much more since their first meeting, but Zalia didn't want to try the mental healing she had developed just yet. Using it on a "god" was one thing, using it on the fragile mind of a human, a child even, might be dangerous. She wanted to try it on some of the broken men the rebellion was trying to heal first. There wasn't much more damage that could be done to them.

"Any weapons we need to know about?" Alara asked.

"I've got one, an heirloom that can change between bow and sword. And Boreal, of course," Zalia said. "Are General Faian and Lady Indis at this camp? I need to speak to them both."

"Both, yes. You are allowed to enter, though please keep Boreal from killing anyone," Alara said, turning about.

"She'd never," Zalia assured.

They were led into the camp and the small amount of corruption in the air was washed away as a result of the defensive dome. Not that it was needed with how significantly Zalia's Healing Presence overpowered it here.

Within, the camp felt almost like a city, though not one that had grown naturally. It had perfectly ordered roads in a square grid, each space used efficiently. Four-man patrols marched by on different routes, all in unison and perfect form. Others went about various camp duties; a hunting party moving to leave the camp, and messengers running by with rolled pages or envelopes.

Despite the surface-level organisation and cleanliness, looking closer, Zalia could see the real state of things. The guards had armour that wasn't yet cleaned of blood, or had damage to it. The hunting party was larger than normal, each person armoured rather than wearing lighter clothes designed for hunting, and they had dark patches under their eyes. The buildings were orderly, yet there were refugees sitting in corners or under eaves, as if there wasn't enough space for everyone despite how large the camp was.

Zalia also noticed odd glances coming her direction, ranging from confusion to admiration. She thought she might have some idea as to why she was receiving those.

Boreal was definitely part of it, back in her armour and showing off, Aylie on her back once more. The full meaning behind the glances came when they moved through a central square in the camp.

"What the hell is that?" she asked, pointing to the centre.

Standing there atop a rocky base was a life-sized statue of herself, bow in hand, with a much smaller Boreal at her feet.

"Ah, Lady Indis is responsible for that I believe," Alara said.

Zalia stared at it in utter disbelief.

CHAPTER THREE

Answers

Zalia

"*hy am I so small?*" Boreal asked, looking at the statue.

"Why exactly is there a statue of me in the middle of the camp?" Zalia asked.

"For an answer to that, you're going to have to ask Lady Indis, I'm afraid," Alara said.

"I think it best you take me to her right away, then," Zalia said, looking at the statue with a mixture of confusion, annoyance, and disbelief.

A statue of her was the last thing she wanted, she wasn't some damn war hero to be celebrated for their heroic deeds. Well, if her actions were spun in a certain way and key facts, like her being alive, were ignored or unknown, her actions might be shown off as such, but the reality was much different.

Boreal was up at the statue, gently tapping the small version of herself with a paw.

"*Why so small?*" Boreal asked again.

"That is how small you used to be," Zalia explained.

Alara looked at her weirdly.

"Oh, she speaks to me with her mind," Zalia added.

"Rrright," Alara said.

"*I wasn't smaller, world was bigger,*" Boreal told her.

"I— Yes, sure. Can we go now?" Zalia asked.

The statue was making her a little uneasy. The unease was made a little worse by the wide-eyed Aylie staring at the statue, like she believed Zalia was a hero too.

Boreal hopped down, some passers-by looking between Boreal and the statue, then Zalia and the statue. This was not good.

They continued onwards, deeper into the camp. Before long, they arrived at what was a miniature fortress mixed with a bunker within the camp. Thick stone walls of a large circular building greeted them, three small doors set into the walls through which a flood of activity moved. Alara moved forward and began trying to push through the crowd into the building and quickly found her way free once Boreal tried making her way in. She received a few alarmed looks as she allowed her fear-inducing aura to slip through, people moving quickly out of her way. Boreal wasn't a wait-in-line kind of girl.

Zalia followed closely behind, garnering not a few odd looks herself.

They entered into a bustling room filled with various administrative types, at desks and not, using magic to note down information or messages. Pieces of parchment were then handed to a few people who sent them flying through the room to various locations. Alara pushed through, the bustle stopping for just a moment, as Boreal strolled through the middle of it all, following after her.

They left that entrance room through a door at the back, entering another similar yet less busy room where people were reading through pieces of parchment that landed on their desks and noting down parts of them before they were filed away at their sides. Some of the pieces were wiped entirely, the clean sheets put aside for reuse.

"Seems a little inefficient to have all that at the door," Zalia noted.

"Stops people from getting through to speak to the leaders personally unless it's actually important," Alara said.

Zalia shrugged; the explanation didn't make a huge amount of sense to her. She wasn't a leader or an administrator, though, so it wasn't really her forte. She did take note of the guards posted all about the place, more so than she would have thought necessary for the building despite its importance. Had something happened to warrant those measures?

Finally, they left that room via a door to the right, entering another room with three tables set in a U shape. At the middle table sat General Faian, General Ballast, and another she did not know. On the left was a group of three who could have been the administrators in the room they had just left, for all Zalia could tell the difference.

At the final table were two people she didn't recognise and Lady Indis, on her feet, hands flat on the table, in the middle of a heated argument.

"I don't care if we don't have the resources, there must be a way to house these people!" Indis was almost yelling.

"I might be a magician but I am not a miracle worker, Lady Indis, expanding the wall would mean taking down the defences, and we simply do not have the personnel to do that right now. Especially so if the enemy takes note of our actions and chooses to attack at that time. We have simply run out of space!" the first of the three closest to Zalia at the administrator table replied.

"We—" Indis started.

"Lady Indis, everyone. I believe we should take a short recess to cool down and deal with other more important matters at this time," General Faian interrupted, having seen Zalia walk through the door.

"What matters are more important than the—" Indis cut off again, having turned to Faian before following her gaze to the door.

Zalia had to admit to herself that she enjoyed the torrent of emotions that crossed over Indis's face as she saw her. Surprise, worry, confusion, shock, worry again, before finally settling on joy.

"Zalia?" she whispered.

"Hello *Lady* Indis," Zalia said, giving her best dramatic bow.

Boreal jumped forward, basically throwing her body weightily at Indis's in greeting. Indis stumbled, catching herself and looking at Boreal with an equal measure of shock as Zalia had received.

"Yes, I happen to be not dead. May we talk in private?" Zalia asked.

The administrators were talking between themselves while the three generals were walking around the table. The two others that were at Indis's table were staring at Zalia as well.

"You're certain this isn't one of them?" Faian asked Alara.

"Most assuredly, Fin was the one to check," Alara replied.

"Good, you may return to your duties then. We will be fine from here," Faian said.

"As you command," Alara said stiffly, a clank of plate armour sounding as she turned and left.

"How are you alive?" Indis asked, watching Boreal inspect the room, Aylie still on board.

"I have a few questions of my own—somewhere private first," Zalia insisted.

"Zalia!" Ballast exclaimed, coming up to give her a shake of the hand, his giant hand covering her own.

"General, good to see you still around," Zalia said.

"And you! I told them you weren't dead, you've got the look of a survivor about you," Ballast exclaimed.

"Through this way, please," Faian said, gesturing to a door.

Ballast led the way, with Faian saying something quietly to the other general before he walked off. Zalia followed Ballast, Boreal and Aylie close behind, and Indis after that, her stare boring a hole in the back of Zalia's head. She had never really known much to shock Indis into silence before, but if anything were to do so, coming back from the supposed dead would be it.

Ballast led the way through a corridor, past a few doors into the one at the end, arriving in a sparsely decorated office. A desk sat front and centre, the walls bearing the banner of the rebellion as well as some decorative weapons, and some not so decorative ones, hung upon hooks or sitting on shelves.

There were only two chairs in addition to one on the other side of the desk, so

Zalia forfeited taking one and lifted Aylie off Boreal to sit her down instead. Ballast leant against the wall to the left after taking a bowl of some type of nut from the desk. Indis stopped behind Zalia, and she turned around to finally greet her friend.

"It's good to see you," Zalia said, meaning it despite all they had been through.

"We thought you died," Indis said, her voice cracking.

"You should have known me better than that," Zalia said, moving forward and giving the younger woman a hug.

"Where have you been?" Indis asked, still in the embrace.

"All in good time," Zalia assured her.

Faian came in and sat in the chair on the other side of the desk with a deep sigh.

"Right, let's be about it quickly then. Still much to discuss," she said.

Indis sat down in the second chair, almost dropping down in contrast to her usual controlled movements.

"First, and most importantly, this is Aylie. She has lost her family and needs to be taken care of. I'm no parent, nor am I really cut out to be, but I would still like to see her safe. Can that be arranged?" Zalia asked.

"Certainly, shouldn't be too difficult," Faian assured.

"Good, I'd like to be kept up to date on that," Zalia added.

"Very well. Zalia, where exactly have you been and why are you not dead?" Faian asked.

"Ah, yes. Well, that is a very long story. I don't know if the others knew this, but the only idea I could come up with as we were fighting atop that tower was to use a certain herb that has a reversing effects on rituals, in the hope that doing so would disrupt something badly enough to break the whole thing across the continent. It looks like that succeeded, to a degree. It had the unfortunate side effect of dragging Boreal, Juniper, and I into Cormaine, however," Zalia explained.

"Cormaine!?" Indis said aghast. "That's where you have been this whole time?"

Zalia nodded, pacing around a bit.

Boreal was staying close to Aylie, as a comfort.

"And Juniper?" Faian asked.

"Dead, then dead again," Zalia said.

". . . Dead again?" Faian said questioningly, looking with a raised eyebrow towards Ballast, who just shrugged.

"Have you come across the undead here yet?" Zalia asked.

"We have not, I assume there were many in Cormaine then, being the realm of the dead," Faian said.

"Well, Cormaine isn't the realm of the dead but yes, there were many. An entire city of undead Bathar, actually. Juniper became one when she died there, turned by the aura that pervades the entire place," Zalia explained.

"The aura, yes, we can feel it when we leave the defensive barrier and again in the parts of the world that seem to have died due to the rituals. It is quite annoying," Faian said.

"Annoying is one word for it. The one you feel here is weak, like an echo of the real thing. There, it has the power to kill you if you do not have a certain type of healing. It can raise those it kills to become the walking dead. It comes from those that live in Cormaine, thousands upon thousands of shades, and the . . ." Zalia trailed off, shuddering at the memory of the godlike entities that emitted the debilitating aura.

"And the what?" Indis asked, concern in her voice and expression.

"I'd rather not speak of them, just yet. The aura killed Juniper, and I released her soul from its undead prison shortly thereafter. I had to spend a lot of time there simply surviving, but I've learnt much about fighting our enemies. I've also learnt a lot about where they actually come from and what their purpose here is. Before we get into that though, I need to know. Indis, Faian, Ballast, whoever can answer the question: What the hell is with the statue of me?" Zalia asked.

"Ah," Faian said, giving a low chuckle.

"Well, you—" Indis started.

"You're a bloody hero," Ballast said.

Zalia looked at Indis who was a little bit flushed and very embarrassed.

"Well, after you . . . died, I didn't want to let the memory of what you had given for a kingdom that isn't even your own die as well. When I arrived here, and after the initial days of fighting, I told anyone who would listen what you had done. One thing turned to another, and the soldiers began seeing you as a war hero, praising your name and fighting harder for it. After all, if a stranger can die saving your kingdom, why shouldn't you be able to do the same? The statue, well, it turned from a matter of keeping the memory of your actions alive to a matter of morale. They seem to look up to you," Indis explained, avoiding eye contact and looking down.

"And where are Ember and Zen? I couldn't help but notice that Zen has not been mentioned by any of the people I've talked to so far," Zalia said, a little coldness in her tone.

"After the ritual went off, we thought it was all done. The one you disrupted didn't explode or summon creatures like the others. Zen asked that he be left out of anything to do with the rest of the war and left for his home, his farm. Oh, Ember was able to heal him from the wound he received, thankfully, though a scar does remain. No, he wanted to leave it all behind and be left out of it, so I promised he would be. Once we realised things were very wrong, we backtracked to go find him but found his home destroyed. There were no signs of him or his family, and we haven't seen him since," Indis started.

"As for Ember, well. She and I had a disagreement about the way I went about praising your name and actions. She said that you would not have wanted it, which is true, I realise now. I guess I felt guilty about my part in your death, and that blinded me to what you really would have wanted. I'm sorry for that too," Indis finished, getting quieter over the course of the explanation.

Zalia felt relief at hearing Zen was alive, then dismay at hearing he was missing. Indis seemed as much of a constantly-in-motion-trainwreck as she had been when Zalia had left, which didn't surprise her.

"And where is Ember now?" Zalia asked.

"Don't know. She returns every now and then with a group of refugees or important information before leaving again. She doesn't really work well as part of a chain of command and prefers being out there, helping however she can. You know her," Indis said.

"Yeah, I suppose I do. I'm not surprised by that at all," Zalia said, giving a smile and letting out a deep sigh. "It's good to be back in this world again. It's a beautiful place."

"What happened to you in Cormaine?" Indis asked.

"One day I'll tell you the whole story. For now, Faian, we need to go over a few things that might help with the war," Zalia said.

"I was hoping you'd have something for us," Faian said with some hope.

"I might just," Zalia said.

CHAPTER FOUR

Location Hunting

Zalia

After a long-winded conversation, Zalia was able to tell the others in the room everything she knew about their enemy so far. That began with a deeper explanation of the undead; the shades everywhere in Cormaine; the corrupting aura and where she thought it came from; the low-ranked, four-legged, spiked creatures; the Bronze creature that had chased Aylie; the flying demons that she had first seen outside her cave home; and finally, the larger godlike ones.

"They're . . . they're horrible. They have four legs that end in spikes, a twisted torso covered in thousands of eyes, and wings like a bat yet covered in a dark flame. They have no head, only a gaping maw where their neck should be. Despite all that, the most terrible thing about them is the aura they have. It's like the corrupting aura, yet so, so much stronger. It feels almost alive, a little different than the one the others all have, controlled by the twisted creatures. When it comes down on you, you feel as if all hope is lost, and the meaning in fighting is gone. If you're strong enough, you can fight it, but the effect it would have on the army if one of these did decide to join the fight would be . . . disastrous. And there is one in the capital, I can feel its aura even here. Though it's so weak at such a distance, the fact it reaches this far is terrifying. I would hold no hope that the people in that city are alive anymore," Zalia explained.

There was silence at her proclamation, the people present all very aware of what that meant for the kingdom. Many of Endaria's most important or most powerful people had been living in that city, but more impactfully, many people that the soldiers would have known. Friends, family, loved ones. All most likely dead, even more likely to be undead now if Zalia was right.

"But, you must have been able to survive it somehow if you're here now. You have a way to fight them, right?" Indis asked, hope in her voice

"No. A friend, Ro-ak, otherwise known as Nateysta, god, spirit, whichever you choose, of nature and mystery. He was the one to save me, a divine being whose own aura matched that of these monsters. I don't know if he is now dormant once more, reduced to an afterthought by the very beings he saved me and Boreal from. Perhaps he lives, though the chances of that being true and him being able to find his way to this world are slim," Zalia said.

She had to very carefully remember select parts of her last hour in Cormaine, avoiding the big, painful lump that sat amongst the memories.

"Well, that is unfortunate," Indis replied, deflating back into her seat.

"Yes, though some might be able to fight still, such as any Gold rank and above, if we have any. Larel would probably fare better than any of us, for one. Speaking of, where is Larel, did she survive her fight with the Hidden? What happened with him?" Zalia asked.

"After Juniper vanished, he surrendered and told us we couldn't trust him. Obviously in agreement, he allowed us to . . . imprison him. He now lives crushed into a tiny cube deep below this building, where he will stay until this is over. As for Larel, she is well but busy. As one of the only Gold rankers amongst our ranks, she is kept moving any second we can get her to be," Faian explained.

Zalia didn't really know how to feel about that. She had been close, or had thought she had been, to the Hidden. To Hidey. His betrayal was a deep wound, yet not one that was really his fault. Juniper had been the real hand behind that particular shadow puppet.

The fact that he had allowed himself to be imprisoned rather than run the risk of him doing any more damage definitely pointed to him really being on their side. Perhaps he had even been the one that had left the note for Larel to come save them in the first place.

"Well, that is one worry to put aside, at least," Zalia said.

"One of a flock, unfortunately," Faian added with a grimace.

"I overheard one of those issues, and I might be able to help, just a little," Zalia offered.

"How so?" Indis asked curiously.

Zalia explained the Druid Grove ability as well as her ability to grow plants that were more nutritious than normal. That part of it wasn't anything super special, but the Grove itself was very unique, or so the others' reactions told her.

"Very interesting, how long would you need to set it up?" Faian asked.

"A day, maybe? Things would be sped along quite a lot if you could provide me with various plants and seeds that are edible, rather than me having to collect them myself," Zalia replied, shaking her hand in a "maybe?" gesture.

"That can be done easily enough if you would provide extra space for people to live," Indis said immediately.

"I must warn you, it won't be a huge space. It could fit maybe twenty, thirty people comfortably? Forty, if you really stretched it, but it needs space for plants to grow for it to work," Zalia quickly explained.

"Done. We will have some plants and seeds ready for you by the time you've finished finding a place to set it up. Is there anything else you can think of that will help?" Faian asked.

"Immediately? No. I learnt a lot about the history of Cormaine that I would like to go over, but it can wait for now. Something about the Bathar that you would definitely enjoy learning," Zalia said, turning to Indis at her visible excitement at the word "history."

"Thank you, Zalia. If there is anything we can do for you, for the help you are providing and the help you have provided already, let me know," Faian said.

"I'd love to know what exactly happened with the army after we left for Endelbyrn. Did you know we would fail?" Zalia asked.

"We didn't know, but we did plan for it. I can explain it all to you later, if you wish. For now, we have to get back to the meeting you walked in on," Faian said with a sigh.

Indis looked like she was about to protest but didn't say anything. General Ballast crunched on a nut with an unhappy look.

"Well, you aristocrats enjoy your meetings, I'm going to go walk in the sun and fresh air," Zalia said with a smile. Things *were* bad, but they were better than when she had appeared in Cormaine not so long ago.

"Would you like to come find a nice place to set up a magic forest?" Zalia asked Aylie, leaning down.

Zalia noticed she had been staring into nothing the entire conversation, as if she wasn't really there. The child definitely needed a distraction, and the creation of Zalia's Druid Grove was a very pretty sight.

Aylie nodded uncertainly.

"Come on, it'll be good. We can find a place safe from the weather, and with a nice source of water. You'll love the Grove, it's a good safe place," Zalia encouraged.

Aylie looked at Boreal.

"Boreal will come too, of course. I wouldn't want to set up our home without Boreal's agreement," Zalia promised.

That seemed to convince her, so Zalia lifted her onto Boreal's back and they left, the trio behind them looking miserable at the prospect of reentering their previous argument.

They had a little more trouble forcing their way out than they had entering, partly due to the people being less surprised by Boreal, and partly due to the fact that there was a group of people *waiting* for Zalia to come out. Whispers spread like wildfire as she walked into the room; the crush of people, some there for administration and others for her.

"Are you Zalia?" someone called out.

Some of the low talking paused as they waited for a response, and Zalia stopped to consider the task of shoving through so many people. Many of the administrative people were looking at the packed group in annoyance. Zalia understood that quite well.

Zalia sighed.

"Yes," she answered warily.

A burst of chatter came from the crowd, a few questions drowned away by the noise.

"Can you take this outside, please?" an administrator to her left asked.

"I'd prefer it not be happening at all," Zalia retorted. "I don't know how to get them out of here."

The administrator stood up.

"If everyone would please leave the premises, Zalia will be leaving now and will answer your questions *outside*," he said.

It took a little bit for the message to spread through the crowd, but they began filtering out through the doors. Zalia gave the administrator a look that was a mix of thanks and accusation.

He just shrugged like it wasn't his problem and went back to what he had been doing.

She followed the crowd out, Boreal close behind her. As she left the building, she was bombarded with questions mixed with thanks for what she had done for the kingdom. What the hell had Indis told these people?

She opened her mouth to answer one of the questions but thought better of it. She wasn't responsible for this gaggle of idiots; she wouldn't be the one to deal with them.

"Lady Indis will provide answers to all your questions in the future, please be patient while they deal with the information I've brought. For now, it's best you all go back to your duties," Zalia yelled over the crowd before walking off.

She ignored the protests, people asking how she was alive, where had she been, how had she stopped the ritual, and could she reverse it. Some tried to follow, but Boreal's fear-inducing aura stopped them from doing so. She was the best friend a woman could ask for.

"*Let's get the hell out of here*," she thought to Boreal.

"*Stinky people*," Boreal agreed.

Zalia quietly chuckled and moved away from the group of people as quickly as she could without running.

She made her way through the camp, giving her statue an evil look as she passed, before finding the gates once more. She was allowed out but was informed that she would have to undergo inspection again when reentering, a reasonable precaution. She gave Alara a nod on her way out and stepped out onto the plains before the walls.

She wanted to find somewhere nice for her Grove, definitely somewhere that put the camp between herself and the city in the distance. The hilly landscape behind the camp would also have a high chance of having a river she could set up near. While not necessary, it would make life a lot easier if she was going to provide shelter for some people.

She was second-guessing that decision a little, but enforcing a no-crazy-people rule wouldn't be too hard. Her Grove was meant to be a safe space, no fanatics who thought her a hero allowed.

It took a little while before they found a place they all agreed on. Aylie definitely got into the role of "critical eye," only agreeing to a location with a silent nod when Zalia told her she would be able to move some of the earth around to form a better space for planting.

It was a small gorge with water trickling down a stone wall, leading into a small waterway that formed a pool near the entrance of the gorge. That entrance had a good, clear area around it, with trees dotted about the place, but not too thick. The gorge was formed where the bottom of two steep hills met, forming a little V section that would provide good cover from the wind.

Zalia widened out the little gorge a bit and made its walls steeper so it formed into something more akin to a wide crevice—at Aylie's insistence, the first words she had spoken since telling Zalia her name. Then, the spot was ready. Zalia would need to plant a few things as well before being able to form the Grove, but it was a good start. It was only ten minutes' walk from the camp to its east, putting the camp between it and the city.

"Ready to see how a Grove is made?" Zalia asked Aylie.

She nodded excitedly, a little bit of joy forming in Zalia's heart to see her anticipation after what she had been through.

Zalia began pulling out plants from her storage.

CHAPTER FIVE

Blue Sky, New Grove

Zalia

I t took Zalia some time to set up what was necessary, especially with the odd shape of the space she was working with. She set up one of her living rituals, much like she had in Cormaine, but found a way to combine them into one. The protections on the Grove had been three separate living rituals that blocked senses, spiritual senses, and spiritual attacks, respectively. Here, Zalia made good use of Adastem, as well as the components of each individual ritual, to create a single large one that would adjust itself as needed.

Aylie seemed fascinated by the process as Zalia planted the various required cuttings and moved on, using Healing Presence to grow the plants, and Preparation to trim them to her needs as she planted the next. This kind of multitasking was something that she wouldn't have been able to accomplish if not for the Bronze rank mental attributes she now had.

The hardest part came when she had to form five separate components for the initiating ritual and then apply the entire thing across the large area she had prepared. Dried, crushed, cut, and whole herbs drifted through the air, forming from nothing but mana as Zalia focused on her intent. Boreal, helpful as ever, started running around, smashing through gathered patches of herbs as they collected where Zalia commanded. Aylie, who was currently riding the large feline, actually let out a joyous laugh as Boreal raced through a swath of herbs.

Once everything was in place, Zalia had to pour quite a large chunk of her mana into the ritual before it settled over the area, the plants grasping the magic as their own and beginning to fuel it even as it fueled them.

Zalia could visibly see the dome formed by the ritual go up before it altered itself, slowly becoming less and less visible until it seemed like nothing but a part of the nature around it. She could feel the very weak corrupting aura disappear immediately, the initial ritual easily strong enough to counter it. She had a feeling it even made that part of its function weaker to allow the other parts more strength.

With her planted Adastem, Bitterbalm, Manifest, and Dodge-vine, the area looked a little nicer, the plants well cultivated in an aesthetically pleasing pattern. Aside from the plants, there were a few trees scattered around the area, and the little gorge, of course.

Zalia began the process of forming the Grove, now that the prerequisites were complete. She walked around the perimeter of the space she had chosen, lightly brushing her hand over the trees and looking up into the bright blue sky above. The chirping of the birds faded into the background as she closed her eyes, letting the ability and her instincts take over. She walked up the slight slope to the gorge and walked along the small stone path to the end, where the water dripped down the wall. She cupped her hands and caught some, drinking it before moving back out.

She went to the centre of the space and knelt, hands against the sapling that grew there. At once, the power of the Grove began growing outwards, forming the land and space to her needs.

The sapling before her grew in a matter of moments, becoming a large tree with a thick trunk. From that trunk, a curving staircase grew to its boughs above.

Other trees in the area grew similarly, forming their own staircases, railings with leaves growing from them; and within the branches, paths began to form. Little winding walkways were formed by the branches as they grew larger and intertwined with their neighbours. Within the treetops, small homes grew. Small homes that held nothing more than beds grown from the walls, yet made comfortable by the warm lights that began appearing.

All across the ground, dome-like huts made from earth pushed from the earth, grass growing across their surfaces. Warm light came from small windows set into their sides, revealing interiors decorated with wooden furniture similarly grown from the roots of the trees that now formed smooth yet patterned floors.

All along the perimeter of the Grove, sharp and tall hedges formed, leaving only a single small archway that people could move through.

The tree that Zalia had her hands on grew an archway of its own set right into the trunk, which would summon the entrance to her vault, should she will it so.

Finally, the pond that sat near the gorge deepened, blue lights appearing in its depths as it did so. The lights moved around, bringing back memories of Zalia's first time seeing the collective's old home. The comparison brought tears to her eyes, but she stayed focused on the growth of the Grove as it continued into the gorge itself. The walls were shored up, and far at the back, a little cave was dug into the wall behind the trickling water, turning it from a running river to a small waterfall. Behind that waterfall, the cave grew until it was big enough to hold an altar, an altar that grew from the ground, an altar that she knew all too well.

It was the altar of Nateysta, the story of his origin written along its surface, along with the story of his sacrifice to bring Zalia to safety once more. A story that Zalia herself was trying so hard to avoid remembering.

With that final touch, the changes to the space were finally finished. Each one of them was visible within Zalia's mind as if she had seen them herself, even as she remained kneeling in front of the tree, eyes closed.

She opened her eyes, taking in the sight of the Grove that was connected to her. Aylie and Boreal were running around, exploring the changes for themselves, dashing up a flight of stairs into the treetops to explore the homes now built there.

The warm and protective aura of the Grove settled over the space, providing healing and a boost to resilience. The trees, now much larger, threw shade across the entire space, and little beads of yellow light floated around, providing more than enough light to see by. Further away from where the homes had been built near the gorge, yet still within the hedge, land had cleared in preparation for the planting Zalia wanted to undertake.

She smiled, happy to have finally set up the Grove once more. There really wasn't anywhere she felt safer. Despite . . . despite what had happened in the last one.

The memory flashed through her mind, a small body crushed in a large hand.

She stood up quickly with a jolt.

"Hey, guys! We should go grab the seeds so we can begin planting food," Zalia called out.

"*Have to?*" Boreal asked.

"*Yes,*" Zalia said, a little bit of the anguish she felt making its way into her tone.

Boreal came running down a different staircase, Aylie hot on her heels, yet definitely not keeping up. Boreal slid to a stop in front of Zalia and bumped her head into her.

"*Zalia ok?*" Boreal asked.

"I was thinking about Delphi," Zalia whispered.

"*Delphi was good friend,*" Boreal said sadly.

Zalia hadn't shown Boreal the memory of what had happened to Delphi, nor had she explained it. She had only said that the collective had died during the fighting to save them. The very visual memory of their death was not something that Zalia wanted Boreal to have in her mind. It wasn't something she wanted to have in her *own* either.

Aylie finally arrived as well, puffing as she slammed into Boreal's side, sinking into her fur.

"Right! We should go get some of the plants they'll have ready for us," Zalia announced, helping Aylie up onto Boreal's back for the journey.

There was quite a bit of farmable land within the bounds of the

Grove—perhaps not by the standards of her old world, but with the extreme growth the plants would experience due to the continuous Healing Presence, it would be more than enough for the odd thirty or so people that could live there.

They made their way back to the army camp and after a short inspection by the same nervous man as before, they were let in. This time, Zalia managed to get him to explain what the inspection was actually for.

"We have encountered a type of Cormaine creature that is able to disguise itself as people. It was something we didn't really figure out until an officer got his head ripped off by one of the damned things. Let me tell you, they are not happy when they're discovered," he said.

Well, that explained his nervousness, at least.

He was able to detect things with an ability he had, something Zalia unfortunately wouldn't be able to replicate. She just hoped that her Healing Presence would have some sort of effect on the creatures, as that would allow her to discover them too, if necessary.

She found a couple wagons and a group of people waiting for her as she made it through the gates.

"You'd be Zalia then, eh?" a weathered-looking older man asked.

"Uh, yes. You have the seeds and other plants Faian is giving me, I see. Shall we get going, then?" Zalia asked back.

"You don't look much of a hero," he said, ignoring her question.

She immediately liked the man.

"Well, that's good, because I'm not. I'd prefer not to be treated like one either," Zalia replied.

The man grunted.

"Alright, lads and lasses, let's get this thing rolling, shall we?" he called out.

He had a gruff voice, as weathered as his own skin was, doubtless a result of long years spent working the fields in the sun.

"You're a farmer?" Zalia asked as the others in the group began taking up the leads of the animals hitched to the wagons.

Paying attention to them, she realised they were the thick-furred cow creatures she had seen so long ago in a farm near Alston.

"That I am, my whole life. Not about to stop that and become a soldier just because the kingdom hit a little rut in the road," he said.

Zalia smiled, finding the rough positivity to be nice.

"That's good, a kingdom can't live without people like you," Zalia replied.

The man looked at her from under bushy eyebrows as if reconsidering his initial assumption of idiocy.

"Well, ain't that refreshin' to hear," he said with a huff.

"You don't happen to be from the north, closer to Alston, do you?" Zalia asked.

"Why d'ya ask that?" he said.

"I think I've met one of those cows before," Zalia explained, looking at one of the beasts hauling the wagon.

"Not sure what a cow is, but that Burris there has been with me for a good many long years. Ole Feral won't let a little apocalypse stop her," he said with a chuckle.

"Did you just call her 'Ole Feral?'" Zalia asked in surprise.

"Yep! Found her stomping a Garroi's head in once, you know. She's a mighty beast," he explained proudly.

"Ole Feral," Zalia muttered.

They were let out of the gates, and Zalia began inspecting each of the members of their small expedition. The farmer she had been speaking with was Bronze rank, expected from an older man like him. The others were a smattering of Tin and Iron ranked youths, all of whom Zalia figured to be farmhands of the older man. The way they seemed to defer to him gave her the impression they had been working with him for a while. He didn't strike her as the kind of person to deal with nonsense.

"Got a name I can call you by?" Zalia asked.

"Jus' call me Mate like everyone else does," he said.

"Alright, Mate, you and your lot plan to move into the Grove, or are you just delivering all this for me?" Zalia asked.

"Thought I'd have a look, I'm real sick of having to live in the war camp, being of no use to anybody," Mate said.

"Well, I'd like to set a few rules then. Firstly, no one is to touch my plants. My plants happen to be every single plant that is in the Grove at the moment. They're quite important and a part of the defences that are set up. Understood?" Zalia explained.

"Yeah, fair enough, I'd do the same," he replied, nodding as if the request was completely normal.

"Good. Secondly, if you or any of your people ever call me 'hero,' you're out," Zalia finished.

"I'd take myself out before I'd let it happen," Mate assured her.

"Sounds like we're going to get along just fine then," Zalia said, giving him a warm smile.

"Don't bloody smile at me," he grumbled, not entirely in a serious manner.

Zalia gave him a low chuckle.

"Fair enough."

CHAPTER SIX

An Old Friend

Zalia

The small line of carts trundled through the arch in the hedge, the younger farmhands spreading out to take a look at their new home just as the sun was dipping below the horizon.

"How long you been building this place, then?" Mate asked.

"Just today," Zalia said.

"That's some pretty heavy enchantments you've got running in the place for 'just today,'" Mate said disbelievingly.

"It's an ability, mostly," Zalia explained.

"Got some pretty rare class, then, do you?" Mate suggested.

"Something like that," Zalia agreed.

Mate looked around, then up the hill towards where the homes were built.

"Just take any of the buildings, then?" he asked.

"That's the idea, none of them are occupied just yet," Zalia said.

"Good, I'm not goin' up in the trees. Too many stairs for my liking, though some of the youngins will be thrilled, I'm sure," Mate replied.

He didn't look *that* old, but Zalia guessed that's what happened when you had Bronze rank physical stats to keep you moving. Juniper hadn't looked that old either, now that she thought of it.

"Fair enough, and hey, Mate, you're in charge of these lot. Make sure they don't break anything, please?" Zalia said, turning to him.

"Yeah, I'll do my best, no promises with these heavy handed fools, though," Mate assured her.

Despite his less than assuring words, Zalia could tell that he would make certain of it. His farmhands were probably not as bad as he made them out to be either.

"Alright, that's me then. Get settled in and take tomorrow to have a look around. Or get started planting if you'd like. This big section near to the entrance and in a semicircle around the buildings is all yours, barring the small sections with herbs I've planted," Zalia explained.

He just gave the space a grunt of acceptance, glancing over it with a critical eye as he walked up the hill.

Zalia looked around, feeling a little like she had been running at full tilt so long she didn't know what to do now that there wasn't any immediate danger. Sure, there were some demons in the world now, but the atmosphere wasn't trying to kill her and there wasn't some prophesied danger she was trying to prepare for. Could she relax? Before Endaria, she had once enjoyed little wood carving projects in the evenings when it got dark out; maybe it was something she could pick up once more.

"I'm a little lost on what to do next, got anything in mind, Boreal?" Zalia asked, turning to where Boreal was keeping a watchful eye on the farmers.

"*Explore?*" Boreal suggested.

"Might be good to get a solid sense of the land around the Grove," Zalia agreed.

Boreal took that to mean they were going to do so at that very second and started leaving.

"Wait just a second. Aylie, are you feeling tired at all?" Zalia asked. "Or, now that I think about it, do you need to eat something?"

Aylie shook her head to the first question, looking a little sheepish at the second.

"No need to feel bad about it, you're going to need to eat a lot more often than Boreal or me. Not that I remembered that," Zalia said, internally reprimanding herself.

She walked past Boreal towards the entrance.

"Come on, what are you waiting for?" she asked.

A half hour later, the three of them were sat around a small fire controlled by Zalia as a little creature cooked above it. It was the first time in a long while that Zalia felt bad about a kill she had made. While it was necessary to feed Aylie, it had also been almost unfair how she had done it. The thing had tried to hide away in its burrow, but Zalia had just used the intangibility from her armour and the vibration sight to push her arm down through the earth and pull it straight from the ground. Like pulling a potato from the earth.

Still, she couldn't very well feed Aylie just off the berries and nuts she found scattered around, so little potato it was. She used Bitterbalm and a few herbs she found nearby to season the meat before cooling it enough that it would be easy for Aylie to eat. She'd used Preparation to properly butcher the creature and sat next to Aylie as she handed her stripped, green wood sticks with skewered meat on them.

It was nice, sitting by the campfire under the stars. She looked up into them and felt a tingle go down her spine as the stars began glowing a little brighter. She felt the presence shortly before she saw the one responsible for it: a large, translucent, starlit wolf, winding its way through the trees towards them, and tailed by its pack of smaller wolves. Zalia put her hand on Aylie's shoulder.

"Don't worry, it's a friend of mine," Zalia assured her, noticing the girl had gone stiff.

The wolf came and sat by the fire, towering over them.

"It's good to see you again," Zalia greeted, bowing her head in respect.

"And you, Zalia of the Druids. You have progressed much since we last met, and have another blessing from a good friend of mine. A friend that I had thought lost," the wolf said.

"It lives within Cormaine still, though they were fighting against dire odds last I saw them. They may have returned to dormancy, I'm not certain," Zalia explained.

"Ah, so that is where you went. I did not see you below the stars for quite some time. I had thought you to be trapped out of their sight somewhere, and I suppose you were," the wolf replied in understanding.

"Seeing the stars once more brings me more joy than I can explain. I'm sorry Nateysta could not be with me here to see them," Zalia said, her voice filled with sadness.

"As am I, young Druid," the wolf agreed.

They sat in companionable silence for a time, watching the stars above as the fire crackled quietly by their feet.

"The land is fouled by corrupt creatures' presence. I have tried to move some of the others to action, yet they languish in their resting spots, becoming more and more dormant, returning to their natures. I do what I can, but there are just so many of the demons. Some of which I am not strong enough to fight," the wolf said, looking towards the capital of Endaria.

"Returning to their natures?" Zalia asked.

"We cannot die, but we can fade, becoming so deep within our natures that the line between the two turns from blurred to non-existent. Feeling the blessing you have gave me hope that Nateysta had returned, he always was one of the strongest willed of us," the wolf explained, letting out a deep sigh.

"I wouldn't be here without him," Zalia murmured in agreement.

"A story I'd like to hear some day," the wolf said.

"One I will hopefully be ready to tell. Where do the others rest? Maybe I can convince them to action," Zalia suggested.

"I'm afraid not, child, not all of us are so accepting of humans. I fear many would wipe the land clean of your race as soon as they would save them. Most simply do not care for your people either way," the wolf explained.

"Why, are we not a part of nature as well?" Zalia asked, frowning.

Inside, she knew the answer. It was just something different to hear it from a creature that was meant to be like a god. A god that was really just a person with much power, when it came down to it.

"*Because humans, amongst a few other races such as the Astar to the east, do not live with nature, they live despite it. This does not bother the others so much, yet they do not care to protect you as they would otherwise because they do not understand that this is your nature. I try to tell them that it is not you they should fight for, rather, the nature that is being destroyed, but they believe it is one problem taking care of another. They will not help,*" the wolf replied.

"That is not such good news," Zalia said.

"*No, and though I will do what I can myself, my power comes in guidance from afar, not directly such as many of the others,*" the starlight wolf explained.

Zalia nodded thoughtfully.

"And what guidance have you come to give this night?" she asked.

"*That is the question, isn't it,*" the wolf said warmly.

Zalia sat watching the starlit wolf as members of its pack appeared and disappeared amongst the nearby trees. Aylie had finally untensed, yet sat still, hands shaking ever so slightly.

"A question you'll answer?" Zalia asked.

"*If only it were so simple. Guidance is not about answers, it is about showing someone the path they might take to find those answers themselves,*" the wolf explained.

"So you are here to help lead me in the right direction, then," Zalia stated.

"*Lead you in the right direction? No, that is not the way I would describe it. Rather, I wish to help you see the paths so that you might choose one for yourself. I fear that if you do not, you will be put on a path not of your choosing but by the powers around you,*" the wolf further explained.

"And who is to say that you are not one of those very powers trying to put me on a path you would prefer me to take?" Zalia asked.

"*Of course I am. I would see you travel a path that would save this world from those invading it. Nateysta, if they are still as I remember them, would see you travel a path that would save his world. Your human friends would see you travel a path that preserves the kingdom, and the demons would see you travel a path that leads to death. What path would you travel, Zalia?*" the wolf asked.

Zalia frowned.

"I don't really know yet. I want to rid both worlds of the demons and their corruption, that is for sure. To do that, I will need to grow strong enough to combat the creatures that spread that corruption, yet reaching that seems so far from where I am now. I want to return the favour given to me by Ro-ak . . . Nateysta, and save him just as he saved me. I want to see my friends safe, and those friends who have been harmed, avenged. I think, above all that, I want the wild places of the worlds to stay that way. I want nature to keep its beauty and its freedom," Zalia explained, trying to put her jumbled thoughts into words.

"*Then you already know where you wish to end up, it is only the path there that you must find. As is my duty as the spirit of the stars, my guidance is yours. You will find the beginning of what you look for in the north, where heat meets stone meets ice,*" the wolf told her, standing from its settled position.

Zalia knew better by now than to ask what exactly the wolf meant by "find the beginning of what you look for." She was more than used to the cryptic ambiguity from dealing with Delphi.

The wolf turned to Aylie.

"*I am sorry for your hardships, young one, and while I cannot promise the future holds any less pain than the past, I can give you the means to light your own path. Do you accept this blessing? I seek nothing in return for this gift,*" it said.

The wolf leaned down closer to Aylie, and she turned to Zalia.

"It's up to you, Aylie, I have accepted a blessing like this myself," Zalia told her.

Aylie turned back to the wolf, whose muzzle was now only a few feet from the girl, and nodded nervously. The starlight wolf touched its nose to Aylie's forehead and there was a bright flash of light. Once it faded, there was no sign of the wolf or its pack, the forest lit only by the crackling fire and the stars above.

Zalia turned away as Aylie stared wide-eyed into the distance. She turned her attention inwards and for the first time in a long time, read through the notifications of her level ups. She had been ignoring them ever since . . . that day.

Congratulations! Kill Shot has gained two levels, reaching Bronze 3.
Congratulations! Hunter's Mark has reached Bronze 2.
Congratulations! Fight or Flight has reached Bronze 2.
Congratulations! Hunter's Sight has reached Bronze 2.
Congratulations! Survivalist and associated skills have gained two levels, reaching Bronze 3.
Congratulations! Hunter class has reached Bronze 2.
Congratulations! Preparation has reached Bronze 2.
Congratulations! Druid Grove has reached Bronze 2.
Congratulations! Herbal Magic has gained two levels, reaching Bronze 3.
Congratulations! Healing Presence has gained two levels, reaching Bronze 3.
Congratulations! Aura Observation has gained eight levels, reaching Iron 15.
Congratulations! Low Light Vision has gained four levels, reaching Iron 13.
Congratulations! Mobility has reached Bronze 2.
Congratulations! Teaching has gained two levels, reaching Iron 9.
Congratulations! Flight has gained seven levels, reaching Iron 12.
Congratulations! Weapon proficiency - Bow has reached Bronze 2.
Congratulations! Weapon proficiency - Sword has reached Bronze 2.

Previously, going almost a week ignoring level ups—especially over the course of such a fight-filled time—would have resulted in a large amount of level ups. She didn't know if the reduction in levelling speed was a result of being in the Bronze rank, or if it was because she had been right about the theory of catch-up experience due to taking a class so late in life, but it was definitely slowed.

Aura Observation had gained a large amount of levels, though—a result of being bombarded by godlike beings' auras, she thought—so hopefully that would reach Bronze soon too.

"You alright?" Zalia asked Aylie.

The girl jumped, as if she had forgotten Zalia was there. She gave a quick nod and Zalia turned her head to see Boreal looking *grumpy.*

"What?" Zalia asked.

Boreal let out a low . . . grumble, and turned her head away.

Zalia stood up, rolling her eyes. She walked over and tapped Boreal on the head.

"Come on, out with it," she urged.

"*Blessing,*" Boreal said.

"What, you want one too?" Zalia asked.

"*Blessing!*" Boreal yelled.

She turned in a flash, launching a surprise attack and whacking her nose right into Zalia's forehead, a mirror to the starlight wolf's own blessing. Zalia fell backwards, Boreal following after, landing and knocking the wind out of her.

"Ow," Zalia complained, letting out a half wheeze, half laugh.

Boreal rolled off her, giving her a gentle bap to the side of the head on her way out. Zalia rolled over and launched her own attack, using her strength—and a little bit of wind magic, thanks to a Zephyr ritual—to throw herself onto Boreal's back. Boreal gave a surprised yowl and Zalia wrestled her to the ground, avoiding her soft, swiping paws. Boreal used some of her own magic to freeze Zalia's arms to the ground and managed to escape, but Zalia's own control of the element allowed her to quickly break free. She stood up, giving a light laugh before a little missile latched onto Boreal's side. Aylie had tried to knock Boreal over with her top speed but Boreal barely seemed to notice.

Zalia wasn't quite sure what caused her to stop and turn around. It might have been an instinct or her brain subconsciously reading the vibrations now easily visible to her. As she turned and stared into the dark forest beyond the halo of the campfire's light, she didn't see anything at first. Then, as she could see just fine in the dark, she saw a little bird come flying towards her, landing right on her shoulder. She turned her head to look at it, and it looked right back at her.

"*Um, hello?*" she said in its mind.

The message that came back was not in words, but more akin to how Boreal first communicated with her. It was a sense of a concept, and this concept was *danger.*

"Danger where?" she asked out loud.

Boreal was looking at the bird like it was a flying snack but Zalia gave her a warning look. This bird was friend, not food.

Danger, the concept came again and the bird flew off. Zalia extinguished the campfire with her abilities, lifted Aylie onto Boreal and ran after the bird.

"*Get Aylie to the Grove, into one of the treetop homes, and come find me,*" Zalia communicated to Boreal.

Boreal sprinted off towards the Grove entrance and Zalia continued following the little bird, flying at speed through the forest. She idly remembered the part of the Grove's description that said animals in and near the Grove would sometimes provide aid, and wondered if this was a result of that.

Fly, little bird, fly, Zalia thought.

CHAPTER SEVEN

Fire

Zalia

Zalia followed the bird for a little while, finding herself quickly approaching where the Grove stood. What danger could be near the Grove? She had searched the nearby area already before setting it up, though not as thoroughly as she might have.

The bird took her up the hill just behind the Grove before flitting down to sit upon the grass.

"What is it, little friend?" Zalia asked.

Danger, the concept came. The bird began pecking at the ground to emphasise.

Zalia frowned, walking over to see what it was doing. There, in the side of the hill was a little crack. She knelt down, summoning her armour onto her body as she did, and put her face next to it.

Looking through, she could see there was a wider space inside. She tapped on the dirt, watching the vibrations carefully. It looked like there was a passage that led even further in.

"What is in there?" Zalia asked the bird.

It didn't answer, hopping about nervously, pecking at the ground.

"You may go, thank you," Zalia told it.

It immediately took off, as if it had been waiting for her to release it. She watched it go, wondering as to how humane the ability was. Did it force the animal to do that? Did it coerce it?

She would have to test that more at a later time, for now she had a danger to solve. Another one.

Boreal came hurtling up the hill, sliding to a stop beside her.

"*Fight?*" Boreal asked, looking at the dirt.

"I don't know," Zalia whispered.

She began moving the earth with her manipulation skill, Boreal helping the process along. The entrance soon became wide enough for her to squeeze through. She was incorporeal, so it was much easier than it might have been as parts of her simply passed through the dirt. The little chamber that she had to crawl through led deeper into the hill, and she began to notice that the walls were marked. As earth became stone, those marks became clearer, more defined. They were scratches, like the claws of something digging into the hill.

The first thing that came to mind was the Silver rank centipede she had encountered back in her first months in Endaria. She almost started backing up, but realised there would be a good amount of the poison it commonly dripped all over the walls if that had been the case. Steeling herself, she pushed further in, Boreal shoving her way behind.

They actively worked to widen the passage as they crawled, the tunnel behind them becoming much more comfortable to travel if a quick escape ended up being necessary.

"*Any ideas what it could be?*" Zalia communicated to Boreal.

"*Smells . . . corrupt,*" Boreal answered with a low, quiet growl.

A shiver ran up Zalia's spine, memories of all the times she had fought or encountered the various corrupt creatures flashing through her mind. She started to feel it, the aura of corruption, oozing out of the tunnel from further in. Perhaps it was a good thing she had set up the Grove where she had, if she had discovered some hidden . . . nest?

She cast a few rituals, minor ones that gave both her and Boreal protection from senses and harm. She also tried to restrain her Healing Presence as much as possible to prevent them from being detected.

"*Ready for a fight, if need be?*" she asked Boreal.

"*Always,*" Boreal's reply came.

With that, she pushed forward.

Zalia's sight widened, the vibrations within the earth and air providing all the clarity and confirmation to what her sight told her. Within the chamber that the small tunnel led to, was most definitely a nest. A nest of corruption, dozens of creatures swarming about. As she watched, she could tell that none of the creatures within were of a high rank, many still only Tin. Was it some sort of breeding ground for more of the corrupt?

As she watched, a few of the small, bug-like corrupt creatures entered the chamber. They were similar in form to the other flying demons she had encountered, with cracked obsidian skin and six wings, yet not humanoid. They might have been the young of the larger and more powerful versions from all she could tell.

The little bug corrupt were dragging a body behind them. It was an Ironfur rabbit, the metallic sheen of its pelt unmistakable. As she watched, it was swarmed, and pieces of the animal were torn off and shared between the nest. Zalia had seen quite enough.

Knowing that no higher-ranked were in there, but not knowing if they resided nearby, she decided on a quick blitz tactic.

She marked ten of the creatures, cast the spreading cursed fire ritual, and threw herself from the hole.

Fire erupted and screeches echoed through the space. She set off an explosion ritual on the opposite side of the chamber even as she began cutting down as many of the corrupt bugs as she could. Boreal was close behind, tearing through them with a single bite, swipe, or pounce each. Ice spread out like the roots of a tree, occasionally lancing upwards to impale one of the bugs and holding it there like a morbid piece of art.

Boreal quickly moved off and began stopping the creatures from leaving but Zalia was quicker. She used Nature's Wrath, gaining control of the very elements making up the nest. The tunnels closed off, the air rushed towards the cursed fires, fanning them and fueling their power.

Soon, there was no oxygen left in the chamber but Zalia did not care, as she held her breath, controlling the fires, fueling their power now only with her magic. She made them burn ever hotter, spreading them across the entire nest.

A flash of memory, a hand, closing.

The heat grew further, the ashes of the dead beginning to fall.

The hand closed with a crunch.

The heat grew to a point that even she began to feel it. Still, she continued pushing more and more power into the fires.

The two allies that Nature's Wrath summoned, elementals of stone, began their own slaughter. They quickly became charred and cracked as the heat rose, yet they continued on their path of destruction. Each of the elementals was now Iron rank, rather than Tin, and a force in their own right.

"*Zalia*," Boreal said in her mind.

She ignored it for the moment, feeling the fires burn ever stronger, cleansing the corruption as thoroughly as she could.

The top of the nest exploded as two Bronze ranked demons entered the space. She sealed the entrance they had made immediately, condensing the flame around the two newly arrived creatures as their screeches of pain filled the chamber too.

They didn't last long; Zalia was now hanging suspended by earthen arms as she performed her grisly work.

"*Zalia!*" Boreal said louder.

What did she want? Couldn't Boreal see that she was busy?

The smell of scorching flesh reached her nose as the momentary burst of fresh air cast smoke across the room, and yet she fueled the fires ever onwards.

Nothing remained of the corrupt but ashes and melted stone; lava was pooling along the floor, and the roof had been turned to a scorched mess.

"*Zalia!*" Boreal yelled once more.

Another flash, the dead collective littered the floor.

She felt a pressure building within her as the flames burned brighter, scorched earth cracking.

Ro-ak, surrounded by two horrible creatures.

"*Zalia!*" Boreal yelled a final time.

Nature's Wrath ended.

The earthen arms holding her in the air broke apart and she dropped to the floor, panting. She realised the smell of scorched flesh was her own as her skin began flaking off, already healing from her own power. She knelt there, breathing heavily as new air filled the chamber through a hole in the ceiling as the molten stone collapsed.

Boreal appeared at her side, ice gently covering her and cooling her.

She was unharmed, but Zalia could see the concern in her body posture.

"Don't worry, it's over," Zalia croaked.

Her two elementals collapsed in a pile of cracked, scorched, and melted stone.

She leaned heavily against Boreal as exhaustion took over her body, a deep headache pulsing within her skull.

"Do—don't worry," Zalia repeated, her voice slowing and her mind shutting down.

Her vision started narrowing and she collapsed onto Boreal.

Zalia woke up, blinking bleary eyes at the canopy of leaves overhead. She didn't remember going to sleep, where was she?

Memories came back, a tunnel, the cave, fire burning.

It all came back in a flash and she sat up straight, her head pounding still.

"*Boreal?*" she called out telepathically.

A head popped into sight from above her, Boreal looking down from a little icy perch a little behind her own piece of floor.

"*Zalia!*" Boreal exclaimed.

She hopped down and circled around before calmly sitting in front of Zalia.

"Thanks," Zalia said, scratching at her arm a bit.

Boreal exhaled sharply, like an exasperated breath.

"*Zalia out of control,*" Boreal pointed out.

"Yeah, I . . . yeah," Zalia conceded.

She didn't know where it had come from. It was the first time she had ever actually used so much mana that she had passed out. Usually her abilities didn't use quite enough mana, especially with her having the attribute that increased her mana pool significantly, to cause it. Nature's Wrath was able to burn through it all now, apparently. In a very literal sense.

She frowned. She hadn't felt out of control at the time but thinking back to it, she definitely had been a little . . . overzealous. She'd turned those two Bronze rank demons to ash in moments. That shouldn't have been possible for someone of her rank but, well, her abilities were a little different from most.

She looked around, realising she was in one of the treehouse homes that were a part of her Grove. The little bird that had first warned her of danger flew through the doorway, landing on Zalia's arm.

"Hey there, little friend, how are you?" Zalia said to it.

It chirped a few times, inspected her arms, then flew off again. It was cute, only palm-sized with red and blue colourings. Zalia particularly liked the two little horns it had.

She stood up with a groan, Boreal stepping up next to her in case she needed help.

"Oh, don't worry about me, just getting into my later years now," Zalia said jokingly.

Boreal bumped her gently with her shoulder, then walked outside.

Stretching her arms, Zalia followed.

"How long was I out for?" she asked.

"*Two days*," Boreal said.

"Two *days*!?" Zalia exclaimed.

"*Sleepy Zalia*," Boreal informed her.

"Yeah, apparently," Zalia agreed.

She walked out into the light, looking out across her Grove, and was struck by the changes that had happened.

Dozens, if not hundreds, of birds flitted through the treetops, singing their songs. Far below, various animals were grazing, from Ironfur rabbits, suspiciously not attacking anything, to one of the magical deer creatures she had hunted once. Something akin to a badger was digging a little home in the ground.

"What happened while I was asleep?" Zalia asked incredulously.

"*Friends!*" Boreal said.

Zalia slowly walked down the stairs to the forest floor below and was shocked by the sheer amount of *life* she found. The farmers had obviously been busy as many rows of sown ground already had plants sprouting from them. A few Ironfur rabbits looked like they were helping sow more earth further along as the farmers worked using various magics.

A large cat, like she had seen on her first day down from the north hunting an Ironfur rabbit, sat contentedly in the boughs of a tree, keeping an eye on the entrance to the Grove. Zalia, in a daze, wandered over to where Mate was.

"What's going on here?" she asked.

"Was hopin' you'd tell me that," he said.

"Where did all the animals come from?" she asked instead.

"They just wandered in the day after you came back all unconscious, and started helping," he told her.

"Started helping?" she asked, still confused.

She knew the Grove description said that animals may form bonds and help, but this was . . . odd.

"Yeah, that's what I said. Some help us farm, the birds 'ave been bringing us seeds from all over, others help us sow the earth. Some like that one in the tree there seem to keep watch. I dunno what you did, but they certainly seem grateful to ya," Mate explained.

"Huh," she said.

"That's all the explanation you've got for me? Huh?" Mate asked, some incredulity entering his own voice.

"Yeah," Zalia said, still looking around in wonder.

He just stared at her with an odd expression on his face.

CHAPTER EIGHT

Remembering

Zalia

Zalia wandered about the Grove, greeting many of the animals who very calmly greeted her back. Birds landed on or near her to carefully inspect her before flying off to their comings and goings. Ironfur rabbits hopped around her feet before dashing off. The large feline animal that was lounging in the boughs of a tree didn't greet Zalia, but stared very intently at Boreal. It was Bronze rank—none of the other animals had reached that rank—and definitely a dangerous creature.

Zalia left Boreal staring down the other feline; the target of her gaze was more akin to a cheetah, but less fluffy, more lithe. Boreal was larger and definitely more muscular, but Zalia had a feeling the other feline would outrun even her.

As she didn't detect any hostility, more mutual curiosity, Zalia wasn't worried about a fight breaking out. Boreal would win that fight even if it did, anyways.

For now, she had something a little more important to look into, something she had perhaps been putting off for longer than she should have. Before the collective had . . . died, a jumbled mess of memories had been shoved into her brain. And her memory of receiving those memories was also stored away.

She hadn't yet tried to decipher them, not wanting to bring forth the memory of, well, the memory of what had caused that to be there in the first place.

Now, she was safe in the Grove—relatively safe, at least—and wanted to attempt figuring out the odd memory.

She walked through the Grove until she reached the secluded little waterfall, walking behind it to the small space that held the altar dedicated to Ro. Leaning against it, she closed her eyes and tried to recall the memory.

It felt similar in a way to the memory she had first seen upon using the gauntlet, the end of a Bathar researcher's life. That memory had not been her own, disjointed and without place in her mind, yet the collective had used their own power to help guide her mind to an understanding of the memory, allowing it to fit into place.

She had no such help now.

There were flashes, images seen through eyes that were not her own, a very different way of seeing things.

She saw herself in the keep of the city of Hetheir, fighting a battle against undead. A flash of the city from afar, yet in its former glory, bustling with life and buildings intact. A river flowed nearby and there was no sign of the floating islands. Another flash, and the same city from the same view point, yet as it was now, destroyed and desecrated, filled with the roaming undead.

Her eyes opened and she slid down the altar to sit on the floor, head aching as recalling the memory made her remember another. The battle for survival and the death of the collective.

Tears came to her eyes in that secluded waterfall hideaway, her own memories of times spent with Delphi flashing through her mind. She could feel that the memory given to her by the collective was much, much more than the three images she had just seen, yet even trying to decipher more made her head pound.

"Why did you do it?" she whispered, a shiver passing through her body as a tear fell to join the waterfall.

Had it been the only path they had seen to take that would lead to her return to Endaria? They had mentioned something about the future of their world, did they foresee that she would free Cormaine from the corruption?

She knew the collection of memories the collective had been reduced to would hold the answers to those questions, if only she were able to see them.

She sat there in silence, allowing the memories to fade away once more into the vault where they lived.

She stood, running her hand over the surface of the altar.

I hope you still live, wherever you are, she thought.

Ro was strong, if anyone she knew had the power to survive fighting two of those monsters, he was the one. She thought she could almost feel him, holding her hand to the altar. He was intrinsically connected to it in a way she didn't fully understand. The power of faith was something that stretched across worlds, apparently.

She left the cave, returning to the Grove proper. There, Boreal and the other feline were busy in the middle of a fight. Her heart jumped for a moment before she realised it was a playful fight and they were not attempting to kill each other.

Shaking her head at her silly friend, a bright point in the darkness of her memories, she walked to the entrance of the Grove. She needed to talk to Indis and Faian about meeting with the Hidden. Not only that, but she needed to tell Indis quite a few things about the history she had discovered while in Cormaine.

Unfortunately the only things she had brought back in her vault were a sword, a demon's body, and a few shiny collectibles belonging to her crow friend.

"*Boreal*," Zalia sent to her friend.

She must not have heard Zalia as she continued her fight, wrestling the other feline to the ground.

"*Boreal*," Zalia tried again.

The two of them rolled about in the grass, crushing it beneath them.

"*Borreeaaalllll*," Zalia yelled.

She finally noticed and stopped fighting, standing up to clean herself inconspicuously.

"I'm going back to the camp, want to come with?" she called over.

Boreal bounded over and the other feline watched her go. Zalia was tempted to invite Aylie along, but when she found the girl sitting on a log surrounded by small, cute animals that she was telling a story to, Zalia decided against it.

She waited a moment for a pause in the storytelling.

"I'm just going to head back to the camp for a little bit, you'll be ok?" Zalia asked softly.

She received a small nod of the head in answer and Zalia left the girl to her important activities, leaving the Grove with a wave towards Mate.

Zalia and Boreal arrived at and reentered the war camp after another inspection by the person on duty, not the nervous man this time. They made their way, as stealthily as possible to avoid any attention, to the large building where Zalia knew to find both Faian and Indis. Assuming they stayed there at night, that was.

It was dusk, most people thankfully now in their homes, if they had any. This meant that they had an easy time of getting in the building since the doorways were not near as packed as they usually were. As they moved into the second room, Zalia was surprised to find that Indis was seated at one of the tables there amongst the other administrators. Indis looked up at the same time as Zalia entered, her eyes holding something akin to rage.

"Where *have* you been?" Indis asked in an angry whisper.

"Passed out from overdrawing my mana pool. Why do you seem so upset?" Zalia asked back.

"Well, for one, we've been waiting for word that we can send more people up to your little Grove for housing, and two, I've had to spend the majority of my last two days answering questions as to your whereabouts—where you have been before this, what you have been doing, so on and so forth. Endless questions to which I have only the bare bones answers to," Indis hissed.

"A problem that you started and that you will be dealing with. I will absolutely not be spending my time dealing with idiotic masses asking about my every movement because *you* decided to *literally* put my image on a pedestal," Zalia retorted.

That seemed to give Indis pause, and Zalia felt slightly victorious at having made a solid point in an argument with her that wasn't immediately dismantled.

"You know, for someone who is usually so good at controlling what emotions they display, you really suck at not being angry at me," Zalia pointed out.

"You're an incredibly frustrating person, at times," Indis muttered.

"As are you, sweetheart," Zalia said sarcastically.

Indis looked at her with an expression of offence plastered on her face.

"Now, if you're done quietly yelling at me, I have come back to tell you some of the things I've learnt in my time away, if you're interested. I learnt some things that will win an argument you had with Ember a long time ago," Zalia explained.

That immediately got Indis's full attention. Zalia thought it would.

"Let us go somewhere a little bit more private," Indis suggested.

"Fine by me," Zalia agreed.

They moved out of that room toward one of the doors they had walked past on their way to Faian's personal office last time. Inside was a small sitting room, though still set in a utilitarian way. It was somewhat more of a space for private conversations of importance rather than idle chatter to pass away the time.

There, Zalia told Indis all she knew about Hetheir, the Bathar, and the fall of their world. What she knew disproved Ember's idea that the Bathar had once been the owners of the land that the kingdom of Endaria now resided in. They had been something of an ally to the kingdom of Endaria in its very earliest days and had evacuated many of their number there before Cormaine fell. She even drew out a map of Hetheir as best she could from the memory of it stored within the vault.

Through all of this, Indis was mostly silent, only asking questions when she needed further clarity on something. She even pulled out a little notebook and started taking notes.

When Zalia mentioned that there were a lot more documents back there in the keep that she hadn't read, Indis managed to get angry *again*.

"How could you not bring them back with you!" she said, voice raised in agitation.

"I didn't really have much time," Zalia explained.

"That is priceless history, history that could help us now with the invasion of our own world. It could explain what is happening here and help us stop it," Indis said.

"Please, I know you have a lot of pressure on your shoulders right now, but calm down," Zalia pleaded.

Poor choice of words.

"I will *not* calm down. We have tens of thousands of homeless people relying on us to take back our kingdom from these invaders. Countless are dead, more every day. Refugees stream to us on a daily basis, bringing news of more and more towns devoid of life. The land dies around us and you could have found something there that could help our efforts greatly if you had read it all!" Indis yelled.

"You don't understand what it was like there. The very air tried to kill us, the landscape was filled with death and the dead. We were alone, finding only a few others there who were even *alive*, let alone willing to help us. I had to kill and struggle my way through every day, every moment spent breathing poison. I didn't know each day if that would be my last, if I would finally be killed by some demon or a twisted being, flying across the sky with a thousand eyes. I saw a kingdom, shattered and turned to dust, the citizens nothing more than tortured souls trapped in undead bodies. I had no way out, no respite from the life-and-death struggle. Then, I saw one of the two friends I made in that *hell* crushed into paste before my eyes. The other might be in as bad a state, for all I know. I was violently torn from that world and thrown back to this one as a last-ditch effort by my only remaining friend there. Don't yell at me for not thinking about a few stupid pieces of parchment. You have no idea what it was like," Zalia said, starting out coldly but her voice turning ragged towards the end.

The memory surfaced, unbidden, as she tried to explain what exactly life had been like there and Zalia found herself holding back tears.

"I'm sorry Zalia, I didn't think—"

"No, you didn't. You're not the only one that has been through some shit, so stop acting like I'm trying to wrong you at every turn. I'm doing my damn best."

Indis fell silent, looking both a bit guilty and thoughtful.

"Who did you mee—" Indis started.

"I don't want to talk about it. I'm . . . I'm not ready," Zalia interrupted, desperately trying to push that *damned* memory back into the vault.

Taking in a shuddering breath, Zalia tried to compose herself. Boreal was sitting silently on the floor near her feet, wise enough not to say anything.

"You can start sending people to the Grove. The farmers will also be ready to start harvesting as well; the nature of the Grove means things grow there very quickly," Zalia said, changing the subject. Anything to get away from that memory.

"Alright, I'll get it organised," Indis promised quietly.

Zalia stood to leave.

"Zalia," Indis called.

She turned around.

Indis stepped up and gave her a quick, light hug, then stepped away once more. "I'm sorry."

"Don't be. I chose my own path and have come to terms with what that has meant for me. You should too," Zalia said, before leaving.

She didn't blame the young woman. Indis did have a lot of pressure on her shoulders for someone so young, from the collapse of her house, the loss of her closest childhood friend, and the events of the past few months, anyone would be stressed and quick to strong emotion. She didn't blame her, but Indis also needed to understand that she wasn't the only one in a similar situation.

As she left, Zalia decided against finding Faian. She had wanted to talk to the Hidden while she was here, but the stress and emotional exhaustion from her conversation with Indis . . . well, she wasn't feeling up to it. The conversation with the Hidden, Hidey, would probably be similarly exhausting.

Instead, she asked one of the administrators where she could find the building holding the mentally scarred. She didn't ask *if* there was one, she knew there would be.

She was directed to a nearby building and made her way there. There was a theory she had come up with in Cormaine that she wanted to test. A combination of Frozen Heart major and Living Trapvine minor that would create a healing ritual focused on the mind. It hadn't had a super strong effect on Nateysta, though it hadn't really been him at the time, just a piece of his power given semi-sentience. Regardless, the scale of power she was able to produce relative to someone like Ro-ak, or compared to an Iron or Bronze ranked human, well, it wasn't even comparable.

She entered the dimly lit building and found pretty much exactly what she expected to find. Rows of white linen beds, separated by hanging curtains, in which soldiers in various states of mental shock or trauma lay. Some muttered to themselves, others stared sightlessly into nothing and others yet scratched the walls or tapped patterns on their knees. Regardless of whatever mindless behaviour they were doing, they all had one thing in common. Their minds weren't quite all there.

With the small amount of Living Trapvine she had, Zalia wouldn't be able to heal them all. Hell, it might not even work in the first place, but she needed to try. So, she walked up to one of the doctors that saw to the needs of the traumatised soldiers and asked if she would be allowed to try the experimental healing ritual she had devised.

With a little explanation, she was granted permission and she soon got to work.

CHAPTER NINE

Mind

Zalia

Zalia knelt next to the low bed of the soldier closest to the door. He was sat facing down, knees to his chest, hands over the back of his head, rocking back and forth. He was muttering something, gibberish or a language so dissimilar to Endarian that her translation powers didn't work on it.

"Hey, I'm going to try something to help you, ok?" Zalia told him gently.

He didn't reply or even take notice of her words, from what she could tell. Deciding to go ahead, Zalia summoned the few materials she had. She was a little worried about causing more damage to the mind of the man so decided to include Adastem in the mix. Not only would it weaken the overall strength of the ritual, it would also provide it with an adaptability that might be more than necessary for what she was attempting.

Frozen Heart desiccated in an instant, floating up and crushing to a fine powder that hung in the air as a swirling ball. A good amount of it too, a small handful. Living Trapvine was next, a little cutting of the giant bulbous plant that lived in Cormaine. This one crushed slowly into a paste, little more than a small drop that floated next to the Frozen Heart.

Finally, came the Adastem. The ever-changing plant was left as it was, already in a form usable for her magic.

The Frozen Heart and Living Trapvine, at Zalia's command, gently floated over to form a little ritual circle in the air between her and her patient. It began glowing a light green, the colour of new growth and life reborn.

The Adastem soon joined it, twisting and forming until it made a slightly larger ring around the central one, its shape still changing, yet glowing a deeper green than the centre ring, the colour of old growth and times past.

Zalia activated the ritual, yet managed to slow the speed at which it was released. Gently, the materials turned to a fine mist over the course of a few seconds, flowing towards the man whose head was lowered.

It spun around him before sinking into his skull, vanishing from sight. The rocking and muttering stopped.

Zalia waited a few tense minutes, unsure whether she should disturb the man. She decided not to, knowing that the mind was a brittle thing and interrupting the ritual may not be a good idea. Better to let it do its work.

Finally, the soldier raised his head, blinking bleary eyes as if truly seeing for the first time in a very, very long time.

"Hello," Zalia greeted him softly.

"I-I'm. Who, where. Where am I?" he asked.

"You're in a ward for people who need healing. What do you remember?" Zalia explained gently.

"I-I was, I mean, we were just . . . we were just following orders. The blood, oh gods, the blood," he croaked, his speech devolving into sobs.

"It's alright, you're safe now. It's alright." Zalia comforted him, awkwardly giving him a pat on the shoulder.

"W-what happened to me? Everything is so . . . so blurry. How long?" he asked, his words jumping between too quick thoughts.

"Don't worry about all that. You've been out for a while but you're in a safe place. The people here have been taking care of you. Rest, get some rest. You can tackle it all in the morning."

"I . . . gods. I knew it was wrong. We knew it was wrong . . . but the king. Orders. We had orders."

"Don't think about it, alright? Rest and when you wake up tomorrow, you can go see the sun once more," Zalia urged.

"The sun. I'd like to see the sun again," he murmured, already falling backwards to sleep.

Zalia focused a little bit more of her Healing Presence on the man, letting its comfortable warmth pull the man into the embrace of sleep.

She let out a deep sigh, utterly exhausted after healing just that one man's mind.

"Excuse me, Zalia? How did you heal his mind?" the doctor who had been hovering over Zalia's shoulder asked.

"Magic, herbs, and a little bit of hope," Zalia replied.

Zalia looked around, trying to find Boreal but finding her nowhere in sight.

"Could you teach us how?" the doctor asked.

"Not really, unless you know herbal ritual magic?" Zalia inquired.

"Well, no. We could learn though," the doctor suggested.

"Well, you'd have to find someone who knew how to teach you. I certainly couldn't. It's all part of the class," Zalia explained.

"Damn," the doctor muttered.

Zalia agreed with the sentiment but she had also just healed the mind of a man who had been so thoroughly broken, and words meant nothing to him. Well, "healed" might have been an overstatement. It was more akin to picking up the pieces of a shattered glass, putting them back in their place, and telling them to fix the cracks on their own. She wouldn't be able to do that part for them. She could help, sure, but for the next steps others were now a better alternative than she was.

"I'll come back another time and heal who I can. I don't have much of this plant left and want to see if I can grow more before I use it all," Zalia said.

"What is it? We can get some more for you," the doctor asked.

"I highly doubt that," Zalia said.

There was only one place she knew of to find the plant, and she sure as hell wasn't going back to Cormaine anytime soon.

She left the ward, following the instinctive knowledge of where Boreal was at all times that was a part of the bond they held. She kept all her stealth abilities active, blending into the darkness now the sun had fully set.

She found Boreal in the process of assaulting someone who had just entered the war camp with a barrage of body checks and paw taps. It looked like she was trying to determine if the person was real or if she was imagining them. Zalia had to make sure she was seeing right as well, as she saw Ember.

"Boreal? What in the name of the gods are you doing here? You're huge! Is . . . is Zalia with you?"

Ember was looking well, from what Zalia could see. She still had her old twin-bladed sword and heater shield, though it looked like she had managed to acquire a new set of armour somewhere. She had always worn a lighter set of armour made for mobility, a set with even less protection than Zalia's first set of armour. Now though, she wore what was essentially a full suit of plate armour. Despite what must have been an extremely heavy set of armour, she moved in it as if she had been born to it, lithely and with ease.

Zalia felt a little . . . nervous. She hadn't been nervous meeting Indis again, but Ember had always been a compassionate and caring person. Someone who had shared a deep part of her past with Zalia that she had not shared with any other.

Putting her nerves aside, she made her way towards the two.

"Where have you been?" Ember was saying to Boreal.

"Hey, Ember," Zalia greeted.

Ember's head shot up and she stared at Zalia.

She blinked, once, twice.

"How the fuck are you alive?" she asked.

Zalia laughed and gave the woman a long hug. "Good to see you too," she said warmly.

"You're . . . different," Ember noted, pulling away and holding Zalia at arms' length, giving her a critical look.

"As are you," Zalia said, pointedly looking at the full plate Ember now wore.

"We've all had to adapt a bit as of recently," Ember said grimly.

"Yeah."

"But seriously, how the fuck are you alive and where have you been?" Ember asked.

"Long, long story. The short of it is when I messed with that ritual, it dragged me, Boreal, and Juniper, into Cormaine of all places. Juniper is dead now, while I survived. We can have a long chat about the whole thing at another time and place," Zalia explained.

"Fair enough."

"And you, I heard you are going about on your own as usual, saving people and giving all you can and whatnot. Had much trouble out there?" Zalia asked.

"Have you been out there at all?"

"Yeah, yeah I have. It's a welcome respite from the experiences of my past weeks? Months? I'm not even really certain how long I was there for," Zalia said.

"A welcome respite? Bloody hell, Zalia, it's a nightmare out there. How bad was it in Cormaine?" Ember asked in concern.

"Bad."

"You and I need to go get a drink," Ember decided.

"Alcohol doesn't really do anything to me, remember?" Zalia pointed out.

"Oh ho, no? Well, I'm certain Harrick's brew will mess you up something good if you aren't careful," Ember disagreed, moving off into the camp.

"Harrick?" Zalia asked, following along.

"Gold rank chef with the brewer specialisation. Can you believe that? Gold rank!? It's almost unheard of in a class like that," Ember said.

Zalia frowned.

"Why is that?" she asked.

"What?"

"Why is it that it's so rare to find Gold rankers of any type, but especially non-combat-focused ones. Not to mention, I've not seen an Emerald or Diamond ranked person at all. I would have thought if such people were to make a showing, now would be the time," Zalia explained.

"Well, as you know, levelling is much, much easier when you go about fighting things. It's hard to get enough levels to reach Gold within a normal person's lifespan through a non-combat class. Harrick, though, well I managed to get the secret out of him. He has found a way to make an age-slowing drink! Won't let anyone else have it though, too dangerous, he says. As for higher-ranked people, well . . . you know I'm not really sure. I've only ever heard tale of people reaching that rank, I've never actually seen any," Ember said.

Zalia pondered it. She knew that Ro-ak and the thousand-eyed demons were *far* beyond those ranks, and there had been some Emerald rank elementals popping up towards the end of the rituals, yet still, no humans of that rank to fight them off.

"Have the elementals still been attacking?" Zalia asked.

"Nah, not since the ritual happened."

"I wonder why that is," she muttered.

"Doesn't matter much at the moment, does it? One less thing to worry about," Ember said cheerfully.

Zalia gave her an odd look.

"You've definitely changed. I don't think I've heard you talk this much *ever*."

"Well, a lot has happened, you know? Indis has gone and drowned herself in even more responsibility, from some kind of guilt she has around your death. Well, supposed death. Zen, ah man, Zen. Fuck knows where he ended up. I still hope I'll find him out there . . ." Ember explained, trailing off.

"How much impact have you had out there?" Zalia asked.

She had noticed that Ember was also Bronze rank, unsurprisingly.

"I've made a big difference in some people's lives. Saved a lot of people from horrible fates. It never feels like enough, though. I've come pretty close to meeting one of those fates myself a few times too. There are a lot of terrifying creatures out there."

"Yeah, that there is."

They arrived at a dingy little building that had a surprisingly pleasant interior. There were only a few tables with three other patrons inside, all of them having a casual drink.

The warmly lit space also had a little bar fit into a corner where a large, jolly man leant against the wall, idly twiddling his moustache.

"Harrick!" Ember called when they entered.

"Ahh, Ember. Back from your little escapade again I see. Same as usual?" Harrick asked.

His voice was pleasant, smooth and neutral with a slight accent to it that Zalia didn't identify as Endarian.

"Of course, the same thing for my friend here too."

"Coming right up!"

They sat at a little table against one of the walls, nobody blinking an eye as Boreal pushed through and between the tables to sit next to them. Having a look around the room, Zalia realised the other patrons were all Silver rank. They had probably seen crazier things than Boreal in their time.

"I'm surprised Harrick doesn't have more patrons for a Gold rank brewer," Zalia said.

"He prefers it this way."

"Right, fair enough."

"Now, tell me all about where and what you've been doing," Ember said, leaning forward intently.

For the second time that day, Zalia began telling the story of her recent experiences.

CHAPTER TEN

Catch-Up

Zalia

D amn, Zalia, that is one wild story," Ember said with a low whistle.

"Yeah, it has definitely been an experience. I'm glad to be out of there, back to fresh air and lively forests," Zalia agreed.

They were still seated at the little table in Harrick's bar, amongst a few other higher-ranked people minding their own business. Ember was drinking a brightly coloured cocktail with the top of a plant Zalia didn't recognise sticking out of it. She had her own, though, and was making her way through it significantly slower than Ember was.

Ember was uncharacteristically peppy, joyous even, which confused Zalia a little bit, having known her before the entire kingdom went to shit.

"Now, do you want to explain to me why you're so happy?" Zalia asked.

"Happy? I wouldn't say that. I am feeling a lot more hopeful, though."

"Yeah, why is that?"

"Well, as bad as things look, I've been out there helping people, saving lives, basically since you vanished. Before the demons appeared, people were selfish, greedy, indulgent. They would kick down their neighbour if it would give them an advantage, more often than not. Now though, I see people helping others despite danger, despite having next to nothing themselves. This shared adversity has brought many of the people out there together, as if they understand that this isn't about personal gain but the survival of the kingdom, perhaps the world. That gives me hope," Ember explained.

Zalia mulled it over. While that certainly was true, she was a little bit surprised to find that Ember had found hope in a seemingly hopeless situation. She hadn't seen what Zalia had seen, though, so maybe that would change. She hoped not.

"Alright, fair enough. What now? Are you going to go back out there?" Zalia asked.

"Yeah, I'll give it a day, get some supplies, and make my way down south west this time."

"Might I convince you to come north with me instead?"

"Oh? Possibly—why do you want to go north?" Ember asked.

"Well, remember that starlight wolf god spirit thing that blessed my bow a while back? It told me that the first step to achieving some of my goals lies in the north, in the snow. I figure that means with Those Born of Heat and Stone," Zalia explained.

"Oh shit, I forgot about them in all this. I wonder if they're doing ok," Ember said.

"I hope so. They did have one of those ritual sites on the mountain above them. Though, they were united as a race even before this happened, I'm sure they're doing just fine," Zalia said.

The conversation brought back memory of the other types of races similar to Glemp's. Those Born of the Watery Depths and . . . Those Born of Wind and Sky? She didn't quite remember the exact names Delphi had given them. Delphi . . .

Shaking her head, she absently tapped on the table.

"Alright, I'll come north with you. I want to go by all the towns we can on our way there though, deal?" Ember said.

"Deal," Zalia agreed.

Having Ember along would be helpful, as she was a Healer herself. One that could do a lot more healing in a shorter time than Zalia could, though she was more of an extended fight kind of fighter herself.

"What happened with Zen?" Zalia asked.

"Zen? I don't know. Haven't you asked Indis about him?"

"I did, she said that Zen wanted nothing more to do with it, that he asked to be left out of everything," Zalia explained.

Ember nodded.

"That's right. Though I wish she had kept you out of her scheming and political bullshit as well. I assume you've seen the *wondrous* statue of yourself in the centre of the camp?"

"Uhhhh, tell me about it. It's a nightmare come true. Do you know there was a *mob* of people asking me where I've been and what I was going to do about the demons on the first day I arrived here?" Zalia asked incredulously.

"I'm not surprised, the way Indis has been talking you up," Ember said with a chuckle.

"So I told them all that Indis would answer all of their questions, and she's had one big headache for the past two days. Definitely glad I did that," Zalia said, smiling as well.

"I'll bet she hated that. Did she know where you had been yet?"

"Nope."

"Even better!" Ember said, laughing.

Zalia laughed too, happy to be in good company.

Boreal was busy attempting to sneak up on Harrick to perhaps steal some food or drink from the man, but no matter what she tried, the man saw her and stopped her. Zalia would have stopped the behaviour but Harrick didn't seem to mind, simply laughing at Boreal's antics.

"You do know that what I've discovered means that Endaria *didn't* steal these lands from the Bathar, right?" Zalia asked Ember, after a short moment of silence.

Ember shrugged.

"Yeah, I'm not worried about that, quite the opposite, really. It's good to hear that my own kingdom hasn't committed a huge crime against an entire people and in fact, actually took in those said people as refugees. I'm just a bit confused as to how that history has been lost. Surely someone should have known about this, where are all the documents and tales or anything that points to these events in history? That's what I'm more concerned about," Ember explained.

Zalia frowned, it was a good point.

"Hmm, maybe when they evacuated some of the demons got through with them? Maybe this isn't the first time that something like this has happened before?" Zalia pondered.

"Well, that's a little concerning."

"Also a good thing. If this has happened before, then the invasions were fought off those times too," Zalia pointed out.

"But if that were the case, the state of the kingdom left behind must have been so dire that no history or recollection of those events endured. That doesn't bode well," Ember said.

"Hmm, well, maybe not then. I don't know, maybe they didn't write things down back then. From what I've read and seen, it looks like these events happened a very long time ago, closer to the formation of Endaria as a kingdom at all. Who knows what has transpired since then?"

"Possible. No point wondering about it, it's not like we can find any answers to those questions right now," Ember sighed.

"Actually, I might be able to. The starlight wolf would have been around then, maybe they know something. I wish I'd asked Ro-ak when I had the chance . . ."

"He sounds like a good friend," Ember said.

"He wa—is a good friend. There was much I could have learnt from him, I just had so much to think about in those last days in Cormaine that I didn't get the chance," Zalia explained.

"I can see why, I think I might've been the same way," Ember empathised.

"Oh, you should come by and see my Grove," Zalia exclaimed.

"Your Grove? I thought you said that was in Cormaine?" Ember asked in confusion.

"Well, the first one was, yes. Looks like I can kind of, um, move it around a bit. Well, if it is destroyed I can set another up. Or if I release the magic . . . anyway you get the idea. I set the Grove up nearby, Aylie is there along with a whole bunch of ani—"

"Aylie?" Ember asked.

"Oh, right. Yeah, I found Aylie being hunted by a demon, a type like a feline with a disjointed jaw and slime coating it."

"Ah, yeah, I know the type. I've killed a few, nasty fuckers."

"Speaking of, what kind of abilities did you get from becoming Bronze?" Zalia asked.

"Besides everything becoming more . . . well, more, one of my Healer class abilities transformed to help me a lot in my recent activities. It is a little, uh, strange? Or, well, reactive, I guess, to what I'm doing at the time. It is kind of a bit odd. It's a little bi—"

"Ember, please, just read out what it does," Zalia interrupted.

"Ok, so, when I activate it, the ability helps a community in an impactful way dependent on what I am doing at the time," Ember explained.

"That's a little vague," Zalia said.

"I know right? It is very, very vague. But I've found it really helpful! This one time, I was trying to get a group of refugees to safety from a group of Iron demons. I could have taken them on my own but with their numbers . . . let's just say they were getting around me. One second, a whole bunch of them were moments away from killing the people I was trying to protect, the next, they were protected by a large dome. Another time, it created a whole bunch of food for a town I was trying to help feed. It does things like that, always to help whichever community or person I'm trying to help. It really has helped take care of a lot of things I wouldn't have been able to help with previously."

"It does sound very useful," Zalia admitted.

"What about you?" Ember asked.

"I've got a few nice bits and pieces. The extra five abilities I have on most others have been shining, as of late. I've got away with a few stupid moves that I wouldn't have otherwise, simply because I am stronger than your conventional Bronze ranker."

Zalia went on to describe the basics of what her abilities could now do and how they were slowly evolving to create synergies between classes.

"I've had similar experiences, such as my combat passive gaining an ability that increases the amount of healing I receive based on how wounded I am," Ember said.

"Hey, I've got one that does that too."

"Healing abilities used often in combat usually get something like it."

"That they do. Want to come see the Grove now? I've got a spare bed or twenty," Zalia asked.

"Don't mind if I do, let's go!" Ember agreed, standing from the table with a little wobble.

Zalia felt it as well, just a bit tipsy from the one drink she'd had. She wasn't surprised Ember was wobbling based on the four empty glasses in front of her.

Since they'd already paid—or rather Ember had, and a not insignificant sum at that—as expected after drinks from a Gold rank brewer, they left the bar with a wave and a stumble.

With Boreal helping hold up Ember, they left the camp, Zalia lithely leading the way and Ember wobbling after, and they soon found themselves at the Grove.

"Woahhh, look at that," Ember said in awe as they walked through the entrance arch.

While during the day, the Grove was a beautiful sight, the nighttime was absolutely stunning. The warm lights floating about under the treetops cast dancing shadows amongst the boughs and trunks. In the leaves of the canopy above, little worms were emitting a light blue glow that was somehow both conflicting yet complimentary with the warmth of the lights, and a reflection of the stars glittering far above.

"Welcome to the Grove," Zalia said, the warmth of the lights entering the tone of her voice.

CHAPTER ELEVEN

Fun in the Sun

Zalia

You weren't kidding about the Grove," Ember said a little breathlessly, turning about in place.

They were standing in the centre of the Grove now, staring up at the glittering starlight worms above.

"It's a place of safety for nature, me, and my friends, above all else," Zalia explained.

"It definitely seems like it. This feeling . . . is it healing us?"

"It is, it also helps protect everyone inside against harm."

"And there is . . . something else here. Another aura maybe? I can't quite tell," Ember said, looking about curiously.

"It is a living ritual that helps protect and hide the Grove. It is something I figured out how to do separately, a way of using the natural aura of all living things to a certain effect," Zalia explained, pointing to a few of the plants around that were components of the ritual.

"How did you figure out how to do that?" Ember asked, turning to her.

"I learnt a great many things in Cormaine, not much other choice, really," Zalia said, shrugging.

"Well, we'll definitely be better off because of it."

"I hope so. Oh, hey, I purged some kind of demon nest further up the hill two days ago, should I have told Faian or someone about that?" Zalia asked.

"Ah, no need, they pop up all over the place. Another will find its way somewhere else in these hills before long. They're all across Endaria now, it will take a long time to remove them all once this war is over," Ember assured her.

"That's horrific."

"Yeah, it is," Ember agreed. Then she frowned. "How did you and Boreal manage to purge one of those nests by yourselves? I usually have to find a few others to help."

"I pulled it off mostly by myself," Zalia replied, a little distracted by a light that was trying to land on her face.

"You did what?"

"Yeah, Nature's Wrath has become quite a, um, how do you say, powerful ability," Zalia explained.

"You did it with a *single* ability!?" Ember asked, her expression becoming even further shocked.

"Well, no, it was a mixture of that plus a Herbal Magic ritual to light the fire. Though, I guess I could have started a fire without the ritual."

Ember stared at her.

"What?" Zalia asked.

"I'm glad you're back!" Ember said with a chuckle. "Anything else I should know about that you picked up while you were there?"

Ember looked pointedly at the decidedly plant-like artifact attached to Zalia's hand.

"Oh, yeah. Well, Boreal got her own set of heirloom armour, as did I, along with this heirloom storage device. It kind of merged with one of my abilities and also has the properties of the Grove, as well as being able to store a good amount of things."

Ember looked down at her own ordinary plate armour with a slight *clank*, then looked back up at her.

"Your cat has heirloom armour," she stated.

"Yes."

Ember looked down at her armour again.

"Can I have the next set?" she asked, looking back up.

Zalia laughed. "Sure, sure. Next one is yours, if I find one. Want to check mine out?"

"Absolutely!" Ember agreed excitedly.

Zalia summoned her armour onto her body and stood still as Ember did a circle about her, inspecting it.

"Very, very cool. What does it do?" Ember asked.

"Well, it gives me incorporeality, suppresses my aura so people can't see my rank or find me through it, silences my movement entirely, aaand lets me step through a plant to a nearby similar plant. Pretty good overall," Zalia explained.

Ember gave a whistle.

"Daaaamn, that is something else. I'm quite jealous," Ember said.

"You'll get your own one day," Zalia assured her, giving her a silent pat on the back.

"The absolute silence is a little unnerving," Ember muttered.

"Imagine how unsettling it would be if I was trying to kill you!" Zalia exclaimed.

"Thanks for the mental image," Ember said, sounding a little bummed out.

"Hey, look, if you want to go through a month or two in *the realm of the dead,* as Indis put it, and all you get out of it is bad memories, dead friends, and a few cool trinkets, be my guest," Zalia offered.

Ember raised her hands in a surrendering gesture.

"Woah, woah, wasn't getting on your case about it. You have been through a lot for the things you've gotten, I know. Don't need to come out the gate on the offensive like that," Ember said.

"Sorry, just had a *little* bit of a bout with Indis earlier on a similar topic," Zalia apologised.

"You? And Indis? Having a bout? Nahhh, wouldn't have guessed it. I've had my own gripes with the woman recently as well," Ember said.

Zalia snorted a laugh. "Yeah, I heard. I also heard you were against her martyring me, which I appreciate greatly."

"It was wrong of her to do that."

Zalia sighed. "Yeah, maybe so. I don't mind it *that* much if it helps the soldiers fight harder. Did they have to build a statue though? I mean, come on," she complained.

"Of course! A great big statue for the great big hero of Endaria, Zalia! Stopper of rituals! Killer of demons! Tamer of Boreals!" Ember announced, waving her hand like she was revealing a grand sight.

"Please stop that," Zalia groaned.

"Alright, alright. I should probably catch some sleep. See you in the morning?"

"Yeah, see you in the morning."

"Oh, hey, do you even need to sleep anymore?" Ember asked as she backed away towards the tree's stairs.

"Not really," Zalia said.

"Huh, cool. Enjoy your free time then, I guess," Ember said with a wave. "Goodnight!"

Zalia waved goodnight as well, then went to find where Boreal had gotten off to. She found her with the guardian feline, the two of them cleaning each other.

She gave them a smile and a wave before walking off to the cave behind the waterfall, where the temple to Ro-ak was situated.

She opened up her vault and pulled out a few little shiny trinkets that were sitting in one of the closest vault slots and put them on top of the altar. It was a coin, a shiny pebble, a piece of tin foil, and a shiny damaged spoon. The little sparkly bits and pieces that Ro-ak had brought her before he had awakened to his form of Nateysta once more.

"I've not forgotten you, my friend, I will find you once more, one day," Zalia said under her breath, kneeling at the altar with her eyes closed.

She felt like she could almost feel his presence beside her, the little crow with his gravelly voice and shiny trinkets.

"Stay safe, keep fighting."

Zalia woke up, blinking at the sun just rising above the horizon. She had fallen asleep lying on the grass within the Grove, more comfortable beneath the stars than she was inside. She yawned and stretched luxuriously, feeling relaxed. Boreal, who was acting as her pillow at that moment, made a complaintive growl.

"Oh, I know, the others will be up and disturbing us soon anyways," Zalia mumbled.

Boreal rolled out from under her, and Zalia's head dropped to smack the ground with a dull thud.

"That was cruel," she complained.

Boreal let out her own complaint at the world before standing up, looking down at Zalia's face.

"Do I have to get up too? Maybe you could just scare them all away from me while I lie here for a bit longer?" Zalia suggested.

Boreal started licking her forehead with a raspy, sandpaper tongue. Fighting away the skin-shearing weapon of destruction, Zalia managed to make her way to her own feet.

"I'm up, I'm up."

Boreal gave a big, long stretch before looking up towards the treehouses.

"Want to go wake up Ember as well? It's been a while since we got to do that."

Boreal bounded forward with glee, making her way up the stairs at a significantly faster pace than Zalia cared to manage.

She arrived just in time to see Ember under assault, blankets flying and the sounds of battle resounding. She ended up lying on the floor, plate armour strewn about and her blanket essentially tying her up as Boreal flopped on her chest, holding her down.

"Good morning, Ember," Zalia greeted.

"Ge thih fuffy deah sirit off e," Ember complained, her voice muffled by the ton of fur burying her.

"What was that?" Zalia asked innocently.

Ember spat out some fur before replying.

"Get this fluffy death spirit off me, *please*," she repeated.

"Boreal get off her, please," Zalia said.

Boreal pretended not to hear.

"I'm sorry, Ember, but you must have slain the beast in your battle. We need to work together to move the corpse," Zalia informed her.

Ember groaned.

Zalia stepped over Ember's breastplate and put her hands under Boreal. Together, the two of them managed to shove Boreal off of Ember and she stood up.

"Such a shame for such a majestic creature to die such a painful death," Zalia said mournfully, shaking her head.

"You two are ridiculous," Ember stated.

"I don't know what you me—"

Zalia was interrupted as Boreal leapt from the ground in a sneak attack, hitting Zalia and throwing both of them out the door, off the walkway, and all the way down to the ground below. Zalia managed to get off the Zephyr ritual halfway down which slowed their descent enough that she wasn't crushed under Boreal's weight.

"Boreal," Zalia said as Boreal jumped up and started running away.

She stopped and slunk back.

"Gotta be careful playing so rough, you know, not everyone can survive being thrown from that height," Zalia reminded her.

"*Zalia strong!*" Boreal reminded Zalia.

Zalia rolled her eyes.

"Yes, yes, but you have to be more careful with, say, Aylie. Alright?" Zalia said.

"*Aylie cute, no throwing,*" Boreal scolded Zalia.

"I wasn't saying to throw her!" Zalia said indignantly.

Boreal gave Zalia a judgemental look and Zalia stared back at her.

"You little rascal," Zalia said in a playful growl.

"*Big rascal!*" Boreal announced, before sprinting off.

Zalia watched her go with a shake of her head. She was just the same as she had been growing up. She had been a little more serious in Cormaine, but it seemed like being back in her natural world was having a relaxing effect on Boreal too.

Zalia was drawn from her thoughts as Ember jumped the last few steps down from the treehouse and rushed over.

"Are you alright?" she asked.

"It'll take more than a surprise attack from Boreal to take me out," Zalia assured her.

"She is a menace, no surprise with you raising her," Ember said.

"What's that meant to mean!?"

Ember gave her a look like, "Seriously?"

"Alright, fair, I take your point. She's a fun menace, though," Zalia countered.

"That she is," Ember agreed with a laugh.

"Should we start getting ready to leave?" Zalia asked.

"Hmm, maybe. Thinking it over last night, I believe we should take Aylie with us," Ember said.

"What? Why?" Zalia asked, her humour vanishing to sobriety.

"I actually talked to her last night, she looks up to you a lot. She even told me the story of how you saved her life. I don't think she'd be very happy being left behind."

"You managed to get her to talk?" Zalia asked, surprised.

"Yeah, a bit. She's been through a lot but . . . well, so had I when I was that young. I feel a bit of a kindred spirit in her," Ember explained.

Zalia mulled that over for a minute.

"I don't think we should take her out into the world, though. It's damn dangerous out there. The Grove is safe. Besides, Faian said she would find a home for her," Zalia objected.

"Phh, she's going nowhere. I don't think you'll be able to be rid of her."

"Well—I—Ember, I can't raise a child!"

"I don't think you'll have to. She's already had a strong pull into reality, I think she's already significantly more mature than Boreal. Though, saying that . . ." Ember drifted off as she looked over Zalia's shoulder.

Zalia turned around to see Boreal running in circles with Aylie firmly attached to her tail, being dragged around in the grass.

Zalia sighed, closing her eyes and settling her thoughts. It didn't seem like she would be handing off Aylie to a family after all, and she didn't know if that made her happy or not.

CHAPTER TWELVE

About Old Friends

Zalia

A war camp is no place for a child either, Zalia. At least if we take her with us, we know she will be safe. If we leave her with some family here, who knows what will happen," Ember urged quietly.

"Look, I don't like it, but I'll let her decide, ok?" Zalia said to Ember.

"Fine, we'll let her decide."

"But, here and now, her safety takes priority over everything else," Zalia added.

"I agree. I don't think I could take it if something did happen to her because I convinced you to take her with us. You want to ask her?" Ember asked.

Zalia sighed.

"Yeah, let's go. We should probably be off soon."

They walked over to where Boreal and Aylie were still playing, and Boreal was thankfully being extremely gentle. Apart from dragging her around on the grass, but that was fine. A little dirt never hurt anybody.

"Boreal, Aylie, we're going to be leaving for the north soon," Zalia informed them.

Boreal sat still, looking at Zalia as Aylie pulled one of her whiskers.

"Aylie, you can either stay here or come with us, I'll leave the decision to you. It's very important you understand that it will be dangerous though, alright? We'll try our best to take care of you, but there are many creatures out there like the one we saved you from. Otherwise, you can stay here in the Grove until we get back."

Aylie looked a little unsure, nervously twisting her hands in front of herself.

"Will you be long?" she asked in a small voice.

"It will be perhaps a few weeks. It depends on if we get slowed or interrupted," Zalia said.

Aylie looked like she might be about to cry.

"What's wrong?" Zalia asked.

"You . . . you told that general lady to find a family for me. Please don't leave me too," Aylie said, her soft voice falling apart as she began to cry.

"Oh, no darling. I won't, not ever," Zalia promised, pulling the young girl into a tight hug.

They stayed there for a while, Zalia trying to comfort Aylie while the girl cried. She really shouldn't have had Aylie there for that conversation and she berated herself for her idiocy in that matter. She just forgot to take things like that into account.

"Aylie, I'm sorry for saying that. I'll always be here if you need me, ok?" Zalia said softly, still holding the girl.

She felt Aylie nod against her shoulder and she hugged the girl even tighter. Zalia really did feel like an idiot.

She pulled back and held the girl by the shoulders.

"If you want to come with us, you can. Would you like to?" she asked.

Aylie looked at Ember over Zalia's shoulder, who nodded encouragingly, before giving a nod as well.

"I'll come," Aylie said, voice still trembling.

"Alright, but you have to listen to us when we're out there, ok? We'll avoid any trouble as much as we can, but it is important."

She nodded once more, so Zalia didn't push the matter any further.

"Alright, we'll have to get you some travelling clothes as well as some much warmer ones for the north. We will probably need a tent as well, though—no, we can sleep in the vault. I can probably store some . . ." Zalia's rambling faded away to silent thought.

"I'll go with Aylie to get some clothes then, Zalia, I know a good tailor at camp," Ember suggested.

"Sure, yeah. There are a few things I need to get stored into my vault . . . Oh, hey, did you ever get my bag back?"

"Your bag?" Ember asked.

"You know, the one they took when they captured us," Zalia said.

"Oh . . . no. We kind of left it there, we didn't really see any point in taking it," Ember said, scratching at her neck a little self-consciously.

"You . . . never mind. Do you have some gold I can borrow, then? All of mine was in that bag."

"Oh, sure, yeah. Gold ain't nothing much these days, though. Most people will trade for food, clothes, that kind of thing. Gold won't help you much in these times," Ember explained.

"Right, maybe I can find something to trade then. I got this cool sword and . . ."

"What's that?"

"Nothing, I just remembered I need to go speak to the Hidden before we leave," Zalia said.

Ember's expression darkened.

"We haven't been able to get him to say a thing, bloody traitor," she hissed.

"He might talk to me," Zalia said quietly.

"What makes you think that?" Ember asked. "He won't talk to any of the rest of us."

"Just a feeling. Go on, I'll come around to the camp later. I've got a couple things to do first," Zalia urged.

Ember walked off and Aylie followed after, sparing a glance backwards at Zalia like she was making sure Zalia wouldn't leave without her.

Giving Aylie an assuring smile and a wave, Zalia turned about to Boreal. "Right, we've got some errands. If you could hunt something nice for us to trade, I want to go take a look at the nest we burnt out."

Boreal licked her lips, an excited energy entering her body at the thought of a hunt. She ran off out of the Grove as well.

Zalia smiled, casting the ritual of flight on herself, the wispy air wings forming across her back. She took off, flying towards the burnt nest. She'd gained a level in Nature's Wrath from burning it down, though she hadn't seen the message until some time after waking up and checking.

She flew low up the hill, finding herself at a scorched hole in the ground before long. She looked down into it to see a spherical chunk missing from the land, the sides and base frozen solid in an image of flowing liquid. She really had done a number on the cave.

Flying down, she found herself wondering at the power of the ability. She had pumped her entire mana pool into it, true, but it seemed absurd. It reminded her of the strength of the abilities the shadowy twins had, the two whose abilities were stronger working in tandem with each other. They had summoned acidic rain and shadowy arms that had helped take down the Gold rank elemental that the mine had become. She wondered how those two were doing—all of Endelbyrn, for that matter. The other two leaders of the Morning's Shade were surely still there, Hildebrandt and . . . Marcus? She didn't remember the other man's name.

Still, the fact that her abilities stood up to that of two other Bronze rankers working in tandem gave her a little bit of confidence she sorely needed. Sure, she had managed to survive against some steep odds in Cormaine, but the things they were fighting . . .

She recalled the emotion flowing through her as she had fueled the fire ever higher. Anger, a pure rage at the demons for their invasion of Endaria, their corruption of nature, for killing Delphi.

A pair of eyes and a crunch.

Zalia shook herself back to the present, ignoring the little flames that had ignited around the place and the floor that was beginning to melt again, and took off back into the open air. She flew back down into the forest, following along the tug of the bond that let her know where Boreal was. Making sure her armour was on so as not to create any sound, she gently alit upon a high tree branch, watching Boreal stalk her prey below.

It was only that tug of the bond that let her even see Boreal; the feline's sight, sound, heat signature, and vibrations were so well hidden that Zalia had trouble even then.

She seemed to be hunting a strange four-legged animal with a low-hanging body and a neck that pointed forward, a diamond-shaped head on its end. It was one of the more bizarre creatures Zalia had seen in her time in the new worlds, and that was saying something, yet she felt bad about its soon approaching fate. Almost bad enough to call out to Boreal to stop—but with a quick pounce and some frenzied movement, it was soon over.

"Good catch!" Zalia called down.

Boreal looked up proudly, a little bit of blood dripping from her maw. It was blue, another oddity about the creature.

"I'll store it in the vault," Zalia informed her, jumping down and doing just that.

The two of them left the forest and went to the war camp, having to go through the inspection process *again*. It was becoming a little tiresome, though it was performed by the extremely nervous man again who was at least quicker than the other person had been.

As they walked through the camp, Zalia kept her armour on to try and maintain some type of anonymity. It was kind of hard to do that with the large wildcat at her side, but while she looked like the smaller Boreal on the statue, it was at least enough to deter some assumptions. Not all of them, though, as they still received awed looks here and there.

They found General Faian in the administrative building, busy with a whole stack of paper she seemed to be struggling with.

"I didn't think being a general would include so much paperwork," Zalia commented, standing on the other side of her desk.

"Neither did I, though I've become more of a camp administrator than a general these days. We can't assault the city until our other forces catch up from the other parts of the kingdom, and we can't leave the city to go help them lest the garrisoned troops decide to leave and cause us other issues. It's quite frustrating," Faian agreed.

"Certainly seems so."

"Now, what can I help you with today?" Faian asked, putting down the sheet of parchment she was holding and looking up at Zalia.

"I want to talk with the Hidden," Zalia said.

"I thought you might, at some point. I'll get Indis and we can go down to see him then."

"No, just us. I'd prefer Indis isn't there."

"And why would that be?" Faian asked, raising an eyebrow.

"We had . . . a bit of a fight and things need to cool down. I'll see her before I leave for the north most likely but that can wait for now," Zalia explained.

"You're going to the north?"

"Yes, I believe I might be able to find some help and . . . something else I'm looking for. I have a friend up there I need to see."

"Alright, I won't say no to more help, though I'll admit you've got me curious," Faian said.

"Have you heard of Those Born of Heat and Stone? I believe your people call them goblins."

Faian furrowed her brow at Zalia's use of the term "your people" but didn't comment on it.

"Yes, I know of them. Are they the help you speak of?"

"Correct. They are quite powerful and are quite a bit more accepting than most people I've met. They would be a valuable ally," Zalia explained.

"Curiosity sated. I'll lead you to the Hidden now, if you wish."

"That would be appreciated."

"Very well, this way," Faian said, standing up and walking towards the door.

She led them out of the office and back through the calmer administrative building, and through another door in that chamber to a large locked iron gate that Zalia could tell was definitely magically reinforced. They weren't taking any risks on him escaping, it seemed.

Faian took a key from her coat pocket and unlocked the door, swinging it open on quiet, smooth hinges.

She led Zalia and Boreal down a steep set of winding stairs leading deep into the ground. They ended at yet another door that Faian unlocked, moving into a circular chamber with a single pedestal in its centre. Atop that pedestal was a dark cube with wisps of shadow flickering around its edges.

"*Hello, Zalia,*" the Hidden said.

CHAPTER THIRTEEN

Ready

Zalia

H idden," Zalia replied by way of greeting.

"*It is good to see you're alive,*" he said.

Zalia paid close attention to his tone and words. She didn't want to miss a single hidden meaning or obfuscated truth in the conversation.

"Despite your efforts," Zalia reminded him.

"*. . . yes. I would explain, but I believe you already know much of the truth. My predicament does not excuse my actions, however. I only wish I could have done more to help,*" he replied sadly.

"If it helps settle your mind just a bit, Juniper is dead. You're free of her control now."

"*I am glad to be free of* her *control, though I feel sorrow at her death. Despite the actions she took towards the end of her life, she was still a close friend and a good person for most of the rest of it. Thank you for delivering this information.*"

Zalia couldn't help notice the emphasis he put on the word "her." Within the context, it almost felt as if he was trying to say that she hadn't been, or wasn't, the only one with control over him.

"I don't suppose you would be able to tell us your true name, so we can free you and bring you to our side?" Zalia asked.

"*I cannot, it is impossible for a shade to reveal their true name of their own volition. I would not have you release me until the war is over, either way, however, despite the free will I currently maintain. The risk of the damage I would be capable of doing is not worth the reward of having me join this fight.*"

His emphasis on "currently" confirmed Zalia's suspicions. He had obviously been ordered not to tell anyone of his status being controlled directly, yet it seemed the way it worked must have been by the letter of the order, not the meaning of it. He did not have to keep good faith with a command as long as its literal definition was not broken.

"Were all commands given to you by Juniper broken upon her death, or do some remain?" Zalia asked.

"The confirmation of her death does indeed free me from the restraint of her commands. I can see within you that you were the one to release her soul from her body. That is a mark not easily forged," he explained.

"Good, then answer me this. What did Juniper hope to accomplish by her actions? Why did she perform that ritual?"

It was a question that had been in the back of her mind for a long time, something she hadn't expected to find the answer to.

"She . . . discovered the rituals before many in Endaria, though she was not the one to initially begin performing them. She intended to subvert a part of the power of the ritual to summon Zayes from Cormaine, a plan ruined by you when you interrupted her ritual."

Zalia frowned at the way the Hidden had paused. Almost as if he didn't mean "discovered" so much as "was told about." Zalia's mind raced at the thought, trying to figure out what that actually meant. Assuming, as their previous information told them, that the king was the perpetrator of the rituals, had he told Juniper for some reason?

The only logical path that train of thought took was that the king knew about Zayes being alive and had told Juniper in a ploy to get the Morning's Shade on his side through her interference. A gamble, but one that had obviously panned out, assuming it was the truth of the matter. There was only a single point she could think of to counter that: Why would the king take the risk of Zayes being summoned to Endaria? He was in prison in Cormaine for a reason, or so Zalia thought. The only proof she had of that was the visions and dreams sent to her by Zayes when she had been in Cormaine herself . . .

Faian was watching Zalia closely, as if she was having the exact same thought. She knew everything that Zalia did about the situation, as Zalia had told Faian herself. The general probably knew even more than Zalia, considering her numerous informants and the previous position she had held.

"Why would she put all of Endaria at risk to bring Zayes back? Couldn't she see what that would mean for the world?" Zalia asked, just a little confused.

"You underestimate what love can make a person do. She was also . . . different in those final months. Not fully there anymore."

"I don't quite believe that explanation. There must have been something else, something we don't know. What of Darren, her son, do you know where he is? Perhaps he knows more."

"Darren is with the king. I do not believe you will be able to reach him nor get anything from him of import if you do."

"That is . . . unfortunate."

"You are being a lot more forthcoming, care to explain why?" Faian asked.

"*With the confirmation of Juniper's death, I am able to tell you what I know.*"

Boreal looked bored, pacing around the room and giving the cubic Hidden the odd glance here and there. Knowing Boreal, she was probably trying to figure out if it was a good idea to eat him or not.

Zalia had a thought.

"How old are you?" she asked.

"*I do not know. I have no memories from before my awakening.*"

Unfortunate. She had hoped he would have some answers about the times long ago, when the Bathar had come to Endaria.

"It's been good seeing you again, Hidey," Zalia said.

"*And you, Zalia. Do come by again soon,*" he replied.

Zalia moved to leave, motioning for Boreal to come with her.

"I'm going to stay here, ask him a few more questions," Faian said.

"Alright, I'll be leaving for the north now, though," Zalia informed her.

"Understood, stay safe. I await your return with allies, should you succeed."

They left, leaving Hidey and Faian behind. Zalia meant what she said, it had been good seeing him again. A little hole in her had healed slightly at realising Hidey really was doing everything he could to help. She saw no other reason for his turning himself in and readily answering her questions as much as he was able. Unless it was all some long ploy to gain their trust again. Well, before she put any complete trust in his words or actions again, she would find out his true name and pull the truth out of him that way. It was the only way to be sure.

They left the command building and made their way back to the front gate, where Ember and Aylie were waiting for them.

Aylie had a new set of clothes on, comfortable looking travelling clothes, a light jacket, and a broadbrim hat. She looked a little like a farmer.

Ember was in her plate armour, as usual, but held a bag by her side.

"Hey, nice. Looks like you two found what you were looking for," Zalia said in greeting.

"Sure did, my tailor sorted her out real quick. Got a little something for you too!" Ember said.

"Oh?"

Ember pulled another of the big, broadbrim hats out of the bag, the sides flopping a little bit, and presented it to her with a big smile. Aylie looked at her hopefully, so Zalia put aside her sudden regret at ever meeting Ember and took the hat, putting it on.

"Happy?" she asked dourly.

"Absolutely," Ember said.

"I hope you got one for Boreal as well." Zalia said.

"I did not, Boreal is just perfect as she is," Ember said in a matter-of-fact tone.

"And you think I would be improved by this hat?" Zalia replied, only mildly insulted.

"Of course."

"What else have you got in that bag?" Zalia asked, changing the subject.

"Have a look," Ember said, handing it over.

Inside were some very small and very warm-looking clothes that she had no doubt were for Aylie when they got into the snowier sections of the north. There was also a bigger set of clothes that matched exactly what Aylie was wearing.

"So you two can be matching," Ember explained.

"What's wrong with my clothes?"

"Well, despite those extremely good self-repairing and cleaning enchant-ments you have on them, you are somehow managing to damage them. Look, there are threads hanging out all over the place, your right shoulder has a hole in the shirt, and the pants are looking a bit rough on the hems. Besides, you two would look cute wearing matching outfits," Ember explained.

Zalia was definitely going to find an inconspicuous way to get Ember back for this. It wasn't like she was about to wholeheartedly disagree in front of Aylie, who was looking so excited about the idea.

"Alright, sure," she agreed.

She would change later and enjoy her last moments of freedom before they left.

"Anything else left to do? I wanted to get a few food supplies before we go to keep in the vault, as emergency supplies," Zalia added.

"Nope, I'm happy," Ember said cheerfully.

Zalia had the body of the animal that Boreal had hunted in the vault still, but wanted to get some herbs and spices as well. She quickly opened the vault, surprising Ember and Aylie who hadn't seen it yet, and went inside.

"What the fuck, Zalia," Ember said, stepping in after her.

"I did tell you I have a vault, didn't I?" Zalia asked absentmindedly.

She took the body of the creature out from the storage and used Preparation to butcher it quickly and efficiently. She took the pelt of the creature, storing all the meat back in the same slot.

"Yeah, but I didn't think it would be this big. It's cool, and it's got an herb garden at the back. Oh, hey, what are these swirling misty things back here?" Ember rambled, walking further back.

"They're . . . I'll explain another time. Please leave them alone," Zalia pleaded.

"Alright, alright, I won't pry," Ember said, surrendering.

Taking a deep, settling breath to calm herself, Zalia left the vault with the pelt and Ember close behind.

She found a little market with Ember's help and managed to trade the pelt for the few cooking herbs, salt, and spices that she wanted. Storing those in the vault, and with Ember having nothing else to get done, they left the war camp to begin the journey northwards.

CHAPTER FOURTEEN

Saint Ember

Zalia

Zalia finished pulling on the shirt Ember had bought for her, having just thoroughly cleaned herself in a bubbling river. She pulled on the floppy broadbrim hat with a sigh, completing the farmer look that was a matching outfit with what Aylie was wearing back at their temporary camp. Her vault was open there, the others resting within its safe and comfortable confines. Zalia was actually considering if she could shape the plants in the herb section at the back to make seats or comfortable cots. Perhaps some living vines could be fashioned into hammocks.

She bundled up her old clothes and walked back to the vault. Upon stepping through the door, Aylie dashed up to inspect her, looking up under the brim of her own floppy hat.

"Now we match," Zalia said, managing to dredge up a pinch of enthusiasm to put into the words.

Aylie grabbed her hand excitedly, dragging her to the back of the vault. Zalia managed to dump the old clothes into a storage slot in passing, to where Ember and Boreal were. There, Boreal was sitting sullenly, and it took Zalia a moment to realise why. Some of her fur had been braided into twin braids running from behind her ears down the length of her neck. Twined into those braids were some little blue flowers.

Zalia couldn't help but smile and chuckle to herself at the sight. At least she wasn't the only one suffering a makeover.

It had only been two days of travel, with another two weeks ahead of them at the pace they were moving at. Since Ember and Aylie needed to sleep eight hours or so *every day*, it was slow going. Boreal and Zalia could probably have made the trip in a week to a week and a half.

So far, there hadn't been any major run-ins with demons, though they had seen some from afar. Zalia had gone on cleansing the corrupted parts of the world, doing her best to make sure they didn't overcome the nature around them.

Ember was sitting on the ground, still in her armour, smiling up at Zalia.

"Suits you," Ember commented.

"I'm sure it does," Zalia grumbled.

The beige shirt and thick brown pants were simple at least, that much was a comfort. It honestly wasn't that different than what she had worn before, though the hat felt a tad unnecessary.

Boreal was giving Zalia a careful sideways glance that looked like she was asking for help. Aylie had sat down and started twining a few violet flowers into the braids now.

"Looking good, Boreal, I like the flowers," Zalia said cheerfully.

Boreal lay her head down on her paws in surrender, letting out a sigh. When had she learnt that mannerism?

"Alright, alright. We better get going again, then. Ready to walk a bit more?" Zalia said, directing the question at Aylie.

She seemed reluctant but didn't complain or argue, standing up to leave the vault.

Ember also stood up with a clank, picking up her sword, sheathing it, and slinging her shield. Zalia remembered when she had needed to carry around her bow, sword, and armour with her. What a hassle it had been. Her armour was visible on a mannequin at the back of the vault, something that had only formed after Zalia's constant use of the space to store the armour.

They left the vault, Zalia closing it with a little popping sound, and a whole bunch of flowers dropped to the ground from the closed portal—the ones Aylie hadn't had time to tie into Boreal's braids.

They began their travel again, ever northwards towards the mountain home of Zalia's friend Glemp and whatever unknown goal the starlight wolf had hinted would be there.

Aylie, for her part, was thoroughly enjoying the trip, inspecting many of the plants they passed by. Zalia often used Flora Identification to read about a little bit of the history and the uses for the plants Aylie took particular interest in, and told the child about them. When Ember started to give Zalia looks like she was wondering if Zalia was making the details up, Zalia informed her that it was a Bronze upgrade of one of her abilities.

Things actually started to look a lot better the further north they travelled. Fewer areas of corruption were showing up and the ones they saw were smaller than normal. Zalia started to see the tracks and traces of more active wildlife, as if they weren't being hunted so thoroughly here as they were back south. She wondered if that was because the point of disruption for the ritual had been as far northwest as you could get while remaining in Endaria, while she had entered in the southeast. It was a reasonable conclusion to make.

On the fifth day, they ran into a town that still had inhabitants.

It was a tiny town, no more than twenty buildings in all, by Zalia's count. They could tell there were still people about because the few still in the town ran at the sight of them, slamming doors behind them as they retreated.

"Well, that wasn't what I expected," Ember said.

"These are some pretty dangerous times, I'm not that surprised. What if we were here to steal their possessions?" Zalia said.

"Then a few doors wouldn't stop us."

Ember walked down the street.

"Hey! There's no need to fear us, please. We want to provide any help we can," she called out.

At first, there was nothing but slowly, ever so slowly, a few people began to come back out of hiding.

"Y-you, wait, are you—are you the Saint Ember?" a man called from a doorway.

The what? Zalia thought.

Ember paused for just a moment.

"That would apparently be me, yes," she agreed.

Perhaps she didn't feel like arguing with the townspeople on the specifics, simply wanting their cooperation so she could help however she was able.

"A passing refugee told us you could perform miracles," another townsperson, a woman, called out.

Many of the people were leaving their doorways now, moving out into the open and towards the small group. Aylie looked like she was starting to get a little anxious so Zalia picked her up and placed her on Boreal. She always seemed to feel safer there.

The people slowly gathered around them, asking questions and making comments, all of which Ember bore with infinite patience, answering calmly and politely. Zalia was in awe, seeing something that she would never be able to do, not if she were Silver, Gold, or Ascendant: deal with *that* many people with such patience.

After some time of Ember asking her own questions and drawing out of the people what troubled them and what they needed, Zalia felt a warping in the air. It was originating from Ember, an ability perhaps?

She watched as the few injured townspeople had their wounds healed and a table with a bounty of food and water appeared. Some of the houses also had mild repairs made to their frames, holes in walls, or damage from what had obviously been from some type of fight. An old woman had a cane put in her hands and it looked as if she stood a little straighter, perhaps having had some injury healed.

It was, well, without better words for it, a miracle, as the townspeople had said. Ember had listened to each and every complaint and need of these people, and when activating her ability, it had apparently tried to resolve all of those issues.

Looking at the finer detail, though, Zalia could see that it was still a bit past the strength of the ability to deal with everything. Some cuts were only scabbed over, not fully sealed. The food was mostly very basic rations that weren't anything fancy, though they would last. Some of the houses didn't get repaired, one still with a hole in its roof.

"Please, I cannot do more for you now. I urge you to take what I have given you and leave this town to go south. After five days' travel, there is a camp being run by the rebellion and those fighting back against the invasion. They have food, supplies, and most importantly, defences that can keep out the demons. We have just come from there ourselves and there was not much danger along our path," Ember said as the townspeople listened with expressions of . . . hope on their faces. There was a little bit of awe, and they still looked exhausted with bags under their eyes and dirt on their faces, yet there was hope now, too.

After her little speech, Ember turned to walk away as the townspeople began talking amongst themselves, arguing the sides of listening to Ember's plea.

Zalia helped as she could as well, letting her Healing Presence finish healing the rest of the wounds, even catching some type of growth in one of the men . . . Was that . . . cancer?

Filing that revelation aside, she let the Healing Presence flow into a pair of fruit trees nearby as well, the trees blooming and fruits growing.

Then, she did something that she hadn't really been expecting to do herself.

She knelt, pulling out the tiny altar to Nateysta she had in her vault using the Druid Grove ability. She placed it on the floor in front of her and summoned some of the cave fungus as well, placing it atop the altar and using Preparation to turn it to dust—dust that floated about the altar and began glowing a light purple.

"May the lord of the forests keep you hidden amongst the boughs of his trees, within the roots and behind foliage. Let the animals of his domain keep you safe from the invaders that seek to eradicate life on this world. Let the stars of the shining wolf guide you in your travels to whichever destination you so desire. This is my will," she intoned.

The light purple dust formed both sparkling, deep blue motes and misty, dark patches. Slowly, the entire formation dissipated into the air and Zalia put the altar back into her vault.

The townspeople were giving her odd looks as if they didn't exactly know what to make of whatever she had just done. She didn't really know what to make of it herself, to be honest.

"What was that?" Ember whispered.

"I've got no idea," Zalia whispered back.

Ember gave her a look that let Zalia know she would be interrogated about it later. But, for now, Ember waved goodbye and they left the town, returning to their journey.

CHAPTER FIFTEEN

Idle Chatter

Zalia

Zalia looked sideways at Ember, quickly looking away again when the woman caught her staring.

She looked again, Ember turning once more to meet her gaze.

"What!?" Ember asked, her voice a little louder than she might have intended.

"So . . . Saint Ember, hey?" Zalia said innocently.

They were walking down a little path that led down the length of a fence. It might have once held a herd of animals but was now empty.

"Don't even start," Ember warned.

"Well, that's not fair, you gave me a little bit of heat about the giant statue in the middle of the war camp. I think I owe a little back."

"Ugh, it's started happening the past few towns I've gone through. Unbelievable, really. Like someone actually just helping out others makes them some kind of mythical saint or something," Ember complained.

"I'm not surprised people here are a little bit more superstitious, with magic existing and everything," Zalia said.

"What?"

"Well, a lot of impossible things can already happen; gods have a very proven state of existence, even. It isn't a much bigger step from that to you being a saint, or me to being some kind of war hero, I guess," Zalia explained.

"The place you're from sounds quite weird. No magic, you say? I couldn't imagine life without it."

"It wasn't so bad, though magic is *absolutely* an improvement in all regards so far. Well, we didn't have demons, I guess, but there were plenty of other things that weren't so different from them."

"Really? How could you have had something as bad as them without magic?" Ember asked.

"Megacorporations," Zalia said with a shiver.

She wasn't exactly sure how that translated for Ember but the woman gave her an odd look.

"Is that . . . some kind of beast from your home?" she asked.

"The worst kind," Zalia said, nodding her head.

"Maybe one day we can hunt one down, to help free your world?" Ember suggested.

"Maybe," Zalia said, considering that prospect.

What would she do if she ever managed to return to her old world? Would she keep her magic and abilities?

If so, she wouldn't necessarily have some kind of huge advantage at her current level of power. A gun would probably still be enough to kill her, not to mention the huge variety of military weapons with more destructive power than something like a handheld gun.

Well, either way, if she did end up back in her old homeworld with no way back she would just live on the edges of civilization again. She had no intention of rejoining that particular society again.

They came upon a large patch of corrupted land, though it was small compared to what was down south, and Zalia began to cleanse it with Healing Presence.

"I'll never get used to that," Ember commented.

"Hmm?" Zalia hummed questioningly.

"It's just . . . stunning to see the nature come back to life and begin thriving again with such little effort," Ember explained.

Zalia shrugged.

"You could do it too, if you had a healing ability that was more of an area thing, rather than the extremely targeted healing you have now," Zalia said.

"Maybe, but I don't think so. None of the other healers I know, even some with area healing abilities, can do it. I prefer the stronger, single-target healing anyways, so I'm not so bothered."

Ember had an extremely strong targeted healing ability that required her to be close to the target, as well as an emotional healing ability—something that Zalia had definitely noticed her using on Aylie from time to time. She was more grateful than words could express for that.

She was also able to detect injuries and their severity, something that Zalia could not do, and she had an aura that increased the healing received of allies in the area. That tied in extremely well with Zalia's own Healing Presence, leading to even stronger passive healing for them all.

"Have you lost a limb in battle yet?" Zalia asked.

"I have, actually, not a fond memory," Ember said, scrunching up her face at the question.

"Not a very fun experience," Zalia agreed. "How long did yours take to grow back?"

"A leg, and it took all of about five seconds. You?" Ember asked.

"I wish mine took as little time as that. A couple minutes for me, though I wasn't quite Bronze at the time. My healing ability was, though, so not much difference there," Zalia replied.

"Damn, two minutes would have been torturous," Ember said, wincing.

"Not so much, actually. I was in shock for most of it, still in battle for a good amount of the time as well. It was mostly just . . . itchy. The emotional trauma was the worst of it. I still get a phantom stabbing pain from when that one undead shoved their sword through my chest."

"From when they *what*?" Ember asked, a little shock on her face.

"Sword, chest. All the way through. Would have taken my head as well, if it weren't for the protective ability that activates when I'm going to be killed," Zalia explained.

Ember shivered. "Maybe don't say that so loudly," she whispered.

Aylie and Boreal were only a dozen steps behind them, playing some kind of game that involved a lot of hopping.

Zalia grimaced, having forgotten herself. She would have to be a little more careful with her words. Luckily, Aylie didn't seem to have heard.

"I'm fine now, at any rate. Just have a collection of bad memories," Zalia said.

"Don't we all," Ember agreed.

They fell into silence, each of them deep in thought. Zalia didn't miss that Ember started using her emotional healing on her, however, as a calm soothing blanket fell on her mind. She didn't ask Ember to stop, though she didn't feel like she particularly needed it at the moment. Well, except for that one memory . . .

She came to, shaking her head and finding Ember looking over at her.

"What was that?" Ember asked.

"What was what?"

"You forget that I can detect injuries. That includes emotional ones, Zalia."

"Yes, and?" Zalia asked, genuinely confused.

"Well, I just felt a huge emotional wound appear and disappear," Ember explained.

"Oh, right. That's just a memory from my last few moments in Cormaine."

"You never did tell me how you got back."

"It's not important."

"I feel like it might be a bit more important than you're letting on," Ember said softly.

"Drop it," Zalia said sharply.

Ember fell silent, and so did the giggling Aylie behind them.

Zalia turned around and found her looking with wide-eyed worry.

"Don't worry," Ember said soothingly.

Zalia immediately felt a stab of regret. She shouldn't have snapped at Ember, especially not with Aylie around.

"Sorry," she said quietly.

"It's alright. I can see it's a sore spot for you. I'm here if you ever need to talk about it," Ember said, her voice still soft.

Saint Ember indeed.

"I'll keep it in mind. Thank you," Zalia said.

Aylie and Boreal had gone back to their game, but Zalia could see by the expression on Aylie's face that she was still worried. She would have to explain later.

"Keep walking, I'm going to see if I can find something to eat for tonight," Zalia said, beginning to walk off.

"Are you going to be alright?" Ember asked.

"I'll be fine, I just need a little time alone," Zalia said.

"I'm just going to go find something for the others to eat tonight, keep Aylie safe," she sent to Boreal.

She got a mental confirmation and so walked off to the left, where the small trail led off into the forest.

She let her mind focus on the task, reading the tracks and tells of the forest. She had told herself that when she got somewhere safe that she would allow that . . . memory back into her mind. That she would process what had happened in a calm and safe environment. The Grove would have been the perfect place to do just that, yet she found herself here already, walking into the dangerous wilds.

Did she really have to process it? Couldn't she just leave the memory in the vault?

It already popped up whenever a topic surrounding the memory came up, the experience fresh as the moment it had happened. Perhaps leaving it in the vault would not be possible. Well, she would deal with it later. For now, she didn't have the time, so she would just bottle it up for a time that she was able to deal with it.

It didn't take long for her to find food for the evening, the sun already beginning to reach the end of its daily journey and dipping below the horizon. The forest was dim and cold, but neither of those things were even mild annoyances to Zalia anymore, with her abilities allowing her to ignore both.

An Ironfur rabbit was her reward for a short hunt, a small Tin ranked one that would be enough to feed the voracious Ember and the small Aylie.

Zalia and Boreal had already eaten three days prior, and probably didn't need to eat for another day or two.

Congratulations! Hunter's Sight has reached Bronze 3.
Congratulations! Harvester has reached Bronze 2.
Congratulations! Low Light Vision has gained two levels, reaching Iron 15.

She was also awarded a couple levels, as she used Preparation to harvest the few herbs she walked past. They were all very common ones, Bitterbalm and Dodge-vine the most common amongst them. Nothing special to talk about, but also free experience to level her Herbalist abilities, so she wouldn't say no.

She found her way back to the others who had set up camp just off the small path, a little bit into the forest. Her internal compass that pointed directly to Boreal was helpful as always.

She wordlessly walked up to the camp and, using her passive Heat Resistance, lit the small fire that one of the others had already set up for her. She quickly prepared the meat, cutting it into small chunks, and skewered it onto a few sharp sticks.

Congratulations! Preparation has reached Bronze 3.

She used a bit of salt and Bitterbalm to garnish the meat. It wasn't anything fancy, but better than nothing. She had been considering if any of her current Herbal Magic combinations would allow for some type of flavour-enhancing ritual but hadn't come up with anything just yet. She might have to find a new herb for that one. Or perhaps would need to use the base effect combination from Herbal Magic's Bronze ability. Though, even that didn't seem to have any combinations that would work. How was it that she was able to come up with any number of powerful, harmful effects, but something so simple as making food more tasty was unachievable?

Well, she would have to keep an eye out. For now, though, neither Ember nor Aylie complained as they chewed their food.

"So, Aylie, are you ever going to tell me what that blessing the starlight wolf gave you was?" Zalia asked, trying to spark conversation.

"Oh? You didn't tell me about this," Ember said, turning her gaze to Aylie as well.

The girl shrunk under their combined gazes but had a mischievous look to her eyes.

"Yeah, the starlight wolf came to find me shortly after I returned to Endaria. Aylie here was given a blessing by it, somewhat unlike the blessings I've received so far, I might add. My two blessings have been on heirlooms I own, whereas the wolf blessed Aylie herself," Zalia explained.

"You were blessed by a god?" Ember asked Aylie.

The girl nodded, still chewing.

Zalia eyed Boreal, who had decided on a surprise boop to the forehead at the time the blessing had happened. She wouldn't be caught off guard again.

"Are you going to tell us about what it did?" Ember asked.

Aylie looked thoughtful for a moment, then shook her head.

"You won't?" Ember asked, faking an aghast look.

"You won't keep it from Ember forever, will you? She doesn't like mysteries and secrets," Zalia explained wisely.

Neither did she, but she wasn't about to explain that to Aylie. That would just make the girl do it more. She had learned a lesson or two about cheeky younglings from Boreal.

Ember looked at Zalia with a real aghast expression while Aylie looked at Ember with the expression of a pyromaniac who just found a flamethrower.

Zalia just shrugged at Ember and picked up a chunk of wood that had missed the fire. She turned it around in her hands before storing it in her vault using the ability from Druid Grove. She would need to find some whittling tools. Times like these when she had an entire night on her hands and these two would need to sleep would be perfect for picking up wood carving again.

Aylie jumped up and ran over to Zalia, whispering in her ear.

Zalia nodded, then nodded again.

"I see, I see," she said sagely.

"What did she tell you?" Ember asked as Aylie went back to her little seat fashioned from stone. Zalia had made those.

"Oh, just the secret about her blessing," Zalia said innocently.

"You told her before me?" Ember asked Aylie, mock hurt in her tone.

Aylie nodded sharply like, "Of course!"

"Ouch," Ember said, holding a hand to her heart.

Aylie started to look regretful, so Zalia turned to her.

"Can I tell her?" she asked.

Aylie looked at Zalia for a moment before nodding her assent.

"Aylie said her blessing will give her a class option when she is the right age for the choosing," Zalia said.

"Oh?" Ember asked, her mock hurt turning to genuine interest.

"Yeah, she didn't say what the message actually said to her except for that, but it could be really powerful, I think. I mean, a class granted by the blessing of a god? That is something anyone would want," Zalia explained.

"You can say that again. A class? I've never heard of that happening before," Ember mused.

"I guess most people don't tend to attract the attention of a god for any reason without already having a class," Zalia suggested.

"Yeah that would be right, I suppose. Still, I'd be interested to see what that ends up being," Ember said.

"As would I."

CHAPTER SIXTEEN

Aura

Zalia

Aweek later, they were walking through another forest, Aylie trudging along slowly and the others keeping pace. She was valiantly continuing on, but after upwards of a week of constant walking, Zalia could see that she was getting exhausted. Every now and then, she would get so tired that Zalia had to lift her onto Boreal for a rest.

They were in a part of Endaria that Zalia recognised from the first time she had met the rebellion. They were soon approaching where the old war camp had been, and she was a little surprised to find that there was no sign of their passing. Shouldn't an entire army moving across the land leave more of a mark?

She remembered when they had first met General Ballast, how his army had mages to move the terrain out of the way and then put it back untouched. Perhaps that is what they had done here.

"How much longer?" Aylie asked.

"Another week or so," Zalia said.

Aylie let out a long pitiful groan, looking for all the world like she was about to collapse.

"Let's take a rest," Zalia suggested.

Aylie obviously agreed, as she immediately dropped. Zalia hopped forward and caught her, forming a stone seat for her to sit in. It wouldn't be super comfortable, but better than the ground.

There were still another three days of walking before they would hit the snow, though Zalia thought it might be soon approaching winter, as she noticed ice forming across the landscape during the nights and their breath puffing into little clouds in front of them. Zalia herself didn't notice the cold since she was still wearing the outfit Ember had bought for her, but Aylie wore her warmer clothes and a giant puffy coat with a hood, the whole thing made out of extremely soft wool.

Zalia did what she could to help as well, using the heat manipulation given by Heat Resistance to stop Aylie from cooling down too much.

"How you doing?" she asked Ember.

"Yeah, fine. It's a bit of a journey, hey?" Ember said.

"Yeah, for sure. I wish we could fly but I don't want to risk attracting any of the Silver demons. They seem to watch the sky. Maybe when we are closer to the mountain, if there appear to be less demons around."

"That would be magnificent," Ember said, smiling.

While she could definitely cast the flight ritual on all of them, she probably couldn't keep it up for long before running out of mana. That was something she definitely didn't want to risk. If it came to fighting a Silver ranked demon, which it might, with Aylie as slow as she was, she would need every drop she could get. She wasn't certain, but she felt like she, Boreal, and Ember would be able to take one. They were a pretty strong trio.

They had come across a few demons on their way so far, each of them swiftly put down by the three of them. Aylie was terrified of the demons, but Zalia always stayed by her side during the fights, using the distraction of Ember and Boreal to release arrow after arrow.

"How old are you, Aylie?" Zalia asked.

It wasn't something that had occurred to her to ask, yet it popped into her mind as she started thinking of what class opportunities the starlight wolf's blessing would provide.

Aylie looked at Zalia, then held up her hands with fingers splayed.

"Ten?"

Aylie shook her head, holding up two more fingers.

"Twelve?"

From what she remembered from talking with Zen and the others previously, people usually were able to take classes from around fourteen onwards, yet could take one early, as in Ember's case. She might have to wait a while to find out what classes Aylie would be able to take, then.

Zalia summoned the little chunk of wood into her hands from the vault, looking it over again. It had occurred to her that she might not need whittling tools to shape it, that perhaps she could do so with her Healing Presence.

She pushed her aura into the wood but tried to focus it on one side in particular and found that she was indeed able to promote growth in a specific area. It wasn't perfect but perhaps would be enough to make some rudimentary shapes.

She tried using Preparation on it and, to her pleasure, found that she was able to carve it down. With this she would basically be able to change a singular piece of wood into any shape she desired. Interesting.

Unfortunately, as she tried to carve something a little more deliberate out of it, she found herself failing entirely. It felt like she should be able to change it to whichever shape she wanted yet she lacked . . . control. A skill to learn, then.

She sat down, forming a chair under herself as she did so, right next to Aylie. Boreal walked off to investigate the immediate area and Ember stayed standing, looking towards the north.

"Do you think we will be able to convince Glemp and his people to join the fight?" she asked.

"I don't know, to be honest. They don't really like to leave their cave. Maybe they wouldn't be opposed to taking in some refugees though, that would provide another escape for some of the people further north here," Zalia suggested.

"Hmm, that would help, I guess. What about this other 'start to your goals' the starlight wolf mentioned?"

Zalia had, of course, told Ember about *why* she wanted to travel north. The reasons were twofold; she hadn't explained in detail the conversation she'd had with the wolf, though.

"Well, I told the wolf I wanted to walk the path that led to my friends being safe, or avenged, and Endaria being preserved, and nature being . . . well, nature. Apparently the first step to that large range of goals lies in the north where heat meets stone meets ice. Or something like that," she explained.

"Right. I hope it isn't the avenged part of that. I hope Glemp and his people are ok," Ember said, frowning a bit in worry.

"So do I," Zalia agreed quietly.

Just then, she felt something strange.

It was kind of like the aura she had grown oh so used to in Cormaine but . . . different. It was hard to explain. Maybe it was just the feeling of power great enough to create a physical feeling.

This one, unlike the one in Cormaine, didn't feel as . . . angry. The aura of the horrific creatures Zalia had come to know in this world's hell felt angry, and it attacked with a very real power.

This new one felt uncaring. It didn't seem to give off any emotions or feelings, simply existing as an enigmatic well of power.

She stood up, alert, noticing Ember did just the same as Boreal came running from afar to group up. Aylie didn't seem to notice, yet looked at the three of them with alarm either way.

"What is that?" Zalia asked in a whisper.

The strange feeling had a direction to it; she could tell it was coming from the tree line some fifty metres away.

"Never felt anything like it. Want to run?" Ember asked.

"No, not yet. I want to know what this is."

They waited, ever so patiently, as the aura grew stronger. She had started to notice slight auras around people as Aura Observation reached higher levels. It wasn't anything significant, most people unconsciously kept their aura largely contained, unless they were in a heightened emotional state.

She hadn't really found a use for the ability as such and had only really noticed it four days ago when Ember had been laughing at Aylie and Boreal.

The auras were very obviously stronger, based on the power of the creature they came from. Even some higher-ranked plants emitted auras. This one felt like it came from a creature of Silver or Gold rank.

That should have made Zalia scared, as fighting a creature like that would undoubtedly be a life-or-death fight for them. She wasn't, though, for whatever reason, and looked towards that tree line with curiosity.

Finally, she saw the owner of the aura. A humanoid creature with a dark blue complexion, floating serenely with toes pointed to the floor. It had runes inscribed across its body, and long, black hair flowing down its back slightly further than its feet.

Another left the tree line, looking quite similar to its brethren, yet with slightly shorter hair.

What made the creatures otherworldly to her eyes was their lack of mouth and nose. They had featureless faces, only two eyes that, even from this distance, looked as if they were pits leading into an endless abyss.

"What the hell are they?" Zalia whispered.

"I think . . . I think those are the Astar," Ember whispered back.

She had heard of the Astar; Indis had spoken of them some time back. They were a race that lived to the east of Endaria of which very little was known. That was because they didn't leave their lands and did not take kindly to humans encroaching upon their lands. At least, they weren't supposed to leave their lands.

"What the hell are they doing here?" Zalia whispered.

She let the little chair she had made for Aylie melt and crouched down to reduce her profile. Ember did the same, and Boreal was already as low to the ground as she could get. Aylie was lying down.

"Why are you asking me?" Ember whispered tensely.

Zalia summoned her armour, Boreal doing the same, not wanting to get caught off guard by the creatures. She swore they must have been quite a high rank, but as they serenely floated closer, she noticed they were only Bronze.

? - Bronze rank.

How could that be possible?

Their auras were so strong, rivalling that of someone like Hidey, had he not kept his aura very well hidden. They weren't even close to the strength of Ro-ak or the thousand-eyed demons, but they were still far above Zalia's or Ember's own auras.

"Should we talk to them?" Zalia whispered, unsure.

They had the strength advantage, three Bronze against two, if it came to it. That made the situation a little less worrying. Unfortunately, she was unsure what exactly Bronze meant for this race. It meant something entirely different for Zalia than it did for Ember.

"They aren't really known for being talkative," Ember whispered, uncertain.

"Well, it's not like they would just attack us outright, would they?"

Ember didn't reply. A possibility then.

"Alright, maybe they will. Still worth a try, though? Maybe they sensed the demons and have come to figure out what is happening in Endaria. Maybe we could get their help with the war!" Zalia said urgently.

If that was possible—and considering their aura's absolute strength, even at Bronze rank—they would have a much better chance of winning. Even a single Gold or Emerald ranked Astar would probably outmatch a thousand-eyed demon in raw aura power.

"Alright, fuck it. Why not? Let's go," Ember said, giving in.

"Stay here, Boreal, take care of Aylie," Zalia said before standing up.

Ember stood as well, and they walked towards the Astar. It took a surprisingly long time for the two to notice them, finally turning their endless gaze upon the duo.

Zalia looked at Ember and she gestured for Zalia to go first.

"Um, hello?" Zalia said.

The two stared at them wordlessly. Hmm.

Seeing as they didn't have mouths, maybe they didn't communicate verbally?

"*Hello*," Zalia greeted mentally.

Still, they stared. A deep thrumming began building within the two creatures' chests. It was like nothing she had heard before, not a purr like Boreal or a groan like a human. It was an endlessly reverberating bass.

"Uh, Ember, I don't like that sound," Zalia said quietly.

"Neither do I."

The thrumming grew louder, and Zalia was about to summon her weapon when space folded, the two Astar disappearing in a flash as the sound of a water drop hitting a still pond permeated the air.

"Oh, what the fuck?" Ember swore.

CHAPTER SEVENTEEN

Love for the Warm One

Boreal

Boreal watched as Zalia stared into the empty space where the Astar had been.

"They just vanished on us, not a single word," Ember said, looking a little pissed off.

Boreal stood, wondering if the Astar were tasty.

"Maybe they weren't here to talk?" Zalia wondered out loud.

Boreal started walking over, Aylie following suit, no longer seeing any need for secrecy.

"I think they have terrible eyesight," Zalia said.

"What makes you say that?" Ember asked, finally looking away from that empty space.

"Did you catch how long it took them to notice us?"

"Well, yeah, but that could have just been them not caring until it was obvious we were approaching them," Ember pointed out.

"Could have been," Zalia admitted.

"Always asking questions you can't answer," Boreal thought, shaking her head at Zalia.

Her dear friend was very powerful, that was true, but she wasn't very good at thinking the right things. Like how the Astar would taste. That was the real question.

The first thing Zalia had said was "hello" not "what do you taste like?" What kind of thing to say was that? Hello?

Well, she couldn't blame Zalia, she was limited by the form she inhabited.

She watched as Aylie pottered up to the two warm ones. Boreal wasn't entirely sure how most warm ones created new children, but she didn't think that saving one from a not-very-tasty demon was the normal way. What did she know of the subject, though? It wasn't the right question to be asking anyways.

As Ember and Zalia continued talking about what had just happened, Boreal padded off to scout out the road further ahead. She had definitely felt the power of those creatures, yet she thought she could take one on in a fair fight. Even a higher chance of success if she ambushed one, which would be easy enough considering how long it had taken those things to see Ember. Ember wasn't even sneaky at all.

Boreal scented the air, breathing in the varied forest smells of earth, greenery, trees, and sun. She loved those smells, much better than the acrid and sulphurous smell of Cormaine. She didn't know why Zalia had taken so long to get them out of there but was very happy when she had. It was unfortunate that their little mind-friend Delphi had fallen along the way. She would honour the small, cold one each and every time her hunt took her in the direction of the foul-tasting creatures that had killed them.

Padding into the forest edge ahead, she smoothly navigated her way through the undergrowth. It wasn't her natural environment, that being the snowy mountains where the warm one, Zalia, had saved her. She still remembered that day, her first mother lying dead from the attack of the flying creature. That creature had seemed so big back then, but she knew that the world had shrunk since. She looked forward to paying them a visit soon.

For now though, she had to make sure that Aylie stayed safe. She knew Zalia got very easily distracted, knew it intimately from when the world was bigger and she had slipped away many times for adventures. Aylie wasn't as prone to that, but knowing her warm one, Boreal knew she would misplace her somehow.

She discovered no animals or Astar hidden in the trees, much to her displeasure. She was hoping they had just teleported a short way to hide, but that wasn't the case. She just knew that those strange, glowing runes would make the floating ones taste *way* better.

She walked up to where Ember and Zalia were and found them *still* talking about the Astar. Silly warm ones, what did they think they could achieve by talking about it so much? They could have walked far enough to find some more by now if they tried.

She moved up and sat right in front of them and meowed.

"Boreal?" Zalia asked.

Boreal stared into her eyes, focusing as intently as she could.

"What?" Zalia said.

She waited.

"Is something wrong?"

Then, Boreal stood up and walked off.

Aylie was still with those two, so she would be safe. Boreal just wanted them to finally stop talking.

"Yeah, alright, we'll keep going," Zalia called from behind.

Finally.

They travelled for a time, Boreal didn't really know how long. She didn't pay attention to things such as the passing of the warmest one far above. Zalia usually took care of those kinds of things. She had needed to keep count when Zalia accidentally slept for two days, and that had taken all of Boreal's attention to make sure she got the number right. She knew Zalia would want to know the right number when she woke up.

Time passed, and along their travel, they found another town where both Ember and Zalia said their words to the people and the people said their words to them. Boreal didn't find much meaning in those words, much of it was conveying things that could already be seen. Of course they were lacking for food, you could see it in how skinny they had grown. Of course you could see that their homes were damaged, some of the people wounded and their clothes worn down. Couldn't Ember already see those things? Why did she have to ask what troubled them?

Well, eventually they moved on again and Zalia asked Boreal to hunt something for the others to eat that day. Finally, something fun to do. She was feeling a little hungry herself, though she felt like she didn't get as hungry now as she used to when the world was bigger.

She slinked off into the woods, scenting the air and watching the tracks just as Zalia had taught her to do.

Zalia had told her only to catch something small, so she ignored the very obvious tracks of a big, four-legged creature and found the tracks of something big enough that it would feed them all but small enough not to break Zalia's directions.

She hunted it for a time, following its winding path through the undergrowth until finally she saw it. It was round and Boreal knew that meant it would be good eating. Round things often were.

She was downwind from it where she sat, an obvious advantage for the hunt. She wanted to try something a little more fun today, though.

Where she was, she used the passive given to her by the bond she shared with her warm one to create an icy replica of herself that shifted and crouched into the undergrowth, remaining perfectly still. Then, Boreal stepped through the shadows so that she was upwind of the round creature. She purposefully made a little noise as she charged Pounce.

The sound, along with the sudden scent she allowed to drift downwind, alerted the round one and its tiny head popped up. Boreal sprinted forward, and it immediately took off away from her. It was pretty fast for something so edible, managing to outpace Boreal in the short term.

Unfortunately for it, the little creature ran straight to where Boreal had left the trap and it got caught by the icy replica, her own pounce following shortly behind to finish it off.

She picked up her slightly mauled, round snack in triumph, making her way proudly through the forest back towards Zalia.

Her warm one could be pretty stealthy when she wanted, perhaps even stealthier than Boreal herself. That was something she definitely appreciated about her. A warm one like Ember was great and all, but she just couldn't sneak as well as Zalia could. She couldn't hunt as well either. Those were two very, very important skills, or so Boreal thought.

She came out of the trees, blood dripping down her maw and her kill held tightly, dropping it on the floor in front of Zalia.

"Nice catch, Boreal, what is it?" Zalia said, whistling in appreciation.

What is it?

"*Round snack,*" Boreal informed her.

Zalia looked at her through the corner of her eyes

"You could be a little more specific. What did it look like before it got completely mauled?" Zalia asked, looking at the mess of flesh.

Boreal looked down at it too, then looked back up. What did it look like?

"*Snack, but round?*" Boreal suggested.

Zalia rolled her eyes at her, but Boreal wasn't really sure what else she wanted to know. It was food, that was all.

While Zalia went through the process of cooking the meal, Boreal went off into the trees to find a puddle. There, she cleaned herself thoroughly. Blood was all well and good, but being presentable was important. Plus, she didn't want to make Aylie uncomfortable at all.

When she came back, Zalia was still cooking, so Boreal walked over to Aylie and sat down. The little warm one seemed to take comfort from her presence, much like Boreal took comfort in Zalia's presence.

Zalia said they were going to see her friend, Glemp. Boreal just vaguely remembered the thin one that the name belonged to, but it was so soon after the death of her first mother. A lot of her memories surrounding that time were quite vague.

Well, if the thin one was able to help them fight the foul-tasting ones, Boreal wouldn't object.

Once the food was cooked, Boreal waited patiently as some was given to the little warm one first, then Ember.

"*Hungry,*" she informed Zalia.

Zalia handed over a bit for her as well, and Boreal gladly chomped it down. It was good, not the best that Zalia had ever cooked, but she seemed to have a very small number of things to make it taste better with. Still much better than eating it raw, though that had its appeal as well.

It was approaching night time now, and Zalia opened her vault for the other two to sleep in and pulled out a chunk of wood. Boreal had noticed that she had been fiddling around with it recently but made no comment on the pastime.

Boreal herself liked making little scenes out of ice every now and then as well. How different from wood was it really?

Well, she didn't want to sit around while that happened and so decided to climb a tree. She easily clambered up the surface, her sharp claws digging further into the wood than might have been normal. She managed to get far up enough into the branches of the tree that she was able to see out over the top of the forest. There wasn't much to see up there, but she did notice a little dot flying far off in the distance. It looked like . . . one of those that had killed their friend, Delphi. A foul-tasting one.

It was flying away, a shame really. She was looking forward to paying those creatures back for what they had done. Another day, perhaps.

She sat there for a time but got bored pretty quickly. There wasn't really anything to see up here other than trees and more trees. There was the odd break in the forest as a small hill rose out of it, or less heavily overgrown areas that stretched on into the distance, but nothing of real interest.

She yawned and climbed back down. Zalia was still there fiddling with the chunk of wood, bits falling off and other parts growing back. Maybe "fiddling" was the wrong word, as Zalia wasn't even holding the thing; the chunk floated in front of her as she focused intently on it.

She loved her warm one, for all the oddities about her, the strange questions she asked, or the odd manner in which she acted sometimes. Despite it all, she was caring and compassionate, a great friend, and an even better teacher. A second mother to her, one who had taken her in after her first mother had died.

If it wasn't for her warm one, she probably would have been a snack to one of those flying creatures long ago.

CHAPTER EIGHTEEN

Old Places with New Sights

Zalia

Zalia sighed, putting down the chunk of wood. She was getting better at fine-tuning her control, she could feel it. If she just kept working at it she knew she would get it eventually.

Boreal was laying on the ground nearby staring at her, having climbed down from the tree not five minutes after climbing up it. While Zalia definitely had more patience than her furry friend, she did understand how she felt. The eight-odd hours they had to sit around while the others slept were quite boring. She was almost tempted to walk off and climb some trees herself, but it was safer if they ensured the other two could sleep safely within the vault.

Meeting the Astar had been odd in a way that meeting the people of Endaria hadn't been. The Endarians were still human, at least. These people had been odd, serene, and quiet, yet with an intensity about them that spoke in volume. Her own aura wasn't something that had ever been visible to her, probably due to it being slightly reined in due to the Stealth passive, and even further so from the effects of her armour.

She sighed.

"Boreal, do you have anything interesting to do?" she asked.

Boreal looked up at her, rolled over, closed her eyes, and put her paw over her face.

"Alright, then," Zalia muttered.

Cheeky little cat.

She stored her chunk of wood, having already given up on practicing with it for the day.

* * *

The next few days were spent in similar boredom, the plains and forests turning to the denser snowy forests as they entered a section of the north cold enough to sustain a coating of snow. Zalia had to work harder to keep Aylie warm, yet her eyes were kept on the mountain that grew ever larger on the horizon. That was the goal of their journey: the home of Those Born of Heat and Stone and the first friend she had made in this world, Glemp.

She was the same rank as them now, though they very well might have ranked up to Silver in the time she had been away. It wouldn't surprise her, as the amount of time they spent meticulously measuring and performing their alchemical studies was astounding. There wasn't really much else for them to do all day though, stuck in the mountain.

She could see far, far above the mountain where the little wispy trails were left behind the wings of the flying creatures far above. The first time she had seen the mountain, she had thought them simply a formation of clouds, but knew them for what they were after travelling there for a short time. She also swore she saw the occasional flicker of movement on the mountaintop, though while her sight was excellent, it wasn't quite good enough to see that far clearly.

She also noticed that Boreal often looked up at the wispy trails as well. Zalia wondered if she remembered the creatures that had taken her mother from her, the large birds that breathed ice, the ones responsible for the trails of clouds.

It was another two days before they finally reached the mountain, yet some odd sights she had seen from afar were confirmed as they did.

Along the outside of the mountain, many and various structures had popped up. They looked to be made of obsidian, formed as if the flowing lava had cooled into the shape by design. That was very likely, considering the abilities of the race of people that lived inside. They also apparently lived outside the mountain now too, as she saw forms move between the structures along winding paths. There were also the odd streams of lava that flowed through the air behind the people moving along the mountain face.

Her astonishment at the new buildings was overcome by further surprise as they made it to the entrance she remembered. Well, it was definitely not as she remembered, that was for sure.

Where there had once been a smooth invisible door, sealed from the inside by stone bars that were controlled by powers of the people within, there was now a fortress. There were towers atop high obsidian walls, the crenellation spiked and the wall face rippling. It was a daunting sight, one she might have reconsidered approaching if she didn't already know the people who lived inside.

"That's a little different," she murmured, staring from the edge of the forest towards the fortress.

It seemed that without the ice elementals scaring them away from the surface, Those Born of Heat and Stone were more than willing to spread their wings, as it were.

"Just a little," Ember agreed.

Aylie just shivered a little and Zalia helped warm her up, pulling the heat dissipating from her body and pushing it back into her. Like a magical blanket.

"Well, we should go up and knock, right?" Zalia suggested.

"Why would we knock?" Ember asked in confusion.

"So they know we're there."

"Why don't we just yell at them?"

". . . We could do that too," Zalia conceded.

She left the tree line and walked towards the walls. It was getting a little tiresome having to enter through all these walled fortresses as of late, but that was what happened when everything went to shit, demons roamed the lands, and the world was being killed piece by piece.

"Hey, we would like to enter!" Zalia called up.

A little, hooded head popped over the wall, looking down at her.

As the other three stepped up beside Zalia, the large gates began to glow slightly. They then swung open and a torrent of lava flowed from the entrance, forming a jagged wall around them. A dozen Heat and Stone denizens rushed out after it, each of them chanting in unison and controlling their own streams of lava. Then, to her surprise, six humans ran out and formed a shield wall, slowly approaching with spears pointed forward.

Not having missed the little squeak Aylie had let out at the surprise, Zalia instinctively put a comforting arm around her head and shoulders, pulling her close.

"Um," Zalia managed to get out.

"We really mean no harm!" Ember called.

"From where do you come?" one of the women in the shield wall called out.

"We've come from the rebellion's war camp some distance east of the capital. I'm looking for a friend here, Glemp is their name. Have you heard of them?" Zalia asked.

The humans said nothing as some of the Heat and Stone denizens began chattering amongst themselves in that language Zalia didn't understand. Then, one of them came forward, lava still flowing around them.

"Have heard, yes. I will bring, yes, straight away," they said.

"Ahh, ok, sounds good," Zalia agreed.

She waited as the one that had talked ran off. The others stood still in formation, six humans in front and the Heat and Stone denizens split to either side.

"So, what exactly are other humans doing here?" Ember asked.

"We're here for our own reasons. Surely you've noticed what the hell is happening in Endaria," one of them said.

"We have," Zalia said.

"Hey, do any of you know a Zen, by chance?" Ember asked.

There was silence for a long while, until the woman who had spoken first spoke up again.

"How do you know that name?" she asked.

Zalia's heart skipped a beat. That was almost a confirmation.

Ember took a step forward.

"He is our friend, part of our team, once. Is he here? I can't believe we didn't think to look here when we were trying to find him. Of course he would have brought his family to somewhere safe," she rambled, lost in her own thoughts.

As she took that step forward, however, Zalia could see that the entire contingent of . . . soldiers in front of them tensed.

"Hey, Ember, just relax a minute, yeah? If he is here, he's waited this long," she said carefully.

Ember finally seemed to snap back to reality.

"Right, yeah."

Soon, the Heat and Stone denizen that had run off came back with another figure in tow. A figure Zalia remembered quite well.

Glemp - Silver rank.

"Glemp!" she called out.

"Zalia? No, no, no, no. I was told of your fall, yes, not alive," Glemp said, walking up past the other Heat and Stone denizens.

"Very alive, actually. Come on, you know me better than that!" she said.

"Yes, if one was to perform something quite unlikely, yes, you would be them," Glemp agreed, walking all the way up to her.

"Can we come in, then?" Zalia asked.

"Mmm, possible. Your hand, yes," Glemp said, gesturing.

She hesitated, took her arm from Aylie's shoulder, and held it out palm up.

"What is this abou—" she started. "Ow fuck!"

Glemp had drawn a jagged obsidian blade and slid it across her hand in a sharp gesture, staring into her eyes as they did so. Her healing quickly took care of the wound, but she still shook her hand vigorously.

"What the hell?" she asked.

"Yes, not one of them. Real, yes, very real," Glemp said.

She could hear their tone change from wary to warm, a little wobble in their voice. Had they missed her that much?

The thought brought warmth to her heart, so much so that she ignored the oddity of being stabbed and put her hand gently on her friend's shoulder.

"Of course I am, I wouldn't die without saying goodbye first," she said warmly.

Glemp let out a little clicking laugh and the other humans and Heat and Stone denizens let down their guard. She'd passed some kind of test.

"I'm a cousin of Zen's. I'll take you to him. I've heard quite a lot about you lot, though I didn't dare believe it was actually you. From what he said, you're meant to be dead, Zalia," the woman who had first spoken called over.

"A cousin!" Zalia exclaimed.

She didn't know Zen had cousins.

"One of many, come on, I'll show you the way," she said, gesturing for her to follow.

? - Iron rank.

While she wasn't Bronze rank, the woman seemed to hold her weapon with practiced ease. A result of good training, or so Zalia thought.

She led their whole group through the cave entrance, one that Zalia remembered well, into the mountain. Aylie let out a sigh of relief at the warmth inside, actually going so far as to take off the thick jacket she wore, as it got too hot. They were led up through winding passages until they came out of the mountain to the buildings on its side. Zalia gave a light laugh as Aylie had to put her jacket back on.

Around the mountain a short way, walking single file along a winding path, they were led to one particular building that was much larger than most. Zen's cousin led them inside to a bustling hive of activity. There were at least ten people in the main room, some cooking, others cleaning, a few seated about. One older-looking fellow that reminded Zalia of Zen was sitting in the corner, working on a piece of leather with a thick needle and twine.

After noticing all that, the person that caught Zalia's attention almost immediately, and kept it, was Zen. He was sitting on a chair with a young child that he was rocking to sleep.

CHAPTER NINETEEN

Family

Zalia

The entire room bustling with motion came to a stop as everyone in there stared past their guide at Zalia and Ember.

"Um, hey. Zen?" Zalia said into the silence.

The entire room turned towards Zen as he looked at her with disbelief.

"You're alive?" he asked incredulously.

"Wish people would stop saying that," Zalia muttered.

The entire room went back to their separate tasks after seeing Zen confirm he knew the visitor. He stood up, passed the child off to one of the other adults in the room and stepped carefully past a few people on his way to the door.

"How are you here?" he asked, giving her a hug that she returned with more strength than she intended.

She'd missed him more than she realised; all of her worries after she last saw him with a blade through his chest dissipated in one tight embrace.

"It's a long story," she said into his shoulder.

"I'll bet, come, sit down," he said, pulling away and gesturing to the room.

"Space for a furry friend?" Zalia asked.

He looked past her towards where Boreal was standing, now almost fully grown and reaching up to Zalia's chest. She would probably grow just a little bit more from Zalia's estimation.

"Boreal?" Zen asked in surprise.

"She's a fast grower," Zalia explained.

Ember grabbed Zen in an embrace as well.

"Good to see you're alright, Zen," she said.

"And you. I wanted to try and find you and Indis after realising how wrong things had gone, but had to get my family to safety," Zen said.

He pulled away and moved into the room behind them, gesturing to a couple free seats.

"This is my father, Anton, my mother, Annette, twin younger siblings, Harry and Jaz, my grandmother, Polina, and my cousins, Jasper, baby Ingrid, Terrance, Garrett, and Fiona, who you have met," Zen said, introducing each person in the room in turn.

Zalia was overwhelmed by the list of names she definitely wouldn't remember but tried her best to return the courtesy.

"I'm Zalia, this is Ember, Boreal, and little Aylie," she introduced weakly, giving an awkward wave in greeting.

Despite the somewhat large room, she felt just a little bit claustrophobic at the sheer number of people in the room already.

"We've heard that you died, by Zen's accounting. I hope you've got a good story to entertain us with," the older man who was working some leather, Zen's father Anton, said.

"Well, it's probably not what I'd call entertaining," Zalia explained, stepping past the young twins, Harry and Jaz, as they ran up to meet Aylie and Boreal.

Deciding Boreal would be able to keep Aylie somewhat safe from the joint harassment of two terrible twins, she took a seat pointed out to her by Zen.

"What happened after we left you to walk the rest of the way to your home?" Ember asked Zen as she sat crushed up next to Zalia, armour still on.

It was quite uncomfortable, yet somehow comforting.

"Well, when I got home, everything was fine for all of half a day. I caught up with my parents, got to see my little siblings again. Even cousin Fiona was there, a pleasant surprise," Zen started.

"I managed to avoid the mass drafting for the war. I used to be a guard in Alston," Fiona supplied.

"Yes, so I was happy to find that she was alive and well, not some thrall as part of the king's army. Well, it didn't take long for the first of the demons to find us. We fought them off easily enough, a small group of the flying Tin ranked ones. I knew what it meant, though, that none of Endaria was safe," Zen continued. "I sent Fiona to go get her family while we packed to leave. Dad didn't want to leave his farm for anything, he'd lived there his whole life, after all. Well, that changed when Fiona came back some hours later with her other siblings in tow, all of them bathed in blood. The demons got to them too, and their parents didn't make it out."

There was silence in the room as Zen explained. Zalia noticed the downcast expressions of Zen's cousins—they had experienced the death of their parents to those monsters, then.

"That convinced dad well enough, and we left. I brought them here because it is the closest thing I knew to be safe. I didn't want to go to Endelbyrn as I had no trust in the Morning's Shade any longer, nor did I wish to try and travel through half of Endaria to reach the army, an army I didn't know whether it was destroyed or not. So, I came here. Glemp was kind enough to take us in, and we started helping out how we could. A few times I've been back to Endaria to see if I could discover what was happening there, and have brought back groups of refugees fleeing one town or another. The rest you can probably figure out from there, really," Zen finished.

"I'm glad you got out safe," Zalia said.

"Not all of us did," he replied.

That left Zalia in silence. It would be a long time before the kingdom recovered from the recent events. If it even survived them.

"What about you, Zalia, where in the worlds have you been?" Zen asked.

"Ember first," she said, not quite ready to retell the story again.

Ember went on to explain how after she and Indis had encountered their first pack of demons, they had gone back to find the farm where Zen lived. The farm had been destroyed and there was no sign of the family in sight. Having no idea as to where Zen had gone, they had then left to see if they could help the army in any way, not wanting to abandon their people. She explained how the army was still holding on and had, in fact, managed to put up quite a fight; they were now trying to find a way to take back the capital so they could launch a cleansing campaign against the demons from there.

In most ways, Indis and Ember were two very different people. Their temperament, actions, way of thinking, and many other facets of their personalities were different, if not directly at odds with one another. One thing that they had in common, however, was the urge they had to help the people of Endaria. Indis felt this way because she saw herself as a leader of the kingdom, somewhat rightfully so, since her family was previously one of the largest political houses, and she was a childhood friend of the king. Ember was moved to help simply because of her kind-natured heart and her moral compass.

It sometimes seemed that the current events within the kingdom were one of the only reasons they could still stand working with each other.

Once her side of the story was done, Zen and the rest of his family turned to Zalia. Apparently, these people liked to sit in circles and tell each other stories. Even the twins had stopped inspecting Aylie and were sitting on the floor by the warm fire crackling in the fireplace.

Zalia started out a little self-consciously, some memory of Indis's reaction to her retelling of events sitting in the back of her mind. At the lack of interruption, and a gentle mental thought of support from Boreal, she finished retelling what had happened to her and Boreal—what they had been through, and how she had made it back. She left out some of the details of the more gruesome or traumatic parts, partly because of the children present and partly because she couldn't emotionally handle it at that moment.

"Quite a story lass," Zen's father said, once she was finished.

Lass? She wasn't *that* much younger than he was. She definitely wasn't a young woman either.

"It has been a rather eventful few months, yeah," she agreed.

"Not that I am not happy to see you, but why did you come north?" Zen asked.

"Zen!" Zen's mother, Annette, exclaimed.

"What?" he asked confusedly.

Shaking her head at Zen, finding amusement at his somehow continued obliviousness, Zalia gave his mother a warm smile.

"I actually came to see if the Heat and Stone denizens would fight with us," Zalia explained.

Zen frowned.

"Well, I don't speak for them, but I don't think they would leave this mountain, to be honest. Why would they? It's defensible, not surrounded by enemies, secluded, and, most importantly, safe."

"Because if the army fails, those demons aren't going to stop with Endaria. They will take over this whole world, consume it piece by piece. I've been to Cormaine, I've seen what happens when they are left unchecked. It is not something anyone wants to experience, I promise you that," Zalia argued.

"Well, I can understand that, but they might not see it the same way. They have lived in relative safety within this mountain for a very long time, from what I can gather."

"Not as long as you might think. They did not originate in Endaria. Glemp's people come from Cormaine, in fact," Zalia said.

"What?" Zen said.

"Delphi, the oracle friend I mentioned, told me of a memory they and their collective had kept stored for many, many years. A memory of Glemp's own people and other types of the same race that came to the collective to ask questions. The collective were created on Cormaine, back when it was not a hell but a thriving, living world," Zalia explained.

Most of the people in the room were quiet, processing the information she brought. It heavily challenged the beliefs of a lot of people, the fact that Cormaine wasn't the afterlife but a sister world to their own, one that had fallen to the very demons that were invading Endaria at this moment. Where those demons had come from in the first place, neither Ro-ak or Zalia knew.

"For what it's worth, we and the other Endarians living here are behind you. We would love to do what we can to help in this war. I think I can speak for us all when I say we want our homes back," Anton said.

"Well, will you come with me and try convince the Heat and Stone denizens to fight for this world as well?" Zalia asked.

"We'll do what we can."

CHAPTER TWENTY

Druids, Stars, Dreams

Zalia

Zalia stood outside the house, breathing the fresh, cold mountain air. After she had told her story, the claustrophobic space had become too much for her, so she'd left to take a breather.

Having found Zen, she finally felt like things were back together again. Her team was all alive and well, even if they weren't technically a team anymore and might never be again. Glemp was alive and well, and she planned to go find them again later. They hadn't come to Zen's house, probably having some other duties to attend to. Well, she remembered where their house was, unless it had moved to some other part of the caves.

The starlight wolf had said that the first part of her goals would be in the north, where heat met stone met ice. She had assumed that meant the home of the Heat and Stone denizens and in part, it made sense. One of her goals was to see her friends protected and those who had already been harmed, avenged. Had the starlight wolf meant for her to find Zen here?

For some reason, though, she didn't feel like that was all it had meant. Sure, protecting Zen was part of those goals, but it seemed like he was doing just fine. Hell, the people here were doing better than most of Endaria was, from what she could tell. They were relatively safe from the goings on of the kingdom, perhaps even far enough that the demons didn't come here at all.

She turned as she heard the crunch of feet on snow behind her to find Zen walking up.

"Hey," she greeted.

He walked up to lean on the tree next to her, looking her up and down.

"You seem healthy."

"Hard not to be when you have healing constantly flowing through your body," she pointed out.

"Fair point," he said, letting out a quiet chuckle.

"What happened with the ritual site up on the mountain here?" Zalia asked. Zen frowned.

"You know, I never asked. It didn't seem like Glemp's people even knew about what was happening until we showed up on their doorstep."

"Perhaps I'll ask them later."

They fell silent for a while, looking out over the snowy landscape filled with trees interrupted by the odd spike of a mountain here and there.

"I'm glad you got most of your family out safe," Zalia said, interrupting the silence.

"Most," he echoed.

"I'm sure you did all you could," Zalia comforted.

"I did but . . . it wasn't quite enough. It feels like a running theme in my life, of late," he murmured.

"None of us have had a good time recently. You've done well for yourself and your family, considering what we're up against."

"You didn't tell the full story in there, did you?" he asked.

"No, no I didn't. I left out the worst of it or glossed over the details. It's nothing the younger ones need to hear."

"They're stronger than you think, all of them are. They've all been through their own share of horrors."

"It feels like we've all been changed by this. You have mellowed down, Ember has somehow become more outgoing, Indis has gone from poised and in control to an absolute mess, though I suppose she always was, but was just better at hiding it. At least Boreal is still a cute menace; I hope that never changes."

"I've missed all of you quite a bit. Boreal has grown a lot for the time you were gone," Zen said.

"Yeah, she seemed to grow quite a lot as she got closer to ascending to Bronze rank. I wonder if those are related at all."

"I believe someone actually studied that at one point. There is a link to the life stage of animals and the rank they have. One advancing quicker than the other can actually drag the slower one ahead," Zen said.

That made sense to Zalia. She had definitely advanced in rank significantly faster than was normal, that was for sure. She had thought it was because she had gotten her classes so late in life, compared to the average person. Did the speed at which Boreal reached Bronze, certainly faster than was normal for her species, make her grow bigger quickly?

If that was true, did that mean by ranking up, Zalia was actually becoming older? Or did it only affect the growth, not the real age of a person?

Questions for another time, maybe.

"That's interesting. How old were you when you got your class again?" Zalia asked.

"I was seventeen, and I think I remember Ember saying she got hers at eleven, why do you ask?"

"Aylie in there was given a blessing by the starlight wolf, and she said that it would give her a class option. I was wondering when she would be old enough to actually choose one," Zalia explained.

"Well, if it gave her a class option, she should be able to choose it now. People should be able to take a class as soon as one pops up."

"Really? Why hasn't she taken it yet?" Zalia said, more thinking aloud than asking Zen.

"Why don't you ask her?" Zen asked.

"I will, I will. I just need another minute," Zalia murmured.

She really did enjoy the snow. It brought back memories of her time in her own world, living in the wilderness with no more worries than what she was going to be eating over the next week and what preparations needed to be made for the coming season.

"Do you ever just want to pack up everything and leave?" she asked.

"Sometimes. I kind of did that coming here, though I guess I still want to help the kingdom however I can. Where would you go?"

"North, further north. Maybe I could go east and find out what is up with the Astar. I met a nice woman in the south who could probably show me around the desert. Do I really need to be here to help the kingdom, won't it be ok without me?"

"Maybe, maybe not. You're the only one who has been to Cormaine, the only one who has come back with their mind intact at least. A feat that I still don't fully understand. You are also the only one who has been able to heal the damage that has been done to the land by the corruption," Zen said.

Zalia remained silent, letting out only a small sigh.

"*Boreal, can you bring Aylie out here, please?*" she sent to Boreal.

She got a mental affirmation and waited.

A few moments later, Ember opened the door of the house from the inside and let Boreal and Aylie out, closing it behind. Zalia gave Zen a meaningful look and he gave her a nod before leaving. He walked past Aylie on the way to the house as she came over and stood next to Zalia.

"You told me that the blessing gave you access to a class. Are you able to accept that class now if you want?" Zalia asked.

Aylie hesitated, looking up at her with wide eyes beneath a thick fur hood.

Zalia could see the answer in her expression but still waited until she got the affirming nod.

"Why haven't you taken it?" she asked.

"It's scary," Aylie whispered.

"How so?" Zalia asked, crouching down to Aylie's height.

"Mum never told me about this class," Aylie explained.

"Well, maybe if you tell me what it is, I can help you understand what it means?" Zalia suggested.

"It says . . . it says Druid, and the only specialisation option says Starlight Priestess," Aylie whispered even quieter.

Zalia was taken aback. She hadn't met anyone else who had the Druid class, as it was a combination of her other two classes that formed a unity class. Aylie had the option to take it as her main class.

"Well, luckily I can help there. One of my classes is the Druid class. Do you want to know what mine does and what it means for me?" Zalia asked.

Aylie nodded.

"Well, there are a few parts to it. The first thing is the abilities it gives me. Do you feel the calm and warm presence around me? That is an aura the Druid class gives me that lets me heal people. It also gives me access to two very strong abilities that let me control nature to fight my enemies and protect my friends. Those are only part of it as well; it gives me . . . instincts that help me to understand nature a little better, which helps me protect nature in turn," Zalia explained in an even, calm voice.

She had noticed Aylie's expression light up at the mention of Zalia also having the class. Despite that, she still seemed unsure as to whether she wanted to take the class.

"Why do you hesitate?" Zalia asked.

"Big decision," Aylie murmured.

"It is, though I was much less indecisive to take the classes I did, I'll admit. I took the first ones I could get my hands on. Take your time, think it over. I think you should, though. Druid is a strong class, and the specialisation is obviously part of the blessing given by the starlight wolf. It's not every day you get an opportunity like that."

Aylie hesitated still, then nodded, her expression changing to resolute. It looked like she had decided.

"Are you certain?" Zalia asked. "You can still think on it some more, there is plenty of time."

Aylie nodded again.

"Yes, I want to save people like you saved me," Aylie whispered.

"Alright. I'll be here with you the whole way. Whenever you're ready," Zalia said, holding onto Aylie's arms now.

She could see the moment Aylie accepted the classes, as her expression went through a journey. She remembered going through this herself, the slight burning sensation, the disorientation, and the many, many messages that appeared.

She held her steady throughout, with Boreal standing nearby, looking mildly concerned.

Eventually, Aylie blinked as if she had just woken up, looking about.

"Well?" Zalia asked.

"So much," Aylie said quietly.

"It is a lot to take in. Do you want to share your abilities with me? I can try to help you figure them out if you'd like."

Despite that, she could already feel one of them. It was a feeling very much like one she knew so well, one that had kept her alive many times. She was glad that Aylie had it. A slight warm comfort permeated the area coming from Aylie, the effect of Healing Presence.

Aylie nodded, and the second she did, a list of abilities came scrolling through Zalia's own messages.

Profile - Aylie
Health - Excellent
Mana - Full
Stamina - Full
Class One - Druid - Tin
Linked Attributes - Resilience, Vitality
Active Skills
Plant Manipulation - Tin
Nature's Wrath - Tin
Dreamweave - Tin
Passive Skills
Healing Presence - Tin
Spiritual Connection - Tin
Specialisation - Starlight Priestess - Tin
Linked Attributes - Wisdom, Intellect
Active Skills
Starfall - Tin
Starlit Portal - Tin
Passive Skills
Astral Walker - Tin
General Passives
Cold Resistance - Tin
Weapon Proficiencies

Druid
Active Skills
Active 1 - Plant Manipulation - spell - targeted.
Tin - You are able to manipulate plants within a small distance from yourself.
Active 2 - Nature's Wrath - spell - area.

Tin - You invoke the wrath of nature. Nearby enemies are bound by vines, sinking sand or other area-related hazards. Enemies are also subjected to a damage-over-time effect related to biome that lasts until the restraint has ended. The damage-over-time effect deals moderate damage per second.

Active 3 - Dreamweave - spell - varies.

Tin - You may weave the dreams of creatures that are asleep. The more familiar you are with the creature, the further away you may use this.

Passive Skills

Passive 1 - Healing Presence - passive - aura.

Tin - Your very presence grants life to all around you. You, nearby allies, and any flora and fauna you so choose within your aura are affected by a heal-over-time effect. The heal-over-time effect heals for low health every second.

Passive 2 - Spiritual Connection - passive - enhancement.

Tin - You have a strong spiritual connection to the world. You are able to interact with the spirits and souls of creatures and plants alike, living or deceased.

Starlight Priestess

Active Skills

Active 1 - Starfall - spell - area.

Tin - You may cause stars to fall in target area, dealing a high amount of damage to enemies in the area.

Active 2 - Starlit Portal - spell - target.

Tin - You may teleport a short distance.

Passive Skills

Passive 1 - Astral Walker - passive - enhancement.

Tin - Part of your soul walks the astral plane, allowing you insights into otherwise invisible or unknowable things.

"Oh, wow. You've got a good set of abilities there. Some of them are a bit . . . undefined, but many of them seem pretty strong. Plus, I can see many of them becoming quite powerful with future rank-ups as well," Zalia said, reading through a second time.

Some of them were simple, abilities such as the Nature's Wrath one she had, and Starlit Portal probably was easy to use with just a simple activation. Others like Astral Walker, Dreamweaver, and Spiritual Connection were a little more complicated. Zalia feared she wouldn't be able to help with those ones.

"Would you like to try out some of the abilities now, or would you rather wait a bit longer first?" Zalia asked.

"Try!" Aylie said, the excitement in her voice spreading to the expression on her face.

"Alright, start with something small first. How about Plant Manipulation? Focus on that tree and try and move it around," Zalia urged.

Aylie turned about as Zalia stood up, and looked at the tree. Slowly, the branches began bending around and the trunk rippled, the entire thing changing shape as Aylie willed it. It grew thinner and taller, the branches forming wild patterns, before changing back to become exactly as it had been.

"Very nice," Zalia said.

"Its soul. The shape changes but its soul doesn't," Aylie whispered.

Zalia frowned.

"Well, that must be one of your abilities showing you that. Want to try out some more?"

CHAPTER TWENTY-ONE

Starfall

Zalia

Zalia stood by Ember as they watched Aylie from a short distance away. "Whenever you're ready," Zalia called out again.

Aylie was looking a bit stressed, the cause of the emotion being that Zalia and Ember were waiting for her to use one of her abilities on them. Starfall, a spell with an extremely long cooldown of two days, was one of if not the strongest abilities Aylie had. The name of the spell along with the short description was more than enough for them to understand what was coming. That taken into account, though, Aylie was still only at the very beginning of Tin rank and the chances of her spell, even one with such a long cooldown, being able to do them serious harm was very unlikely. Taking into account that all three of them were healers now, and Zalia had an anti-death measure, it wasn't really as dangerous a situation as it might have looked at first glance.

"Are you sure?" Aylie called over, her voice still somehow quiet.

"We're sure," Zalia assured her.

Before the sky darkened, Zalia could see Aylie muttering something to herself, the words too quiet for her to hear. It was daytime, yet the light from the sun faded away and the land was cast in shadow. Glimmering, pinprick stars began glowing in the sky, yet as she looked up, Zalia noticed that a few of the stars looked like they were growing brighter. She knew what was coming, yet couldn't help but feel a small amount of awe mixed in with a drop of fear as she noticed they weren't growing brighter, but bigger.

Then, two glowing balls of solid light collided, leaving a starry trail behind them.

Both Zalia and Ember were thrown to the ground with force, and she actually felt some of her ribs crack, the stabbing pain arching through her body. She grit her teeth, not wanting to scream at the pain because she didn't want to cause Aylie any concern. It felt like the light of a star had been given the solidity of matter and had been thrown at her; a slight burning feeling accompanied the massive force with which the light hit.

She rolled over and pushed to her hands and knees, getting one foot underneath her as she managed to stand, the healing already fixing the damage that had been done.

Ember looked a little worse for wear but her condition was improving at incredible speed, her own healing working much quicker as well as benefitting from Zalia's.

She looked up to see Aylie rushing over with panic written all over her face but Zalia just gave her a broad smile.

"Wow! That is a really strong ability. It should be able to take out most enemies of your rank on its own as long as you have time to cast it," Zalia exclaimed.

Aylie careened into her, hugging her with as much strength as she could muster.

"Don't worry, we're both just fine. I just wanted you to see that you have power now, a lot of strength for someone so young. It means you can defend yourself from some creatures in this world, better than even many Iron rank people might be able to. Even better again than those who have classes such as farmers or craftspeople."

"Sorry," Aylie said into Zalia's side.

"Oh, don't be sorry, we did tell you to do it, didn't we?" Zalia assured her.

Aylie pulled her head back and looked up at Zalia, and she could see that the worry on her face had been replaced by something akin to excitement.

"It's good, isn't it? You have some control over your own future now. No one can take this from you, your powers are yours to use as you see fit. Just remember that it's important to help others when you can, as long as it won't cause you to be harmed yourself, alright? Can you do that?" Zalia said.

Aylie nodded.

"I want to help people how you help people," Aylie murmured.

"Well, now you can," Zalia said, giving her a smile and a tight hug back.

She was reminded how down-to-earth Aylie was for someone of her age. She had seen too much for someone so young, hell, for anyone at all. No one should have to go through what Aylie had.

"Right, now that one is out of the way, would you like to try some of the others?" Zalia asked. "Starlit Portal seems like it could be fun."

"I would like to see that one as well," Ember said, still lying in the snow.

"What are you doing down there?" Zalia asked, turning her head to look at her.

"Just relaxing. It's comfortable," Ember explained.

Zalia rolled her eyes.

"We're trying to help Aylie experiment with her powers, remember?" she reminded Ember.

"And I can't do that while I'm comfortable?" Ember retorted.

"Well, Aylie, how about it?" Zalia said, turning back to the young girl.

"Sure, I can't figure out this one," Aylie said.

"Oh? What are you having trouble with?" Zalia asked, furrowing her brow.

"Seems strange," Aylie explained.

Ember sat up, putting her arms behind herself as support.

"You said you have a teleport now, Zalia, why don't you show her? Maybe it will help?" Ember suggested.

"Good idea."

Zalia activated her own teleport skill, Mobility, shunting a short distance away with a rush of air, a small breeze created by the sudden disappearance and reappearance of her body.

"Just like that!"

Aylie's face scrunched in concentration and a light starry portal appeared behind her and folded, swallowing her in a fraction of a second. She appeared in the next instant next to Zalia. Strangely, she didn't displace air like Zalia had.

"Well, you picked it up pretty quick," Zalia said, happy to see Aylie's natural skill in her abilities.

She hadn't really seen anyone else go through the process of learning their skills yet, and while she hadn't had any trouble figuring out any of hers, she wasn't certain if that was normal. It seemed like most abilities came with a certain degree of instinctual knowledge in how to use them.

"Could see how you did it," Aylie said.

"What do you mean?" Zalia asked.

Aylie shrugged.

"Is it one of your passive abilities, then? The one that lets you see into the astral, maybe?" Zalia suggested.

"Maybe," Aylie said.

"You'll probably have to work on those two strange ones and the dreamweaving on your own, though I'd be happy to help however I can. I don't really know what they are either."

"I can weave your dreams?" Aylie asked in a small voice.

"Sure, why not? Just don't make them anything bad, alright?" Zalia said after a short pause.

She didn't *really* want someone meddling with her dreams, but she only slept for an hour or two every few days now, so why not?

Congratulations! Healing Presence has reached Bronze 4.

Well, at least something good had come of being flattened by a falling star.

"Hey, Aylie, want to come meet Glemp? They're a good friend of mine."

They were still out on the mountain, just off one of the lower paths. Boreal was nowhere to be seen, maybe exploring what was her natural home. She was sneaky enough when it came to normal terrain, an effect that was amplified when in her natural habitat. Even without magic, she would blend in extremely well with the snowy, rock-filled landscape. With it, she would likely be impossible to find unless she wanted to be.

Aylie gave a nod of affirmation, so she started trudging through the snow towards a cave entrance.

"Hey, you just going to leave me lying here?" Ember called.

Zalia looked over.

"Are you stuck?" she asked.

"Sure," Ember said, a mischievous twinkle in her eyes.

Zalia rolled her eyes but walked over to help Ember up.

She offered a hand and pulled Ember up to a standing position. Ember gave her a radiant smile and a hug.

"Thanks," she said, then pushed Zalia over.

Or, tried to.

Zalia managed to keep her feet beneath her, months and months of experience against Boreal's shenanigans coming in handy as she managed to stay upright.

"That's just rude," Zalia said, tsking at Ember.

"That's cheating! You must have used some kind of magic there." Ember sulked.

"No, I'm just faster than you," Zalia teased.

Aylie was already halfway towards the cave, having decided to walk on ahead, so Zalia started walking off. She heard quick footsteps as Ember began to chase her, so Zalia took off as fast as she could. They very quickly overtook Aylie, who also joined in the chase, running after Ember and Zalia, albeit much slower than they could manage.

Just as she was about to reach the cave entrance, the snow to her right exploded and a large, furry form slammed into her and Ember, knocking them both over. Half-buried in snow, Zalia saw Aylie appear from thin air at the entrance to the caves. She only got that one blink of sight as Boreal proceeded to try and bury Zalia in the snow using her powers.

"Hey, stop that!" Zalia yelled into the building pile of snow, struggling free.

She managed to pull herself free to a standing position and used her own power to bury the struggling Ember just a little more, sprinting to the cave.

She was overtaken by Boreal moments before making it over the line, and the three of them watched Ember finally free herself and trudge towards them.

"See?" Zalia said as Ember made it to them.

"Aylie made it here before you," Ember pointed out.

"She cheated," Zalia said.

"What!?" Aylie gasped.

It was the loudest she had ever heard the little girl talk.

"Teleporting was definitely against the rules," Zalia said sagely.

"And what about setting your big kitty cat on me as a delaying tactic?" Ember retorted.

"She did that of her own volition. Besides, she buried me too," Zalia said, side-eyeing Boreal who was inconspicuously cleaning herself.

"Well, if you used your powers to bury me, Boreal used hers to bury us both, and Aylie used hers to teleport, I think I win since I didn't use any of mine at all," Ember said, a smug expression on her face.

Zalia looked at Aylie and an understanding passed between them.

"No," they both said at once.

"And do you agree with them?" Ember said, looking at Boreal who paused mid–paw lick.

Zalia and Aylie both stared at her as well, and Boreal suddenly looked anxious under the weighted gaze of all three of them.

Boreal vanished into a shadow, no doubt teleporting somewhere else through them.

"Looks like she has abstained from voting, which makes it two to one," Zalia declared.

"Fine, fine, Aylie wins." Ember surrendered.

"Damn right, she does. Now, let's go find Glemp."

CHAPTER TWENTY-TWO

Repressed

Zalia

H*ey, Zen, we're just going to go see Glemp,*" Zalia sent to Zen, still in the nearby house.

"*Gah!*" the reply came.

Smiling at his reaction to the mental communication she acquired in Cormaine, Zalia followed the other three further into the caves. They were on their way to find Glemp and figure out what exactly it might take to convince the Heat and Stone denizens to join in their war. She thought it might be hard to accomplish, considering the safety they currently had within the mountain they called home.

She also just wanted to see her old friend, the first one she had made in Endaria. It would do her good to spend a bit of time with a friend she made when things were a lot simpler. She had been considering using the mental healing ritual she had used on the soldier back in the war camp on herself but had come to the conclusion that what she was dealing with wasn't worth the expenditure of materials. She hadn't tried growing the Living Trapvine just yet but had a sneaking suspicion she wouldn't be able to. The piece she had was only a small part of the larger whole, a tiny cutting of a living creature.

Instead, she considered whether it might be worth offering to use it on Aylie, but she didn't really know if there were any long-term effects of using the ritual. She didn't want to cause anyone any harm, the only reason she had used it on that soldier in the first place being that the man had been so broken as to be basically catatonic.

As they walked through the caves, and now that she wasn't preoccupied with the thought of seeing Zen again, she noticed that the caves had a distinctly more military feel about them. There were guards posted about, and people walked with purpose rather than with the idle meandering of a carefree society. Not for the first time, Zalia was in awe of the unity in which the Heat and Stone denizens lived. She had no idea if they had any ruling body or person of any kind, and had never asked, yet these people still acted with joint purpose.

She still remembered the day the three ice elementals had attacked the mountain and the people here had performed a joint ritual of some kind, combining all of their power to overcome two Silver and one Gold ranked elemental with ease. Some had died and others passed out from the effort, but the speed at which they had accomplished the task was amazing. Even Larel, someone whose powerset was built for fights with a single slow enemy, took a long while to defeat a Gold rank. A human squad of one hundred–odd people from the kingdom of Endaria hadn't even been able to take down one of the Gold ranked elementals by themselves.

Well, Zalia would need to find a way to make the Heat and Stone denizens adopt the joint purpose of cleansing the world of the demon invasion. She just hoped she was the right person for the job; she wasn't exactly known for her social or political prowess.

They found themselves in the small workshop Glemp called home, benches all along the perimeter and centre of the room forming the workspace in which Glemp performed their many experiments, one of which they were currently engrossed in.

"Hey, Glemp, how are things?" Zalia asked in greeting.

"One moment, yes," Glemp said, focus unwavering.

She waited, keeping an eye on Aylie as she wandered around the room. There were more than a few dangerous components and liquids in this room.

A single drop fell from the dropper Glemp was holding steady, plopping into the stone vial in their hands.

"Right! Yes, Zalia. Ember, of course, yes, a powerful name. Boreal, she of the ice and . . . the small one," Glemp said, greeting them one by one.

"Aylie," Aylie informed them.

Aylie was currently still rugged up in the thick hoodie and was standing before Glemp, managing to actually reach the same height as them.

"Aylie of the small humans, yes. Welcome," Glemp said.

"Aylie is a child, Glemp. You know, a young of our race," Zalia explained.

"A child . . ." Glemp said, trailing off.

Zalia tried to figure out how to reply when something occurred to her.

"Hey, you know the language properly now?" Zalia asked.

"Hmm, yes, yes, learned from Zen," Glemp said offhandedly, still looking with confusion at Aylie.

"Right, yeah, makes sense. Two adult humans can have children if they wish, and that child will grow up to be another adult human. How exactly do you make more of your race if not like that?" Zalia inquired.

She had never seen any children Heat and Stone denizens but had just thought they might live somewhere deeper or safer in the mountain.

"Formed from stone, heat. Yes, no growing required," Glemp explained.

"Huh," Zalia said.

She then noticed that Ember was glaring at her like, "Really, you're talking about reproduction right now in front of Aylie?"

Zalia coughed lightly into her hand.

"Mm, anyways. Glemp, I was wondering what it would take for your people to come help us fight back against the demons invading this world," she said, changing the subject quickly.

"Mmm, no, no, no. Our people will stay, resist. Fight we will not, no," Glemp said, looking to Zalia.

Her heart sank.

"There's no chance? None at all? This is something that affects us all, not just the humans of Endaria. If the kingdom falls, the demons will come after your people and all peoples next. This world will be consumed by them," Zalia said urgently.

"Zalia, no, you do not see. We are made of the stone, yes, the heat. Here we are born, yes, here we live. We do not belong in the outside, in the kingdom. Here we are safe. Our memories are long, we remember when the humans treated us without respect, yes. You may be a good one, but many are not," Glemp explained.

Zalia leaned against one of the benches, letting out a long sigh. It hadn't been good odds of them joining, but she had really hoped there might be some kind of chance. The hard shutdown of the idea after the long journey really was painful. She might have come up here just to see if Glemp was ok anyway, but she had definitely been hoping for more.

"Well, I can't say I blame you or your people. It's not a good place out there right now," Zalia said. ". . . Hey, what happened with your ritual site here up on the mountain, did it explode or did any creatures come from it?"

Zalia sensed that Glemp was not going to change their mind, so she dropped the subject. Perhaps she could come up with some way to convince them but had nothing as of yet.

"Ah, I remember you speaking of this. Nothing that we experienced at all," Glemp said.

"What?" Zalia asked.

"Nothing, yes, yes," Glemp repeated.

Nothing at all?

"All of the ritual sites we knew of seemed to have done something, how could yours not have?" Zalia asked.

The mountain *was* close to where Zalia had interrupted the ritual, yet it seemed like closer ones had still activated. If the one on the mountain hadn't, did that mean it wasn't part of the main ritual, or did something else stop it from working?

"Well, good to see you were all alright, at the least."

"Yes, we live on ever as we have," Glemp said, nodding.

They had turned their attention back to the stone vial on the bench, perhaps observing it through an ability Zalia couldn't see.

"Do . . . do you know that there were once others of your race? Those Born of the Water Depths and Those Born of the Wind and Sky?"

Glemp's head flicked up to Zalia, meeting her eyes.

"How do you know of them?" they asked.

"I was told by a . . . a dear friend. They told me that your people used to visit them, long, long ago. Back when your people lived in the other world."

"No, no, no, no. Have you been there? Not possible," Glemp murmured.

"Cormaine, yes, I have. What do you know of it?" Zalia asked.

"I . . . we must speak with the others. This news is important, yes, very important," Glemp said.

"Important how?"

"It is told that we came from such a world, as you say. A closely guarded secret, yes, very closely. Who is this dear friend, yes, of which you speak?"

"A friend I made when I was there, one who was part of a larger whole. The collective, small creatures on their own but powerful together. They kept the memories of Cormaine alive for a very long time," Zalia explained.

"So you have met some of the . . . the . . . how would the word translate? The seers, maybe?" Glemp asked in awe.

"I did, yes they could see the future quite clearly. They—" Zalia cut off.

The memory surfaced: Delphi crushed and the bodies of the collective strewn across the ground of the Grove.

Zalia shook her head and smashed a fist down on the bench next to her, causing Glemp to jump and the vial to tip over. That damn memory.

"Sorry," she murmured.

She could feel the eyes of Ember and Boreal on her back, their gaze burning into her skin. Aylie was looking up at her with worry and a tiny hint of fear.

"What is it Za—" Glemp started.

But Zalia couldn't stand it. She vanished using her teleportation and fled from the room. Why did that memory keep coming back? Couldn't it just stay in the damn vault where she put it?

She ran through too-warm corridors, caves, and up stairs. She just needed to breathe, why was it so hard to breathe in the mountain? The air was thick, tinged red with a sulphurous hint to it that made it so damn hard to breathe. Where was she? Had she really escaped or was this all a cruel dream?

She burst out of an exit to the cool, fresh, open air, taking in gasping breaths.

Slowly, she began to calm, but soon, tears came to blur her vision of the expansive snowy landscape beyond.

She felt a hand on her shoulder and twitched slightly at the touch.

"Hey," Ember said softly.

She was on her knees, she realised, sitting in the snow where she had fallen.

"Hey," Zalia replied, voice choked with pain.

"What's wrong?" Ember asked, kneeling next to her and drawing her into a tight hug.

"They . . . they're dead."

She hadn't told Ember about the death of the collective.

"Who are? What happened?"

"The collective. They died as I escaped Cormaine. They knew it would happen, but they died so that I could escape. They sacrificed themselves because they knew there was no other way," Zalia explained, her voice rough as she tried to hold back tears.

"I'm sorry that happened. Losing a friend is always hard," Ember empathised, gently rubbing Zalia's back with one hand as she held her in a hug still.

"Them, and Ro-ak, they were the only ones there with me and Boreal. That entire world, there is no other life there. Now it's possible even Ro is gone too," Zalia added, tears finally flowing only to freeze lower down her face from the frigid wind blowing across the mountainside.

Zalia could feel a gentle aura that felt as if it were caressing her very soul, calming her, healing her.

"That's what that emotional injury that appeared before was, wasn't it. How are you hiding it like that?" Ember asked.

"I . . . Remember those swirling orbs in the vault? Those are memories. Memories stored from my mind. One of them is my last hour in Cormaine, stored away so I don't have to remember it, only . . ." Zalia faded away, but Ember seemed to understand what she meant.

"Oh, Zalia, no," Ember murmured softly.

"I . . . I know, Ember . . . I know."

CHAPTER TWENTY-THREE

Healing

Zalia

Zalia knelt in the snow as Ember comforted her.

"Zalia . . . how exactly does this memory storage work?" Ember asked softly.

"It lets me store a memory and leaves only vague ideas of the memory behind. It also . . . takes the emotions linked to the memory away."

Ember didn't say anything to that, but Zalia could almost hear Ember calling her an idiot in the silence.

A few moments later, she heard footsteps as Boreal and Aylie found them. Boreal immediately came up and flopped against Zalia, almost knocking both her and Ember over. She was then joined by Aylie as she dropped on top of Boreal to give Zalia a hug as well.

"Hey, you two," Zalia greeted.

Her tears had stopped but she no doubt had red, puffy eyes and her voice was hoarse.

She received a complex set of thoughts and emotions from Boreal that conveyed her own grief at the loss of their friend, followed by the words, "*I miss them too.*"

She hugged Boreal closer.

Despite her seemingly carefree approach to the world, and the joy with which she performed every task, Boreal wasn't unaffected by the loss of their shared friend either. She didn't have a vault in which to store her memories either, though it had turned out to be more of a detriment to Zalia's mental health than a benefit.

She had promised herself that she would restore the memory when she reached a safe place, and the Grove would have been an excellent place to do just that. When she'd been there though . . . it had slipped her mind while she had focused on telling the others everything she had discovered in Cormaine.

Well, she was safe here, wasn't she?

"Why haven't you restored the memory if it has been harming you like this?" Ember asked, mirroring her own thoughts.

"I . . . because it is so bad that I don't know if I'll be able to handle it," Zalia said shakily.

"Well, why don't you do it now? You have all of us here to help you," Ember suggested.

Could she do that? Weren't there more important things to take care of right now?

She needed to try and find a way to convince the Heat and Stone denizens to join the war . . . but they had said no. Maybe she could convince them to take in more refugees though, a middle ground where they could maintain the safety of their mountain and save some people from horrible fates.

"It can wait for later, we need to—" Zalia started.

"Zalia," Ember said firmly.

"Ember, I don't know if I can do it," Zalia said.

"You can, I know you and I know you can. I don't know what it must have been like down there and I won't pretend I do, but if anyone can come through alright, it's you," Ember said.

"I . . . I'll try," Zalia agreed.

She could feel it there still, a memory on the edge of her consciousness waiting to be retrieved at a moment's notice should she ever require. A memory with torn edges, one she had ripped out of her mind very shortly after it had formed.

She grabbed it and fit it back into the hole in her mind where it had come from.

She could feel the memory begin to settle as power flowed from Ember and the torn edges started healing. Strength and support came from the bond she had with Boreal, shoring up her pained mind. And Aylie. Aylie clung on to her with all her newly increased strength. Aylie needed her to be well and strong.

And . . . it wasn't as bad.

The grief was there, the pain, the fear, the stress, and the misery of that last hour in Cormaine were all there, yet with the support of her friends, her . . . family, something she hadn't really had in a long time, it wasn't as bad.

Would you like to form a bond with 'Ember'?

What? she thought.

She hesitated. Her bond with Boreal had been incredibly useful in the past, and she had no doubt that one with Ember would be just as, if not more, useful.

She looked over at Ember who was watching her intently, and accepted.

> **Congratulations! You have formed a bond with 'Ember.' You and Ember are now able to slightly sense each other's locations in relation to each other, as well as gain a vague sense of each other's emotions, as long as the other person is willing.**
>
> **Congratulations! Your bond with Boreal has deepened. You and Boreal's ability to sense each other's location is more accurate, in addition to gaining a deeper sense of each other's emotions, as long as the other person is willing. You and Boreal are able to provide strength of the mind to each other.**

She shuffled around in the cuddle puddle of people to look at Ember, who just smiled warmly at her.

"I didn't know that could happen," Zalia murmured.

"It's not so uncommon between people. Much rarer to be able to form that kind of bond with another species like Boreal," Ember said in reply, her voice equally soft.

She didn't miss that Boreal's bond had changed in its wording a little bit. It didn't refer to it as a beast bond anymore, instead, it was just a normal one. Did that mean that whatever the mysterious system was, it now thought of Boreal as a person, not an animal? Or was that due to Zalia's own perspective?

And she could feel them there in her mind. Another presence—Ember, and a familiar one, now stronger than ever. Boreal was still lending strength to her mind, helping take the burden of her pain.

So Zalia lent some back.

The torn edges of the memory had started to heal, the hole in her mind now occupied by the wound, somehow less painful than the void it had left behind. She wasn't sure why the memory had such a . . . reduced effect now that she accepted both what had happened and the memory itself. Maybe the manner in which she had roughly torn it out had lent to the strength of the pain she felt when remembering it through the vault.

"Thank you," Zalia whispered, to no one in particular.

They all helped her in their own ways, and she was more grateful for that than she could ever put into words.

CHAPTER TWENTY-FOUR

Fireside

Zalia

A few hours later, they were all seated in the large yet somehow small living room of Zen's family. After they had seen Zalia come inside, a complete mess being supported by the others, the family had somehow found places to be that weren't in sight.

Zen was there too, looking a little confused but supportive. A state of affairs that Zalia was more than used to seeing in the young man.

"What now?" Zen asked.

They had just finished explaining that Glemp's people would not help in the war, something that didn't surprise Zen at all. Perhaps he had already tried to convince them.

"We go back, do what we can. Though . . . we did see some of the Astar on our way here. I have a strange feeling that they are a part of this somehow. Why else would they be in Endaria, now of all times?" Zalia said.

"The Astar? What were they like?" Zen asked, leaning forward.

"Well . . . strange. They had an aura that was much too strong for their rank, floated along, and had runes covering their skin. The aura felt . . . careless and cold. Sterile."

"I would have liked to see them," Zen murmured, leaning back in his chair.

"It wasn't really anything special. They vanished as soon as we tried talking to them," Ember added.

Zalia looked at Aylie, who was looking strangely between her and Ember.

"What is it?" she asked.

"You . . . both are different," Aylie whispered.

Zalia frowned.

"Different?" she asked.

"Like there is a bridge," Aylie murmured.

Like there is a bridge?

Then it struck her. Aylie was talking about the bond that had formed between them.

"Like there is a bridge?" Zen asked, his confusion deepening even further.

"A . . . bond," Zalia explained.

"Alright, someone better explain. What exactly happened in the short time between you leaving to see Glemp and coming back here?" Zen asked.

"A bonding experience," Ember supplied unhelpfully.

"I'd rather not talk about it just yet," Zalia added.

"Alright, sure. I just hope you're all ok?" Zen said.

"Yeah, we're good. Much better, actually."

"Just working some things out, Zen, nothing to worry about," Ember explained, smiling warmly at Zalia.

Zalia looked at that warm smile and found herself looking quickly away, a slight heat rising to her face.

That was something she was *not* used to.

"Do you think the Heat and Stone people will be alright with taking in more refugees?" Zalia asked, changing the subject.

"I think so, yeah. They seem ok with the few people I do bring back when I venture out to Endaria now and then. They might have some problems with it if it becomes too many people, though," Zen answered, looking deep in thought for his own part.

Zalia really should have asked him about the current situation between the refugees here and the Heat and Stone people before she went and asked Glemp about joining the war. He probably knew them better than she did, now that he had spent so long in the mountain.

"Well, there is that, at least. I think the army will be happier being able to send people here, rather than south towards the desert. At least this is somewhat close to the kingdom and with a known place of safety. I've no idea what destination the people going south are moving towards. Though, it is a longer trek, I guess," Zalia said.

"And it gets less dangerous the further north you go. We saw fewer demons and corruption from the rituals coming up this way. It is way worse down south," Ember added, her tone taking on a sadness.

Zalia knew Ember did all she could to help the people of Endaria, but she also knew Ember would never think it was enough.

"You do all you can, Ember, no one can ask more of you," Zalia said, finding Ember looking away from her own warm smile.

"I know, I know. I still see so much bad happening out there despite my best efforts," Ember murmured.

"Did you know people have started calling her Saint Ember?" Zalia said to Zen.

"Saint Ember?" he asked incredulously.

"Hey!" Ember protested.

"Right? I mean, they aren't wrong, but still. It was quite funny to hear the first time," Zalia said.

"You're one to talk, walking around blessing them like some kind of priest," Ember shot back.

"Priest?" Zen asked in confusion.

"Oh, I may have a friend or two who are gods and call on them to give guidance to people every now and then, but that doesn't make me a priest. Unlike Aylie, who, according to her classes, actually is a priestess," Zalia said.

"You have a statue!" Aylie announced.

Zalia buried her face into her hands. Betrayed, betrayed by the one she saved.

"A statue!" Zen said, bursting into laughter.

"Yeah, a bloody statue. Guess whose fault that is?" Zalia muttered.

"Indis," Zen guessed immediately.

"Yep! You somehow managed to avoid *all* mention whatsoever, though. Unfair I say," Zalia added.

"Hey, that is unfair. Why don't you have to deal with any of this statue and saint nonsense?" Ember said, narrowing her eyes at Zen.

"Well . . . some of the people here *do* treat me with an unnerving amount of respect," Zen said.

"It's what happens when you save them, apparently. Just don't get to the point where they start *worshipping* you," Zalia whispered, shivering.

"I don't know if I would call it worshipping," Ember argued.

"No? They built a statue," Zalia said.

"Well . . . alright, I'll concede that. At least they haven't started making sacrifices to you," Ember said.

Zalia stared at her.

Ember stared back.

"Why would you even put those words out into the world?" Zalia asked.

Ember just smiled.

This time Zalia didn't look away, narrowing her eyes at Ember.

They hadn't spoken about the bond yet, specifically what they could now do. Sensing each other's emotions was . . . somehow different to her than being able to do it with Boreal. It felt a little more personal.

Maybe that was because Boreal wore her emotions in the way she stood, through posture and positioning. She wasn't hard to read at all, to Zalia at least.

People were different, she hadn't ever been very good at reading people, so having the ability to now . . . well, it was different.

"I guess we're going to have to walk all the way back down south now," Zalia said.

"Yeah, seems like it. Anything you want to check out on the way down?" Ember asked.

"Actually, yeah. There is that town . . ." Zalia trailed off.

Damn, her memory sucked sometimes.

"Ostoss!" she said, remembering. "Tristan lives . . . lived? . . . there, remember?"

"Oh! Yeah, Tristan. Shit, I've not been up this far north since the ritual went off. I do wonder if he is doing ok. From what I remember, that town was pretty shored up, not a small number of guards there. They might be doing ok," Ember said.

"There were a few good people there. Many of them I fought with against the first corrupted I met," Zalia murmured.

"Bloody corrupted," Ember muttered.

"What has happened to them anyways?" Zalia asked.

She realised she hadn't seen any of the madmen since coming back to Endaria.

"Oh, you see them here and there. Most of them went back to the capital, I think, though some still run around committing atrocities," Ember said, vitriol in her voice.

Zalia couldn't just hear the emotion, but feel it from the woman too.

"*We need to talk*," Zalia sent to her.

Ember nodded very slightly in agreement with her.

Naturally, Zalia allowed her own emotions to get through to Ember as well. They hadn't just formed a bond in name, but in reality as well. Ember had been there for Zalia more than a few times, the most recent time being quite significant.

"*Alright*," Ember sent back.

Zalia sat back and got comfortable.

"*We can sense each other's emotions and locations . . . How do you feel about that?*" Zalia asked telepathically.

"*I have no issue with it, I trust you . . . as long as you have no issue with it?*" Ember replied.

"*None at all. It's just, well, a little new to me. We don't have anything like this where I come from. Even if we did, I would have been the last person to form one. Coming here has changed me quite a lot, to be honest,*" Zalia sent back.

"*And less than you might think. I'm glad to have formed a bond with you, you're one of the most caring people I've ever met, despite your tendency to hide it,*" Ember sent.

Zalia felt her face flushing at the compliment.

"*Thank you. I just didn't want to overstep my bounds with the bond is all,*" Zalia sent.

"*Don't be silly. One wouldn't have formed if I didn't also want it. I'd let you know if you overstepped,*" Ember sent.

"Are you two ok?" Zen asked.

Zalia blinked, realising she had been staring into Ember's eyes, and Ember had been staring back. How had she not realised before that the vibrant brown of Ember's eyes glowed so brightly by firelight?

"Yeah, fine, fine," Zalia said.

Boreal was currently so close to the fire that Zalia feared she might try and slide into it. She was also a little more scared that she might actually be able to do that without being harmed. With Aylie resting on Boreal's side on the floor, and two of her closest friends by her side, Zalia felt . . . better.

She had definitely had times in the past weeks in Endaria when she had felt good, but with the constant background threat of that memory hiding in her vault gone, a weight had been lifted. Accepting it had turned it from an occasional, unmanageable misery to a dampener she could cope with.

Her friend had died, but they had died for a purpose they believed in, for a reason. She had to make sure that the purpose they had died for wasn't abandoned.

Delphi, Ro-ak, and the collective had put their trust in Zalia to come back one day and restore Cormaine to the beautiful world it had once been.

She could see it now, beautiful glittering lakes, expansive forests, and the cities of the Bathar that were half stone and half plant. They had lived with nature unlike any race in Endaria did, other than the Heat and Stone denizens.

The image flashed away, and Zalia realised it had come from the other memory in her vault, the one given to her by the collective before she had left.

She would go back and she would free Cormaine. She would save Ro-ak once more.

The starlight wolf had been right. Coming up north had brought her towards the first step of her goals. She knew what she wanted to do, now she just had to find a way to do it. The first step of that was to beat back the demon invasion in Endaria, she was sure of it. Then, she could convince whichever armies remained to continue the fight into Cormaine. to get to the root of the problem. To make sure another invasion never happened again.

Ember was watching her again, perhaps having felt the decision she had just come to through her emotions.

"Zen, if we send refugees your way, will you make sure to take care of them?" Zalia asked.

"I . . ."

She could see what he wanted to say. He wanted to say he would come with them, help them in their tasks. He wanted to say he would fight with them for the kingdom.

They both knew it wasn't true. In reality, he wanted to stay with his family and protect them. He was a lover, not a fighter.

"I will, yes."

"Good. When we go to Ostoss, we might end up sending quite a few people back your way if they still live. Otherwise, we might also end up having the army send refugees up this way just until we can manage to take back the kingdom. Obviously, I'll talk with Glemp about it before we leave," Zalia added.

"And . . . when will you be leaving?" Zen asked.

Zalia met Ember's eyes and an agreement passed between them.

"We should leave tomorrow morning. There is still much to be done, and every day we wait will be lives lost," Zalia replied.

"I thought as much, though I wish you'd stay longer, I do understand," Zen said.

"I know, I wish we could stay longer too," Zalia said softly.

"Besides, it's not like this is the last time we will see you, Zen," Ember said cheerfully.

"I don't like the way you say that," Zen mumbled.

"Well, not to worry. I'll keep Zalia safe," Ember informed him.

"Oh? You'll keep *me* safe, huh?" Zalia asked.

"Of course, who else?" Ember scoffed.

"Well, I look forward to it."

"I'll bet you do," Ember teased.

CHAPTER TWENTY-FIVE

Heat and Stone

Zalia

Zalia was sitting on one of Glemp's benches watching them work. It looked to her like they were trying to recreate whatever experiment they had been working on that she had destroyed the day before.

They were due to leave today, but Zalia didn't want to go without saying goodbye.

"I'm sorry for knocking that over yesterday."

"No, no worries are needed. Not the most of import, no."

Zalia sighed.

"Well, I'm glad I didn't ruin anything."

Glemp put down what they were working on and turned to her.

"I know you do not like that we will not join you, but you must understand, yes, that we need to stay here."

"You . . . *must* stay here?"

"Yes."

"Why?"

Glemp looked at her for a long time, their eyes flicking between both of hers. "Come."

Zalia furrowed her brow, following the much shorter Glemp out of their workshop.

"What are you showing me?"

It was a few minutes of walking before they replied.

"You need only see to understand, yes."

Oddly, they took her on a path that she recognised. The last time she had left the mountain Glemp had taken her down to the very bottom to grab some of the plant that was Flame-root. Now, however, she could create as much of the plant as she wanted simply by growing it herself. They started descending the stairs to the floor-level chamber.

"I didn't see anything strange last time we went down here."

"You did not know how to look, no."

"I did not know how to look . . ."

Last time Glemp had taken her down there they had said it was for a gift, or something of the sort. She had assumed that meant the Flame-root, but had it really been for something different? Had they been testing her?

They both stepped up to the little doorway before the chamber, and once again Zalia felt the heat from being this close to the lava source. It was significantly cooler than the last time she had been there, though, a result of her Heat Resistance being so much higher in rank rather than the actual temperature being lower.

Rather than ask what Glemp wanted her to see, a question she felt they would not answer, she tried to look closely into the chamber.

At first, she saw nothing out of the ordinary. The pits of lava were calm and still; Flame-root grew out of the stone and the air shimmered with heat.

It was odd, not what she would expect a volcano to be like, but she didn't really know how the laws and forces of nature worked in a world of magic. She knew enough to know that natural ecosystems formed their own sort of balance by the magic emanating from them. A place of nature was self-sustaining.

As she watched, she slowly came to understand what Glemp had brought her here for.

"Is . . . is one of the spirits in there?"

Glemp nodded.

"Like the starlight wolf?"

"The wolf has visited before, yes, like the wolf."

It made sense to her then. The starlight wolf had said that the older gods, spirits of nature, were slowly becoming that which they encompassed in their power. This one must have been a spirit of fire and stone, something of the sort.

She could see and feel it now, a vague aura that was almost indistinguishable from the heat permeating the mountain. A force of nature, strong as the mountain it stood within, its heat creating the home in which Glemp's people lived . . . perhaps even making Glemp's people themselves.

They had said they were formed from Heat and Stone, just as their name stated. She had never questioned that, assuming that they themselves created new Heat and Stone denizens. What if it was the powerful spirit that lived here who did that?

"Why were your people made, Glemp?"

Glemp looked up at her with unblinking red eyes.

"Why? No why. No, no, no, there is no why, except the why we make ourselves."

Despite the revelation, it made a sort of sense to Zalia. They had always been more . . . in touch with nature than the other races, even the Bathar. They were unified in purpose, as if each Heat and Stone denizen was only part of a greater whole. Perhaps that metaphor wasn't so much metaphorical as literal. Perhaps they *literally* were part of a greater whole.

"May . . . may I speak to it?"

"You already are."

"Then, why, why really, won't you join the war?" she whispered.

"We are the heat and the stone, yes. We do not take part in wars or politics. No, no, we are a force of nature, not an army to be commanded. You may take refuge in the heat and stone, but the heat and stone will not rise to fight at your bidding, Druid. Not yet, at least."

The voice came from Glemp, except it wasn't Glemp. The voice was different, deeper, much deeper. The voice grated and flowed, its timbre somehow both rough and smooth.

Not yet? she thought. "Then . . . will you rise to fight at another time?"

"You listen but you do not understand. We are a force, Zalia of the Druids, not a being to be bargained with."

Her brows furrowed, an anger burning within her much like the lava in the pits.

"Then will you let those demons invade this world and destroy all nature?" she snapped.

"We cannot simply stand up and stop them, it is not in our nature. Stone moves slowly, over hundreds, thousands of years. Do not think of us as callous or cruel, Zalia of the Druids. We simply are as we are. We have been so since the beginning, and we shall be till the end."

"Then is there nothing you can do? Nothing you will give to aid in this fight other than refuge for those who cannot?"

There was silence then. A minute, two, passed before they spoke again. Slowly indeed.

"Bring the one you call Ember to me. Her namesake is that of heat and her morals are of stone, solid and unyielding. Protective of those in her care and a fiery demise to those who oppose her. We will grant a blessing. We can give no more than this."

A blessing. Another blessing, that was. She was pretty sure these blessings were an extreme rarity, yet was about to witness her fourth one. No one had disturbed these spirits of nature for a long, long time, however, so that might be having an impact on events.

"I . . . I will. I will return shortly."

Zalia turned about and dashed up the stairs.

She sprinted her way up through the mountain, past Heat and Stone denizens that had greeted her with hostility when she had first entered this mountain but now treated her with respect at best, indifference at worst. Up she went until she burst out onto the mountainside where the houses built for refugees were placed.

She wasn't sure why they were built out here in the cold and not the warmth within, but now was not the time for such questions.

She exploded into Zen's house and her eyes quickly found Ember's.

"What's wrong?" Ember's expression turned to one of worry and there was an edge to her voice.

Zalia wasn't even slightly out of breath despite the run.

"Nothing, come, I'll explain."

As Ember joined her, she moved back towards the mountain with an urgent step, though walking so she could explain.

As she did, Ember listened attentively and said not a word until Zalia told her that the spirit wanted to bless her.

"Bless me!?"

"Yes."

"I . . . don't know how to feel about that," Ember murmured.

"Will you turn it down?"

"Is that an option?"

"Of course, I honestly don't think the spirit will care either way."

Ember's step slowed for but a moment, confusion obvious on her face.

"Then why is it doing this?"

Zalia had been wondering that herself.

"I think, despite its many assurances otherwise, there is a little bit of . . . a person in there. Whoever or whatever that spirit was before, it has returned to the nature and power it was born from, but I think a little bit of its self remains yet."

"And . . . is it safe for me to accept this blessing?"

"I think if it meant to harm us, it could do so very easily whether we consent or not. I've felt the aura of a similar being and I'm certain it could have been rid of us at any time we were in its mountain."

"That was before you bothered it, though."

Zalia didn't respond. She knew Ember wasn't wrong about that.

"Look, I know the starlight wolf sent us up here for a reason. I thought that reason was Zen, and partly it is, but maybe it knew I might have a chance of convincing this spirit to help. It told me that a few of the other nature spirits would rather be rid of humans than help them, but I feel it would have told us if this was one of them. Besides, why would it allow all these refugees here if it didn't care and wanted to help in some way?"

"Alright, those are good points. I'll accept it. Anything that can help fend off this invasion is good," Ember agreed as she moved down the steps behind Zalia. "Besides, can't let you hoard all the blessings, can I?"

Ember chuckled but Zalia could hear the nervousness in it, so she turned around and took both of Ember's hands, giving her an assuring smile.

"Look, it's going to be alright. The blessings I have gotten so far have been beyond helpful and have most likely kept me alive. Besides, you might finally get that heirloom armour you wanted so bad."

Ember smiled back.

"Well, now that you mention that, what are we waiting for?"

Zalia dropped Ember's hands, and they dashed off again.

It wasn't long before they reached the bottom and found Glemp waiting for them there.

"Are you ready?"

Ember, still wearing her armour, looked nervously at Zalia.

"Yes."

"Then let us begin."

A warm glow began to emanate from Ember as a halo of light formed around her.

CHAPTER TWENTY-SIX

Ember of the Flame

Zalia

Zalia watched in awe as stone grew oh so slowly up from the floor around Ember's boots. It sped up, beginning to flow more than grind its way into shape as it formed to the plate armour Ember was wearing.

The glow brightened, and the stone grew hot enough to turn a deep orange.

All the while, Ember kept eye contact with Zalia, showing no sign of pain at the considerable heat now emanating from her.

The stone began to cool, solidifying and turning to a dark, glassy obsidian, the glow diminishing with the dissipation of heat.

The armour was glossy and dark, not rough but sleek and form-fitting with jagged, pointed spikes growing from the shoulder pads. The joints were perfectly crafted to slide smoothly allowing a wide range of motion, and barely visible lines of glowing lava flowed through the armour like molten veins.

Still, despite noting all of this, Zalia kept the eye contact that Ember had held throughout the process.

"You look good in that armour."

Ember stretched out, testing the range of motion she could now attain.

"I know."

Glemp walked up and tapped it in a few places.

"Yes, very good armour."

Their voice had returned to normal and Glemp made no comment on the fact a spirit had just spoken through them.

Zalia noted Glemp's familiar absent expression as Ember read through the notifications that must have swarmed her vision and used her own abilities to see what she could about the armour.

> **Flamekeeper Plate (Heirloom) - Bronze rank.**

She also noted the feeling of excitement and appreciation that filled Ember despite her relatively calm exterior.

Zalia walked up and poked Ember in the side of the head.

"Now you gotta bond it!"

Ember shook her head.

"Nope."

"What do you mean 'nope'?"

Ember smiled, her eyes flicking up to focus on Zalia's face.

"Nope, looks like the process of the blessing already did that for me."

Zalia chewed her lip thinking about it. She couldn't really call that unfair, as both of her heirlooms had formed a deeper bond upon receiving their blessings.

"Well, what does it do?"

"Well, other than be an extremely strong suit of regenerating armour? Have a look."

A little screen popped up in Zalia's vision.

> **Flamekeeper Plate (Heirloom) - Bronze rank**
> **Tin - You can choose to leave footprints of fire behind you as you walk.**
> **Iron - While the prints of fire are active, you may stomp your foot to cause a small eruption of flame on a nearby surface.**
> **Bronze - While the prints of fire are active, you are surrounded by a halo of flame that burns your enemies and heals your allies.**

"Woah."

It was pretty impressive, certainly a more combat-capable set of abilities than her own armour had. She was a little worried about what exactly leaving behind prints of fire would mean for Ember when fighting in a forest, but it was something that Zalia herself would be able to both contain and make use of, if it came to it. She would always be able to regrow anything Ember burnt down.

Besides, the abilities fit very well to Ember's own namesake. Zalia liked that and even thought the abilities fit to Ember as a person somewhat. She certainly was as protective of her friends, as Zalia also tended to be. She was protective and helpful to anyone in need, really. It was part of what Zalia loved about her.

Zalia looked back towards the lake of lava.

"Thank you for providing this blessing!"

No reply came.

Glemp stepped up beside her, looking happily over the lava.

"They of Heat and Stone have returned to their slumber."

"Give them my thanks if and when they wake up next then, would you?"

Glemp looked up at her with those red eyes.

"That may be a very, very long time."

"Surely they can't sleep that long."

"This is the first awakening to be recorded in a few hundred years."

Zalia turned away from Ember to look at Glemp.

"I stand corrected."

Ember poked Zalia back.

"We really should be going soon, I'm sure Boreal and Aylie would be ready by now."

Zalia turned around.

"Yeah, we should."

Then she paused for a moment, thinking.

"Though, while we are here, I would like to go up and see the ritual site further up the mountain."

Ember looked at her in surprise.

"That . . . is actually a good idea."

"Why do you sound *and* look so surprised?"

"Remember when you thought it was a good idea to reverse Juniper's ritual and get yourself sucked into Cormaine?"

"Yeah?"

Ember looked at her blankly.

"You don't think it was a bad idea to do that?" she asked pointedly.

"Nope, you're not the only one that gets to sacrifice for your friends and the kingdom as a whole."

Ember didn't argue that, knowing that Zalia was definitely right about that one, even if she didn't like it.

"Up the mountain we go, then."

"We can fly up, it won't take too long," Zalia suggested.

Ember basically jumped in excitement.

"I would love that!"

Zalia smiled, eyes twinkling.

"As would I."

"Quite interesting, yes, very," Glemp muttered.

"I'm sure you wouldn't be interested, what with you being a person of the stone and all."

"No, actually, it would be an interesting experiment, yes. Unfortunately, I have not the time to waste, no," Glemp corrected.

"I still think we could have flown the entire way here," Ember said.

"That would have drawn the attention of every other flying creature and demon in the area, and it takes a lot of mana for me to sustain that for a lot of people at once," Zalia explained. Again.

Ember muttered a little.

"Well, that makes some sense, I guess."

Perhaps she had been hoping for an easy method of travel back to the war camp.

Zalia started moving quickly up the stairs.

"Sorry to disappoint, darling, let's go!"

"Darling?" Ember asked, her tone teasing.

Despite the tone, Zalia could practically feel Ember's heart skip a beat, a combination of her ability to sense vibrations and the bond they now shared. She stopped for only a moment to turn and give Ember a sly smile before continuing her quick pace up the stairs.

"Hey, now that isn't fair!" Ember called after her.

Zalia heard the sound of heavy footsteps as Ember clanked up the stairs after her.

Smiling to herself, and her own heart beating faster than it should have, Zalia led Ember on a chase towards the surface, purposefully staying just ahead of the significantly slower Ember.

Up they went, until Zalia burst out into fresh air and snow once more. Ember came out behind by only a few moments, stumbling over a patch of thick snow.

Zalia caught her by both arms, and Ember grabbed onto Zalia's arms for stability to regain her balance.

She found herself standing close to Ember, both of them holding the other. A little bit too close, not because Zalia *didn't* want Ember in her personal space, but because she found that she *did* want Ember there. A little bit more than she realised.

Zalia stepped back, brushing down her clothes with a cough.

"Hmm, right. Let's go find the other two then, shall we?"

Ember smiled at her and nodded.

"Sure."

Zalia could feel her face was flushed, because of the cold, obviously, and yet found that Ember was completely at ease. Damn, confident, intelligent, beautiful . . .

She turned about and walked towards Zen's house, completely aware that Ember could feel her emotions just as she could feel Ember's.

"Boreal, come out here with Aylie, please," Zalia pleaded.

It was but a few seconds before both Boreal and Aylie exploded out of the house in a puff of snow. Boreal slid to a stop, and Aylie bumped off of her to get ahead, running towards Ember and Zalia.

As the other two approached, Zalia called out.

"We're going to fly up the mountain, get ready!"

She began channelling the wings of air ritual, using Hunter's Mark on herself and the other three so that the ritual targeted at herself would affect the others as well.

Just before she took off, Boreal looked Zalia up and down, her ears aeroplaning a little bit, and a thought of amusement drifting over their bond. Even Boreal was teasing her now?

She jumped into the air, her wings strong where her legs were feeling weak.

"Come on, you two!" Zalia called down, watching as Boreal took off.

Aylie jumped and attempted to control the wings, only barely managing to stay airborne yet getting better by the second. Ember, on the other hand, didn't even manage that far.

She looked up nervously and tried to fly up but failed, falling a short distance back to the ground.

"I . . . I don't know if I can do this," Ember called up.

"You've got this!" Zalia called back down.

Ember failed once more, so Zalia flew down and landed.

"Just think of them like extra limbs, limbs that can make you fly. Flex them, flap them, and join me in the sky," Zalia explained.

"You're going to have to carry me," Ember said, her tone final.

Zalia looked at her nervously.

"Carry you?"

"Mhmm, I can't do this in a short time, and we need to be off soon. Just carry me up. Here, I'll even store my armour to make it easier," Ember added, her armour vanishing.

Her bonding had given it its own storage space, something Zalia's armour didn't even have despite another of her abilities allowing her to do something similar.

"Should be easy enough," Zalia murmured.

Her heart was beating wildly, but she steeled her nerves and scooped Ember up.

Before she could question her own sanity, she ascended and began to travel up the mountain, going slowly as to allow Aylie a little more time to adjust.

Ember clung to her, arms wrapped around Zalia's neck and her face pressed to her shoulder. Every point of contact sent little fiery beams through Zalia as if the blessing Ember had received made her hot to the touch.

Zalia managed to maintain their course, however, as controlling the magic was an almost subconscious action to her now.

She wasn't particularly worried about running into any of the Bronze birds that flew about, knowing full well that the three Bronze ranks in their own party could easily win that fight.

They flew up for a long time, Zalia managing to settle her nerves and just enjoy the flight with Ember in her arms, before they arrived at the place she remembered the ritual to be. She made sure to keep Aylie warm with a little magic on the flight up.

They landed and looked out at the ritual site to find that . . . absolutely nothing had changed.

Zalia stared at the wind-torn ritual site.

"This looks . . . entirely the same."

Ember came up beside her, eyes scanning.

"Yeah, doesn't seem any different to me."

It was exactly as Zalia remembered it, blood stains flaking away in the alcove set into the mountainside.

"Does it seem . . . older than some of the other ones we have come across?"

"What?" Ember asked.

Zalia kicked some of the flaking substance and watched it scrape away and shatter to dust.

"Well, the blood seems older."

Ember knelt down and scraped some away with her hand.

"It could have been one of the first ones that were performed, plus it is in quite a hostile environment."

"Hmm, that could explain it," Zalia murmured.

She had a feeling that this ritual was different than many of the others she had come across. All of the other rituals had some effect, even the one that Zalia had disturbed in the first place. Well, she didn't know that for sure, as she didn't know where every ritual had been placed, but there were quite a lot of demons roaming the lands and many dead spots that she had to heal.

Despite all that Ember said, though, Zalia felt like she knew this ritual hadn't been activated. Whether it was an instinctual or a subliminal power given by her magic, she just *knew* it.

"What if . . . what if this is a ritual from a time before?" Zalia suggested.

Ember turned to her, frowning.

"What do you mean by that?"

Zalia watched Boreal walk around the site, sniffing at the ground occasionally. Aylie was keeping close to her, one hand holding onto the hem of her shirt.

"Well, remember we theorised that this might not be the first time this has happened? What if this is a ritual site from another time," Zalia explained.

Ember turned back to the ritual and walked to the middle of the room, frown still present.

"I guess it could be, but why haven't any other sites like this one been found? Remember the map of them that was being made by the Morning's Shade? This one fit perfectly into the huge circle that was being made by the rituals."

"Hmm," Zalia hummed.

She noticed Aylie shiver a little bit.

"Let's get down from here, nothing more for us to see, really."

Ember came over for another lift and before they left, Zalia looked at the site, closed her eyes, and carefully stored the image of the site into the vault, a light mist leaving her eyes and twisting down her body to enter her hand.

She met Ember's eyes, receiving a teasing smile that caused her heart to skip a beat before she scooped the woman up and began flying back down the mountain.

Aylie was already in love with the flight, twisting this way and that as she performed aerial manoeuvres that shouldn't have been possible for someone so new to the task.

"*She's a natural,*" Zalia sent to Ember.

"*Definitely a lot better than me,*" Ember thought back.

"*I feel like you're better than you let on,*" Zalia accused.

"*Maybe,*" Ember replied innocently.

This woman.

She could see her smiling up through the bottom of her vision and Zalia held on just a little tighter.

They landed and she put Ember down gently.

"Let's say goodbye to Zen and make our way towards Ostoss then, shall we?" Zalia suggested.

"Sounds good to me," Ember agreed.

Aylie floated up beside her.

"Ostoss?"

Zalia pointed in the general direction of the town.

"It's a town to the west and further south a little, back in Endaria."

She let the wing ritual fade as Boreal landed, dropping Aylie into the snow. She could see even just that short flight up and back down for four people had pretty much emptied her mana. It wasn't enough for her to be in danger of passing out due to mana drain, but it was still alarming to see how quickly that particular ritual drained it.

They walked over to the big house that belonged to Zen and his family and entered, knocking the snow off their boots as they did.

None of them had boots made for the snow, though they were all thick and sturdy. For Ember and Zalia, this wasn't really a problem; their increased strength and dexterity were more than enough to make up the difference. Aylie wasn't so lucky and did slip about quite a bit.

"Hey!" Zen greeted as they pushed into the room, feeling a blast of heat pass over them.

A lot of his family weren't there, probably out performing various tasks. Zalia had noticed that his parents were quite high-ranking, and she assumed they were trying to find a way to farm up here on the mountain. That was what they had spent their lives doing, after all.

"Hey, Zen, we're about to be off," Ember said as Zalia got lost in thought again.

Zen looked up from where he sat.

"Time to say goodbye, then."

She could hear a hint of sadness in his voice.

"We'll see each other again," Zalia promised.

"I know, just keep safe out there, alright? Boreal, I trust you to make sure they don't do anything stupid," Zen said.

Boreal bowed her head and managed to pull off a smug expression.

"You really have faith in the wrong people," Zalia explained.

"*Zalia silly*," Boreal sent.

It came with an image of Zalia and Ember running toward the cave entrance as Boreal launched her surprise attack and buried them both in snow.

"*Boreal sillier*," Zalia retorted.

She didn't say anything back, but Zalia noticed her tail flick aggressively. She'd have to watch out for more surprise attacks in future.

Zen came up to them, arms wide open.

"Well, see you later, Zen," Zalia said, stepping up to hug the large guy.

Ember also received a hug, Boreal got some scratches, and Aylie received a pat on the head that she looked mildly affronted by.

They left, and Zalia's mana was recharged enough to allow for her to activate Flight for the short distance to the bottom of the mountain. As they landed, Zalia put Ember down and they began their journey out of the snow.

CHAPTER TWENTY-SEVEN

Tornado

Zalia

It took about a week for the four travelling companions to reach Ostoss. Along the way they did have to fight one Bronze demon, an easy take down for the three Bronze in their group, and Zalia messed around with her woodworking skills each night. This led to gains in a couple skill levels.

> **Congratulations! Kill Shot has reached Bronze 4.**
> **Congratulations! Fight or Flight has reached Bronze 3.**
> **Congratulations! Survivalist has reached Bronze 4.**
> **Congratulations! Flora Identification has reached Bronze 2.**
> **Congratulations! Preparation has reached Bronze 4.**
> **Congratulations! Harvester has reached Bronze 3.**
> **Congratulations! Herbal Magic has reached Bronze 4.**
> **Congratulations! Herbalist has reached Bronze 2.**
> **Congratulations! Healing Presence has reached Bronze 5.**
> **Congratulations! Low Light Vision has gained three levels, reaching Iron 18.**
> **Congratulations! Aura Observation has gained four levels, reaching Iron 19.**
> **Congratulations! Mobility has reached Bronze 3.**
> **Congratulations! Teaching has gained three levels, reaching Iron 12.**
> **Congratulations! Flight has reached Iron 13.**
> **Congratulations! Bow - Weapon proficiency has reached Bronze 3.**
> **Congratulations! Sword - Weapon proficiency has reached Bronze 3.**

It was quite a lot of level gains for a few reasons. The first and main reason was that since she had arrived in Cormaine—and even further, since she had gotten back to Endaria—she hadn't had the time nor the mental capacity to continue her training very often. With the extra time she now had as the others slept, she practiced her sword and bow work, formed and broke apart the chunk of wood, set up protective living rituals, closely observed her friends' auras, and went for runs.

It was a lot, but it helped pass the time much quicker than her usual sitting around and waiting. She also sometimes used her wings to practice how her sword work and archery skills would need to change when fighting in the air rather than on the ground. Obviously, it wasn't as good practice as the real thing, but every bit could count.

Not only that, but now that Aylie had her class, Zalia spent a good portion of their days walking around while teaching Aylie about the skills they shared and trying to help her figure out the skills they didn't. She also taught her some basic tracking skills, knowing they were useful for anyone, really, but especially another Druid. Additionally, she actually tried to help Aylie learn some simple mathematics and letters. It was at this time that she realised she didn't actually know Endarian letters, and Ember took over that half. With bonded mental attributes, it wasn't such a hard task but still something she thought the young girl should learn. Maybe it wasn't the norm in this world, but the education system within her own was something she took for granted. Aylie hadn't been taught anything at all and probably would have spent her life as a farmer or other trade worker and wouldn't have needed anything other than simple addition.

Still, she learned quite quickly and Zalia wasn't surprised. She took to any task with fervor, as if she wanted to learn every little piece of information and advice Zalia had to give. It was simultaneously heartwarming and heartbreaking. Zalia knew that Aylie clung to her words and what she had to teach with such strength because of what had been taken from her. Inside, the little girl was desperately clutching for any kind of grounding after having her life shaken so thoroughly to its core. Just old enough to understand what had happened yet not old enough to know how to deal with it. So, Zalia taught her all she could.

Soon enough, with time passing much quicker due to her busy nighttime schedule, they arrived at Ostoss. On the way, they had headed past what was Juniper's old farm but had found it entirely burnt to ashes and Alston, the town nearby, was still somewhat intact, yet entirely devoid of life. The people had obviously fled, hopefully some having been saved by Zen and his group in the north.

Ostoss itself, though, was heavily fortified with walls and guards, and as they arrived, Zalia found it still occupied. Occupied and under attack. There were guards up on the walls, slinging spells, arrows, and valiantly defending against a veritable horde of flying demons as they tried to break into the town. The reason that the town had not fallen yet, or so Zalia assumed, was the big dome of energy that arced and crackled overhead as demons tried to break through.

"Boreal, take Aylie and run around the other side of the town and see if you can't get in," Zalia said.

"I can help!" Aylie protested.

"I don't doubt you can, but this isn't the time for that. This is too dangerous, there are too many of them. I won't be able to keep you safe down there," Zalia quickly explained.

Aylie looked like she was about to protest but Ember spoke up.

"Please, we can take care of this just fine," Ember said softly.

Zalia could see it in Aylie's eyes. The fear that she would be the only one left again, that even her saviour would die while she lived on. She didn't want to be left alone again.

She knelt down to take both Aylie's hands in her own.

"Don't worry. I lived in the homeland of these creatures, and they couldn't take me down. I'll live through today and every other day, and I will *always* return to you, ok? One day you'll be big, old, and strong enough that you can join me in these fights, but for now I need to know that you're safe, alright?" Zalia explained calmly.

Aylie nodded, so Zalia lifted her onto Boreal.

"Keep her safe," she whispered, giving Boreal's head a ruffle.

Boreal sped off and Zalia activated the wing ritual for both her and Ember. They weren't far away from the battle, but she wanted to get in there as quickly as possible. She recognised the enemies, the small Tin and Iron rank flying ones that would be absolutely no challenge to her. It was time to show Ember how exactly she had purged one of those dens practically by herself.

They sped on wings of air towards the battle, and Ember was actually able to fly with ease despite her pretense at being unable to a week earlier on the mountain. Zalia smiled to herself as she shook her head, entirely sure the woman had just wanted Zalia to hold her.

As they flew, Zalia was able to see with incredible detail due to her Flight passive and she spotted Tristan on the walls, yelling orders. She was glad to see her friend alive and kicking, looking like he was leading the town's defence force, no less. Well, she would take these demons off his hands and help lighten the load.

She dove from above, and the speed of her drop allowed her to smash through a few of the demons before they realised what was happening. She dove straight to the centre of their ranks and as Ember was about to join her, Zalia activated Nature's Wrath.

The elements became hers to command, two air elementals forming like twin whirling vortexes. They immediately flew out of the swarm and began using air to push the demons closer to Zalia at her wordless mental command.

She took a hold of the very winds with her mind, pulling and pushing them into a much, much larger swirling tornado around her as the demons struggled to escape. But their attempts were futile, as wind speeds picked up and any little demon trying to escape was immediately shoved back in by the two elementals guarding the perimeter.

Zalia wasn't done, however. The winds themselves were not enough to harm the creatures greatly so she started ripping up chunks of earth from below and allowing them to be whipped up into the swirling maelstrom. Thuds of earth on flesh could be heard, the cries of the impacted whisked away in the wind. Blood and torn bodies soon filled the whirlwind and the effect was multiplicative as the broken bodies of the already dead demons caused chaos amongst their brethren.

It was all over in a matter of seconds, perhaps half a minute of stone and wind and flesh colliding in a morbid tornado of pain. She allowed the winds and the stone to drop, the broken bodies of her enemies dropping with them.

She looked up to see Ember hadn't joined the fight, simply floating in the wind above with shock and awe coating her expression and body language.

Zalia dropped down to land, knowing that her mana would surely be close to out. She checked, and sure enough, it was at less than a quarter. Ember dropped down too, obviously having put two and two together about the very same thing.

"Zalia, what the hell was that!?" Ember exclaimed as she landed.

Zalia used heat manipulation to gather enough warmth to start little fires that she used to burn the blood and gore from her armour.

"That was Nature's Wrath," Zalia replied smugly.

She felt good showing off for Ember, especially considering she hadn't really done much other than shoot the occasional demon since they had found each other again.

"I know, but . . . how?" Ember asked.

"It has an extremely long cooldown, remember? It also used almost all of my mana to do that. I could have achieved the same over a much longer time through other methods, as I'm sure you could too," Zalia explained.

"I don't really have any . . . area of effect abilities like that," Ember said sullenly.

"Aw, don't worry, I've got enough for the both of us. Besides, it's nothing compared to what Aylie's Starfall will be like at Bronze rank. Mine is a six-hour cooldown, hers is two days. It can already hurt us at Tin," Zalia pointed out.

She had a scary thought. What would that ability be like if Aylie ever reached Ascendant? Would she be able to drop an *actual* star on someone?

She hoped not. She didn't like the idea that anyone could have that kind of power.

"Come on, I saw Tristan from up there. Let's see if we can get inside, shall we?" Zalia suggested.

Ember still looked like she was recovering from Zalia's display, so she stored her armour, grabbed Ember's hand in her own, and started walking towards the gate.

"Are you two safe? Did you get inside?" Zalia sent to Boreal.

"*Safe, inside,*" Boreal sent back.

A picture of the two of them walking down a dirty street with thin, hungry-looking people arrived with the words. Zalia had a feeling that Saint Ember would have her work cut out for her here.

The gates opened as they neared and Zalia saw Tristan run out to meet her.

"Zalia!? By the gods," he yelled as he ran, "I thought I saw you in the middle of all that but I never imagined—"

"Tristan! Long time no see," Zalia said, smiling as she held Ember's hand tightly.

"How in the worlds did you do that?" he asked as he finally reached them.

Zalia looked at the many, many kill notifications and the two levels Nature's Wrath had gained.

"Well, I have a loooong story for you," Zalia said, getting ready to explain *again* what had happened to her and where she had been.

"That can wait, come inside. We'd be happy to compensate you however we can," he interrupted.

"I'd love to."

CHAPTER TWENTY-EIGHT

State of Ostoss

Zalia

Zalia found herself seated at a table in a long, low dining hall with Tristan seated opposite her and Ember seated beside her. She could sense Boreal's location and knew that she was making her way through town towards them.

On their way to the dining hall, Zalia had seen many sights, such as what Boreal had sent to her. Starving people, disorder, and absolute chaos reigned within the confines of the walls. Where the army camp was a symbol of order in the face of dark times, this town had become a cesspit. She had seen several younger people stealing from others and sprinting away, mothers in gutters with children barely alive next to them. She had even seen a man dead in an alley, a knife wound in his chest and blood pooling.

She wanted to stop and help each and every person in need, and she knew that Ember felt the same. She could feel that emotion as bright as daylight shining from the midday sun. She also knew that they would be able to help better by working with the military force within the city walls. The dining hall they sat in might have originally been set for that purpose, but it now looked to be a barracks for the military force, one half of the space cleared and containing various bedrolls and low bunks.

Zalia leaned forward.

"What's going on in this city, Tristan?"

He shrugged.

"Same as what's happening in most of the rest of Endaria, I guess."

"No, no this is not the same. Things seem *really* bad here."

"If I were one of the people on the streets, I'd rather leave than try to live in this place," Ember murmured, her eyes focused on the doorway.

"That's easy to say with a class like yours. Many of these people are farmers, cooks, clothiers, and all other types of non-combat classes. They wouldn't last a day out there," Tristan snapped.

Zalia raised her hands placatively.

"Hey, we aren't trying to attack you in any way."

Tristan took in a deep breath and sighed heavily.

"Sorry, it's just that some of my soldiers actually did that. They got it into their heads that the others were holding them down and decided to leave on their own. I have no idea if they live, or are dead, but they left our defenses in shambles."

Ember's gaze focused on Tristan.

"I'm sorry that happened."

"As am I," he agreed.

"You said 'your soldiers.' Are you in charge?" Zalia asked.

"Sort of. I'm the only one in town with actual military experience. Everyone else who now fights is either a guard or some type of adventurer who has stood up to help. The shield dome is created by a Silver rank Enchanter with the Barrier Mage specialisation. That in itself has saved us time and time again. Well, since I was the only one with military experience, I kind of ended up in charge. Nothing official, mind you, but people do listen to me."

Zalia leaned back, ideas flashing through her mind.

"A Silver rank Enchanter, hey?"

"Yeah, they live centrally and are pretty reclusive. Part of the reason for the Barrier specialisation, I'd guess."

"Do you have any food stores left?"

"That . . . yeah, a bit, but not much. While we have plenty of farmers, we don't have much farmable land and no conjurers of any sort. While we have been thinking of expanding the dome to get a little bit of farmland they can work, we were stretched thin before those idiots decided to leave. Enough about us, though, I want to hear where you've been and what happened. You joined up with the Morning's Shade right? You must have some kind of idea what the hell has caused all of this."

Zalia turned to look at Ember.

"Yeah, we know a bit."

She went on to explain the entire deal around the rituals, the king, Juniper, and what had caused this entire mess. Then she described their final fight atop the tower at Endelbyrn and her further . . . adventures in Cormaine. She kept that all to a minimum, not seeing any reason he needed to know everything, and while she found herself growing emotional when coming to her escape from Cormaine, she managed to get it out without breaking down entirely.

Ember took over and explained what had happened after the rituals had gone off on her side, about the army still fighting down to the south and what she had been up to in the meantime. Hearing that, Tristan started to look hopeful, but as Ember noticed as well, she told him she had not run into his missing people.

Then they explained about the mountain to the north and Glemp's people, how it was a safe haven. There were major issues in bringing such a large population there, however. Mainly in that these people probably wouldn't even fit within the mountain, even if the Heat and Stone denizens weren't also living there.

"Well, you two have certainly been around a lot. I can see how you have such freedom of movement with you being so strong now, Zalia," Tristan said.

She gestured to the doorway.

"And there is someone else for you to meet."

"Oh?"

Tristan turned around as Boreal and Aylie walked in the door, the latter riding the former.

"Oh shit!"

Tristan stood up from his seat and summoned a large double-edged axe from out of nowhere.

"Wait!" Zalia exclaimed.

But recognition had already dawned in Tristan's eyes as the blade vanished again. "Is that *Boreal?*"

"Yeah, she grew a little bit," Zalia said nonchalantly.

"A little bit!?"

"Yeah."

"*World just smaller,*" Boreal sent to them all.

"What do you mean the world is smaller?" Tristan asked, apparently too overcome with the size of Boreal to be shocked at the mental communication.

"And this," Zalia said, interrupting, "is Aylie."

Aylie waved from atop Boreal's back.

"Aylie, this is Tristan. He is a friend of mine and a strong fighter."

"Zalia?" Tristan asked.

"Yeah?"

"Whose child is this?" he asked.

"What do you mean?" Zalia asked, frowning.

"Well, last I checked you didn't have a child," Tristan explained.

"Ah. It's . . . complicated," she said.

"*Her family was killed, I managed to save her from a demon. She's been with me ever since,*" she explained mentally.

Tristan's eyes widened just a little bit at the explanation, but he seemed to finally begin to relax, taking his seat again.

"Tristan, I'd like to do what I can to help these people. Is there any way you can organise a small squad to give out food safely?" Ember asked.

Tristan looked up sharply.

"You have food?"

Ember explained her ability. It wouldn't feed everyone in the city by a long shot, but it would definitely help some people. At this explanation, his eyes seemed to light up.

"Oh, that's excellent news!"

He called over an older boy, perhaps fourteen years old, and asked him to go collect a few people he named.

The boy ran off to do as instructed.

"I can start today, if you'd like?"

"Absolutely. Is there anything you need to get started?"

"No, just a minute or two to cast the ability," Ember said.

"I actually might be able to help as well. Do you have any type of park or place inside the walls that could be farmed?" Zalia asked.

The excited light in Tristan's eyes dimmed just a little.

"Some farmers did actually try to take a central park and start growing food and were successful, until a group of thieves came and stole it all. Killed one of the men too."

It was horrible that people could do such a thing to the only ones in the city capable of growing food for everyone, yet it was not unexpected. Zalia was actually surprised she hadn't seen more of that in the time since the rituals.

"Well, I can cause plants to grow at extremely increased speeds. Perhaps I can help?" Zalia suggested.

"I'm sure some people would be willing to try again with your help," Tristan agreed, "especially with how strong you've grown. Not a lot of people, if anyone, in this city could contest you in a one-on-one fight."

That brought a little shock to Zalia's system. She was a lot stronger than she had been, but surely in a city this large, there were many powerful people. The Silver ranked Enchanter, for one, but . . . well, their powers would probably be more keyed around utility and enchanting items, rather than instant and powerful attacks.

She tapped her chin in thought.

"Good, I'd love to give it a go. I have some tricks up my sleeve that may help us out here. Some things that the Enchanter might be interested in working on as well."

A group of people made their way through the barracks towards their table and settled in next to them.

"Trist, we already ran a food tent today, what's this I'm hearing about you wanting to run another?" one of the men asked.

"We've got some good news. These are the people that took out the demons so quickly. One of them has an ability to conjure food on a daily basis! We can do more now," Tristan explained excitedly.

That set the whole table to murmuring, and some of the other nearby guards turned to listen in.

Tristan stood up from the table.

"Well, what are we waiting for!"

The guards ran off and each started gathering some items. One of them actually pulled out a large, foldout cover attached to four posts, others yet grabbed weapons and tables.

They all moved out of the barracks and into the city, and Zalia, Ember, Aylie, and Boreal quickly followed.

The group walked a little ways away, down a main street to what Zalia remembered as the city square where Tristan had made a call-to-arms speech so long ago. That had been the start of a lot of current events, for Zalia at least. It was the time she had seen her first corrupted man, made her first kill on a person, and helped stop the raids on Ostoss and the nearby farmers. It only occurred to her then that the town probably hadn't recovered from those raids once this entire invasion had started. All around, it seemed like a bad time for these people as of late.

The few guards quickly set up the cover and tables, and some hungry-looking nearby people started lining up. Some ran off to presumably get friends and family so that they could be fed too.

"Gather around, gather around! We have some good news!" one of the guards yelled out.

Tristan gestured to Ember.

"From now until this woman decides to leave town, there will be an extra handout of food every day! She is able to conjure some each day!"

Murmurs spread like wildfire through the people gathering about and Zalia saw on their faces the dawning light of hope. These people had suffered a lot in recent times, and she was glad that they could give something to these people other than more blood and pain.

Ember started focusing, and unlike how her ability had worked last time, a huge table behind the tent started shimmering into existence, and a bounty of food outlined in the glowing visage.

Zalia heard someone murmur, "Saint Ember."

She wondered how word of Ember's deeds had reached even here, yet she also knew that some people did manage to make it across parts of the land unharmed. By the looks of it, there were definitely more people in Ostoss than there previously were when she had come through on her way to Endelbyrn.

The whispered words spread through the crowd even as more people pressed in from the nearby streets. They were obviously used to this kind of thing happening each day and managed not to attack each other in their fervor to get food.

Ember finished casting the spell and stumbled a bit. Zalia quickly caught her as the table apparated behind them.

It wasn't anything fancy, only very basic stews and bread, filling yet bland food. Zalia could tell that much by the smell and the appearance of it all.

She didn't doubt that Ember could make something fancier with her ability, but the sheer volume of food she had summoned took away from the quality.

People pressed forward and were quickly sent away with bowls of steaming stew and toasted bread. Zalia held onto Ember as the team of guards moved with practiced motions, smoothly and quickly handing out what they could.

Despite the huge volume of food, there were still people lined up when it ran out, their disappointed and downtrodden faces bringing pangs of pain to Zalia's heart as they slowly walked or stumbled away.

She had tried to push her healing through people as they lined up and did notice that some people looked better for it. She hoped to be able to eliminate any disease or wounds that existed in the town, knowing that doing so would reduce the food and water requirement of the people. Being injured or sick was hungry work.

Once it was all done, the table summoned by Ember vanished into a golden, glowing dust that quickly disappeared as well. The guards solemnly packed up their things and began the walk back to the barracks. Zalia could see in their posture and expression that they wished they could do more, yet there wasn't anything to be done. At least the people would be able to eat better from now on and, hopefully, that would reduce the chances of people trying to raid whatever Zalia managed to set up in terms of a farm.

"Want to show me the way to the central park?" Zalia asked Tristan.

"Sure, yeah. Let's go now."

He waved at the other guards.

"See you back at the barracks."

He led them back through the town square and to the left, moving east past some straggling refugees. The road led to what had probably once been a beautiful park but was now somewhat dead and devoid of life. The trees looked sad and wilted, the grass yellowed.

"Everything's soul is so . . . pained here," whispered Aylie.

Zalia hadn't been paying attention to Aylie, too deep in her own wandering thoughts and the things she was seeing. She wished Aylie didn't have to see any of this, the horrors happening to her people.

She let her Healing Presence flow out over the park and the grass began to lift back up, looking lively and green again. The leaves on the trees unfolded and took on a glossy sheen, the boughs of the trees seeming to shake less in the wind.

CHAPTER TWENTY-NINE

Seek

Zalia

Zalia watched in satisfaction as the park's beauty returned as she walked through it, pleased with her power's ability to do something so . . . simply good. A lot of her abilities were used for pain, killing, and assisting in that regard. At least, that was how she often used them.

Healing Presence, though, it was entirely about rejuvenating what was damaged.

Tristan was walking slightly ahead of her to watch the plants being restored.

"Wow Zalia, I . . . that is something else."

"I never get tired of seeing it," Ember added with a broad smile Zalia felt.

Boreal, Ember, and Aylie were all behind her as she did her work, though it was more of a casual stroll than an active effort.

Tristan turned to her walking backwards.

"You're different."

"It's been a while," Zalia pointed out with a smile.

"Not long enough for the change I see in you, not to mention you've reached Bronze already!"

Zalia shrugged.

"I guess you could say that I've been in a place that I had to change a little bit to survive in."

They passed over a wooden bridge, grown from the roots of a tree to span over a little bubbling brook.

"And where was that?" Tristan asked, now walking forward again as he admired her handiwork.

"Cormaine," Zalia said.

"She would be the person, if any, to survive that place," Ember chipped in from behind, and a growl of agreement soon followed from Boreal.

Tristan stopped and turned to face her once more.

"How in the worlds did you get there?"

Zalia leaned against the railing of the little wooden bridge.

"Well, I suppose you could guess it was because of that little ritual that went off," Zalia said, breathing out a soft sigh.

It was time to explain where she had been *again*.

Tristan nodded his head a few times.

"Ah, yes, that *little* ritual. Well, that explains it a bit."

Then, he began walking off again.

Zalia pushed off the railing and looked at Ember quizzically.

"Not going to ask about it?" Zalia asked, following after him.

"No. You'd tell me if you needed to talk about it. Besides, I'm sure it isn't a fun memory to recall," Tristan said over his shoulder.

Zalia quickly stepped up beside him.

"No, it isn't."

"I get it, I have my own memories I prefer not to recall," Tristan replied, his wandering gaze seeming to stare into nothingness.

"Thanks," Zalia said, bumping her shoulder into his.

They meandered through the rest of the park, coming out the other side and back into the dirty city filled with hungry refugees.

Zalia stopped and sat against a tree, looking back out over the park.

"What do you think?" Tristan asked, leaning against a tree on the other side of the path.

"What do I think?" Zalia asked, looking up at him as the other three settled next to her.

"About the park. Think it can be done?"

"Easily, if you have enough people to work it into a proper field. I'm surprised it isn't already, with the state the place is in. I don't understand why anyone would have attacked the previous efforts to turn it into farmland," Zalia said, frowning.

Tristan turned to look across at the people nearby.

"They're hungry, and some heard there was grain being used to set up a farm and thought it was better served in their stomachs. Simple as that I think," Tristan explained.

"I don't know, it doesn't feel . . . right," Zalia murmured, looking down at the grass between her legs.

"It isn't right. Not much in war is."

"On that, we agree."

They sat for a while longer before Tristan left to find some people to help work the field. He expected it wouldn't take long, considering how desperate people were for food.

Zalia wasn't quite sure what was going on in the town of Ostoss, but something didn't feel right. It was like a sensation nudging against her senses that she couldn't quite see. Something in the corner of her eye that vanished when she turned to look.

"You healed their souls," Aylie murmured from beside her.

Zalia looked at her, and she was staring across the park in awe.

"You can do that too, you know," Zalia reminded her, giving her a little nudge with her shoulder.

Aylie nodded, still staring at the park.

Zalia knew that with this ability, Aylie would grow up in a very different way than most people. Seeing things' souls and understanding parts of the world that no one else did must have an effect on a person. Especially one still developing like Aylie was, still a child.

"Let's take a walk through the city, hey?" Zalia suggested.

The others agreed, so they stood up out of their little pile of people and walked through the streets.

Zalia was lost deep in thought, considering how to approach the reclusive Silver rank Barrier Enchanter that lived near the centre of town that Tristan had mentioned, when she heard a yell. A yell, then the sound of a blade piercing flesh, followed by a gurgling.

She broke out of her thoughts immediately and spotted the source of the disturbance. Ember quickly grabbed up Aylie as Zalia dashed forward.

A teenager had stabbed an older man in the throat and stolen his bowl of stew.

Zalia watched the expression of pure shock followed by delighted surprise on the older man's face as her healing swiftly closed the stab wound in his neck, but the majority of her attention was on the chase.

She felt something about this teenager that was off, some instinct telling her that everything wasn't quite right about them.

In a dozen quick strides, she caught up with the person and grabbed their wrist.

As she did, she finally understood what was wrong as she felt the corruption flowing through the person's veins. They turned to face her, their face half-melting as a feral snarl came from their mouth. Zalia reacted by using her leverage on their arm to pull them closer, grab them under the arm, and use both her arms and legs to flip the person over her shoulder and slam them face first into the ground.

A few nearby people made themselves scarce as the stunned and shocked-looking demon blinked up at her from the ground.

? - Iron rank.

Its disguise had disappeared entirely, the face of a young teenage boy being replaced by that of a snarling monster in human clothing. Not wanting to let the thing recover, she quickly followed up the ground slam with a kick straight to its face.

It slammed backwards and smashed its head into the ground yet was still not out, so she gave it another kick to the head, finally knocking the thing unconscious. There were a few questions she wanted to ask this beast and she was not about to lose the opportunity to get answers.

Zalia dragged the unconscious demon through the streets until she reached the barracks, stepping through the door, covered in armour and slightly transparent.

Tristan looked up from where he was seated with a few other soldiers and stood in alarm.

"You there! Stop!" he called out, weapon appearing.

The other soldiers in the room all stood as well, the sound of weapons being drawn resounding through the space.

"It's just me, Tristan," Zalia called out, allowing her helmet to disappear back to the Grove dimensional space.

"Zalia, what the hell is that?" he asked, stalking over.

"This is a good friend I just made with my boot. You need to start checking for the shapechangers at the gates," Zalia said, dropping the leg she had dragged the demon by with a dull thud.

Zalia had told Ember and Boreal to take Aylie back to the park while she dealt with this, not wanting the young girl to be anywhere near this creature.

"Got anything to bind it with?" she asked, sitting down at a table.

Tristan nodded to two of the soldiers in the room and they ran off.

"So . . . what exactly is this thing?" Tristan asked once more, poking it with the hilt of his axe. "A little bit more information than a friend you made with your boot."

"Right. Apparently, some of the demons have the ability to shapechange and blend in with people. This is the first one I've met so far, can't say I'm impressed. Though, I guess I might have met more that were just better at hiding," Zalia said as her arm went through the table she attempted to lean on.

"What the hell is that you're doing with your arm?" Tristan asked as he looked over at her.

"Sorry, I'm still getting used to the armour's abilities."

"What, your armour? Where in the worlds did you get that anyway?" he asked.

The two guards from earlier came running back and securely tied up the demon.

"Take a guess," Zalia said dryly, managing to rest her arm on the table this time.

"Right," he said in understanding, a grimace forming on his face.

"You really need to start checking people for this kind of thing at the gates," Zalia pointed out.

"We didn't even know about this!" Tristan protested.

Zalia raised her hands in a placating gesture.

"I know, but you should start doing so anyways," she repeated.

"How do I even do that?" Tristan asked, pacing back and forth.

"Um, sir? Are we just going to leave that thing on the floor? It's a little disturbing," a man nearby asked.

"Well . . . what else are we going to do with it?" Tristan asked.

He looked around at the others that were crowding around and murmuring to each other but they looked equally as unsure how to act.

"Got a lockup or something?" Zalia asked.

"No, why would we?" Tristan said, looking back down at the demon.

"Because of criminals . . . ?" Zalia said, trailing off.

She hadn't really thought about it, but she didn't know what kind of justice system they used in Endaria. Did they use capital punishment here? She didn't really know what could be done about a high-ranked person that had committed crimes other than removing either them or their powers.

"Why would we imprison people?" Tristan asked in shock.

"Well, I don't know, the Morning's Shade had a prison! Why wouldn't you!?"

"Anyone who commits a crime is put under house arrest until the king's judgement can be rendered through one of his judges. Usually, that means they are made to work for the community. What use would there be in locking up a person who can provide for others?" Tristan said, looking closely at Zalia.

She guessed it worked a little differently in a community small enough that everyone would know everyone. Obviously, that was no longer the case with the king being corrupted and Ostoss being cut off from the rest of the kingdom.

"Well, what do you do now?" Zalia asked.

"Well . . ." Tristan said, trailing off and avoiding eye contact.

He didn't have to finish the sentence. She knew exactly what he was going to say.

They were stretched thin, only a few guards left to protect the town from the demons that tried to destroy it. He had said as much already, and she had no doubt that they simply didn't have the people to police the city. It was each to their own, she had seen that for herself already and should have known the answer before she asked.

"Well, maybe something can be made. I can control the stone to a degree, want me to see if I can make a prison for it?" Zalia asked.

"Yeah, I suppose. It isn't like this thing ever has any plans to contribute to our survival. One less mouth to feed, at least."

"Where can I put it?"

She stood and picked up the demon's legs, now bound together.

"Just out the back," Tristan said, gesturing, and the crowd moved apart.

He led her through a door out the other side of the hall where a toilet had been built in a small fenced area between buildings. She quickly worked, moving earth out of the way and filtering out stone until she could build a box out of it. She made the box around the demon, manipulating it into a sitting position where it had only a small opening where its face could be seen.

"Handy ability that one," Tristan noted.

The other soldiers were crowding the doorway but seemed reluctant to leave the hall.

"Yeah, it has saved me a bunch of trouble," Zalia agreed, admiring her handiwork with one hand on her hip and the other on her chin.

"So . . . why exactly is this thing still alive, anyways?" Tristan asked, peering in on its smashed face.

"Well, I figure if it is able to disguise itself as one of us, it can probably speak our language, right? This might be a chance to get some answers out of these creatures that we wouldn't get otherwise," Zalia explained.

"Makes sense, want me to go get a bucket of water to wake it up?" Tristan asked, standing back up from the opening.

"Hmm, no, I might be able to wake it. I want to try something anyways," Zalia murmured, crouching down.

She looked at the small demon's expressionless features and tried to push her Healing Presence into it.

It awoke immediately with an ear-splitting screech.

Her aura was enough to hurt it but as soon as it awoke, she was unable to affect it any longer.

So a creature that wasn't actively fighting against her aura was able to be affected by it, interesting . . .

It stared at both her and Tristan with a look that could kill a Tin ranker.

"Hey, buddy, good to see you're doing alright," Zalia said cheerfully.

It hissed at her.

She hummed as she considered what to do next. She doubted it would be very forthcoming with information, and she didn't *really* want to torture it. In fact, she definitely didn't want to. It might be a demon that was here to kill off the human race and take over not only Endaria but the original world it belonged to, but she just wasn't one to perform something like torture. She was more likely to just kill it and be done with it entirely.

"If you answer our questions we won't kill you. We might even let you out of the city if you tell us enough," Zalia suggested.

Tristan looked at her sharply.

"*I'm not even considering it, don't worry,*" she sent to his mind.

The demon didn't answer and Zalia sighed. She didn't know if it actually did understand her. That was just an assumption she had made.

"I don't think it understands us, we might as well just kill it and be done with it," Tristan suggested, picking up his axe.

Smart man.

"Seems like it. Want me to do it?" she asked, summoning her bow.

But she could see the twisted anger on the creature's face begin to turn to fear.

"Sure, you can kill it without releasing it," Tristan agreed.

Zalia drew back the string of her bow, and a glowing arrow of starlight appeared nocked and pointed directly at the demon's head.

"Wait!" it screeched, its voice like nails on a chalkboard.

Zalia slowly released the tension from the bow.

"So, going to cooperate?" she asked.

It glared at her.

"Wonderful. What the fuck are you doing in this city?" she asked, her voice turning venomous.

"You'll all die, human," it crowed, the voice still grating and cold.

She could feel the corruption from it now, its aura no longer being held within. She made sure to press down on it fully with her own aura and could feel that she was stronger. Not by a significant margin, but enough that she could maintain the suppression with ease.

"I have a good friend who would love to know what you taste like, so I suggest you try and answer. What are you doing in this city?" Zalia tried again.

"You will fall, and we will come down upon you as death comes for all," it chanted.

Its eyes rolled up into its head and Zalia could see the veins beneath its skin begin to glow with a visible light.

"What *is* that?" Tristan asked, looking closely.

But Zalia thought she knew what was happening and quickly closed up the opening in the stone.

"Get away from it!" she yelled.

The soldiers quickly rushed away from the doorway and Zalia stepped back as far as she could in the fenced-in area. She summoned her armour and stood in front of Tristan, who was only wearing some light clothes.

An explosion tore through the stone enclosure, breaking apart the earthen wall she tried to hastily erect in front of herself, before hitting her with a solid force. Luckily it was slowed enough to not harm her; the few bruises she would have received healed in an instant.

The wall of the hall was torn apart, but luckily the soldiers inside had moved far back enough to remain unharmed, and the few who had scratches from stone shrapnel were easily healed by her power.

"Shit, what was that!" Tristan exclaimed.

"I guess they really don't take well to being caught," Zalia muttered, stepping forward to inspect the damage.

She was pretty easily able to use the chunks of stone to repair the hole in the wall of the hall, cleaning up the debris spread around by controlling the stone so it would flow back and repair itself. When she was done, it was as if the explosion had never happened, other than the smoke still clearing away and a sulphurous scent in the air.

"I'm going to have to remember not to keep the next one alive," Zalia said, now inside with Tristan.

"I would prefer if you didn't bring an exploding demon into my soldier's home, yeah," Tristan agreed, sitting with head in hands.

She could see how stressed the man was. Not only was he dealing with guarding the town with too few people, but there was also an insurgent faction inside the city that undoubtedly had the goal of bringing down the town even quicker. It was a lot for one man to shoulder.

"We'll find a way out of this," Zalia promised him, leaning down and putting a hand on his shoulder.

"It's a lot to deal with," Tristan said quietly.

"I know. Look, I can help deal with these shapechangers, and I can also help feed the people. You focus on keeping the demons out and I'll do what I can on the inside. Ember should be a good stopgap measure for starvation until we can get the farm up and running, and I have an idea that might help take care of the shapechangers with the help of the Barrier Enchanter," Zalia explained, hoping her optimism would help cheer the man.

"A plan?" Tristan asked, looking up at her.

"It involves a little something I learned how to do in Cormaine . . ."

CHAPTER THIRTY

Farmplanned

Zalia

Zalia told Tristan about how she had learned to counter the corruption with her ritual magic. It required the living rituals that she had also learned how to create in Cormaine, as well as a power strong enough to overcome the corruption that was being subdued.

"My plan is to work with the Enchanter to weave this type of ritual magic into their barrier. It might take a bit of work to convert what I have learned so I can do their type of magic but I hope that with the same type of magic fueled by a Silver rank person, they might be able to simultaneously weaken whichever shapechangers have made it into the town so far," Zalia explained.

They were seated at a table in the former dining hall that many of the guards of Ostoss had called home. Zalia could feel that Boreal and Ember were on their way back to the hall after her brief spike in alarm when the explosion had gone off. She probably could have communicated that they need not worry but there was no reason for them to stay away any longer.

"Will that work?" Tristan asked, still looking weary and burnt out.

"I don't know. I've been under the effects of a strong corrupting aura bearing down on me and it was pretty tough to do anything at all. Sure, this is only Silver, where that was more akin to Emerald rank in strength, but it should at least give us an advantage. Weaken them, disrupt their ability to shapechange, anything that gets us a step in front of them," Zalia replied, shrugging.

Maybe it wasn't the best plan, but it would at least disrupt the shapechangers in *some* manner and help defend against more attacks from the outside.

"Well, it's something, at least. Any progress we can make towards a better defence is a good one in my books. Should I try introduce you to the Enchanter, then?"

"Hmm, not right now, no. Maybe tomorrow morning would work, though?" Zalia suggested, more focused on tracking her friend's location and emotions than the conversation.

"Sure thing," Tristan agreed.

He stood up and was about to leave when Zalia remembered something.

"Oh, hey! Did you manage to get some people who would like to work on the food growing?" she asked, similarly standing.

"Yeah, actually I did. Not as many as I hoped for, but a few experienced men and women. Some of them never recovered from those damn raiders way back and don't have much hope left now, but . . . Well, let's say they are desperate for something to do, some way to fight back."

"Are they coming here?" Zalia asked, furrowing her brow.

"No, no, I organised for them to meet about this time tomorrow, for Ember's food handout. Feeding them will go a long way to helping their spirits and hope-fully speeding up how quickly we can get established," Tristan explained, gesturing to Ember as she walked through the door.

"And you have enough grain to get started?" Zalia asked.

"Enough, barely. If this doesn't work out, then we'll pretty much be out of food soon after. Better to try and get things going now rather than starve in a couple weeks anyway."

"Well, hopefully, me and Aylie's ability to grow plants faster combined should be able to get them established in minutes, and harvestable not too long after that," Zalia explained.

She wasn't really sure of how quickly her ability was able to grow food, though it certainly was able to cause already established trees to bloom and grow fruit within a very short time. It was also able to, depending on the rank, of course, grow the herbs she had stored within her Grove's dimensional space.

"I hope so. If this goes the same way as last time then we'll have people swarming the farm within a short time of us starting. Are you ready for that eventuality?" Tristan asked, crossing his arms.

She hadn't considered that part fully. Of course, she was absolutely against harming the citizens in any way, despite however they might act. Starvation would cause otherwise good people to do things they usually would never even consider. Well, she had a few ideas on how to deal with the people who came.

"I am certain I can convince them to allow us to continue with growing the food if I promise to feed them," Zalia explained.

Tristan seemed unsure but didn't comment on it.

A bell resounded in the hall and a few of the guards inside groaned as they stood, gathering weapons and armour, preparing for what seemed to be their next shift.

Zalia, though, had been carefully watching one particular person out of the corner of her eye. She had felt their presence, felt the corruption inside of them now that she knew what to look for. She hadn't told Tristan, knowing that the more people who knew, the more likely it was that her ruse was to be discovered.

Well, she had a feeling that the previous farm being attacked hadn't been coincidental or the cause of starvation entirely. In fact, after discovering the first shapechanger and realising what that off feeling she had been having was, she was certain that it was a result of their interference.

She had thought about what cause that shapechanger had for stabbing the old man and stealing his food and had come to the conclusion that it was for a few reasons. To start off with, it seemed odd that the creature would out itself like that, but if people didn't know about them and it was a common occurrence for such things to happen in the town, then it would cause fear, unrest, and distrust for one's neighbours. If you saw or heard about it happening regularly, you would be much less likely to work with others rather than cut them off and survive as best you could.

It was an intelligent tactic, a way of destroying the morale and hope of the people within the walls. Make it seem like even in the town there was no safety, as the person just down the street might kill you for your food.

So, she had spoken about her plans very openly with Tristan in hopes that the shapechanger in the room would listen and make their own plans to disrupt her. Well, they had, and she watched that creature leave the room, hopefully to tell the others in the city. She genuinely did think that working with the Enchanter was a good idea, yet this might be a quicker way of not only bringing out the shapechangers but killing them off. There were surely not too many in the city, otherwise they would have taken over by force already, at least, that's what she thought.

"Right, we should go back to the park and get ready," Zalia said to Ember, Aylie, and Boreal, all of whom had only just arrived from there.

"I'll see you tomorrow morning, then? Will you be alright finding somewhere to sleep? Otherwise you can stay here," Tristan called over from where he was putting his armour on.

"I'll be fine, Tristan, thanks," Zalia waved, leaving the room.

"So, what was all that about? What happened?" Ember asked as they left.

"Well, that shapechanger I caught decided to explode," Zalia said theatrically, waving her hands in a wide gesture.

"Didn't know they could do that," Ember muttered, scratching at her head.

"Neither! But, we know now," Zalia said.

Boreal was looking expectantly at her and Zalia sighed, knowing what she would want to know.

"I told it that if it didn't cooperate, I would let you find out what it tasted like, but the damn creature took matters into its own hands. You'll have to find out another time, Boreal," Zalia explained, patting her friend on the head.

"Silly Boreal," Aylie murmured, comfortably lying across Boreal's back.

Boreal huffed belligerently, obviously annoyed at the improper use of "silly."

"Well, you are a little silly sometimes," Zalia pointed out, looking knowingly at Boreal, a hand on her chin as if in deep thought.

Boreal turned to stare up at her and narrowed her eyes.

"*Yes, but taste is important*," she insisted.

With the admission of silliness, Zalia had no footing on which to disagree. Once again, Boreal had smoothly won the argument seemingly without effort. Taste *was* important after all.

Zalia quickly used mental communication with Ember to get her up to speed with what exactly her plans were and Ember agreed. She would set up a huge ritual around the park that would do exactly what she wanted the Enchanter to do. It would suppress the corrupting aura and hopefully give them an advantage.

However, she didn't want the shapechangers to have any idea of this beforehand, so she would have to wait until the people came to disrupt the planting, assuming they even did. Then, she would activate the ritual.

The only issue with the plan is it would use almost all of Zalia's mana, meaning she wouldn't be able to use Nature's Wrath or Protection of the Wilds. Of course, she could still shoot from afar but the main task would be up to Boreal and Ember to take care of the enemies. She wanted to keep Aylie in the Grove vault just in case, being the safest place in the entire town right now.

She wanted to get Tristan's help as well. She knew that most of the guards would need to remain on the walls or out of rotation just in case an attack came, so she couldn't rely on them, but Tristan was a Bronze rank soldier, someone who trained with the army. His fighting skills were significantly better than her own, or used to be at least. She hadn't sparred with him in a while, she might have caught up by now.

Either way, he would be useful in their fight.

She couldn't really set up traps either, knowing that should they activate on a civilian, she would never forgive herself for that death.

"*I agree with all that, sounds like you've already thought well about this. I'm surprised you came up with it so quickly*," Ember sent.

"*I had to learn to react to situations quickly in Cormaine*," she replied simply.

Ember nodded, well aware of pretty much everything she had been through in that place.

They reached the park and Zalia led them down to the little wooden bridge and pulled out the chunk of wood she had been playing around with. During the bit of practice time she'd had to develop her skills of growing and pruning the wood using Healing Presence and Preparation, she had come up with an idea. Something not necessarily that useful but still a good extension of her practice.

She put the chunk of wood down on one side of the bridge and slowly, piece by piece, grew it outwards as a structure began to take shape.

CHAPTER THIRTY-ONE

Confidence

Zalia

Branches and roots spread out, some pruned and others yet branching out even further. When four particularly large pieces had grown out far enough, they began shooting upwards, forming the corners of the structure as yet more wood grew to fill out the walls.

A doorway formed, windows, another doorway. A second room started to shoot off from the main one, yet another off the other doorway.

"What in the *worlds*, Zalia," Ember exploded, looking at the forming building in awe.

The structure wasn't anything that fancy, the large scale control much easier to maintain than what was required to shape any finer details. If she were to form a perfectly smooth floor or properly squared building, decorations, or an artful facade, it would be a lot harder to manage.

Still, she had to stay focused, not having the attention span to reply.

A sloped roof formed, leaves starting to grow out of it to create a foliage covering that grew ever thicker, thick enough that it would keep the rain out. The roots of the structure grew ever downwards and outwards, some tapping into the little stream running nearby and others into a well of water deep, deep below.

A fourth room split off from the others and Zalia finally finished the structure. There were three rooms with beds that grew up from the floor, made of thin interwoven roots and softened with lush, fresh leaves. Thin beams of light struck through various gaps in the wood and leaves, dimly lighting the space, though even that wasn't necessary for her, Ember, or Boreal anymore.

Congratulations! Healing Presence has reached Bronze 6.

Satisfied with the result, she used Preparation to sever her chunk of wood from the structure and store it back in the Grove vault.

"When did you learn that?" Ember asked, coming up to rest an arm around her shoulders.

"I have a lot of free time when you two are snoring away," Zalia explained, arms crossed.

". . . Snoring?" Ember asked, suspicion entering her voice.

"Mmmhmm," Zalia hummed.

"I do not snore!" Ember refuted.

"If you say so, darling," Zalia said placatively.

"Hey!" Ember protested.

"*I can hear from far,*" Boreal sent to Zalia.

Zalia snorted in amusement, trying to cover it with a cough.

She felt Ember turn her head to glare at Boreal, as if she had heard it too, so Zalia pulled her close with an arm around the waist.

"Don't worry about it! We have a nice little home here that we can stay in while we are in Ostoss. I do need to get around setting up everything else, though tomorrow is a long way away still," she said.

She could feel Ember stiffen, then relax against her side before she rested her head on Zalia's shoulder.

"Maybe we could all just relax for a little bit?" Ember suggested.

Aylie pushed past both of them, finally running out of patience, running up to explore the new house. Boreal, who was equally impatient, and realistically, actually younger than Aylie, followed close behind.

"That sounds nice," Zalia agreed, revelling in the warmth of the woman beside her.

She still wasn't quite used to enjoying other people's company, let alone enjoying someone's company so much that she started to consider a future with them. That was exactly what went through her head at that moment, though, as she stood there with Ember's arm around her and her arm around Ember.

"I still think about leaving this all behind and going somewhere else," she murmured, tightening her arm around Ember just a little more.

"I . . . I'd come with you," Ember whispered.

Zalia almost jumped with surprise. She knew that the kingdom meant a lot to Ember, the people even more so. She was always not only ready but proactively looking to help her people. The fact that Ember would walk away from all of that to go with Zalia shocked her. Did that mean Ember was starting to think of her as she was of Ember?

She could feel the emotions coming off Ember like waves, appreciation, happiness, and attraction. She knew that Ember would be feeling all of the same emotions coming from her.

Just because the emotions were there, it didn't mean that Ember was really up for something like that, mentally.

There was no way to be sure other than to ask.

"Hey, I—" Zalia started.

"Zalia!" she heard Tristan call from somewhere far off behind her, cutting her off.

"What were you going to say?" Ember asked, lifting her head off Zalia's shoulder.

"Don't worry, I should check out whatever this is," Zalia said, pulling her arm away and turning to face Tristan.

Ember dropped her arm as well but, much to Zalia's happiness, stayed close. Her confidence had gone away in the instant she was interrupted but that didn't change her feelings.

"What's up, Tristan?" she called over.

Tristan jogged over but something seemed off to her. His gait wasn't quite as smooth as normal, and there was a very slight nervousness around him that set off alarm bells in her mind.

"Hey, I just wanted to know what the plan was," he said, coming to a stop a metre and a half in front of them.

Zalia adjusted herself very slightly so that she was in front of Ember just a tiny bit.

"What do you mean? I already told you," she said, frowning.

"Yeah, you told me what you wanted everyone else in that room to hear, not what your actual plans are," Tristan added, looking around as if checking no one else was nearby, "I want to know what you actually plan to do about the people who will come. You don't plan on killing them, do you?"

"What? No, of course not. As I said, I believe I can get them to listen," Zalia insisted, folding her arms in front of her.

"Well . . . alright. Are you certain? You weren't there for the last one, there wasn't much convincing those people," Tristan added, the nervousness having disappeared entirely.

"Yeah, absolutely. These are rational people, deep down. I'm sure if we explain that the food is being grown *for* them, not to be hoarded for the needs of the few, they will leave us be. Maybe even help!" Zalia said excitedly.

She could feel the confusion that Ember was experiencing and knew she would need to explain later.

"Ok! You know, you might be right. It's just so hard to be optimistic with our situation but . . . maybe things have taken a turn for the better. I'll see you tomorrow, yeah?" Tristan, no, the imposter, said.

"Yeah, tomorrow," Zalia confirmed, going so far as to step forward and hug the thing.

She felt it for sure, the corruption flowing through it. She had already felt hints of it, but the physical contact made it certain in her mind. It had come to figure out if she did actually have some other plan in mind, and she could only hope that she had been convincing enough to trick it into a false sense of security.

It ran off, perhaps a little faster than it should have to remain inconspicuous.

She had a feeling that it was young, perhaps inexperienced in the art of deception. Why the shapechangers had sent one that was both of those things to perform such an important task, she was unsure. Hopefully it wasn't a part of some kind of larger plan.

She could see far off that some of the people of Ostoss were beginning to walk into the park, as if the life flowing through it were attracting them.

She spent the next four hours walking about the park and growing various plants in the locations she needed them to be for the ritual. It was hard work that required a lot of concentration and not a small amount of adjustment. She kept finding that she had made the distance between sections of plants too small, as if she was subconsciously trying to make the living ritual smaller. She had a feeling that she wasn't yet at the point where it should be possible to make such a large ritual, or rather, that it was dangerous for her to do so.

Despite that, she pushed on, forcing the ability to give her the instinctive insight into placement that it usually did.

It was all made a joyful experience by Ember joining her. They laughed together at Ember's attempts to plant a few of the plants, spoke about nothing yet everything at the same time, and generally spent the time relaxing with each other.

Aylie ran back and forth across the park inspecting different plants and using her Plant Manipulation ability to alter their appearances. Zalia knew she was using Spiritual Connection and Astral Walker to see things about these plants that Zalia couldn't. In a way, Aylie was better—or rather, would be better—as a Druid than Zalia was, and that was ok with her. It was Aylie's main class after all, whereas it was only the combination of Zalia's other two that made her one.

So it was that it brought even further joy to Zalia's heart to see Aylie teleporting around and engaging with nature, Boreal following along on her adventures. It seemed like, despite the state of Ostoss, Aylie was beginning to open up to the world once more. She still stared off in dissociation every now and then, but Zalia felt as if it was now due to the things Aylie could see that none of the rest of them could. She was learning and discovering things about the world that maybe no one else had before. Her class was a blessing given by a god, after all.

Knowing that Boreal was keeping Aylie safe, Zalia allowed herself to open up to the world much in the same way. She had been feeling shut off ever since Delphi's death, but with the healing provided by Ember and the reconnection of the memory, she felt a lot better. The wound still wasn't healed and would leave a scar, but she would carry that if it meant remembering the collective, something that was the dying wish they had sent to her.

That train of thought brought her to the memory still lurking in her vault, the one given by the collective. She had tried to experience it once. Doing so had given her a killer headache and not much progress. That had been when she was still suffering from the repressed memory of the collective's death, however. She would try to decipher it once more, perhaps when she had helped stabilise Ostoss.

After the plants were done and Zalia reached out with Herbal Magic, she could tell that the ritual would work. Well, it would work, provided she managed to push enough mana and materials into it. She also finally built up enough confidence to talk to Ember once more.

"Hey, Ember," she started.

They were sitting, leant back, on a little bench she had grown into the side of the house, just shaded from the sun by the leaves overhead. Ember was leaning into Zalia and she sat with hands in her lap, fiddling nervously.

"Yeah?" Ember murmured.

"I've been meaning to ask, because I want to . . . Well, I'm not sure how customs are for this kind of thing here but—" Zalia started, fumbling over her words a bit.

She could feel herself starting to blush but soldiered on.

"I'm interested in you. Would you be interested in pursuing a relationship? No pressure of course, if you're not," she finished, turning her head to look at Ember.

Ember sat up, turning to look at Zalia as well. She could feel Ember's emotions just as strongly as she could feel her own, as if the woman was projecting them into her very soul. Excitement, anxiety, nervousness. Relief.

"Yes, I am. I'm very interested, Zalia," Ember said, taking both of Zalia's hands to stop her fiddling.

She could feel how Ember felt; she knew that what she felt for the woman was shared back yet somehow, the answer still surprised her.

"Oh."

CHAPTER THIRTY-TWO

Comfort

Essen

Essen rushed away from the park, excited to get back to the elders with the news. It had been a risk going alone to talk to the interloper, but he thought it was quite worth it. Not only would he now have proved himself worthy to be ascended, his skill obviously great enough to deceive the interloper, but he had proof that the foolish human had no other plans than to try and convince them to stop fighting.

He couldn't blame the human, though. It was not their fault that their capability for deep thought was reduced to such a small amount. It was due to the bright sun in this world, or so was his theory. There was simply no need to have such a bright light shining so constantly. Did they not have powers to see without this ungainly orb in the sky?

He nodded his head politely at a duo of guards who were walking the other way. It disgusted Essen that he had to be so nice to the humans when he was disguised but the knowledge that all of their hard work would pay off with a delightful feast at the end brought limitless motivation to remain in disguise.

Increasing his pace, Essen continued the rush to the elders. They didn't have much time until the interloper started growing her nasty plants at a speed that would allow the tension and fear they had been building in the town to diminish. There was just no way that they could allow that to happen. Then, the elders would have the right of preference taken away for this city and the other clans would be allowed to move in. It simply couldn't be allowed. If the other clans were allowed to take part in the assault on this town, the feast would be split between too many mouths.

Essen finally reached the house of the elders and was allowed in, though he did receive an angry glare from the guard on duty. Yelza was far too rigid to play the part of most humans but their guards did tend to be quite similar in attitude. Well, let Yelza play their part as a human guard and Essen would, as the more adaptable one, finally be granted the permission to ascend. Of course, he could ascend without the elders' permission, but that would result in a quick banishment if he was lucky, death if he was not.

"Elders," he greeted, kneeling with arms stretched forward and forehead placed on the floor.

The room he had entered was large and dark, only lit by a few flames flickering in the air at the edges of the room. As always, the elders were seated in shadow towards the far end, cloaked not only in darkness but mystery.

"Essen," the raspy voices of the elders spoke in unison.

"I bring news, Elders, would I be allowed to speak it in your presence?" Essen asked.

One day, he would sit up there amongst them, looking down on his own inferiors kneeling before him. The journey towards that day began today, the real journey.

"Speak," the elders commanded.

"I have spoken to and fooled the interloper elders," Essen informed them.

There was a silence, the flickering flames dimming as he felt an anger through the powerful auras the elders emitted.

"You did *what?*" they asked.

Essen cringed.

"I overheard her and Tristan, the leader of the guards, speaking in the hall they live in. Then she left, so I disguised myself as Tristan and followed. I pretended that I wanted to know the real plans, insinuating that she was hiding them due to the danger of one of us hiding amongst his guards. She told me that there were no other plans, simply that she was to talk the people into not attacking. I could barely read the interloper, but her companion looked extremely confused with my questions! That must be their true plan," Essen explained, shaking a little bit.

However, he still did not lift his head, keeping his eyes fixed on the floor. He didn't close them, knowing that the elders would see if he did.

Another silence ensued and Essen sat there nervously. He didn't quite know how the elders communicated with each other, a mental communication skill, perhaps. However they did it, the silence that was left in the wake of their soundless conversation was unnerving.

"Very well, Essen. We shall attack as planned, then," the elders agreed.

Essen almost let out an audible sigh of relief but held back. Giving tell to his nervousness in front of the elders would not do.

"I am glad to hear it. If I may be so bold as to ask, would you allow me to ascend for the good work I have done?" Essen asked.

"We shall see, Essen, if your information is true. If this leads to a success for us, you shall be given that right. However, if you have doomed us, it will not be us that you answer to but the thousand-eyed one who resides in the capital," the elders said in unison.

Essen shivered, not able to contain the feeling of terror that overcame him at their words. It was a risk he took but one well worth it. The permission to ascend would put him above many of the other clan members, bringing him to the fourth stage. Even Yelza was not that high-ranked.

Zalia

"Oh," Zalia murmured, looking into Ember's eyes.

Ember pulled her into a close hug, her arms wrapping around Zalia just as hers did around Ember.

"I'm glad you asked," Ember said, the joy audible in her tone.

"So am I!" Zalia said, unable to contain the nervousness that escaped her body as laughter.

Ember pulled back and took Zalia's hands again.

"What do we do now?" she asked, a wide grin on her face.

"Exactly what we've been doing, I guess," Zalia said, losing herself in Ember's joy.

It matched her own, their shared emotions bouncing back and forth across the bond, each enhancing the others.

"And what is that?" Ember asked slyly, her smile teasing.

"Making each other happy," Zalia said matter-of-factly.

She could visibly see as Ember's heart pumped just a little faster, the vibration visible to her eyes. It had been a little unnerving to see that kind of thing to begin with, but she had quickly grown used to it. It felt as natural to her now as either her normal or heat vision did.

"Is that so," Ember whispered.

"It is," Zalia said, before leaning in and kissing her.

They spent the rest of the day together, almost locked to each other as they grew used to the new dynamic between them. It had been growing this way for a little while, as they both acknowledged, yet making it a verbally agreed matter changed things. It changed things even as . . . it was the same as before.

It was hard to explain, yet Zalia felt no differently about Ember, still had the same attraction and emotions, yet with her feelings out in the open and Ember's similarly verbalised, the nervousness and anxiety that she felt around Ember was gone. She was free to relax and enjoy the company of her friend . . . her partner, without worry.

Zalia knew that Boreal was aware of what had happened, because she was still there through their bond, both of their emotions and thoughts bare to each other. Boreal was being silently supportive and kept her distance, allowing both

Zalia and Ember to explore this newfound comfort together. She even kept Aylie busy for Zalia, playing games and generally entertaining her. She was possibly the best wingcat that a woman could ask for.

Before long, nighttime came and they went to bed, and while all three bedrooms were used, both Boreal and Aylie slept in separate ones while Zalia and Ember shared a bed, cuddled up and warm.

The night passed quickly, Zalia dozing in and out while Ember slept soundly. While she didn't need to sleep for very long, Zalia still lay there holding Ember as she allowed her imagination to run free, thinking about the future and what she wanted to do when the invasion was finally over. She wanted to cleanse Endaria and take the fight to Cormaine, to take back the world that belonged to her friend Ro-ak.

But now, another path had come up before her, another door that led towards a different life. Ember would obviously come to Cormaine with her if she asked, she would do it not only for Zalia but for the people of Endaria. Removing the demons as a threat permanently would mean that the people in Endaria could live peacefully without fear of another invasion. Not only would it bring that peace, but it would allow people to move on from these events easier.

The other path, however, was a life lived with Ember somewhere else. She had said she would come with Zalia if she chose to leave, so what if after they helped free and stabilise Endaria, they went . . . somewhere else. Settled in to live a nice life with Aylie and Boreal somewhere. Perhaps they could help Aylie grow into her power in a safer environment. After all, Zalia didn't want to take Aylie to Cormaine, not as a child. That would not only be incredibly irresponsible but unfair. Aylie deserved to have a childhood she could look back on fondly. A life filled with pain, fear, and death left nothing to be proud of when one died. There had to be good times to balance out the bad.

It was those thoughts that Zalia had as they lay there that made her begin thinking of this other life, one spent in a comfortable peace. Revenge for her friend was all well and good, but surely it could wait until Aylie was older and most importantly, stronger. Maybe she could even help Zalia to take back Cormaine. Aylie as a Bronze or even Silver rank Druid would be an incredible force of nature to contend with. Not only did she have Healing Presence, a great boon in current day Cormaine, but she had some soul-related abilities that might be incredibly helpful, depending on how they evolved.

Ember woke up in the morning, blinking blearily as her mind exited its unconscious state.

"Good morning, sleepy," Zalia murmured, pulling her in closer.

"You're still here?" Ember asked in a whisper, holding onto the arm Zalia had tight around her front.

"Of course."

She could tell Ember's breathing began to slow again so she shook her lightly.

"Hey, hey, you just slept basically forever."

"Some of us need a lot of sleep."

"Alright, a bit longer," Zalia agreed.

Essen

Essen followed the others nervously. It was the morning after he had delivered the news to the elders and they had agreed to continue with the plans. The guards often gave out a morning breakfast to people a few hours after sunrise and this time was the same. Essen knew from the plans he had overheard that it was taking place at the park, where the farmers were gathering to begin their work.

The elders had decided to wait until the farmers had started, then the majority of their clan in the city would congregate, spreading the news to the people of the city that there was food in the park for the taking. He was a part of a group led by Yelza, the job of leading given to him simply because of his dull-minded loyalty. Essen respected that decision; he would make similar ones when he was in charge of the clan. It was much easier to trust an idiot who was loyal, rather than an intelligent person who feigned it.

Still, despite his confidence in the plan, Essen couldn't help feel a little nervous. A little . . . scared.

He had seen the way the interloper had treated his clanmate, the one she had captured and dragged into the guard hall like a trophy. He had seen what she had done to the probing attack one of the other clans had sent to keep the guards of Ostoss busy while his clan worked. She was strong, much too strong for one of her rank.

They entered the park, and he saw the small wooden house from the day before. Near to it, a little pavilion was set up with the guards giving food out to the farmers. Tristan was there, along with two others.

The interloper and her companion were sitting on a bench, holding on to each other like they feared losing the other should they let go. Essen altered his opinion of the woman.

Other groups were entering the park from different points along the city, and soon there were four or five dozen of them walking towards the centre.

However, the interloper had noticed as well. He saw a bright flow emit from her and spiralling leaves turned into a storm as they rose into the sky. They created a huge glowing pattern that burned brightly and in the instant it finished, Essen felt a force hit him like a hammer. It was her aura, yet stronger and coming from everywhere. He felt his disguise fade, and all around the park his clan stiffened or dropped to their knees as well, many of them losing their disguises. It was a trap.

Essen struggled to his feet, staring at the interloper as she too struggled to stand, the strain of the spell obviously having taken a lot out of her. The aura wasn't fading, though, its force a painful weight upon his shoulders. He saw a wildcat start tearing through some of his clan on the other side of the park and panic took him. He turned to ask Yelza what to do, but a bright, glowing arrow took him straight through the head. Essen watched in fear as Yelza dropped to the ground, dead. Then, he turned and ran as fast as his heavy body would allow.

CHAPTER THIRTY-THREE

Returned to the Dirt

Zalia

Zalia watched as the growing crowd of people walked down the slopes towards the bottom of the park. They came from multiple sides, all looking like people, yet she knew through the feeling in the air, the push against her aura despite their own being held back, that these were not all people.

Aylie was inside the house, further inside the vault that she had open in there. Zalia had told her to stay there and if things turned out to be more dire, Boreal would come and get her out and away from the city if necessary.

She waited until only the trailing ends of the groups were still outside the perimeter of the large living ritual she set up before beginning to cast it.

Masses of the herbs she required for the ritual began appearing from nowhere, flowing into the sky above and forming a huge glowing circle over the entire park. Her mana was ripped from her at a speed even Nature's Wrath didn't manage to achieve, most of it vanishing in moments.

The ritual above glowed brighter as she activated it, and with a final flash, a ripple went out through the air, forming a dome that vanished as soon as it appeared. As that ripple flowed through the crowds of people, however, many of them stopped, standing rigid.

A large number of them dropped to their knees and clawed at their chests in pain as the disguises they had taken were torn away. Zalia only saw this for an instant, however, as she too dropped to the ground in exhaustion. Ember managed to catch her before she fell over completely, holding her half on her knees.

There was but a drop of mana left in her pool, enough that she would not lose consciousness, thankfully. Her main contribution to this fight was this ritual; it would probably take her longer to regain enough mana to do anything more.

She managed to get her feet under herself, standing up and leaning against the house.

"Go."

Ember nodded and ran off.

Zalia noticed that Tristan was ordering the farmers into the house. A good idea, to keep them safe as well. Ignoring that and trusting him to do his job now that her plan had really been revealed, Zalia summoned her bow and turned her attention to the shapeshifting demons closest to her.

Most had still not recovered, still trying to stand up from the ground where they knelt or lay, struggling. A few stood, struggling, yet not nearly as much as the others. Those must have been the Bronze rank ones. They definitely moved with a litheness that the others did not and had a certain . . . dangerous look to them.

She drew and shot, hitting one that wore a guard's uniform straight through the head. This caused quite a few of the lower-ranked ones around it to panic, a few even running away.

Most, however, looked at their fallen comrade and managed to build enough strength to charge.

Boreal was in and out of combat, pouncing from shadows and tearing through enemies. Others yet were dragged screaming into patches of wildlife before being silenced by her ferocious furry friend within. She was so quick that many of the shapeshifters didn't have time to respond and the ones that did, didn't manage to get through her armour.

Zalia shot off more arrows, not able to enhance them with any effects, nor able to place Hunter's Mark on any of the enemies. Still, with the powers of her bow and weapon proficiency, the arrows punched through Tin and Iron rank shapeshifters as if they were made of paper.

Ember was taking on her own group, some six enemies, by herself. With the halo of fire surrounding her, they were unable to get close without being blinded and burned, probably the only reason she was able to hold her ground so effectively. She deflected a blow with her heater shield and used the moment to stab her double-bladed sword through the enemy's chest. Another three of the group tried to take advantage of that moment but she sped up, and with a blur, two of those found themselves with throats slashed as Ember pushed her advantage against the remaining three.

Zalia took care of two of them, Ember switching to the defensive as Zalia's arrows dropped her enemies. The final one fell over backwards as it tried to scramble away, but that only sealed its fate as Ember stomped her foot and a burst of fire exploded from the ground underneath it.

Zalia quickly used her strength and air jumps to get onto the roof of the house. From there, she could see Tristan and his guards fighting a much larger group with practiced proficiency. They worked extremely well together as a team, the guards forming a kind of backup point for Tristan as he moved in and out of combat. The shapeshifters' failing in fighting them was not taking advantage of their numbers. They shoved and fought with each other, trying to be the ones to get into the fight next. Some even pushed their comrades in battle, causing their deaths at Tristan's hands.

Zalia could see that the shapeshifters were struggling to move properly within the confines of her ritual and more than a few had run off already. Despite their initial momentum in the fight, the higher-ranked shapeshifters were taking back the initiative. The group Boreal was picking off started to wise up to her tactics and moved together as a ball, making it harder for her to take them one by one. After quickly disposing of that first group, Ember was quickly losing ground to a larger group of eight. She managed to pick one off but received a wound in return, and though it quickly healed, she had to drop back quite a distance because of it.

Tristan and his guards were also struggling to hold ground. While they had moved far up the hill to begin with to meet the enemies, they now were at the little bridge near the house. Zalia fired off arrows wherever they were needed, taking out shapeshifters to give Ember some breathing room, disturbing the grouped-up enemies for Boreal so that she could pick a few off.

Then, the sun went out.

The battle almost paused as everyone looked up at the twinkling stars that were growing ever brighter in the sky. Zalia looked down off the side of the house to see Aylie, tears flowing down her face and words whispered into the wind.

"Not my family, not again."

The stars came down, one for each of the shapeshifters in the park. Blazing lines were burnt into the air as they struck, many of the lower-ranked shapeshifters dying from the impact. Waves of light burst out from where the stars had landed, washing the field ablaze with a starry fire.

The sun returned.

Tristan, his guards, and the remaining shapeshifters stood still in confusion and awe, yet Ember, Boreal, and Zalia did not hesitate to take advantage.

"*Back inside* now," Zalia sent to Aylie.

She was both thankful and worried for the child.

She didn't look to see if Aylie had listened, quickly taking out one of the Bronze shapeshifters and moving on to the next.

They were significantly harder to kill, some managing to dodge her arrows or at least twist such that they hit less vital parts. Ember managed to take down the two Bronze ranked demons that remained of the once eight enemies she had faced, moving quickly across the battlefield to where Boreal fought.

The group that Boreal had been fighting had fared the worst, however. They had been grouped tightly together when the stars had struck, and nothing much remained of them other than a squished patch of ground.

Zalia marvelled at the power of a single Tin rank ability. It was much more powerful than anything she had been able to do at that rank. Granted, it was a two-day cooldown, but it was still absurd. The power of a god-blessed class was not something to dismiss, even a Tin rank one.

Tristan and his squad similarly smashed down the remainders of his enemies, pulling themselves together before the shapeshifters did.

With that, the battle was over.

Zalia walked across the battlefield, doing the gruesome work of finishing off the shapeshifters that were still alive as she looked through her notifications.

> **Congratulations! Druid Grove has reached Bronze 3.**

The cry of a demon resounded across the park before she stabbed it through the throat.

> **Congratulations! Herbal Magic has gained two levels, reaching Bronze 6.**

She heard the whimpering of a lower-ranked one and pulled aside the mangled body of a larger demon to find it alive, yet missing its lower half. She put it out of its misery.

> **Congratulations! Healing Presence has reached Bronze 7.**

Magic flared to life as she used a Flame-root ritual to burn away the pile of bodies, returning them to ash. A quick manipulation of the earth later, and there remained only a patch of bare ground, Healing Presence quickly growing grass back over it.

> **Congratulations! Bow - Weapon proficiency has reached Bronze 4.**

She could see Ember walking across her side of the battlefield, performing a similar grisly task. Using the bond between them, Zalia sent what was essentially an emotion hug. She received one back as they both continued on.

Tristan was sitting on the bench with his head in hands, his axe lying across his knees with the blade dripping blood. She knew what he had been through before and didn't disturb him; he would just need a little time.

Boreal came over and started helping Zalia, finishing off the still-alive demons as she burnt their remains and buried them. She didn't want Aylie to see what was left of them after her ability. She, no doubt, had received a disturbing amount of levels from what she had done and Zalia would need to talk to her later about it. These may have been demons, but they probably had their own society, perhaps their own bonds between each other. She didn't know much about them on a society level. Sure, she knew where they came from kind of, what they were capable of, and the fact they were here to invade, yet she didn't know how exactly they acted as a people. She had seen fear in their eyes this day as the stars came crashing down. Did they love too?

It was easy to see your enemy as a faceless abomination in war. A monster that had come to take your land, life, and people. Perhaps that was true of the demons as a whole. It was definitely true of the thousand-eyed creatures that haunted her dreams still. What about these shapeshifters, though? What about the lower-ranked of the demons, ones that showed so much fear? Were they here out of a bloodlust or out of fear for their own lives?

All questions that she would need to answer in due time.

"You—you'll all suffer for this."

A voice by her feet, one that Boreal had missed. Zalia kneeled down.

"What do you mean? You lost this fight."

The demon coughed, blood bubbling out of its mouth.

"With—with this lo-loss, the right of pref—preference has also been lost. Struggle against your f-fate all you want, interloper, but now—now you die."

It coughed up more blood, then its whole body jerked.

Zalia grabbed it by the shoulders.

"What is the right of preference?"

It jerked once more, then lay still. She let go of its shoulders and it dropped to the ground, limp. Fire soon swallowed it and the other nearby demons, her power then returning them to the dirt below. Their bodies would feed the plants that the farmers grew, and the misery they caused to the people of Ostoss would be repaid, if only a little. This was the cycle of life and no matter how much they might try, Zalia would not allow them to break it.

CHAPTER THIRTY-FOUR

Morals?

Zalia

After the cleanup was over, Zalia checked to make sure Ember was ok, then found Aylie.

She had gone inside the vault again, thankfully, alongside a whole group of farmers. Zalia kicked the farmers out, sending them in the direction of Tristan, hoping that having something to do would pull him out of his past.

Zalia leaned against one of the benches at the back, watching Aylie manipulate a plant slowly and carefully.

"That was risky."

Aylie turned to look at her.

"So were you."

Zalia nodded once, accepting the point.

"How do you feel?"

Aylie shrugged.

"Your ability did a lot, you don't have any feelings about that?"

Aylie shrugged again.

"Their souls are different. They killed my family. They would have killed you."

Zalia sighed deeply. Aylie had almost whispered that last part.

She walked over and sat next to Aylie, lightly caressing the plant that she was manipulating.

"They are different, yes. We don't know why they do what they do. Perhaps it is a mindless need for violence or some other malevolent reason. A creature of another race from their world did kill your family, and if these ones had their way, they would have killed us all as well. They will probably try to do so again. Do you know why they are doing that?"

Aylie didn't respond for a moment, curling the plant around Zalia's arm before returning it to its original form.

"No, why?"

Zalia leaned back, hands behind to support herself, and looked past the gently floating lights at the ceiling.

"I don't know. I have no idea why they're in this world at all. They are invading, for a reason unknown to me. Yet I still feel . . . bad that this fight happened."

"Bad? Why?"

"They just lost their entire family. Yes, they attacked us, yet why did they do that? Do we know that they did that out of malice, or is there another reason behind it? What if someone is forcing them to, what if they do it out of fear, not hatred? Maybe some of them are stuck between us and something else threatening their lives."

Zalia looked down, and Aylie was staring at her with confusion and a little bit of anger.

"So you're saying we shouldn't fight back against them?"

There was bite to her tone and Zalia didn't blame her. "I . . . No, that's not what I'm saying. I think we should do what we have to do to survive, to get justice for our friends and family. But, I don't think we should be happy or careless about it. And I'm not saying you are either of those things, I just . . ."

Zalia trailed off, unsure how to continue her thought. She wasn't the best at verbalising sometimes but wanted to pass over this feeling, this way of seeing things, to Aylie.

Aylie didn't reply and luckily, the anger had gone from her expression. Maybe she was too young for Zalia to try teach her about this kind of thing, hell, Zalia didn't fully know what she was trying to say either.

"It's . . . it's necessary to fight them. Whatever their situation is, they *are* trying to harm us and our friends, and we can't let that happen. I don't want to let this entire thing turn me callous to the troubles of others, though, to make me see any other living creature as lesser or monstrous. Does that make any sense?"

Aylie nodded slowly, though she did look quite confused. Zalia didn't blame her.

"I'm sorry, I'm not explaining myself very well. I want you to have a normal childhood, to experience love, safety, and warmth. Yet, I can't lie to you about what is happening in your kingdom, your home, and what I, and possibly you, will have to do to protect it. This whole situation is unfair to you."

Aylie quietly latched onto her side and hugged her tight. Zalia leaned forward a little and wrapped one arm around her.

"I'm doing my best," Zalia whispered.

She felt Aylie nod against her side.

"I know."

They stayed that way for a little while, until Ember came in and wordlessly pulled them both up into a tight embrace as well. Zalia could feel that Boreal was out there still, hunting down the tracks of a few of the shapeshifters that had escaped. Zalia probably should have joined her, to rid themselves of as many of the enemy as possible, but the dying words of that demon haunted her.

It had said that the right of preference had been lost. The right of preference to what? The town?

If that is what it had meant, it would mean the town was now open to attack from other demons as well, though hadn't it been already? There had been many of the Tin rank flying type attacking when she had arrived after all.

She couldn't understand what it would mean unless she managed to catch another shapeshifter and ask it questions without it exploding, which didn't seem likely. They would just have to get the entire town protected better, in that case, meaning she would need to talk to the Silver rank Enchanter as soon as possible to determine if her ritual would work on a larger scale with their type of magic.

She sighed. Could it wait? Probably not.

Zalia was with Ember out in front of the house, having left Aylie in the vault. It would do her good to think a little about things before Zalia complicated her thoughts again. The warmth and safety of the vault would be good for her as well, though Ember had said that her emotional state, while certainly not settled, wasn't tumultuous.

Zalia leaned her head onto Ember's shoulder.

"I'm so tired," she whispered.

Ember stroked her hair gently.

"That's because you keep taking on such huge responsibilities, silly."

Zalia closed her eyes, breathing in Ember's scent, now containing a little hint of woodsmoke. An addition from the blessing perhaps.

"I couldn't just leave the town like this. You wouldn't have either."

"I know, that's part of what I like so much about you."

Zalia lifted her head back up and looked over at where the farmers were beginning their work. She could already see Healing Presence helping the planted seeds to sprout, little stalks shooting their way out of the ground. This could be the beginning of a turning point for the town with a large number of the shapeshifters eliminated and food being grown. Those words still weighed heavily on her, however.

"One of the demons told me that we had sealed our own fate and that the right of preference had been lost. That now we will all suffer and die."

Ember frowned, turning to her.

"Maybe it was just trying to unsettle you?"

". . . Maybe. I didn't feel like it was lying, though. What if we did just open up the town to attack from other demons? They never seem to work together, from what I've seen, maybe there is a reason behind that. I've only seen different types working together in those last days in Cormaine, and that was certainly not a normal situation."

"None of this is a normal situation."

Zalia looked at her pointedly.

"Alright, alright. Well, what do you want to do, then?"

Zalia chewed on her lip, thinking about it.

"Well, I want to use this ritual on a larger scale for the whole town through the Silver rank enchanter's power, for one."

"Well, that's something—but, Zalia, if there really are many more higher-ranked demons that will come to attack the town, we won't be able to stop them all."

"I . . . I know. There doesn't seem to be much that I *can* do about it. All I can think of is finding someone more powerful to come help, but who is close enough?"

Ember also stopped for a moment to think, though she didn't look happy when she spoke.

"We could see if anyone from the Morning's Shade will be able to come help. There are a few Gold rankers there, after all."

"Mmm. Maybe, I'll think about it. It's not a bad idea."

Ember pulled her into a hug.

"I don't like it either."

Zalia hugged her back.

"We can't let our personal feelings get in the way of possibly saving the entire town, though."

"I know."

Zalia held on for a moment more before breaking away and striding towards Tristan.

"Hey!"

Tristan looked over from where he was talking to his guards and met her in the middle.

"What's up?"

"Firstly, sorry for not telling you the entire plan."

Tristan frowned.

"Huh?"

Zalia blinked at him.

"The huge ritual, exposing the shapeshifters, and then taking them down?"

Tristan shrugged.

"I thought that was just you being ridiculously strong again. You planned all that?"

"More or less."

Tristan sighed heavily.

"How exactly did you kill the sun and drop the stars on them?"

Zalia scratched the back of her head awkwardly.

"Thaaaat . . . wasn't me. That was Aylie."

Tristan stared at her blankly.

"The child. The Tin rank child."

"Yeah."

"Ok then, let me ask a different question. How did the *Tin rank child* kill the sun and drop the stars on them?"

Zalia watched Boreal walk past towards the river, half coated in blood, before replying.

"She was blessed by a star god. Anyways, sorry for not clueing you in. I kind of needed you to be out of the loop to deceive the shapeshifters."

"She was blessed by a *wh—*"

"I want to go see the Enchanter now, to see if they can do what I did to this park to the whole town. It would be an extremely strong protection if they could."

Tristan sputtered.

"Cool, I'll wait for you over here whenever you're ready."

She walked off, back to the ever-warm Ember.

"Zalia!"

Tristan quickly gave his guards a few orders, then ran after her.

"Sometimes you are going to have to explain things more, you know."

Zalia considered it.

"No, I don't."

Tristan grabbed her arm.

"What did you mean when you said she got blessed by a star god."

"I meant it literally. Ember got a blessing too; stick around long enough and you might get one of your own."

She tapped her chin thoughtfully.

"Though, you'll have to get in line. I definitely owe Boreal the next one."

Tristan gave a resigned sigh, which made Zalia feel a little bad.

"Look, I get tired of explaining all the things that happen all the time to multiple people. Sometimes I just want to be around people without having to explain myself."

Tristan eyed her, but accepted it with a nod.

"Alright, let's go."

He made off and Zalia quickly went inside to collect Aylie. Ember and Boreal followed along and the five of them reentered the city. It was obvious that the passing of the demons had caused a disturbance because people were hiding, some inside and others in alleyways. There was a stench of fear hanging in the air, and it made Zalia sick.

Tristan soldiered on, though, making his way to the centre of town. There, he stopped before a large, mansion-like house. The home of the Enchanter. She could tell because there were several visibly glowing runes on the building and floating over it. There were even more out of her direct visual sight that her heat or even vibration sight picked up independently. This person was not messing around.

"Well, that's scary."

Tristan gave her a crooked smile.

"Oh, they aren't so bad. They're quite nice once you get to know them and they forgive you for existing. And once you get over the fact that many of these runes are there specifically to kill people who want to speak to them. It'll be fun!"

Zalia narrowed her eyes at Tristan, but didn't push for more information. Fair was fair.

"Alright, in we go, then."

CHAPTER THIRTY-FIVE

Incompatible

Zalia

First, Tristan walked towards the house after insisting that they remain behind. Apparently, the Enchanter really didn't like to meet new people. Three new people and an only slightly tame wildcat were not exactly easy to get used to.

Zalia watched him sidestep a glowing rune on the ground, then walk in an arc through a corridor of invisible runes that were only visible to Zalia as vibrations in the air. After reaching the door, he knocked on it. Only, he didn't knock where one usually might, instead putting his hand to the height of his knees and knocking there. It looked odd, performing such a menial thing as knocking in a different way, which somehow caused Zalia's brain to grind a little in confusion.

Tristan waited for a few minutes before the door was finally pulled open. The person who opened the door was . . . basically still a teenager. They looked to be barely twenty and shorter than Zalia, wearing robes that glowed with multitudinous runes.

Despite the unassuming look of a youngster, Zalia knew that this was not someone to mess with. She could see the power radiating from them, undeniably Silver rank. It looked like they might even be close to Gold, according to Aura Observation.

Congratulations! Aura Observation has reached Iron 20.
Congratulations! Aura Observation has reached Bronze 1.
Aura Observation - passive.
Tin - You are able to identify what rank a creature is by sight, unless it has a method of hiding that information.
Iron - You are able to identify a creature's general progress to the next rank.

> **Bronze - Your strength of observation increases. Fluctuations in the auras of undisciplined beings can give insights into their emotional state.**

New information suddenly assaulted Zalia's eyes, another upgrade to a sight-based ability causing her bonded mental stats to work hard to keep up. Not only did the ability do as it said, allowing Zalia to see people's auras almost as if it were a loose, skin-layered coating, but she could also tell the state of them.

She could even see the faded auras of the few Tin and Iron people that were on the street nearby, looking as depressed and hopeless as the people they belonged to.

She looked back over to where Tristan was talking with the Enchanter. He gestured back towards her and the Enchanter met her eyes. She held contact, trying to keep her expression neutral.

The Enchanter nodded, then said something in response.

Zalia was surprised she couldn't hear them. The range of her hearing had grown quite good since gaining access to magic, yet their words must have been blocked by one of the many, many runes that protected the house since she couldn't hear a word. She could still see the vibrations of their speech, however, and did notice that they stopped abruptly at the border of the property. Might it be possible for her to read what people were saying in the vibrations their speech made? Another skill to learn, perhaps.

Tristan looked resigned at something the Enchanter said but trudged back over, looking at Zalia.

"He said that only you can come inside."

Zalia frowned.

"Why?"

Tristan's eyes flicked down to Boreal then back up.

"He said, and I quote, that he does not want to deal with wild beasts or children in his home."

Ember, Aylie, and Boreal all looked simultaneously offended.

"So was he calling me a wild beast or a child?" Ember asked.

Tristan winced and Aylie poked him in the knee.

"He's basically a child as well!" she complained.

"Aylie, don't be fooled by how he looks, he has some kind of magic that makes him younger. Physically, at least."

Zalia sighed.

"Yet he still acts like one. Can I go and talk to him? I might be able to convince him to change his mind."

"Don't worry about it, Zalia, if he doesn't want us in there, then we don't want to be in there. You know where to find us."

Ember gave her a long hug, then a peck on the cheek.

"But do annoy him a little for me, would you?" she whispered in Zalia's ear.

Zalia smiled, a little tingle going down her neck.

"You can count on it. I'll see you three later."

She knelt down to give Boreal and Aylie a hug as well, before standing up and following Tristan to the house. She had to avoid the runes as he did, not wanting to accidentally set off some kind of death trap.

The first thing she noticed as she got closer was how . . . perfectly symmetrical everything about the Enchanter was. From the clothes, to the runes he drew, to the house he lived in, to his face. Even the garden in front, nothing more than a lawn, looked as if each blade of grass were perfectly mirroring another.

Closer now, she could see the aura of power about him in more definition. She could also see that he was indeed close to reaching Gold, a fact that Aura Observation told her.

"Hello."

The Enchanter looked her up and down.

"He told me that you have a . . . *ritual* that affects the demons directly."

His voice was high-pitched and sounded almost whiny. Some Silver ranker they had the misfortune of having to rely on.

"I do. It directly counters the nature of the demon's aura."

He narrowed his eyes.

"And how did you manage that?"

Zalia gave him a look up and down, aiming for an expression of disappointment, like she had just opened her bag of bread and discovered mould. She needed to fulfill Ember's request after all.

"It's based on one of my abilities. It is antithetical to the demon's aura in a more reactive way, the ritual does the same thing but in more of a . . . subduing manner."

She didn't really know how to explain all the things she did on instinct due to Herbal Magic. She just hadn't ever really considered needing to explain how it all worked before. The best way she could describe it was Healing Presence acting like an acid that neutralised itself and the aura it was fighting. The ritual was more like a heavy weight that stopped it from standing up.

"Based on an ability, you say? What is your class?"

Zalia smiled.

"I have a few. Would it be ok if I actually walk in the door, or shall we have this entire conversation on the doorstep?"

He looked like he was actually considering it for a moment, but relented and stepped aside to let them in. Tristan let out a deep sigh behind her, but followed them inside as well. She didn't think he was going to have a very good time, talking about rituals and power specifics. While it was certainly not a big point of study or conversation for Zalia, she at least had abilities related to and an understanding of it. This was about as far from Tristan's powerset as it could get. Yet, he probably wanted to stop her and the Enchanter from killing each other, an event with a nonzero chance of occurring.

The Enchanter led them through a small hallway, past doorways placed symmetrically to the sides, before heading into a small dining room. There was a table, thankfully with four seats around it, not one.

The room itself, as with everything else, was symmetrical. There were more runes decorating the walls, and a large one placed centrally on the ceiling, lighting the space.

"What did you mean by a few classes?"

The Enchanter wasted no time nor energy on idle conversation, jumping straight into things again. Usually, Zalia would enjoy that kind of thing, yet recently she had been a little more . . . ok with other people's presence. She even enjoyed idle conversation sometimes too.

"I have three, though only two of them will matter for this particular task. Herbalist and Druid. One of them gives me Herbal Magic, a type of ritual magic that uses herbs as fuel. The other gives me my aura, which is antithetical to the demon's own."

The Enchanter leaned far forward in his seat, as if trying to view the answers to his questions directly through her forehead.

"Three? How?"

Zalia leaned back, away from his inquisitive eyes.

"That is neither the reason we are here, nor important to this."

She could see the hunger for knowledge burning in the Enchanter's eyes. It was oddly unsettling.

"So be it. Show me the ritual you speak of."

Zalia summoned a tiny little circle on the table using herbs from her Grove's storage.

The Enchanter stared at it and seemed . . . disgusted.

"That is . . . a horrible way to perform rituals."

Zalia stared at him, taken aback. Maybe Tristan wouldn't be the one who enjoyed this process the least.

"*What* did you say?"

His eyes flicked up to hers.

"Inefficient, messy . . . unsymmetrical."

Wonderful.

"Why exactly does it need to be symmetrical? Look, I'm not going to go around giving you bad mouth about how you do your magic, so don't come over here attacking me about mine. Can you obtain the same effect or not?"

The Enchanter grumbled, staring at the little ritual circle.

"What is your medium for permanency?"

"Huh?"

He gestured around the room to all the runes that were glowing on the walls.

"Permanency, what is your medium?"

Zalia was a little confused. Well, she knew what he meant, but did all ritual magic have some kind of permanent version? How then was his fueled, was it in the symmetry of everything he did?

"Plants, mine is plants."

His expression turned from disgust to horror.

Plants, arguably the most natural thing in the world. Nature also tended to stray from symmetry, however. The cause of her own ritual's messiness, or a symptom of it?

"Why do you ask?"

He stood from his chair and paced back and forth. One hand idly scratched at his head while the other flicked like he was dismissing thoughts with a wave.

"You have, perhaps, the least compatible ritual magic I have ever seen. At least, the least compatible with mine."

She couldn't help but agree.

"So are you unable to do it? Convert what mine does to something you can emulate?"

He whipped around to face her.

"I didn't say that! It will just . . . take some time."

Zalia nodded slowly.

"Okayyyy then. What do you want from me? Is this circle enough?"

He looked at her with annoyance, then resignation. Slowly, he closed his eyes.

"You'll have to leave a permanent ritual here so that I may study it. It is easier to do with one that is active."

Ah.

"Right, where do you want it?"

She stood as well, looking about the room. She had to admit, the chaos of her living rituals would very much disturb the aesthetics of the immaculate, bare, symmetrical room. Not that she minded it. She didn't really like that aesthetic anyways.

"The table."

He sounded miserable.

"I can put it in your front yard somewhere, maybe? It might—"

"No, the table."

Zalia didn't argue any further.

"I'm going to need some dirt."

He nodded and a ball of dirt floated through the doorway. Where had that come from?

It dropped to the table, and Zalia got to work. She spread it into a little circle, then put small flakes of plant into place, growing them until they made tiny versions of the real plants. Then, when it was all ready, she activated the living ritual.

The Enchanter sat down in front of it, head in his hands, staring with confusion.

"Are you going to need anyth—"

"No."

Shrugging, but trusting the man to know what he was talking about, Zalia took his words as a dismissal and left. She could say with certainty that she definitely annoyed him. Perhaps even a little *too* much.

Tristan followed her out and led the way through the rune maze in front of the house. She noticed that this was symmetrical as well, there were two paths through. Or . . . were there? If she were the Enchanter, the second path would be the one thing she made unsymmetrical, as a kind of trick.

Though, she was far from the Enchanter.

"That went well, I think."

Tristan turned to look at her, both of them now safely off the house grounds.

"About as well as I expected, yes."

"I didn't even raise my voice or anything. I barely even reacted to him calling my magic messy and inefficient!"

Tristan eyed her.

"Well, compared to the Enchanter's, it does look a litt—"

"Don't you dare, you won't receive as much leeway as he did," Zalia interrupted, finger pointed.

Tristan chuckled lightly.

"Alright, alright. Let's go find your . . . friend."

"Partner," Zalia corrected.

He didn't seem surprised, just giving a shrug.

"Didn't know if you'd put a label on it yet."

"What's that supposed to mean?" she grumbled.

"Oh, well . . . you know . . ." He looked at her as he trailed off.

"Yeah, I know."

Then, he smiled brightly at her, the weariness leaving his face for just a moment.

"I'm happy for you, Zalia, really."

"Thanks, Tristan, I appreciate that."

CHAPTER THIRTY-SIX

Shield

Zalia

They found the other three at the park house and Zalia gave Ember another long hug.

"Did you annoy him?"

Zalia smiled and squeezed a little tighter.

"Just for you," she whispered.

She let go of the embrace and turned to Aylie, fixing up her messy hair.

"And how are you doing?"

Aylie grumbled a little at the treatment but didn't push her hands away.

"Ok."

Zalia nodded. Ok was . . . ok.

"We might be leaving town soon, depending how things go. Are you alright with that?"

Aylie nodded her assent, but Tristan looked concerned.

"So soon? We really could use you here for longer. Obviously if you can't, then that is that, but . . ."

"I might have . . . some bad news."

Tristan's already stressed face looked as if it aged a further ten years.

"Bad news. Out with it, then."

Zalia swallowed, collecting her thoughts.

"Right. Well, one of the dying demons said something about the right of preference, which had been lost with this fight? I don't know exactly what that meant, but it seemed convinced that we were doomed."

A little of the tension left Tristan's face.

"Well, that could have just been some final breath bravado or a tactic to make us panic."

Zalia nodded a few times, though she didn't agree at all.

"Maybe. Don't you find it weird that nothing stronger has attacked Ostoss, though? We have seen a Silver rank demon flying around aimlessly not a few days east of here. Why wouldn't they have come here?"

Tristan looked a little disturbed and Zalia didn't blame him. The thought of a Silver or even Gold rank demon coming to Ostoss and slaughtering everyone was a horrific one. She wasn't certain if the Enchanter would be able to win a one-on-one fight against a Silver rank demon, let alone anything higher.

"What if these shapechangers had dibs on the town, and we just inadvertently opened it up for any of them?"

"Then . . . why would you leave us after finding this out?"

Zalia looked to the sky.

"I don't know that we would be able to defeat a Silver ranked demon. Whatever is left of the Morning's Shade, though . . . well, they might be able to."

She had actually killed a Silver rank creature before, but it had been one of the undead in the Bathar city of Hetheir. Those had been significantly weaker than your usual Silver rank creature and lacked any abilities whatsoever. The truth of the matter was, if she went up against one of these Silver demons by herself she would die. With Boreal and Ember, they might stand a chance but even Delphi and the collective hadn't been able to take one down.

"So you would be going for help, then?"

"Yes, Tristan. We aren't just going to leave you all to die. The army needs us but not nearly as dearly as you do. Hopefully, the Enchanter will be able to get something out of my ritual to improve the barrier you have. Hopefully, you'll be able to survive until we can get back with help."

Ostoss was a week's journey from Endelbyrn, the city that held the organisation known as the Morning's Shade. While such a journey might take Zalia and Boreal less time, she didn't like the idea of splitting up from Ember and Aylie. She was certainly not going to leave them in Ostoss by themselves.

Tristan and his guards would need to hold out for a little over two weeks for her to make the journey and return, assuming she even found any help in Endelbyrn at all. She hoped it still stood, as it had been the centre of a lot of Endaria's powerful people.

Tristan heaved a long sigh.

"I guess we can try. I don't see that there is any other option, really."

Zalia chewed at her lips a little, trying to figure out what else they could try. Getting help from the army was out of the question, as they were even further away and less likely to come. The Heat and Stone denizens would not leave their mountain to help but would take refugees. Could they walk the entire population of Ostoss a week's journey to the mountain?

The logistics and danger of such a task took that idea away from her quickly.

"I don't see any other way either."

Ember looked like she was deep in thought as well, yet said nothing. She was probably having most of the same thoughts Zalia was. Boreal, of course, didn't even seem to be paying attention.

"When will you leave?" Tristan asked.

Zalia looked at Ember who shrugged.

"Tomorrow after Ember uses her ability to feed the people?"

Tristan nodded in agreement and they fell into silence. There wasn't much else to be said. She would help grow the plants and would even set up a living ritual to accomplish that same task but then there wasn't much else they could do but get help. If both Hildebrandt and Matthias, the two who led the Morning's Shade alongside Hidey, were still in Endelbyrn, their help would be invaluable. She just hoped she could convince them to come.

Essen

Essen sat in a gutter, many hours after having run from the park where the interloper had slaughtered his clanmates. It had all gone so horribly. What had that dome of oppressive power been? How could someone so low as Bronze rank create something so powerful?

There would be hell to pay for this, he knew that. The elders would take his life for providing them with such wrong information. He couldn't go back, not after leaving so many of his clanmates to die for a mistake he had made.

He didn't understand. Had the interloper known they were coming all along? Had she sensed his real form when he had been talking to her?

There was nothing for it now. He was doomed, there was no way he could survive what was to come. The right of preference was lost now. There would be no feast or celebration, no capture of the city. The others would come pick over the spoils and their clan would fade back into the background once again.

Perhaps . . .

He had been hoping this would go well so that he could finally ascend. He would be on the same level as many of the stronger members of the clan, the same level even as the interloper. Though she would have killed many that were of her same rank despite the odds by now. Such strength . . . strength that could be his.

Well, he didn't have to wait for permission now, did he? Usually, ascending without permission from the elders would be the end for him but they would already kill him for this, so why not?

Essen slipped through a few alleys, getting lost amongst the desperate of this horrible little town. His hidden form had reestablished itself not long after leaving the oppressive power of the interloper, thankfully. No, he didn't have to wait for anyone to tell him he could advance his own power. The message was asking *him* if he wanted to ascend, after all. Why did some elder get to tell him what to do?

He summoned the message, and it sat there in his sight, a goal just out of reach yet always within it.

> **Would you like to ascend?**

"*Yes.*"

He felt the power flow through him. It was nothing so different than the last ascension yet it was so, so much more. All of his powers were already Bronze ranked, yet they felt even more solid now.

Once he adapted to the new sensory input of being Bronze, he looked about at the cowering filth that had hidden themselves away in the alleys with him. Had they always looked so drab and depressed?

Well, even if they had, they would still bleed just as well. He jumped forward and grabbed a man, tearing into him with claws, teeth and all.

Zalia

Zalia was sitting with Ember watching the plants grow. Tristan had left some time ago to check on things in the city, yet the farmers remained, looking confused but overjoyed at the speed of growth the plants had obtained.

It hadn't really occurred to Zalia, but her powerset would actually work quite well if she were to be a farmer. Not only could she grow plants at very quick speeds but she could also harvest a crop extremely efficiently. All the plants she harvested would even provide more nutrition as well.

It was slightly amusing to consider—a life where she used her powerful Druidic abilities to run a little farm.

Her deep reverie was shattered as the sounds of screaming began to fill the air. She couldn't discern where it was coming from at first, but it started growing louder and louder. Before she knew it, there were shouts as people from the city began fleeing across the park.

She looked at Ember and both of them jumped up to investigate. Boreal and Aylie were somewhere in the house, probably within the vault. Zalia knew she could leave the protection of Aylie to Boreal and so wasn't worried about the two of them at all.

They ran past fleeing refugees and eventually found the source of the commotion. One of the escaped shapechangers had apparently dropped its guise entirely as it leaned over the corpse of a man whose eyes stared sightlessly into the sky above. Ember immediately dashed forward and interrupted the disgusting sounds of chewing with a savagely delivered shield to the head.

CHAPTER THIRTY-SEVEN

Elder

Zalia

The shield bash sent the demon sprawling across the ground, Ember quickly following it with blade at the ready. She didn't activate the fiery powers of her armour, perhaps worried about lighting a fire in the city. In nature, Zalia could easily take care of a fire by healing plants quicker than they could be burned. Here, she would have to use Nature's Wrath to tamp a big fire down.

She followed Ember on the offensive, applying Hunter's Mark and various rituals to the creature as it desperately avoided Ember's blade.

"Wait, wait!"

The voice ground at Zalia's ears like two blades crossing. It did make her pause, however, though Ember didn't falter for even a moment.

Ember began pushing it back, managing to corner it into an alley.

"Wait! I'll show you where the others are hiding! Please!"

It was at that moment that Zalia recognised the demon. It was one of the very first creatures to flee, one that had been standing next to her first kill. As she watched, it did something she very much did not expect. It knelt down and bowed its forehead to the ground, arms reaching outwards.

That caused Ember to pause as well, as if considering its words, though she kept her weapon ready. There was no way they would let it live, yet if it really could lead them to where the survivors were and provide an opportunity for them to clear the rest of them out of the city, wasn't it worth a try?

"*Thoughts?*" Zalia sent to Ember.

"*Might be worth a try.*"

Zalia agreed.

"We'll humour you for now. Lead us there."

Watching the demon closely, Zalia could swear she saw an expression akin to joy pass over its face, though it was hard to tell with its forehead on the ground. Perhaps she could get some answers from this one about a few things.

Slowly, ever so slowly, they left the alley and let it come out. It took on a human form, a sight that was much less disturbing than the bloody-faced demon.

"You'll answer questions as well."

It nodded fervently.

"Good. Walk."

It began walking, only turning its back on them with what was obviously great internal conflict. Zalia wouldn't have turned her back on it, that was for sure.

"What is the right of preference?"

She heard it let out a light hissing sound before it replied.

"Our clan had the right of preference to this town. No more."

Clan. So it must have been as she thought, and the town would now be open to attack. It changed nothing about her plans, however, simply a confirmation of what she feared.

"Who are these others? Why would you lead us to them?"

She wasn't particularly worried about what they might face. There was certainty that a large number of the shapechangers had come to the park and had died there, as it would have been a final breaking event for the city, had they not won. Maybe the strongest of their bunch had stayed in relative safety but she couldn't see that being the case. It was hard to be certain, but she thought that these demons ruled by strength, something shown by this demon prostrating itself before her.

"They would kill me for my failings. They must die first."

Survival then. A valid enough reason, though she couldn't see why they would kill it.

"Failings?"

"I . . . informed incorrectly. You were prepared."

So this was the same one that had come to her disguised as Tristan. She could see why the others might kill it, then. If it had gone back to the others and told them that she was completely unprepared for the shapechangers to attack, it was almost entirely its fault that they had fallen into her trap.

They started passing by people once more and none of them reacted to the demon. It was a little terrifying, seeing how closely these creatures had walked amongst people without their knowledge. She was glad that the army camp back south already knew about them.

"One last question then. How many of you remain and how strong are they?"

"Many, most, went to the park. The oldest of the elders remains. However, many escaped."

She could hear fear in its voice, now human and very much readable as a human emotion. Mulling over this last bit of information, she realised she might have been completely wrong in her assumption that there were no stronger demons in the city. However, from what she could tell, these demons didn't really have any combat-based abilities. At least, none that were flashy.

During the attack on the park, they had simply swarmed and tried to use the strength of their bodies to overwhelm. If it had been the flying demons that could often teleport, the ones that had killed Delphi, it would have been a different fight entirely.

Could they take a Silver rank shapechanger?

Perhaps. Ember and her against one Silver shapechanger. It might be possible, especially with their combined healing. She had no doubt that it would have strong abilities for what its classes were based around, as well as attributes that were much better than her own. Fortunately, she had all six.

She was brought out of thought as the demon stopped.

"There."

It pointed to a house further down the street and Zalia couldn't help notice that there were no people around. If this had been where the shapechangers lived, then most of the people that had come here or had been here had probably suffered a fate similar to the man they had found this demon standing over.

Zalia looked at Ember, a question in her expression.

She summoned her sword as Ember stabbed the demon in the leg. It screeched and tried to avoid Zalia's strike as it dropped to one knee. Her strike took its arm off rather than its head, yet Ember was already following up with her shield, smashing it in the head for the second time that day. It dropped back and Zalia's sword slid through its face and into the stone beneath ending the battle.

It was a prime example of a creature that had bonded neither vitality nor resilience as attributes. It was fast and strong, but pinned between two people who were equally quick, it didn't last long.

She found no joy in killing the demon, no sense of victory. It was perhaps even cruel of them to do what they had done in getting its hopes up. Unfortunately for the demon, it was just as she had tried to explain to Aylie. There was no need to find joy in doing what had to be done, yet it needed to be done all the same. Had this demon been raised in another place or society, maybe it would have been different. There was nothing to be done for it now, however. It had killed and would kill again, given the chance.

"Ready?"

"As ready as I'll ever be. You think it might be a Silver rank as well?"

Zalia nodded.

"Yeah. At the least. Doubt it's Gold or it could probably have taken down the town by itself through simple strength alone. I doubt it has many if any combat-related abilities so we might be able to take it."

Zalia hadn't actually used Protection of the Wilds since it had become Bronze rank. There hadn't been any time when she could have used it efficiently, considering its mana cost, yet she strongly considered it now.

They approached the house, weapons at the ready and both wearing their separate sets of armour. They must have looked like spirits of nature, Zalia an almost ethereal creature made of wood and shadow, Ember a solid bastion of rock and fire.

Deciding to do a little bit of scouting, Zalia walked straight through the wall to the side of the door.

Inside was a dimly lit room with only flickering candles for light. It was enough for her to see by, however, as three figures sat on what may as well have been thrones at the far end of the room. There were no other demons in the room, but three might be more than they could handle. They were wearing no disguise and wore thin decorative strips of cloth that must have denoted rank. The central one was holding a staff that glowed with power. An heirloom.

? - Silver rank.

They all looked up simultaneously as she entered.

"Interloper."

They spoke as one, their voices varied yet in unison.

She stepped right back through the wall.

"Three, in there, though I could only see the central one's rank, which is Silver."

She sent an image of the room to Ember.

"Want to go for it?"

Zalia considered quickly, knowing they only had a little time to make a decision. The one thing that swayed her decision to fight was the damage that this creature could do if it decided to.

"Let's go."

She ran straight back through the wall but this time with her bow. She shot the central one in the chest with an arrow, and it didn't even try to move out of the way. The arrow only dipped half the length of the arrowhead into the demon's chest before stopping.

Zalia ran left, phasing through another wall and then went straight. Her aim was to get behind the demon.

She heard the sound of wood shattering as Ember must have run straight through the door.

Switching her bow to blade, she jumped through the wall on her left once more and swept her blade through the neck of the left-hand demon as she found herself right next to it. It shattered into a fine mist, then formed back.

What the hell?

It turned and swiped at her, barely missing as she dodged backwards.

Ember was busy engaging the other demon of unknown rank, illusions perhaps, while the Silver rank one had its eyes closed as if in deep focus. Not wanting to take any further risks, Zalia cast Protection of the Wilds.

Active 2 - Protection of the Wilds - spell - area - counter-execute.
Tin - You call upon the protection of the wilds. You and nearby allies are protected by a biome-specific shield and are subjected to a moderate heal-over-time effect. The heal-over-time heals exponentially more based on how low the target's health is and remains until the shield is broken.
Iron - Protection of the Wilds now has a more ethereal and moving visage. You and allies within a shield created by this ability may still see and move as normal. Additionally, you may enhance this ability with a single effect replicable by the Iron rank ability of Herbal Magic.
Bronze - Upon activating Protection of the Wilds, you and your allies within the shields are not only healed over time, but the healing effect becomes more potent as the shield absorbs damage. The shield's resilience increases with the amount of healing it provides, creating a symbiotic relationship between protection and restoration.
Mana - Very high mana.
Cooldown - 6 hours.

A thin ethereal light layered itself over both Ember and her, providing a protective layer that immediately began pulsing with a healing light. Taking a moment, Zalia pushed Healing Presence into the demon in front of her and found . . . nothing. An illusion after all.

She tried to shove past it but found herself pushed back as it scored lines through her newly formed defence. Backing up quickly, she met back with Ember closer to the front of room.

"Give up, interloper," the three said in unison.

Zalia initiated mental communication with Ember.

"They're illusions, yet they can harm us easily enough."

Ember nodded and they changed tactics a little.

Seeing that she still had some mana, Zalia applied Hunter's Mark to all three of the enemies and began casting some rituals of her own. Ember ran forward and for a short time, held back both illusions. She fought as if she were on the level of both her enemies, turning away strikes, twisting her body so any hit was deflected rather than causing severe damage.

A fire engulfed the demons as Zalia finished casting the cursed flame ritual, its effect increasing as she consolidated the heat of the flames into the bodies they burned on using the manipulation element of Heat Resistance.

Ember failed to dodge a strike, long claw marks forming in the ethereal shield over her.

Zalia cast a protective ritual on Ember using Dodge-vine, then used Fight or Flight and ran straight past the two illusions. They tried to grab at her to stop her passage, yet with the ability active, they moved slowly enough that she dodged with ease. Sword in hand, Zalia attacked the Silver demon, breaking its reverie.

Her bow was unable to inflict much damage to it but her blade cut a long wound straight across the chest of the demon, enough to force its eyes open.

It hissed in frustration as the glow from its staff faltered.

The glow started up again but Zalia pushed the attack.

It was slow, almost sluggish compared to her even once Fight or Flight ended. She had no doubt in her mind that it had neither Dexterity nor Strength bonded. Unfortunately, despite how many times she managed to cut it, the demon didn't seem to become very injured. Even the cuts she made, glowing with the burning starlight, looked as if they were healing.

The fire that blazed across the demon barely even disturbed it, and Zalia began to get frustrated.

She needed Ember to be up here with her to harm it, yet she was busy with the illusions. The illusions, controlled by the staff?

Zalia hopped forward, cutting at the arm holding the staff and as it hissed in pain, she dropped the sword and ripped the staff from its grip.

She knew the illusions had gone as heavy footfalls sounded from behind, quickly followed by Ember charging past and body slamming the demon into, then through, a wall. Zalia followed behind and together, they repeatedly stabbed the demon as it tried to get to it feet.

It wasn't done yet, though.

Its form shifted and changed into that of some monstrous beast, with a thick hide, two beady eyes, and six legs, three on each side, sticking out like those of a spider. Its arms ended not with hands but with large blades. Both Zalia and Ember quickly backed away and yet, something seemed off to Zalia.

There was no need to risk fighting that thing in close combat, even if it was another illusion like she suspected. Its other illusions had been real enough to harm them, after all. Luckily, she had regenerated enough mana to cast the strongest of her spells.

Nature's Wrath flared to life, two stone golems ripping themselves free of the walls and grabbing onto the arms of the demon. Controlling the stone of the house around them, Zalia ripped it apart and began to bury the demon alive.

CHAPTER THIRTY-EIGHT

Just Die

Zalia

Stone crumbled and compressed, turning from dust to stone once more as the pressure exerted forced it into a ball. Zalia heated it as much as she could, the stone beginning to glow with a molten light. It was about to liquify when she came close to running out of mana and let the spell drop, the half sphere of glowing rock slowly cooling in the breeze.

The house around them had been torn down, the pieces of wood that were once a part of their structure strewn across the foundation. The building no longer existed, the tiled roof and stone walls now part of the large chunk that now buried the elder demon inside.

Using the stone manipulation she had outside of Nature's Wrath, Zalia started to dig up the demon at a pace much slower than the one with which she had buried it. After a minute of stone seeming to melt and flow away, she finally revealed the demon and . . . it was still alive.

It had a compressed body, scorched with the inside of its chest visible to the open air. Yet its eyes were open and it took ragged, painful breaths. As she watched, its scorched skin began to flake away and its wounds started healing over.

"Just fucking die!"

She cut at its neck, the sword cutting only a few centimetres in. She cut again, and again. A fourth time. A fifth strike and its head was finally parted from its body.

She stepped back, her armour coated with its blood. Ember stepped up behind her and laid a hand on her shoulder.

"It's done."

Yet, it wasn't done. As she watched, the neck of the creature began to regrow a head, skin and bone slowly forming from nothing. The regenerative powers of this demon were absurd. Were all normal Silver rank beings like this? She had only seen a few other real Silver rank beings die, the corrupted captain that Tristan had killed being one of them. That man must not have had both resilience and vitality as this demon did. The six-legged bear in the north might have, though, and that had died much easier. Perhaps it had only vitality and not resilience. It would explain how the rockfall had injured it so much yet not killed it. The combination of both attributes, perhaps in addition to an ability around survival, resulted in a very hard-to-kill being.

This time, Ember stepped forward. She stabbed through the still open wound in its chest and impaled the heart of the creature, then left the sword there. Slowly, the healing came to a stop.

> **'Druidic Bow, Blessed by Starlight' has ascended to Bronze rank.**

Zalia took her helmet off with bloody gauntlets, almost unconsciously cleansing her armour using a mixture of fire and stone manipulation.

Perhaps she should have used Kill Shot, a natural ability for this situation, especially considering its execution nature. It just hadn't occurred to her, though. She didn't mind either way, happy that her heirloom had ascended. She would check it out once they were back at the farm.

"I'm going to burn it."

Ember nodded her agreement and Zalia manipulated heat from the surroundings into the body until it caught ablaze. It took a while after that for the heat to actually affect the resilient body, but it eventually managed to reduce it to ash. A little manipulation later had the body buried in stone.

She stepped over and picked up the staff she had discarded on the ground after ripping it from the demon's hands.

> **Illusory Mage Staff (Heirloom) - Silver rank.**

She already had a few clues as to what it did, yet found it wasn't exactly the item for her. She neither wanted to nor felt that she would be able to bond with it. Perhaps it would change to something more fitting if she could bond it, but thought it would be better to give to someone else, Aylie perhaps.

Her heart slowed, the adrenaline of the fight gradually fading from her body. She needed to go check on Boreal and Aylie, yet could feel through her bond that at least Boreal was fine. If that were the case, Aylie probably was too. What they really needed to do was leave and find help for the city, someone that would be able to protect them from what was coming. If this elder had been a combat-focused one, they probably wouldn't have stood a chance. She couldn't imagine fighting something that was equally resilient yet stronger and faster, with powers and martial abilities. Well, she didn't need to imagine that. She had seen Larel fight as both a Silver and Gold ranker. With Boreal's help the three of them could perhaps fight one such creature. Any more would be too much.

They left the shattered remains of the house, walking back through the city with armour stored away. She didn't need to help Ember clean her own armour, the aura of fire enough to burn away any blood and gore that stuck to it.

"That thing was bloody tough."

Zalia nodded.

"I'm pretty sure you're along the same train of thought as I am at the moment. We need to get someone stronger here immediately."

"Want to leave earlier than we planned?"

Zalia thought it over. It might be wise for them to do just that. Ember could use her ability to help feed the people for the day, Zalia could set up a living ritual to help the farmland grow, and then they could go.

Deciding the walk was as good a time as any, Zalia looked over the abilities that her bow and sword combination heirloom had gained upon reaching Bronze rank.

Druidic Bow, Blessed by Starlight (Blessed Heirloom) - Deeply bonded Bronze rank.

Tin - Arrows fired from this bow gain a powerful seeking effect.

Iron - When this bow is drawn without an arrow nocked, a Starlight arrow with the 'Starlit' effect will be summoned in its place.

Bronze - Upon firing an arrow, you become invisible and can move slightly faster for a short time.

Druidic Blade, Blessed by Starlight (Blessed Heirloom) - Deeply bonded Bronze rank.

Tin - Druidic Blade, Blessed by Starlight is magically sharp and remains so permanently.

Iron - When wielded by you, Druidic Blade, Blessed by Starlight gains the 'Starlit' effect.

Bronze - After parrying an attack with this blade, your next strike will be infused with a powerful cosmic force.

It seemed like both blade and bow were evolving in a way that promoted a more reactionary and distanced fighting style. It was somewhat counterintuitive to how she was sometimes forced to fight, yet would allow her to fight more how she preferred. From a distance, with a bow. With two abilities now based on parrying enemies, she would be able to hit pretty damn hard. It was somewhat reminiscent of how she liked to set up for fights. Prepare and strike when the time was right. Obviously, that wasn't always possible and she sometimes got carried away, like she just had. Running in there had probably been a stupid idea, despite it turning out well.

As they walked, she also had a look over her few ability rank-ups.

> **Congratulations! Hunter's Mark has reached Bronze 3.**
> **Congratulations! Fight or Flight has reached Bronze 4.**
> **Congratulations! Hunter class has reached Bronze 3.**
> **Congratulations! Nature's Wrath has reached Bronze 5.**
> **Congratulations! Protection of the Wilds has gained two levels, reaching Bronze 3.**
> **Congratulations! Druid class has gained two levels, reaching Bronze 3.**

Happy with any progress at all, she was particularly happy to rank up the Druid class a little. Being bonded with wisdom, each level brought a bit more mana for her to use. Something that had only really become necessary in recent times. She really needed to use Protection of the Wilds more often. Though . . . it being the ability to rank up last and evolve might yield something powerful for her.

She hadn't really decided whether or not it was a good idea to manipulate that or not. Did the purposeful evolution of key abilities yield greater results, or was it better to let the ones she used the least evolve by the simple reasoning of them being the ones she used the least?

Thoughts for another day.

They arrived at the park, now farm, where both Aylie and Boreal were playing in the sun. Boreal must have sensed Zalia's emotions and realised the danger was over.

Tristan was there once more, thankfully, as they needed to tell him of their plan to leave today instead.

Stepping down the slope towards the park, he saw them approaching and came up to meet them.

"Hey, Tristan."

"Zalia, Ember."

Zalia looked at Ember.

"We're planning to leave today instead," Ember said.

"What, why?"

"We encountered one of the demons and actually managed to get some answers out of them. The right of preference is what we thought, the city is now open to any 'clan.' You can expect stronger attacks to be coming, so we need to get someone stronger here to help you immediately."

Tristan seemed to age a decade, the weight of responsibility bowing his shoulders.

"I see."

Zalia felt a little bad as Ember delivered the news. Last she had seen Tristan, before the rituals had gone off, he had been living a wonderfully relaxed life as a baker in his own shop. The joy in his eyes from those days had long since disappeared as he struggled to keep his town safe.

Zalia gave him a hug.

"I know it's hard. I wish you could just go back to your bakery and make us some nice loaves of bread. You'll get back there, I promise. We'll get you back there."

She felt the tear drop onto her shoulder and she held him even tighter. He'd probably not had anyone to be vulnerable with since this had all begun. He had to be the strong one, the leader and guardian of the people. Should they see him lose hope, what should they feel?

The warm and healing power of Ember washed over both of them and Tristan began crying for real. It was at this moment that Zalia realised Ember's power didn't just *heal* emotional wounds, it gave space for them to heal on their own.

In this case, that meant opening up Tristan's emotions while he was in a safe place where he could deal with them.

She held him as his tears took their course, and when he had some semblance of control once more, Zalia let him go.

"Don't worry too much, we'll get help back here before you know it. Just hold out for two weeks, alright? That's all you have to do. After that, you'll have all the help you'll need."

He seemed to take solace in the promise. Now all Zalia had to do was keep it.

CHAPTER THIRTY-NINE

Terror of Rank

Zalia

Zalia stood to the side as the food Ember had summoned was handed out to those in need. She did her part, cycling her healing through all of the people that came close, watching as they stood a little straighter, cuts and scrapes healed, and disease was eliminated.

They were a bit off to the side in the park, away from where the food was being grown. Zalia had already set up the living ritual of Manifest and Frozen Heart that would help grow the grains. All they had to do now was finish handing out the food and they could leave. Technically there was no reason for them to have to stay, but Zalia wanted to heal them all as much as she could.

She was feeling a little uneasy. The city was feeling lighter already, as if the sudden decrease in violence and mistrust due to the shapechangers being gone had brought a new light to the streets. The tension that Zalia felt was in complete disregard of that, the source of it being the knowledge that the city was actually a little less safe now. Sure, on the inside it was better off, but the danger from the outside had only really just begun.

And there wasn't really any way to tell if the attack would come that day, the next, or six weeks from then.

Both Boreal and Aylie were nearby too. She had told them they were going to leave sooner than planned, as they needed to get help as soon as possible.

A thought had occurred to her, that she could leave all three of them behind and make the run to Endelbyrn herself. She was self-reliant enough and stealthy enough to be able to manage that and could make the distance even faster than Boreal due to her Mobility passive.

> **Mobility - passive.**
> **Tin - Your speed is increased. Your stamina is less affected by movement.**
> **Iron - You may step on air one time before stepping on a solid surface once more.**
> **Bronze - You are able to step on air three times before resetting this ability. Additionally, you may perform a short-range teleport with a long cooldown. Finally, when travelling long distances, you are able to maintain a fast pace while maintaining your stamina indefinitely.**

The second half of the Bronze rank effect wasn't something that she had ever really needed, but this was the perfect situation for it. She could probably make the distance, especially since she didn't need to sleep for three or four days. Maybe less, she hadn't seen how quick of a pace she could maintain just yet.

It was deep in those thoughts that her eyes got caught on a little black dot in the sky. She only saw it due to her bettered eyesight, managing to spot it past the occasionally crackling dome that protected the city. It was flying above the city, watching closely. It was also something that Zalia recognised, a creature very similar to the one that had killed the collective.

She ran up to Tristan and Ember.

"Hey, hey, we might have a problem."

She pointed to the dot in the sky and they both left the cover of the little pavilion to see. Ember cursed, also recognising it, though Tristan looked confused.

"It's Silver rank, a much more dangerous Silver rank than the other one we killed. This one is built for one thing and that's killing."

Looking around, Zalia knew they had the best odds they could hope to have against such a creature right here. Five Bronze rank people: herself, Ember, Boreal, Tristan, and one of his guards. It was a lot more than they'd had against the shapechanger.

Her hopes that they wouldn't need to fight were dashed as she watched the dot drop from the sky, landing on the dome and sending a crackling ripple across its surface. It punched once, another ripple travelling across the dome. This time it came with an arcing sound and people started to notice. It punched again, a big crack appearing under it.

With a quick check, she knew that both Nature's Wrath and Protection of the Wilds were on cooldown. She did still have the anti-death measure of Healing Presence, however, something she hoped they wouldn't need but was glad to have.

A third punch and the dome shattered, a hole ten metres wide appearing in its surface. The translucent material fell with glittering light even as it dissipated in the air.

Dropping like a rock, the demon fell towards the city. Two glowing arrows rose from the park to meet it, carving a brilliant arc through the air.

It dodged them both, yet a third struck one of the demon's wings. It didn't seem too affected but its course changed, now in a guided descent towards the park even as the hole in the dome slowly repaired behind it.

The people in the park hadn't missed what was happening, fleeing with screams even as death approached. The farmers also fled, running from the centre of the park into the streets beyond. All three of Tristan's guards tried to stay, but he sent away the two Iron rank ones, knowing they would only get themselves killed. Ember sent Aylie off to the house to hide in the still open vault.

Zalia felt her blood pump and adrenaline release even as she shot more arrows towards the demon. Now that she was clued into where the arrows were coming from, no more landed before the demon itself did.

It slammed into the ground next to Zalia at speed, throwing her off her feet with the impact.

Ember, Tristan, and the last guard all moved forward and engaged it in combat, the crystal shards growing from Boreal's back beginning to glow a light blue as she charged Pounce.

Tristan brought his axe down in a brutal strike that was easily dodged, the guard following through with a jab that scratched over the demon's obsidian skin. They both had to immediately go on the defensive as the obscenely quick demon struck back, slapping the sword out of the guard's hand and then slashing at Tristan with its clawed hands.

Ember came at it from behind, but it had already stepped back from the other two and punched her shield so hard it dented as she was thrown back a few steps.

Boreal took her chance and pounced, slamming into the demon's legs and freezing them to the ground even as she raked her claws across its thigh. Bright blood glimmered in the sun, three light claw marks showing on its skin. It must have bonded resilience then, to shrug off Boreal's claws like that.

Taking advantage of its immobility, Zalia shot it and was rewarded with an arrow that sunk very slightly into its shoulder.

The demon managed to grab Boreal before she could retreat from the pounce and threw her across the park. Zalia watched her spin away but didn't worry, as she saw the damage immunity shield from Pounce was still active.

Ember, Tristan, and the guard all made use of the time the demon had taken to throw Boreal and moved in again. With a quick exchange of blows, during which Zalia started casting some protective rituals on her allies, the three managed to cut the demon twice, a thin line of blood visible on its back and chest.

Seeing her casting something, the demon used its teleport to appear right behind her and grab her by the neck. She'd forgotten about that.

She heard a crunch and felt a stab of pain before she felt nothing. A shimmering skin of light appeared over her and a warmth deep in her core expanded, protecting and healing her. Her anti-death measure. It had been so quick.

The demon dropped her limp body to the ground and she heard screaming as the other three fought it. She could feel the pain and worry of her friends through the emotional bond and eventually, felt her body once more.

Her spine finally healed and she stood from the ground, summoning her bow to her hand and rejoining the fight.

The others had managed to cut it a bit deeper, some of the wounds visibly slowing it down now. Boreal pounced once more from a distance and the demon tried to counter it by punching her mid-flight. Its undoing there, though, was that the one-use invulnerability that Boreal gained from Pounce every so often was active, and its punch accomplished nothing. The others took advantage, and Ember managed to stab her blade into an existing cut and through its leg.

It grunted in pain and ripped the blade from its leg before flying upwards. It was trying to escape.

Zalia fired off a few more arrows in an attempt to take it down and then . . . it hit an invisible wall.

A glowing rune came into their vision and a hundred others followed as a large cube appeared around their fight. The Enchanter.

The demon tried to break through this shield just as it had the other, yet found no success. Zalia's arrows found its back and wings, dropping it from the sky.

It landed hard, turning to face them with anger filling its expression. Anger, and what looked like a little fear. Good.

They attacked again, the others pushing the advantage of their numbers.

The demon managed to break the guard's arm and Ember quickly went to assist. It then tried to use the same move on Zalia, but she was ready and teleported away herself, escaping death. Looked like this thing only had one real trick.

The arm was healed already, Ember and Zalia's combined healing enough to fix it in a flash.

From there, the demon grew more desperate as it accrued more wounds. It kept allowing hits to try and take one of them out of the fight but both Zalia and Ember healed any damage it could do.

It was when it ignored one of Tristan's strikes that it finally fell. It tried to grab Ember's head but was blocked by her tattered shield, and Tristan's axe fell down hard on its arm. He managed to cut halfway through and the arm hung limply from its side. From there, the others began to brutalise it. It tried to teleport away and flee the cube once more, but the power of a Barrier Enchanter solely focused on keeping you in was not so easily overcome. It died in that cube, stabbed, hacked, shot, and clawed to death by the five Bronze rankers after its life.

In the aftermath, they were all breathing hard. The fight hadn't taken long, yet each of their hearts beat quickly as they tried to recover some semblance of calm.

Ember came and grabbed Zalia, holding her tight. She didn't think she could imagine the fear Ember must have felt when it had snapped Zalia's spine. She didn't have to imagine, though. She could feel it.

CHAPTER FORTY

Left Behind

Zalia

It was shortly after the fight with the Silver rank demon, and a decision was growing further into certainty in Zalia's mind. As much as she disliked the idea of leaving her friends and family in Ostoss while she went to get help, she even more greatly disliked the idea of Ostoss being destroyed simply because they were too late.

Without the others, Zalia would be quick enough that she might yet be able to get help.

The Barrier Enchanter had come out of hiding after the fight as well, lending no words to the conversation, simply inspecting the dead creature's body before leaving, back to his house.

Zalia didn't pretend to understand the man. They were probably about as different as two people could get while still fighting for the same cause. Much like Ember and Indis, now that she thought about it.

The farmers had slowly come back to the park after the fight had ended, a little scared-looking, but rightfully so. Twice now they had been attacked as they tried to farm the quickly spreading crops.

"Ember."

Ember looked up from where she sat on their bench.

"What's up?"

Zalia tapped her finger on her leg a few times, going over the list of reasons in her head once more before finally making her decision.

"I think I should go to Endelbyrn alone to get help."

Ember stood abruptly, looking confused.

"Why?"

"Because I don't need to sleep much, am very stealthy and am significantly faster than any of you. I can get there in just a few days compared to a week or more of travel."

She could see the gears turning in Ember's head. She could see as Ember tried to come up with counterpoints or any rebuttal to her idea. She also knew that there weren't any or she would have found them. It wasn't a decision she made idly, as she would have actually preferred the others come with her. It just simply wasn't possible this time.

"Can't you see why? You can continue giving out food to the people while I get help as well. It's what is best for Ostoss."

Ember stayed frozen for a few more moments.

"Damnit, Zalia."

"I know."

"Don't you dare get yourself killed out there."

Zalia stepped forward and grabbed Ember in a tight embrace.

"I won't, don't worry. You better all stay safe here too."

"We will."

Zalia finally pulled away, then kissed Ember gently.

"It'll be alright. We can do this."

Ember nodded, a single tear running down her cheek that Zalia wiped away with her thumb.

"*Leaving?*" Boreal asked.

"Yes."

Boreal started to walk towards the city gates far off in the distance but Zalia stopped her with a hand.

"Not this time. I need you to stay with Ember and Aylie."

Boreal stopped and sat, looking at her in confusion.

"*But . . .*"

Zalia knelt down and hugged her furry friend. They had been by each other's side ever since Zalia had found Boreal atop that snowy mountain. Neither had been separated from the other for more than a few hours at most.

"I know, darling, but I need you to protect them both for me. You're big and strong now, and I need you. Can you do that for me?"

Boreal pushed her face into Zalia, almost knocking her over.

"*I'll protect them.*"

Zalia nodded, finding herself crying now. She cupped Boreal's face with both hands and gave her a kiss on the forehead before standing.

She found Aylie in the house, playing around with the walls, decorating them with her Plant Manipulation ability. Boreal and Ember crowded the doorway as Zalia stepped up and sat on the bed beside Aylie.

"I'm going to go get help on my own, Aylie. Boreal and Ember will be here with you."

Aylie looked up sharply.

"What, why?"

"Because I can get there and back much quicker than any of you. I'll be alright, I promise."

Aylie's voice came out nothing but a little whisper.

"It's not you I'm worried for."

Zalia pulled her in close for a hug.

"I need you to stay safe for me."

She looked up at Ember.

"If anything happens, I want you to leave the city. Don't stay and protect it if it isn't possible. All three of you, get as many people as you can and get out."

Ember nodded.

Zalia knew Ember would usually do everything she could to save people, but she also knew she could trust her to protect Aylie and Boreal before anything else.

She stood up, gave Ember one last hug and looked back at Aylie's fearful face, before turning about and leaving.

She found Tristan first, telling him that she was leaving and Ember was staying. He looked surprised but didn't ask questions, though she was sure he would grill Ember about it later.

Then, she went to the city gates and left.

As city streets turned to empty plains, she sped up her pace until she was comfortably running quicker than most people would usually be able to achieve at a sprint, all thanks to Mobility.

She quickly left the city behind as plains turned to forest, back to plains, and back to forest again. Trees flashed by in a blur as her legs pumped, driving her ever towards her westward goal, Endelbyrn.

She knew that Larel was with the army, performing some task or another at the direction of Indis and Faian. However, the two Gold rankers she was hoping to find, Hildebrandt and Matthias, were most likely at Endelbyrn. She knew that the city still stood, thanks to information she had received from Indis when they'd caught up. She would undoubtedly find some strong people there as it had once been the home of the majority of the powerful people in Endaria, though she knew of only two Gold rankers still amongst their ranks.

If there were more, or even higher-ranked members, she had never met or heard of them. So, her hopes lay in getting both Hildebrandt and Matthias to Ostoss as quickly as possible. Perhaps they could even escort the people of Ostoss to the mountain home with Glemp and continue onwards to the war camp after that. Their chances of defeating the demons would be increased considerably with an additional two Gold rankers, and who knew how many other well-trained and high-ranked people in their numbers.

She could still feel both Ember and Boreal over their bonds, the concern, fears, and anxiety that they felt, emotions she shared.

It felt odd being away from them, an experience she found quite strange.

When she had first come to Endaria, it had been after living on her own for many years. During that time she had grown accustomed to her own company, talking very little and socialising even less. She had been comfortable in the wilds by herself more than she had been in cities filled with people making sounds, smells, and other assaults on her senses.

Since then, though, while she still didn't like being in cities, she had become used to the company of others. She had been around Boreal so long and had been through so much with her that it felt wrong to be without her. Additionally, while her relationship with Ember was new, her friendship with her was not. She had met Ember even before Boreal, and while they had not endured Cormaine together, she had still been there for Zalia more than a few times.

So it came that as she ran through the wilds alone, she felt, well, lonely. It was an entirely new experience, one she didn't like at all.

Three days later, Zalia was still running.

She had stopped after the second day to sleep a single hour before waking and beginning her run once more. Strangely, she didn't feel tired or hungry on the surface whatsoever. Her body felt strong and lithe, ready to take on anything as it often did nowadays.

What she did feel, though, was something deep, deep inside. An exhaustion that had nothing to do with her body. It was as if the Mobility passive had its own separate limitations to her body that would eventually rise to the surface and make itself known.

That eventuality felt far enough off, however, that she would be able to make it to Endelbyrn.

She was half expecting the glowing city to appear over every next hill or past each clump of trees. It had been a long while since she had last been to the city, though she remembered the way quite well due to her increased mental abilities and the fact that she had lived there for quite some time.

She hadn't had to avoid any demons so far, only needing to annihilate a pack of the Tin flying demons with a few quick rituals. Other than that, it had been the simple and boring task of running day in and day out. Step after step, focusing on nothing other than where her next foot would land.

After another hour of her extended running, Endelbyrn finally made itself visible over the horizon. It was much as she remembered it, tall, crenellated walls made of a stone that glittered in the sunlight and a keep far within that absorbed the light, only to emit it during the night.

The big difference she first noticed, though, was the huge hole in the outer wall and the light streams of smoke that drifted from the city proper into the sky above. The keep itself looked fine, thankfully.

She was a little concerned for the state of things, hoping that she hadn't come all of this way for nothing. If it turned out that the Morning's Shade had indeed fallen, she would have to run all the way back and come up with an entirely new plan on the way.

She approached the city and after a little bit of a stumble, managed to convince her legs to drop into a walk. She felt like she had been running forever.

The gates were wide open and she walked straight through into the city beyond, finding it . . . completely silent. It was an odd change to what she remembered of entering the city. Usually, it was one of the loudest places she had the misfortune of walking into, but it felt dead now, without the sounds of bustling city life.

She walked past some houses that were torn apart, smoking remains of structures and even some bodies lay in the streets. Some of them were demons and some were not.

Her path led up towards the keep, where she knew she would find the people she was looking for. Where she *hoped* she would find them.

The entrance was much as she remembered. A carefully cultivated garden with a path leading through it came to a large set of double doors set into the base of the central spire. All around, many other spires rose into the sky, connected to the main one and each other by walkways both ground level and between higher floors.

It was all as she remembered it, as well as the two guards that stood by the front doors.

She frowned, realising she didn't have the little icon they had given to her when she had joined that let her enter usually. She would just have to convince them.

"Hey there, mind if I come in?"

Her attempt at sounding casual came out a little tense.

One of the guards drew their dual sabres and she recognised him with a jolt. It was one of the men who had been guarding the door the very first day she had arrived.

"Hey! You're alive!!"

"Stay where you are!"

Zalia sighed.

"Hey, you really don't have to be so—"

She cut off as the other guard stepped forward and grabbed her by the arm. They roughly pulled her arm up and cut into her palm.

She suffered the indignity in silence, knowing what exactly they were testing for. She wondered if it would become a cultural practice to cut one's palm before entering a building after all this was over.

"Happy now?"

The guard dropped her arm and scratched at their head.

"Sorry about that."

"Ah, no apologies needed. I understand why. Can I go in and see Hildebrandt now?"

The guard stepped out of her way but the other did not.

"You said you knew me?"

"Yeah! You were here on my first day."

Then she frowned. The guard that had given her food when she had been imprisoned in the tower by Hidey had been the other of the two guards that were here on her first day. She wondered idly if this guy had been in on it too.

"Hey, yeah I think I do recognise you. Zalia, right? Aren't you meant to be dead?"

"Loooooong story. One I'd like to tell Hildebrandt and Matthias first."

He finally stepped out of the way.

"Alright, in you go."

Zalia smiled at him.

"Thanks."

Help

Zalia

As Zalia stepped into the floor-level room of the main spire, she was utterly shocked by how unchanged it all was. The kingdom was being invaded, towns were empty, Ostoss was in complete disarray, and yet here, it was like nothing had happened at all.

Pushing away the momentary confusion, she quickly stepped up the main stairwell into the spire. What followed was a long and confusing path between spiralling stairs, walkways, and hallways. It was as seemingly random as she remembered it and she had to stop and ask directions not two but three times. It was in asking these directions that she did start to notice little changes.

People looked exhausted, bags under their eyes and hair a mess, armour or weapons a little uncared for. It was far better than most of the kingdom had suffered though, so she didn't feel too bad. She was sure many people would have much preferred being a little tired or having a bad night's sleep. It was better than dead friends and family with the chance of meeting the same fate any given day yourself.

When she finally found herself at the office belonging to Hildebrandt, Gold ranker and one of the leaders of the Morning's Shade, she drew in a deep breath and prepared herself. She had to make a good sell with her next words or Ostoss would suffer a terrible fate.

Raising her hand, she knocked twice lightly on the door.

"Come in."

She opened the door and stepped in.

Looking completely unfit for the position, a giant of a woman in her plate armour sat on a small stool behind a desk. She was trying to write something down on a piece of paper with a wooden instrument that must have been a pen.

"It's good to see you again, Hildebrandt."

The woman stood up in alarm.

"Zalia? What in the worlds are *you* doing here?"

Zalia sighed. Here she went again, explaining everything that happened. *Again.*

"I didn't die, I was pulled through the portal to Cormaine where I survived. Then I spent some time there trying not to die, then I found a way back, then I spent some time here trying not to die *and* trying to help people. Then I found myself at Ostoss with a bunch of people who *really* need help not dying, and here I am."

Hildebrandt nodded twice to herself, but was looking at Zalia suspiciously.

"No, I'm not a shapechanger, yes, your guards at the gate tested me. I'd love to get to why I'm here since we have very little time."

She sat back down again, gesturing to the chair opposite her.

"Alright then, let's get to it. I am glad you're alive, by the way."

Zalia sat down opposite her, stretching her sore legs out with a groan.

"Ahhh. I'll bet I'm more glad that you're alive. Here's the basics of it. Ostoss is in shit, deep shit. There was a clan of shapechangers in the process of destabilising the town so that they could take their sweet time destroying and possibly eating the population. Me and mine went there and ended up killing ninety percent of them, and now they apparently lost something called 'the right of preference.' That basically opens up the town to attack from every single demon everywhere."

She checked again, as she had often over the past days, on Boreal and Ember's emotions. Finding the faint link, she could feel that they were somewhat calm, though definitely both a little anxious and stressed as well.

Hildebrandt leaned forward, metal elbow guards grinding against the desk.

"Alright, I can see the problem. Why are you here?"

Zalia looked her in the eyes.

"It's simple. They are guarded basically by a thin sheet of paper over the city and a couple Bronze ranked guards. I need you to send at least one Gold ranker, more if you can, to protect the city. If you don't, it's likely that most of those people will die."

Hildebrandt examined her closely, as if looking for any kind of lie or deceit. Zalia waited. She had a little past experience talking to the woman and thought it best to be completely blunt and open in her words. Hildebrandt didn't seem like the kind of person to faff around with fluffy words and pointed meanings.

Hildebrandt pursed her lips, then nodded.

"Alright, fuck it. We were thinking of abandoning Endelbyrn anyways. Might as well head somewhere we can actually do some good, we're not exactly getting much done here in the ass end of Endaria."

Zalia blinked.

"You can just decide that? What about Matthias?"

Hildebrandt leant back.

"Matthias? I'll be damned if I know where he is. I've got the twins, who are Silver rank now, a couple other Silver rankers, and about thirty Bronze rankers. I'm the only Gold ranker in the Morning's Shade now with the Hidden imprisoned, Larel having left to join the army, and Matthias vanishing into thin air."

"Matthias is *gone*? That's all we have? I swear there were a lot more out there."

"We've lost a lot, Zalia. Matthias, another Gold ranker, and I were out fighting an Emerald elemental when the rituals went off. The damn thing went insane, killed our friend, and then sunk into the ground once the rituals were done. I haven't seen Matthias since he left that battlefield. We had a lot of people in the field when shit went down, and not a whole lot of them have made their way back here."

Zalia sat silently, considering. There had been a few hundred people in the Morning's Shade when she had joined. Now they were reduced to what, less than fifty?

"So you'll all come to help?"

"Damn right, we will. As a group, we're able to kill pretty much anything out there, I'm certain of it."

Zalia wasn't so sure. She knew of one thing that they wouldn't be able to kill. Well, maybe they could, but she wasn't certain of that fact.

Either way, she could see that this would be how the human race survived. Put all the powerful people in the kingdom together in one spot, protect them against the corruption, and then gradually cleanse the kingdom of all the demons that had invaded it.

It would be a long, long task, but for once, she could see it actually being possible. Now they just had to figure out how to deal with that damned thousand-eyed monstrosity that sat in the capital. She knew that the nature gods could easily take care of it if they moved their asses into gear but, well, she also knew that wouldn't happen anytime soon.

Zalia stood in the marshalling yard, the scene unfolding before her much like one she remembered from so long ago only on an entirely different scale. Back then, she had gone on a mission with twelve people, now there were around fifty. Fifty of Endaria's most powerful people, all of them with classes specifically chosen for the art of killing. While usually not something that could be considered truly good in nature, when it came to saving their kingdom, it could become so.

From where she stood, Zalia could see the twins who were as much a part of the shadows as she could remember. The last time she had seen them, they had summoned a large shadowy storm cloud that had rained acid down upon the Gold ranked elemental that had ripped itself out of the mine further south. They had a way of combining their magic together, much as Those Born of Heat and Stone did but on a deeper level. That way, their magic was much stronger than their rank might lead one to assume.

That day, they had been Bronze ranked, helping to take down a Gold ranked elemental. Now they were Silver, and she was looking forward to seeing what kind of power they would have now.

Hildebrandt was standing nearby, directing operations as people hustled about. Using Aura Observation, Zalia could tell that she was actually close to ranking up. She knew that Hildebrandt had spent some time before the rituals had gone off helping to take down Emerald rank elementals and it had apparently paid off. While Zalia had never seen her actually fight, she knew that anyone who was Gold, and close to Emerald, would be a force to be reckoned with. She might even stand a chance by herself against the worst of the demons.

Despite how quickly Hildebrandt had organised things, Zalia couldn't help but feel impatient. She had arrived the day before, but Hildebrandt had insisted they wait until morning to begin packing. Now that they had started, Zalia just wanted to run all the way back to Ostoss without waiting so she could make sure the others would remain safe while the group travelled.

Letting the impatience get to her, Zalia moved towards Hildebrandt. She had to push her way past a couple people busy packing bags and even a few carts that looked to be self-powered.

"Hey, I wanted to ask. Would it be possible for me to return to Ostoss immediately with just the twins? I fear with how long all of these people will take to get there that it will be too late. The twins and I can get there much quicker."

Hildebrandt looked to think for a short moment before nodding her assent.

"Sounds like a good precaution. Go."

Zalia nodded and looked around for the twins, finding them already standing just behind her.

"Ready?"

They looked at her, their only answer a nod so small as to be almost imperceptible. She couldn't actually recall ever hearing them talk.

"Right, wonderful. Let's go."

She went slowly enough as they picked their way back out through the city. The damage to the city was somewhat superficial, so she wondered where everyone had gone. There wasn't a single person outside of the keep as far as she could tell; it seemed that the entire population had abandoned the city or . . . something worse.

If the majority of the Morning's Shade had been out on some task or another when the ritual happened, as Zalia knew they had, what had the people who were left done? Larel, Indis, and Ember had all left, so had they all gone south, or perhaps north?

She would have to ask Hildebrandt about it later, if the woman even knew. As Zalia knew, she hadn't been in the city at the time either.

Once they left the city bounds, she began speeding up her pace until she was travelling at a comfortable speed once more.

* * *

The entire journey back, it almost felt like she was travelling by herself. The twins were so hard to see most of the time that if she wasn't looking for them, she couldn't see them at all. The only time she actually saw them was while they slept.

While they definitely slept less than Ember and Aylie did, they still had to sleep a lot more often than Zalia did. That meant that the journey back was somewhat slower than it had been getting to Endelbyrn. It took five days of travelling, and even with the increased hours of rest, the beginning of burnout that Zalia had felt while travelling to Endelbyrn made itself much more apparent on the way back. When she ran, her legs were sore and heavy, each step much harder than it should have been. She would have expected Healing Presence to take care of that pain, but it apparently wasn't something that it could heal.

It was the third day that she actually got to see the twins in action as Silver rank beings. They spotted one of the larger flying demons that was Bronze rank, and where Zalia would have thought about whether it was worth fighting or not, the twins performed a piece of joint magic, summoning shadowy arms from the treetops that grabbed the demon and tore it apart, limb from limb, in a matter of moments. Zalia was certain she could have won such a fight as well, but it would have taken her considerably longer.

The power of two Silver rank beings performing joint magic was not something to laugh at. It made her wonder how powerful they would be in greater ranks. As Gold rankers, Emerald, or even Diamond should they make it that far. What feats would they be capable of achieving?

On the fifth day, Zalia began to feel a sense of dread. They were only an hour away by her measure, yet the feeling built within her—until she realised that it wasn't coming from her at all. The emotion was being sent to her by Ember.

She was still too far away to communicate with Boreal despite their deep bond, and the emotion made her speed up despite the pain in her legs. There was no way to tell what the feeling of dread meant, yet she was suddenly glad that she had decided to leave earlier with the twins. It may have yet turned out to be a worthwhile precaution after all.

A few minutes out from the city, she dismissed all notifications so she could focus entirely on what was to come.

> **Congratulations! Mobility has gained four levels, reaching Bronze 7.**

Still running, she was finally able to communicate with Boreal through their bond. She sent a questioning feeling through and received back an image of a group of creatures trying to break through the dome. They were Bronze by the looks of it, about twenty of the same flying creatures Zalia had seen the twins tear apart just days before. The dread faded away, and she actually smiled. It would be ok.

The twins sprinted on ahead, faster than she was by just a bit.

By the time she burst from the edge of the forested clump she had been in and saw the city ahead, things were already well in hand. It looked as if the shadow of the forest was rising up over the city to swallow the demons as they tried to flee for their lives. One by one, they were torn to pieces, until only a few were left. The few managed to escape, but Zalia could see the flickering shadowy forms of the twins running after them, on the hunt.

Zalia didn't worry about giving chase with them, knowing they would have it well in hand. She could feel the flood of relief coming through from Ember and Boreal, her own bouncing right back down the bond towards them.

The ground went by in a blur as she sprinted towards the city, trying to figure out where Boreal had sent that image from. It felt like it had come from the park, so that is where she went.

She ran through city streets that were still filled with people. People that were actually looking a little better than they had. The buildings and smooth stone street beneath her flew by as she found herself running down the bounds of the beautiful green park. At the centre now stood a wonderful little farm, the crops having been propagated and grown further still. Happiness and relief melted away the frozen worry from her veins. Ostoss would be ok.

Her eyes finally found Ember and Boreal, standing near their little living house by the wooden bridge that crossed the stream. That stream was now flowing, with a young mage nearby using some type of spell to create the flowing water.

Her sore legs ached as Zalia slowed down to a walk, striding straight up to Ember and hugging her tightly. It had only been a little more than a week, yet she had missed her quite a lot.

"Hey."

Ember hugged her right back.

"You're sweaty. And you stink."

Zalia laughed a bright happy laugh, not disagreeing at all. She let go and knelt down to hug Boreal as well, receiving a deep bass-y purr in return. At least Boreal didn't complain about how she smelled.

"I missed you a lot too, little one."

She heard Boreal huff and laughed again, before sighing into Boreal's thick fur. Moments later, she felt an impact on her side as Aylie latched onto her.

"You came back!"

Zalia put one of her arms around Aylie and hugged her tight.

"I did, and I think we're gonna be ok."

CHAPTER FORTY-TWO

Responsibility

Zalia

Zalia and Tristan stood atop the walls of Ostoss as the remainder of Hildebrandt's people moved through the gate. They had needed to wait for another three days before the group had arrived, a short enough wait now that the twins were there to protect the town.

The original reason Zalia had come north was to try convince Glemp's people to come down and help out with the war. While she hadn't managed to do that, she felt that the remainder of the Morning's Shade would be an equally powerful ally for what was to come.

They needed to take back the capital and kill or disable the thousand-eyed monster that now lived there. That would mean fighting through a city filled with undead, if Zalia was right, along with fighting off the corrupting aura that would slowly kill them. Her own aura ability protected her from it to a degree, yet it was the power of Ro-ak, otherwise known as Nateysta, spirit and god of mysteries and forests, that had held back that aura enough for her to actually function.

Both the starlight wolf and the heat and stone spirit in the mountain would be able to do the same, if they could ever be convinced to actually take part in the fight.

For now, though, she was happy enough that she had managed to get one group of people to help, even if it did seem like they had been on the verge of doing so anyways.

"What now?" Tristan asked from beside her.

Zalia pushed off the battlements and turned about to look down on the group of powerful fighters milling about.

"I'm not sure. How has the Enchanter done with integrating my ritual into the shield?"

A small smile flickered across Tristan's still weary face.

"Failed to accomplish anything at all, except exuding an abundance of frustration."

Zalia smiled too, though she wasn't exactly happy it hadn't worked out yet. If the Enchanter managed to copy the effects, it would be a great boon to the town. It was just slightly amusing that the Enchanter, despite all of his disdain for her type of rituals, couldn't copy the effects.

"Maybe I should go see if I can help at all."

Tristan turned about to face the city interior as well.

"Maybe, though you've already done a lot for us."

"Perhaps not as much as you think. I want them to go south to help the army retake the capital."

Tristan sighed.

"I thought as much. I've been thinking about what we can do to protect these people. Come with you to the army camp? It feels weird and . . . wrong to abandon Ostoss after we've finally managed to settle things a little. With Ember's help, people seem to be looking a little better. It won't be long until the farm grows big enough to feed us all, with more farmers flocking to help by the day."

Zalia had given it some thought as well. It would be a good opportunity for them to evacuate, if there ever was one. A population this size on the move would need quite a large number of people to protect them. The Morning's Shade would be the perfect group for that. They could go north to the mountain and take refuge with Zen and the others there.

"Maybe one or two of the Silver rank members can stay here to help you defend, once the Enchanter has the shield up and running?"

They only had sixteen Silver rank members in the group, so this reduction would impact their strength. Saying that, though, there were still enough strong fighters that they could make an impact either way.

"That might work, are you sure they would be ok with that?"

Zalia chewed at her bottom lip, considering. Best to ask.

"I'll go ask now. I don't even know that they will come down to help the army."

Tristan nodded.

"I should come greet our saviours as well, I guess."

Together, they came down from the walls to meet Hildebrandt. They had to push through a few people but finally managed to get to the front of the group.

"There you are, Zalia. Want to lead us somewhere a little more private?"

Hildebrandt was looking about at the wide-eyed refugees and townspeople who were watching the large group. Whispers of "Morning's Shade" were spreading through the crowd. Zalia had forgotten that they were a group of people held in a somewhat mysterious light to most of Endaria. Not a lot of people had met a member, let alone knew one properly.

Tristan gestured down the street.

"Please, this way."

Hildebrandt started moving in the pointed direction, the crowd moving out of the way.

"And you are?"

"Tristan, currently in charge of Ostoss's guard."

Hildebrandt patted him gently on the shoulder.

"From what Zalia has told me, you should be commended on your defence of Ostoss, considering how little you have to defend it with. Well done."

Zalia saw Tristan's hands twitch like he meant to salute.

"Thank you, si . . . Thank you."

She smiled. A touch of authority and he fell back into his old military ways. Some things weren't so easily unlearnt.

Hildebrandt looked up at the protective dome as they walked.

"And who is responsible for that?"

Zalia followed her gaze.

"A Silver rank Enchanter, Barrier specialisation. It's quite impressive I have to say."

"I'd agree, I can't see a single flaw in it. That takes quite a bit of expertise to accomplish."

Zalia coughed.

"He is . . . let's just say, obsessed with symmetry."

Hildebrandt looked down at her, stepping around a patch of filth on the road.

"Ah, well, that explains it. I've met a few who go that route with their enchantments. It makes for quite perfect pieces, but their ability to adapt is lacking."

"Oh, really? That explains why he has been having trouble integrating my own ritual into his own work. Do you have any advice around that?"

Hildebrandt snorted.

"Yeah, don't even try. I've seen your rituals, I can't think of any two less suited types of magic to try and make work together."

"That's . . . unfortunate."

"It is what it is. There is a time and place for both types of magic."

While she trusted Hildebrandt's knowledge of magic, both as a high-ranking person and as a leader of one of the most well-informed groups in the kingdom, she had to disagree. Hildebrandt seemed to imply that it wasn't impossible and they should give up, but Zalia felt like there must be a way. Nature was certainly chaotic, whereas the Enchanter's magic was orderly, yet there must be something that both shared, a bridge to make them work together.

She gave it some thought as they walked, losing herself in thought until they arrived at the food hall turned barracks.

They managed to fit all of the Morning's Shade members inside, as space was made for a much larger number of people. Once everyone was settled, Zalia found Hildebrandt once more. She wanted to return to her family who were still at the farm, but needed to settle some details about what came next first.

"Hildebrandt, I want you and your people to come back with me to the army camp so that we might combine forces and take back the capital together. The issue we are running into is that without you here, Ostoss will not be safe. It won't be possible to evacuate all of these people in any short amount of time, and the only idea Tristan and I can come up with is leaving a few Silver rank members here to protect the town. What do you think?"

Hildebrandt looked around at the members of her group, making sure no one was within easy earshot.

"I'll be honest, Zalia, I'm not really sure what I'm doing. Matthias and the Hidden were the planners, the thinkers. My main job leading the Morning's Shade was in defending the city and occasionally leaving to fight some beast or the other. I can show you how to best defend this town but . . . when it comes to the best way to fight off this invasion." Hildebrandt sighed. "I'm afraid that just isn't in my skill set. A result of both my wisdom and intellect not being linked, I suppose."

She laughed nervously, as if she were admitting a crime.

Zalia gave an encouraging smile.

"I feel like I've got no idea what I'm doing almost all of the time, if it's any consolation."

Hildebrandt laughed again, a little more openly this time.

"Well, that's comforting."

Zalia couldn't help but feel bad for the woman. She had been saddled with the responsibility of the entire order after the Hidden had been taken into custody and Matthias had disappeared.

"Then how about this: We leave the twins here to defend Ostoss, as they are the fastest people you've got. Then, we take everyone else here and go down to the war camp where Lady Indis and the generals can do all the thinking about what to do next."

Hildebrandt leaned back in her chair.

"I like the sound of that."

CHAPTER FORTY-THREE

Return . . .

Zalia

It was two days after the Morning's Shade members arrived that they left. Zalia and the twins had finally managed to hunt down the last couple of shapeshifters, a gruesome task, yet a necessary one. It wasn't something Zalia took pleasure in, yet was important for the safety of the town.

She had also tried to work with the Enchanter again, but with the man refusing to take any sort of advice and absolutely refusing to change anything about the way he made rituals, she had given up and left him to it.

Ember, Boreal, Aylie, and Zalia all waited just outside the gates as the last of the members filtered out. They had left Ostoss in a much, much better state than they had found it, something that Zalia often strived to do, though not always with success.

Tristan was staying behind, of course, as were the twins and a few other Bronze rank members of the Morning's Shade. Now that the twins were there, the guard could be a little more relaxed, and Zalia had even convinced the man to take a little time off to get back into starting up his bakery once more. She knew that the simple and relaxing task of baking was something that would benefit his mental health greatly. Something to pull him out of his past and back to the present, lead him back towards being a baker, not a soldier. He was a great soldier, that much she didn't doubt. It was what being a great soldier did to him that neither she nor he thought good.

The final thing Zalia had done before leaving was attempt to lay a blessing on the farm. She had brought out her small altar to Nateysta and used the glowing purple mushrooms she found in Cormaine to ask a blessing on the farm. There was no immediately visible effect other than the ritual itself, yet she felt a little better for having done it. At the request of one of the farmers, she even grew another small altar from her chunk of wood and left it in the house she had grown there.

Hildebrandt had left behind her momentary lapse of confidence and now had her leadership mask on once more. With an end in sight to the indecisiveness that had apparently hounded her, she was more than happy to push on a little longer.

The caravan began to move away with Zalia and her little family towards the front of the group. Aylie would be spending the time attempting to move any particularly overgrown forested areas out of the way with Plant Manipulation, while Zalia and Boreal flattened the ground out for their carts with the earth manipulation they both had from Physical Resistance.

There was an actual earth mage in the caravan that picked up when Zalia and Boreal grew tired, but an advantage that came with needing significantly less sleep was the fact that they didn't really grow tired anymore. Of course, there was mental fatigue, yet a few hours of relaxation had the same effect as a night's rest would have on a normal person. Whatever "normal" was here.

Days began to pass them by as they travelled, their path taking them past a few abandoned hovels and towns that Zalia and her family had passed on the way up. Ostoss was a little further west than the army camp was, so their path led in a south, south east direction.

This journey would take a little longer than the one north had taken, by Zalia's approximation, since Ostoss was also further away from the camp than the mountain home of Glemp and their people was. Still, the Morning's Shade moved quite quick for such a large group. They were also such a strong force that they didn't really have to hide from the demons, often spotting demons fleeing from them instead.

She *was* a little concerned that they weren't able to mask their movements. That concern turned out to be quite well-founded when they were attacked.

A large host of the four-legged spined demons she had fought in Cormaine burst out of a patch of forest within a couple hundred metres of them. Hildebrandt immediately called the caravan to a stop and Morning's Shade members reacted with speed.

Zalia opened the vault and ushered Aylie in, standing in the doorway to protect her. Boreal faded out of sight into nearby brush and Ember stood near the door, ready to protect them both.

Many of the longer-ranged Morning's Shade members began flinging spells. Bolts of magic made of fire, earth, and all other sorts rained down. Arrows were shot, some of them Zalia's own, while area of effect spells were cast.

A patch of demons died as the ground beneath them ruptured, swallowing them into the earth below. Another group was set aflame as fire rained down from above. Many bigger members of the order holding shields or larger two-handed weapons waited in front of the more magic-oriented members, ready to protect them.

Others yet charged ahead, bloodlust in their eyes and smaller, quicker weapons in hand. A Silver rank man with two axes and no shirt became a whirlwind of blood as he danced through the hordes, simply ignoring the fire of his allies.

What struck Zalia most, however, was the sheer presence that Hildebrandt maintained on the field. She stood there like a bulwark, a massive glowing tower shield in her hand. It was an item Zalia had never seen before, and its presence seemed to strike fear into the demons. Most dared not come closer, their charge stopped not only by the number of dead but by fear. The few that did come nearer to Hildebrandt died quick deaths to blurred movement or an ability that Zalia could not see. They simply turned to ash as the woman deflected their blows.

It seemed like a pointless charge, the demons having accomplished nothing except dying. Zalia knew that these hordes of four-legged beasts were controlled by the higher-ranked flying demons, something she had seen in Cormaine, yet she saw none of those demons now.

A sound across the battlefield began to bug her, almost soundless and like a pressure building in her ears. Hildebrandt noticed it too and looked around for its source but found nothing either. Realisation struck Zalia just as a force did.

Two Silver ranked Astar appeared in front of her, the runes on their bodies glowing in mesmerising colours as their auras washed over the Morning's Shade. It wasn't an oppressive force like that of the demons was, yet had an attention-drawing effect just the same.

The entire battlefield seemed to turn towards the three beings—the two Astar grabbed Zalia, and everything disappeared in a flash as the sound of a water drop was heard across the whole field.

Zalia woke up on the cold, hard floor of a room, with the sounds of a language she didn't understand coming above her. She opened her eyes and lifted her head to see the same two Astar in conversation and realised she wasn't on the floor after all. She was on a little floating bench, the stone glowing with power.

Without hesitation, she jumped up and punched one of the Astar in the back of the head. She didn't know what they wanted with her, but she also wasn't prepared to sit here and take whatever it was.

The Astar stumbled forward as the other looked at her in shock, as if surprised by her awakening. She summoned her sword and chopped at its arm, finding that it cut through with ease, blue blood flowing to the ground below.

She was about to strike again when the glowing stone beneath her pulsed, dropping her into unconsciousness again.

The next time she woke, her wrists each had a metal bracelet wrapped around them. She had a moment of panic as she couldn't feel her powers, but feeling a little closer, they were there, just . . . restrained. The bracelets had an aura about them that felt similar to the demon's aura in that it was oppressive. She hadn't felt that an object ever had an aura before.

Healing Presence was still there, still active, yet dulled down significantly. The feeling was claustrophobic, as if she had been pressed into her own body.

Looking around, she identified that she was in some sort of prison room. There was a flat stone bed built into the wall, a stone construction that looked like a toilet—except it was covered in runes, and a cell door, built fully from iron and also glowing with runes.

Naturally, the first thing she tried was to summon her weapon. It took a lot more conscious effort, but she managed it eventually. Her bow dropped into her hands, its weight giving her comfort in the silence of the cell.

Her panic built again as she realised that she couldn't feel the bond she shared with Boreal and Ember. What had happened to it? Was it simply gone? Surely such a thing couldn't just be broken.

She looked closer and felt a tiny, tiny stream of consciousness connected to her own. Boreal.

There weren't any of the normal emotions or thoughts coming across the bond, not even an inkling of a location or direction. She could feel it was there, though. However, her bond with Ember wasn't there, though maybe it was simply subdued so much as to be practically invisible. That bond had not grown as deeply as her one with Boreal, after all.

Next, she summoned her armour onto her body. It made her partially intangible as she hoped, yet when she tried to step through the wall, it failed. To her dismay, she realised the walls and door were most definitely magically protected. Of course they were, you didn't imprison a higher-ranked person without making sure they wouldn't escape.

Uncomfortable realisations came to her then, as she recalled the events of the past few . . . minutes? Hours? Days?

The Astar had captured her, for whatever reason, she did not know. They had captured her, after the Morning's Shade had been attacked by *demons*.

Were they working together?

She heard a lock click and a hatch in the solid door slid open, two depthless eyes peering at her through it.

"Stand back, interloper."

The thought slammed into her mind and she involuntarily took a step back.

The door swung open and the Astar from earlier—at least she thought they were the same ones—stepped in. She pressed herself back against the wall, her bow transforming into a sword as she got ready to attack.

One of the Astar flexed their hand and looked to the other nervously. The same two then, only one had regrown the arm she had cut off.

"What the hell do you want from me?"

"Want from you? Nothing. Your interference has grown annoying, so we have taken you. You will wait here until the envoy comes to meet you."

Thoughts raced through her head. Her interference? With what, the invasion?

Her mind flashed back to when she had been in a similar situation, trapped in a cell as Juniper spoke to them, almost absentmindedly. They had theorised that someone must have given Juniper the information she needed to bring back Zayes. Someone who had an excellent understanding of teleportation. But why? Why would they do this?

"The envoy? Who is the envoy?"

Her bracelets pulsed, much as the stone platform she had been on had, and her focus trembled. Her sword puffed into mist, though her armour remained. They seemed to realise that it wasn't linked like her sword was and stepped forward, but she quickly stored it away. No need to lose the armour.

"You will wait here."

She almost attacked them again, but they stepped out and the door closed with a fatalistic thud.

CHAPTER FORTY-FOUR

An Old Enemy

Zalia

Zalia slumped onto the stone bed cut into the wall. It would probably have been quite uncomfortable for most people, but she preferred sleeping out in the trees and dirt over beds anyways. The only part of it that was uncomfortable for her was the fact that she couldn't see the sky, no trees or stars overhead.

Despite her mostly stationary form, her mind was racing. She went over each and every thing that they knew about the rituals, the invasion, and everything that had happened.

It had been a long time since she had thought about what or why she had been brought to Endaria. Could it have been the Astar who did that?

No, that didn't make sense. Why would they bring her here at all? The plan would most likely have unfolded without much trouble if she wasn't there. Unless . . .

Assuming it was the Astar who had given Juniper the ritual and taught her how to perform it, all to get the Morning's Shade in on the plan as well, maybe they had brought Zalia there to sabotage it so that Zayes could not be brought out of Cormaine, after all? No, that didn't make much sense either.

It wasn't much of a stretch to assume that the Astar had imprisoned Zayes so they could manipulate Juniper and get both the king and the only other power in the kingdom in on the plan, but bringing her there to stop Juniper from freeing Zayes was stupid. It held too much randomness. That kind of plan would be too given to chance.

If she were them, she would have had the ritual that was given to Juniper be one that looked like it would work, but in reality, would dispose of the woman after it was all done . . .

A terrible thought occurred to her.

The Astar had never captured her when she had been running all over in an attempt to stop the ritual, yet they had now that it was done and she was helping build a resistance to the invasion. Maybe it wasn't Zalia who had ruined the ritual. Maybe that was its intended function the whole time. After all, she had only been Iron rank, trying to affect a kingdom-scale ritual powered by many, many different people all at once.

They were all assumptions based on her initial thought that the Astar were working with the demons because they had chosen to capture her during the attack. Maybe that had just been convenient timing for them, an opportunity taken advantage of in the moment.

Who, then, was the envoy?

They had told her she would wait there until the envoy arrived. Well, she wasn't about to just sit around waiting for that to happen. There must be something she could do.

Her magic was definitely subdued, yet not locked away. Healing Presence was still there, weak, but still there. Some of her other magic must work, then.

She tried to teleport through the door using Mobility, and for a moment, her world flickered, yet she hadn't gone anywhere. It was as if she had teleported in place.

With a little focus, she was able to open up her profile menu to look over all of her abilities.

Profile - Zalia Taori
Health - Excellent
Mana - Full
Stamina - Full
Class One - Hunter - Bronze 3
Linked Attributes - Strength, Dexterity
Active Skills
Kill Shot - Bronze 4
Hunter's Mark - Bronze 3
Fight or Flight - Bronze 4
Passive Skills
Hunter's Sight - Bronze 3
Survivalist - Bronze 4
Class Two - Herbalist - Bronze 2
Linked Attributes - Vitality, Resilience
Active Skills
Flora Identification - Bronze 2
Preparation - Bronze 4
Druid Grove - Bronze 3

Passive Skills
Harvester - Bronze 3
Herbal Magic - Bronze 6
Unity Class - Druid - Bronze 3
Linked Attributes - Wisdom, Intellect
Active Skills
Nature's Wrath - Bronze 5
Protection of the Wilds - Bronze 3
Passive Skills
Healing Presence - Bronze 7
General Passives
Heat Resistance - Bronze 4
Cold Resistance - Bronze 4
Aura Observation - Bronze 1
Low Light Vision - Iron 18
Poison Resistance - Iron 7
Mobility - Bronze 7
Stealth - Bronze 4
Trapper - Bronze 4
Teaching - Iron 12
Flight - Iron 13
Physical Resistance - Bronze 4
Mental Resistance - Bronze 4
Weapon Proficiencies
Bow - Bronze 4
Sword - Bronze 3
Throwing Knives - Tin 17
Bonded Items
Druidic bow, Blessed by Starlight (Blessed Heirloom) - Deeply bonded Bronze rank.
Duskwraith Armour (Heirloom) - Bonded Iron rank.
Ethereal Vault Gauntlet (Heirloom) - Deeply bonded Bronze rank.

Kill Shot . . . No, no, no. Maybe Herbal Magic? Nature's Wrath . . .

Of her entire list, nothing stuck out. She tried to move stone with Physical Resistance but managed nothing. Nature's Wrath probably wouldn't be able to do so either. Of course it was protected against magical manipulation.

She needed to get the damn bracelets off to allow her magic to flow properly. Maybe then she could get out.

Then she read over her bonded items. Her vault. Maybe there was something she could do with that.

She tried and tried, focusing as hard as she could on the magic. As much as she pushed and pulled on the magic, however, the vault would not open. Perhaps the bracelets had a stronger effect against spacial magic. It still allowed her to pull items in and out of the storage space there, though, so herbs were on the table. Those and her armour, of course.

She was lucky that the vault gauntlet was entirely built into her hand, making it hard for them to take it away. Well, without taking her hand at least . . .

That was a disturbing thought.

If they did that, she would lose access to the vault, but not her armour. It was the gauntlet that allowed her to open the space and to store memories and objects inside. It was the Druid Grove ability linked to it that allowed her to summon herbs and plants from its space, which included her wooden heirloom armour. She tried to summon her sword and found it worked, then had another terrible thought. She could cut off her arms to take off the bracelets. It would restore her magic, allow her to escape, maybe!

She wasn't quite that desperate yet, though. That seemed like a painful, possibly unnecessary step to take.

Herbal Magic. That was her only chance.

The bracelets limited her magic, yes, but she didn't think they would limit magic that was outside of her. Magic like the living rituals. Sure, she would have to put all her effort into it to make it work, but once it was established, it wasn't part of her anymore.

She summoned her little chunk of wood, and then began growing it. Slowly. Ever so slowly.

A few days . . . she thought it was a few days, it was hard to tell, but a few days passed. She spent most of those days growing her little chunk of wood bigger and bigger. It grew out to the size of the room, kept hidden from her captors when they entered by storing it back into the spacial storage. She even cut off chunks of leaves she grew and stored them as well; she was able to crush them into powder using Preparation.

Her plan was to set up a framework for the ritual with her wood chunk, then plant each plant into place with the powdered leaves as soil. It wasn't the best setup, but she had faith that it would work.

Unfortunately, she wasn't given enough time to test the idea, as there was another click and sliding sound—the hatch opening on the door.

She quickly stored away the wood covering the floor and looked up in time to see the sliding hatch reveal a now familiar face. It was the face of the Astar whose arm she had cut off on her first day there.

They hadn't said anything else to her since, simply coming by and making sure she was still alive before walking away again. She had begun to recognise them by the runes that decorated their bodies. While at first glance they looked the same, she began to notice distinct physical differences. Well, that and their auras. Even with her powers subdued, Aura Observation picked up on their powerful auras, each different from the other, if only slightly.

She sat waiting, expecting the hatch to close and the Astar to walk off, but this time, the door swung open on silent hinges.

Her heart stopped.

Standing behind the Astar was a form she recognised all too well. The memory was engraved into her mind, a clawed hand closing down and crushing her friend, cracked obsidian skin, cruel eyes.

The demon was with the Astar. The envoy. The one she hated above most others.

She thought the trauma and pain of that memory had softened and was in the past, yet seeing the creature made it all come back with a force once more. The edges of her vision narrowed, her mind focused solely on the demon as adrenaline and anger pumped through her veins.

"You piece of shit," she spat.

A voice, grating, cracked, and cruel came from the demon, much as she expected it to sound.

"There you are, filth. You will pay for what you did."

She summoned her sword and stood with fury, prepared to attack the Silver rank demon despite it most likely meaning her death. There was no chance, though, as the auras of the Astar stripped away what was left of her own Healing Presence, only for the corrupting aura of the demon to crash down into her.

It was like she was in Cormaine again, the sheer power of the thousand-eyed ones making her unable to think, unable to move, unable to act. Pain wracked her mind even as pain arced across her body. She felt a slash in her arm from claws both sharp and jagged, yet could not move to stop it. Healing Presence healed the wound, yet she felt another cut across her face.

Congratulations! Healing Presence has reached Bronze 8.

She grabbed onto the notification with her entire being, holding her attention to it like a buoy in a storm. There was no perception of the outside world, only pain, the feeling of her body withering away even as the power of Healing Presence fought back from within, restoring what was lost.

It was hard to tell how long the pain, the oppressive corruption, went on. It could have been a minute or a day, yet when it finally faded away, she found herself lying on the cold stone floor, sweating and panting.

She rolled over with a groan, one arm flopping to her side. Slowly, she reached her perception back out into her body, realising that it was perfectly fine, no damage or pain remaining.

The demon and the Astar were gone, the door shut and then its hatch closed. It was like nothing had ever happened, like it had all been a vague nightmare, yet she knew it was real.

The fucking demon had the nerve to accuse her of doing something bad?

It had killed her friend, crushed them in its hand. What the hell had she done? Survived in the world they had stolen? Brought back a god whose world they had invaded and whose body they had destroyed?

Pay for what she did. Fuck, she would pay it all back tenfold when the chance arose. If it planned to torture her here, she would bear whatever it could bring, then find a way to kill it. She had no interest in torture or any payback of that kind. All she wanted was its head separated from its body.

She stood up, phantom pain tingling across her entire body. Parts of her clothing were cut where the demon had raked its claws across her skin. The clothes would repair and clean off the blood—her blood—coating it in time, but for now, it was a reminder of what she had been through.

There was no time to waste, however.

Shuffling over to the bed cut into the wall, she sat down with another groan and brought out the ritual pad she was constructing, getting back to work.

FORTY-FIVE

Breakout

Zalia

Zalia had no idea how much time passed during the course of her imprisonment. Had she been brought here a week ago? A month? Two?

Her days were filled with pain, almost as if they were trying to scour her soul from her body. She had tried many times to figure out what the demon actually wanted, but apparently, all it sought was the pleasure of bringing her pain. The urge to cut off her arms and let them regrow to take off the bracelets grew by the day. It couldn't be worse than what she was going through, yet somehow she couldn't push past that mental barrier of just doing it. It felt . . . wrong.

The only passage of time that she could perceive was the steady advancement of both Healing Presence and Survivalist. Each additional level of both abilities brought them a little more strength. The healing within her body grew a tiny bit stronger, and her resistance to both mental and physical attacks grew with it.

> **Congratulations! Healing Presence has gained seven levels, reaching Bronze 15.**
> **Congratulations! Survivalist has gained four levels, reaching Bronze 8.**
> **Congratulations! Preparation has gained three levels, reaching Bronze 7.**

Preparation also leveled due to the constant growth and pruning she did of the wooden ritual platform that was under construction.

It was almost done, almost ready for her attempt to break out. She had decided on the same healing ritual she had used to help grow the plants in Ostoss. It consisted of Frozen Heart for its healing properties, Dodge-vine for its protective properties, and of course, Adastem for its adaptive properties. She had tried the ritual individually, and for a moment, the pressure constantly pounding down on her abilities waned. If she could get it to settle as a separate living ritual, she hoped it would be enough for her to have full or at least greater use of all her magic.

Once she had that, she hoped it would be enough for her to do enough damage to the wall to break out. That was with the assumption that she wasn't underground, or the wall wasn't metres thick. At the very least, the breakout attempt would give her knowledge.

Even if all she managed to do was get out into the corridor before she was captured again, she would learn something.

She also felt like she would be able to kill one of those Astar in the right circumstances. The one she had sliced through with her sword had barely any defence against the attack. Maybe it was just that the Astar didn't have resilience or constitution bonded, yet she thought it might be something else. Something related to why they had such strong auras for their rank.

The fact that they could wield that aura like a weapon or tool made her think that perhaps they weren't entirely physical beings. Maybe, they were just a bit more in line with their own souls. She thought Aylie would probably be able to see that, if it were true.

It was a strong advantage, the way that they could pull her aura given by Healing Presence aside so that the demon could attack her directly.

She shook her head and continued working on the ritual pad. There were just few more herbs to plant and it was done. She wasn't exactly sure what would happen when or if Healing Presence reached Silver, but if it had an impact on the pain the demon could inflict on her, she had a feeling it wouldn't risk much past that. It was simultaneously a milestone she so desperately wanted to reach, yet dreaded at the same time. Any major change to the situation like that could cause the demon to kill her.

All she had to do was get out before that.

The ritual pad vanished in an instant as she heard the sliding sound of the hatch opening once more. Depthless eyes peered in, and then the door opened.

As always, she tried to get a peek at what was outside, yet she could only see the same few metres of featureless enchanted stone hallway beyond as always. Most of her sight of that was blocked by the demon.

She closed her eyes and prepared herself as she felt Healing Presence being pulled aside and the corrupting aura of the demon come crashing down.

She woke again, lying on the cold floor panting, covered in sweat. Used to it by now, she sat up and dismissed the notification of another Healing Presence rank up, then continued her work on the ritual pad.

With a final Frozen Heart planted in the correct place, she looked over her work to make sure that everything was as it should be. For a brief moment, she had considered bringing it out and trying to break free while the Astar and demon were in the room, yet quickly gave up the idea. Maybe she would be able to get her powers momentarily, but there was no way she would have the strength to take on three Silver rankers even then.

Something flittered in the back of her mind, a fleeting image of herself stuck in the very cell she was now in. It was a memory, yet not one that was hers. She knew that the collective's memories were still stuck in her vault, almost undecipherable to her, and this felt like one of those. They had known she would end up here, yet had chosen this path anyways?

There was a brief flash of hope in her mind as she prepared to cast the ritual and begin her breakout attempt. This might be the only chance she got. Assuming she even managed to get out of the cell and was caught, they might not take any more chances with her. She wasn't sure she could even stand this much longer without her own mind breaking. Mental Resistance was having an effect on her ability to deal with the pain, but she knew that without the hope this ritual was bringing her, the constant pain would break her.

Her idea was simple. Activate the ritual, hope it blocked the dampening effects of the bracelets enough, cast Nature's Wrath, and destroy whatever she could however she could. The door, the walls, whatever.

She knew that the corridor outside went both left and right. The only hope she had for that was that she would see something in either direction that would lead her towards a decision. Otherwise it was just random choice.

A few herbs began to float about, summoned from her vault. They glowed brightly as she began the ritual.

She wasn't sad, she wasn't scared, she was fucking angry and ready to do something about it.

It took all her concentration to push back the bracelets long enough that the ritual took hold. Quickly, the plants took over the entire thing and began fueling it in a symbiotic relationship. Her concentration waned, but the ritual quickly adapted to push against the bracelets on its own.

With the power of the ritual taking over, she felt free access to her abilities come back once more. Her bonds with both Ember and Boreal flared to life. With one thought, she started sending images and words to the both of them. With another, she activated Nature's Wrath.

The wood of the ritual pad grew roots that pushed and scraped at the walls. Stone rippled slightly as it fought her intentions, its magic holding its shape while hers tried to tear it apart. Finally, the hinges of the door gave as the roots of her plant grew between them, pushing the entire thing apart. The door fell into the corridor with a loud bang.

She used Preparation to cut the roots from the pad and then stored it, the entire living ritual disappearing in a heartbeat. The bracelets took hold once more, Nature's Wrath ending. It didn't matter, though, because she was out.

With quick movements, she sprinted out of the room and into the corridor beyond.

Zalia glanced down both directions within the corridor. The walls were bare, no windows or furnishings. There were no benches or sconces, only the odd glowing rune carved into the ceiling that provided a still, white light.

There were many more iron doors down both directions, yet one of the corridors ended in a wall with the other disappearing from sight up a set of stairs. It was an easy decision.

During the brief moment of her powers being at their fullest once more, she had managed to send messages to both Boreal and Ember about what had happened. Hopefully, they would be able to do something with that. She didn't really know where she was herself though, so wasn't super hopeful about it. If she could just get outside . . .

She ran as quickly as she could down the corridor and took the stairs three at a time. At the top was a small landing with a single Bronze Astar lounging by the door. It didn't even get the chance to wake out of its floating sleep as her blade dropped into her hands and she cut the Astar's head in half.

It dropped to the floor, dead instantly.

She was a little surprised at how easily the Astar had died, a single cut from her blade enough to kill it. Maybe that was why the first Bronze ones she had seen had simply disappeared rather than risking confrontation.

It didn't seem to have any keys or other equipment on it, yet the door before her had no handle that she could see. In fact, it had nothing on it except a single central rune.

She looked down at the dead Astar, whose own runes were slowly fading from a glowing blue to an inert black. There, on its hand, was a rune that matched the one on the door exactly.

Acting quickly, she grabbed its arm and half lifted the body to press the palm of the Astar to the rune on the door.

As the door began to swing silently open, something started to feel off in her mind. This had been too easy.

She knew the demon, not from her own memories but from thoughts now surfacing from the collective's memory bundle. This demon wasn't an idiot. It was cold, calculating and ruthless. It wouldn't have made things this easy.

The door came to a rest and Zalia slowly moved through the doorway. It was nighttime.

Outside, was a huge courtyard surrounded by towering walls. They were formed oddly, out of the same rune-enchanted stone that made up her prison cell. The bottom of the walls was orderly and normal, yet the top started to take on strange shapes and angles, a confusing mess of a design.

The doorway she had moved through was set into the wall of a small building near the centre of the courtyard, a simple cube.

Standing only twenty metres away from her, was the demon.

"You finally come out to play."

It gestured and Zalia's eyes flicked up far above to where the two Silver Astar were floating, observing the entire courtyard.

One of them raised their hand and the bracelets fell from her arms.

There was a sinking feeling in her stomach, a realisation that the demon had been waiting for her to try and break free. All so that it could snatch the hope from her in a single moment.

Its deep red eyes seemed to glitter with excitement, its mouth cracking upwards with jagged movements until a disturbing smile was set upon its face.

"Survive for a minute, and I'll let you live . . . today."

She looked to the stars above, letting out a single, small prayer to the friend she hoped was listening.

"*Help.*"

Immediately, she cast a ritual using Dodge-vine, Bitterbalm, and Manifest. It was what she used as a protection from the corruption in Cormaine.

It came not a moment too late as the aura of the demon came crashing down, trying to slither its way to her flesh.

Compared to what she had endured, it was nothing. Here, Healing Presence was at its full power, the protection enhanced by the ritual. Here, the Astar weren't holding back her own power so that the demon's aura might prevail. It was still a struggle, but there was no pain, no injury.

The demon sneered with disdain, then launched its attack.

She was used to fighting these things by now, her armour appearing on her body as she let the demon's claws slide down the length of her blade, casting Hunter's Mark all the while. Using the increased speed from her sword proficiency and the Bronze rank ability from the heirloom that was her blade, she struck back immediately.

The strike left a glowing, starry arc in its wake as the sped-up blade smashed into the armoured obsidian plate of the demon's right arm. A little crack formed in the surface as the demon was pushed back a single step.

It wasn't a winning strike. It wasn't even so much as harmful to the demon. It was a hit to its ego, however.

Its disdainful sneer turned to fury, and it attacked again with fervor.

She had to immediately activate Protection of the Wilds, enhancing the shield with Dodge-vine using the Iron rank effect of the ability.

The demon only struck harder, shattering little ethereal pieces off her shield and pushing her back up against the wall of the cubic building.

Using Fight or Flight, she sped up and hopped to the side, using the momentum and Mobility to hop once more in the other direction, a second step in the air to push herself forward, and a third to get herself over the head of the demon, twisting to land behind it, bringing her sword down as she did.

It struck, leaving only a scratch down the obsidian of the demon's skin . . . armour?

Another hit, no more dangerous to the demon than the last, yet a small victory for her.

Using a quick ritual, she summoned a wall to block the demon's vision of her. She ran around the side of it straight away, timing it well enough that as the demon exploded through the wall, she was gone. Well, she was around the other side, yet gone from the demon's sight.

A few seconds passed before the demon came smashing through the wall again, but Zalia was ready. A summoned bear trap slammed closed on its leg, the teeth of the metal contraption cutting only a few millimetres into the leg.

The demon stumbled a little, then ripped the trap in half and threw the pieces at her.

She dodged to the side with a slight twist of her body, letting the pieces fly by, then raised her sword in preparation for the next clash.

It didn't come.

The demon walked off, punching the remainder of her summoned wall with a fist.

Standing there in confusion, she only realised what was happening as the auras of the Astar stripped away her own before they landed. An intense power rolled over her and she stumbled to one knee, sword vanishing. The minute was over.

Before they could take it from her, she stored her armour, and moments later, the bracelets clicked back onto her wrists.

When the Astar came the next day, the demon wasn't with them. However, they did open the door and made her move out into the corridor. She had a feeling that her daily torture would take on a new form now, something a little more entertaining for the demon.

She had gained a single level in Protection of the Wilds from the previous day's bout, but really didn't want to have to fight the damn Silver ranker again. There just wasn't any way she could kill it without a whole lot of preparation.

As she stepped out into the courtyard once again, she was met by the sight of the demon, waiting, looking both smug and excited.

"You have a minute and a half."

Her heart thumped, concern and fear flooding her body. A minute and a half. If she survived, would tomorrow be two minutes?

Realistically, how long could she possibly survive before she made a mistake. It wouldn't take much. If she allowed herself to be caught, one strike she didn't manage to dodge . . .

The fight began once more.

At the end of a minute and a half of dodging, casting spells, using desperate measures, and exhausting her abilities, the Astar put the bracelets back on her once more. It was a smart thing they were doing. She didn't want to try another breakout because if she had to use her long cooldown abilities and the breakout failed, she would have a much harder time with the next fight.

The only hope she held was that the starlight wolf had heard her prayer. It would either come to save her or she was likely to die here. There was simply no way she would escape three Silver rankers, two of whom had powerful spacial magic, while her powers were subdued.

She settled in for another long wait between fights, desperately wracking her brain for anything, any way she could escape. Any idea or plan that would allow her to live just a little bit longer.

CHAPTER FORTY-SIX

Desperation

Zalia

Day after day passed. Or maybe not, she couldn't tell.

She had been brought out for another fight, needing to survive two minutes this time. During the fight, she had lost an arm but had survived. It had been the arm without her vault gauntlet, thankfully, and it had grown back.

> **Congratulations! Healing Presence has reached Bronze 17.**

Each time she survived another fight, she sent off a prayer to the starlight wolf, hoping that the prayer would reach it.

Another day passed. She thought another day had passed at least. The demon had come to torture her with its corrupting aura in the cell again.

She had mixed feelings about Healing Presence quickly approaching Silver. It was a reflection of what she was enduring, a milestone. It was also possibly the end for her, once she did get it.

Much later that day, she was taken from her cell once more, to fight the demon again. Two minutes and thirty seconds. It wasn't a long time in most circumstances. You could stand there and wait that long with relative ease, even just close your eyes and wait it out.

The only change in routine was two voices entering her mind.

"Tell us what the humans plan. We will end this if you do."

She looked up to where the Astar floated, staring at the smug bastards. Her hand raised and she flipped her middle finger at them, a gesture they may not understand. Then, she started the fight herself.

When there was adrenaline pumping through your veins, and a stronger enemy in front of you with the will and intent to kill you. When you had nothing but your own skill and power standing between yourself and death. When you weren't sure if anyone or anything was coming to save you, two minutes and thirty seconds became a very long time indeed.

She almost lost her head this time, managing to avoid getting caught by the savage swipe by throwing herself backwards onto the ground. Then she had desperately fought to get back to her feet and continue surviving. She did, barely.

> **Congratulations! Healing Presence has reached Bronze 18.**

A few of her skills levelled as well; Nature's Wrath, Protection of the Wilds, Survivalist, Fight or Flight, Herbal Magic, and Hunter's Mark all gained one or two levels each. She barely even looked at those, though. The only one that mattered right now was the quickly levelling Healing Presence.

When that ticked over, which would probably happen during a fight, she would need to try and get out.

A few times she had flown up off the ground during their fights, mostly to test the limitations of the barrier that locked them in. So far she hadn't found any way to do damage to the thing. Nor was she able to teleport through it.

The only idea she had come up with was definitely a desperate one.

There was a little tree in the courtyard, nothing more than a sapling. She had been slowly growing it bit by bit during their fights, not quickly enough for them to notice what she had been doing. Hopefully.

Zalia wasn't sure if it would even work. Her armour gave her the ability to step into a plant and come out of another plant of the same type within a few hundred metres. Whether the barrier that had been set up would block that or not, she wasn't sure. It was worth a try, though.

Once Healing Presence hit Silver rank, it would be able to grow the tree much quicker than it could at Bronze rank. She just needed to survive long enough to make the tree grow to the point where she could fit inside its trunk. Only then would she be able to test her theory.

Another day passed, and the demon came to torture her once more.

> **Congratulations! Healing Presence has reached Bronze 19.**

How long had she been in prison now? It was hard to keep track.

It had been three weeks, perhaps. Maybe less, maybe more. There was no way to tell how long she stayed passed out for. No one to talk to, or ask. Only the faint bond she had with Boreal to keep her going.

Each time she was released from the bracelets for the fights, the bond with Boreal grew stronger and her bond with Ember became visible once more. It was the strength and support that she felt coming from those bonds that kept her going strong. She knew they were trying to find her, they *would* find her. If she could get out of the keep and into any kind of forest, she knew she'd be able to escape the sight of the demon and its two Astar.

All she would have to do then was follow the direction her bond pointed her. The same bond she knew was directing both Ember and Boreal towards her.

Eventually, the time came for her to leave the cell again. Time for another fight. This would be the one, she thought. The one where Healing Presence reached Silver.

Led by the Astar, she stepped out of the prison complex into the starry night. She sent a quick prayer to the stars above, pleading them to come to her aid.

The demon stood there as always, watching her intently. Was this fight the time it would get to kill her? She didn't know. It didn't know. The thirst to find out was clear in the demon's eyes.

"Three minutes."

Its voice echoed across the silent courtyard, deep, grating, cruel.

Zalia summoned her armour as her bow appeared in her hands. The sapling sat there, visible in the corner of her vision as she started growing it, little by little. She gripped the smooth, comfortable wood of her bow, its solid weight in her hand a reminder of the long journey she had been on to get here.

The demon ran towards her, savage jagged claws ready to tear through her flesh. She shot at it, getting off three arrows in quick succession, moving positions between each shot.

With each arrow, the demon had to adjust its movement as the temporary invisibility granted by her shots allowed Zalia to reposition without being seen.

Still, it avoided each attack and reached her in moments. The bow turned into a sword as Zalia traded strikes, going entirely on the defensive. She only struck when the attack would knock it off balance.

The demon grabbed the blade of her sword and threw it aside. Zalia used Fight or Flight in the same instant, moving quicker than the blade. She plucked it out of the air, turned on her heel and struck the demon hard on the head.

The strike sent the demon reeling, a slight scratch visible down the cracked obsidian of its skin. Without hesitation, Zalia switched out the sword for the bow, shooting it in the chest. Again, only a little cut, yet it allowed her to switch back to the blade during a moment of invisibility and run at the demon.

Another hit to the head and the demon fell over, frustration visible in its expression.

Fight or Flight ran out and Zalia's perception sped up, back to normal. She quickly cast two rituals. The first summoned grasping vines from the ground around the demon, holding it down for a second more. The other was a Dodge-vine major and Adastem minor, which provided her with a good adaptive protection.

The protection immediately adjusted as the demon tried to tear at her with its aura. At the same time, it freed itself from the vines and stood slowly. It wasn't pressed for time, not this fight.

Zalia stumbled a bit at the sudden attack but adjusted to the pain. A step back made the savage strike of the demon turn to a glancing one that tore across the shoulder plate of her armour. Even the indirect hit had enough force to push her back further.

This was always how it started out, the demon using only its strength and speed to try and kill her. After a minute, however, it began to use its magic.

Spikes of obsidian jabbed from the ground around her, the only warning a slight vibration she saw. The first time it had used this magic had been the fight she had lost her arm.

Now, though, she was aware of it. Avoiding the spikes took all her attention, and she didn't dodge the demon in time. A punch to her chest knocked the air out of her and she went tumbling across the courtyard, rolling to a stop some twenty metres away. She struggled to her feet only to find the demon standing over her already. It wasn't playing around now.

Nature's Wrath flared to life and the stone beneath them rose up to envelop the demon. It tore away chunk after chunk, but was eventually buried. She knew it wouldn't last long, yet continued to add stone to the temporary prison. With a strained effort of will, she shoved the entire thing, demon and all, into the ground.

Then, she let Nature's Wrath drop. She couldn't afford to use too much mana on the ability, needing enough to use Protection of the Wilds later on.

She wasted no time, running from where the stone had been lodged in the ground, turning sword to bow once more. The sounds of rock groaning and cracking resounded behind her as she used Mobility to step on the air and reach the top of the central building. There, she pushed Healing Presence into the tree some more, no longer quite worried about the speed of its growth. She counted in her mind, keeping track of how long she needed to survive. One minute left.

Obsidian ripped from the ground and tore into the rock containing the demon. The whole thing exploded, shrapnel flying through the air and bouncing off the ground, walls, and protective dome of the courtyard.

The demon flew up and out of the dust and shrapnel, coming down towards her quickly. She shot at it, scoring three strikes it didn't even bother to dodge. Each left a glowing scrape in its obsidian skin, and in that moment, the difference between a combat-oriented Silver ranker and an illusionist Silver ranker like the elder was stark to Zalia.

She jumped out of the way at the last moment, the demon slamming into the rooftop, cracking the stone. It stood and swiped at her before she had time to even switch her weapon. The strike scraped down the length of her bow with a concerning sound before she switched it for the sword, striking back. The attack was ignored, another glowing line left in the obsidian as a fist punched her in the stomach.

Zalia had the air knocked out of her, bending over as she gasped for breath. The world spun and she heard a ringing as the demon punched her in the head, throwing her off the building to the courtyard below.

She activated Protection of the Wilds, with Zephyr as the enhancement to the shield. It allowed her to float gently to the ground and land safely, breathing hard.

Thirty seconds.

The demon charged again and she barely fended off its furious attacks. Obsidian spines tore her shield away and the demon grabbed her by the throat, tearing her helmet off.

Twenty seconds.

She struggled, trying to pry its hands off her neck. It was too strong. With a twist, it snapped her neck.

Fifteen seconds.

The anti-death measure of Healing Presence activated, healing her snapped neck in an instant and coating her in a protective bubble.

> **Congratulations! Healing Presence has reached Bronze 20.**
> **Congratulations! Healing Presence has reached Silver 1.**

Her aura exploded out of her, reaching across the entire courtyard, further even. So far that it went past her senses.

The demon stumbled, dropping her to the ground as her aura attacked its being. It was on the same level as the demon's own now, matching its power.

Ten seconds.

She jumped to her feet, focusing as much of the aura on the sapling as possible and dashing towards it. The sapling grew to a large tree in a matter of seconds. She got a few steps from it before obsidian spikes grew from the ground and tore it to shreds.

Five seconds.

Zalia spun around, anger and desperation clear in her posture. She summoned her bow and started shooting.

Time's up.

The demon kept coming.

With her aura pressing against its own, the demon had a harder time reaching her. Barely.

She had only a few extra seconds, a few more arrows released, before she had to switch to her sword once more. Fending off its attacks desperately, knowing that if she didn't kill it, it would kill her. There were no more chances.

The fight wasn't destined to go that way, though. Two swipes dodged, one connected. She was sent tumbling again.

The demon stood over her with an easily readable expression of pure ecstasy.

Zalia groaned, trying to lever herself up to a sitting position. The demon got ready to strike.

A fifty-metre chunk of the wall beside them exploded inwards.

CHAPTER FORTY-SEVEN

Not the Only Desperate One

Zalia

The demon jumped away and flew up as the flying chunks of stone collided with heavy, dull thuds all across the courtyard. Standing still in the gaping hole now present in the high enchanted stone wall of the keep was Hildebrandt. She was still Gold rank, yet her presence gave off the feeling of someone so close to Emerald rank that you could practically taste it in the air.

The demon and the two Astar immediately panicked.

Zalia didn't blame them, watching the demon fly towards the Astar as they began to perform some kind of ritual.

Hildebrandt didn't bother chasing after them, simply swinging her mace at one of the Astar. It didn't have time to react as a bolt of energy impacted it.

The bolt turned half the Astar's body to dust. The other Astar continued its spell, but Zalia was able to sense fear in the being's normally neutral and controlled aura.

Zalia stood up groggily from the ground and cast Hunter's Mark on the Astar, watching as Hildebrandt pulled back her arm to swing again. The bolt flashed out, the two remaining enemies vanishing a moment before it hit.

Leaning against the remains of the tree trunk, Zalia closed her eyes and let out a deep, exhausted sigh. She had survived.

"So those were Astar, hey?"

Hildebrandt stepped over a piece of rubble on her way towards Zalia. She didn't sound particularly impressed. The woman was also looking at Zalia in an odd way.

"A few Silver rank ones, yeah."

"And that was a demon with them."

Hildebrandt said it matter-of-factly, though there was confusion and not a small amount of worry evident in her voice.

"An enemy from the other world. One I hoped I had left behind."

Hildebrandt nodded a few times, absorbing the information.

"Alright, we can get to all of that in a minute. I gotta ask though, what in the *worlds* is happening with your aura ability?"

Zalia jumped a little. She had forgotten to check out what upgrade it had received.

Passive 1 - Healing presence - passive - aura.

Tin - Your very presence grants life to all around you. You, nearby allies, and any flora and fauna you so choose within your aura are affected by a heal-over-time effect. The heal-over-time effect heals for low health every second.

Iron - Healing presence now heals the most grave injuries first, and you may focus it onto a single target, increasing that target's healing while reducing the healing other targets receive.

Bronze - Healing Presence now attunes to the specific needs of each individual target within your aura. It adjusts its healing output based on the severity of injuries or ailments, offering targeted healing to each person or creature accordingly. You may still change this manually, if desired. Additionally, once every twenty-four hours, when you or an ally die, you are instead cocooned in a protective barrier as made by Protection of the Wilds and made invulnerable to most things for six seconds.

Silver - Healing Presence expands its reach to the flora and fauna beyond your immediate surroundings. A second layer of aura with only the Tin rank effect of this ability now extends to a wider area, encompassing large swaths of ecosystems, granting them a gentle and sustained healing effect.

All other effects of Healing Presence are still limited to their previous range. This does not interrupt the natural cycle of life within an ecosystem.

Her eyes widened as she read it, then read it over again. She could feel it, spreading out into the far distance, healing the world farther than she could properly sense. It was promoting growth, causing the spread of nature, yet she could also feel it was not disrupting the balance of it.

"I . . . appear to be healing a chunk of the world."

As she said it, Zalia could see that nature was reclaiming the courtyard around them. She would need to be very careful about this ability. It could probably be pushed aside easily by anyone with an aura ability that had some kind of strength, yet the damage it could accidentally do by causing nature to reclaim cities might be an issue.

The grass in the courtyard grew tall and wild, the chunks of tree around her winding and curling to form an odd tree that was almost a sculpture incorporating the obsidian chunks around it. Vines began winding their way up the walls, and within a few minutes of them watching, the keep had been entirely reclaimed by nature. She wasn't sure if this was a result of her subconscious feelings about the place or the nature of the ability, but she rather liked how it looked now.

The odd, jagged, and hard angles of the walls were calmed and smoothed out by the plants growing all over them, turning her place of torture into an artful display of nature.

"Well."

Hildebrandt nodded a few times, looking about.

"Well indeed."

"So my aura ability ranked up."

"I can see that."

Zalia scratched the back of her head.

"It seems a little bit . . . powerful for its rank, doesn't it?"

Since the Astar had left, she had felt the direction Hunter's Mark pointed her towards jump multiple times. It was obvious to her that they were teleporting constantly. It was also obvious that they wouldn't be able to catch up to that kind of speed.

Hildebrandt looked around at the overgrown keep.

"I admit, it seems a little bit powerful, yeah. Abilities usually evolve around what we use them for the most. What exactly have you been using this one for?"

Zalia stood up from her little seat in the decorative tree.

"Eliminating the corruption, resisting the corruption, healing damage done by the corruption."

Hildebrandt didn't say anything but Zalia got her meaning anyways.

"So the ability evolved to do exactly those things as well as it could."

Hildebrandt clicked her fingers.

"Exactly. The ability doesn't really help you any more in fights than it already did, but when it comes to removing the corruption from Endaria? Unrivalled. Sure, it *is* stronger because it is Silver now but that's not the main part of it."

Her expression softened.

"Sorry, I should have asked how you are. Are you alright? What did they want from you?"

Zalia almost broke down then, memories of her torture coming to the forefront of her mind.

"How . . . how long was I gone?" she asked instead.

That must have put together a few key pieces of information for Hildebrandt. Her healing ability having reached Silver already, much quicker than it should have, her loss of time, the situation she had found Zalia in and the absent look on her face.

"A month and a half," Hildebrandt said softly.

"A month . . . Ember, Boreal, Aylie? Are they alright?"

She could feel from their bond that they were, but wanted to hear it anyways.

"They're fine. They were coming with me to find you, but a wolf made of starlight found us and told me I needed to hurry. I left them behind and came here as quickly as I could."

"*A month and a half.*"

"I . . . see."

Almost as if on cue, the stars above shone a little brighter. A shimmering form apparated, stepping down from the glittering dots of molten light.

"*Hello again, young Druid. It is good to see you alive.*"

Zalia bowed her head in reverence, grateful to the wolf for what it had done.

"Thank you. I'm more grateful than I can explain for your help."

"*Do not worry yourself with thanks, child. I heard your pleas.*"

Zalia heard the unstated message in the words. It heard all of her pleas, each and every desperate word. It knew what she had been through.

She raised her head and looked into the depthless, starry eyes and couldn't help but be reminded of the similar eyes of the Astar. Questions pushed to the back of her mind during her time in the prison came to the surface then.

"Why do the Astar work with the demons?"

"*I do not know.*"

The wolf sounded disturbed, and Zalia couldn't help but feel the same. How could it be that the ancient starlight wolf didn't know? From what she knew, it could see and hear everything that the stars could on this world. Had it not known that the Astar worked with the demons?

"What do we do now?" Hildebrandt asked.

She'd been silent, but the weight of what to do obviously weighed on her as much as it did Zalia.

"*Something that I did not dare try until now.*"

That got Zalia's attention and curiosity.

"What? What haven't you tried?"

The wolf sat, staring into the sky above.

"*There are forces beyond even us spirits of nature. They do not wake without being disturbed, neither do they often intervene. They see things on a . . . different scale than even I. I may be able to petition Balance for help. They will not intervene directly, but we may find that Balance can convince one of the other nature spirits where I cannot. I have not tried this because Balance does not tip the weights of fate lightly. It will require a sacrifice.*"

Zalia felt dread at the words. The way in which the wolf spoke of petitioning Balance gave a weight that didn't quite translate in the words.

"A . . . sacrifice?"

"*Do not worry, young Druid. The sacrifice will not be yours to make, nor any of you who live in this world. That shall be my honour.*"

She stared up at the starlight wolf, concern filling her. What did it mean by sacrifice?

"We must go now. Come, I shall bring you to meet them. Hildebrandt, you have done well in this task. Go and take care of our young Druid's friends, we shall meet you soon."

The wolf knelt down, angling itself in a way that would allow Zalia to easily climb on top of it.

"Zalia, are you sure about this?"

Hildebrandt was looking equally worried, eyes flicking between her and the starlight wolf.

"I trust them, go. I'll see you after."

She hurriedly climbed up the wolf's leg and up onto its back, holding on tight. With a slight run up and a jump into the air, the wolf began stepping on sparkling stars on a journey up into the sky. Despite the beautiful sight of the world lit below by the cold light of the stars, only one thing echoed in Zalia's mind.

The sacrifice will not be yours to make, nor any of you who live in this world. That shall be my honour.

CHAPTER FORTY-EIGHT

Petition

Zalia

Zalia was sat on the surprisingly soft back of the glittering starlight wolf who had become her friend, the breeze lightly pulling at her hair and clothes. She had lost the wide-brim hat that Ember had bought for her when the Astar had captured her. Despite her initial complaints about the matching outfit she shared with Aylie, she kind of missed the hat. It had been the first thing that Ember had bought for her, and a piece of fuel for the intense fire that was now the emotions shared between them.

The starlight wolf had brought them far up into the sky, where they now waited.

"Is there anything I should know before meeting this Balance person? Are we meeting them here?"

"*Patience, child, they will be here soon. I have brought you here to be witness to the words spoken, nothing more. Speak if you feel you have something to contribute, otherwise it is best that I explain our position.*"

Zalia adjusted herself a little, getting more comfortable. She wasn't exactly afraid of the height, being able to fly and all, but it was the highest she had ever been outside of a plane before. There was nothing between her and endless open air but the slightly incorporeal form of a wolf made of starlight.

"Alright, I can do that."

She felt out of place, as if what she was about to witness wasn't something that someone of her rank or place in the world was meant to. Shouldn't the wolf have taken Hildebrandt instead? She was almost Emerald rank, after all, with power much more significant than Zalia's own.

"And, you said you would make a sacrifice? What will that be?"

The powerful aura of the wolf, while still mostly unreadable to her, showed a hint of mirth at her continued questions.

"*Everything and nothing. Hush now, they arrive.*"

The air in front of them warped, and then a tiny little creature appeared. It was round and fluffy, almost like one of those small dogs that had their hair groomed and cut to make them look like a little ball. Her first thought was, *Awww*, quickly followed by, *Boreal would probably want to know what it tastes like.*

Both of those thoughts left her mind as she felt the confusing mixture of things her senses picked up. To Aura Observation, it was both not there and everywhere at the same time. She could feel that it was entirely neutral as a being, yet only managed to be so because of the perfect balance of sides. It gave the sense of a board balanced on a ball only by the perfect distribution of the million weights across its surface.

She picked all of that up in an instant, the sense of balance about the creature more accurate to what it really was than the little fluffy ball that it was currently presented as. This creature felt different than the other gods she had encountered in a way she couldn't quite define.

This thought was underpinned by the starlight wolf bowing down to it.

Zalia followed suit, awkwardly trying to bow on the already angled wolf's back.

"*Balance, I come to petition your help. A trade.*"

"*Make your petition, young one.*"

Balance calling the starlight wolf "young one" put her a little on edge. She had seen the story of Nateysta, which explained how the starlight wolf was so old that it had been guiding even the other gods into their power. Yet somehow, it was younger than this being?

"*I have learned that the Astar work with the demons in their attempt to take this world. They disturb the balance of life here.*"

There was a moment of silence; Zalia felt a cold bead of sweat roll down her face as they maintained their bowed posture.

"*Every action has a reaction. Do you understand the price for what you ask?*"

Zalia was a little confused. There seemed to be a subtext to the conversation she didn't understand, or maybe her translation powers were severely simplifying what was said. What exactly had the starlight wolf asked for?

"*I am willing to personally pay the price for my petition.*"

Her heart beat quicker, worry and confusion playing through her mind. Whatever the starlight wolf was asking for, surely it couldn't be worth a . . . a *sacrifice*. What was it losing? What was it losing it for?

"*Very well.*"

Balance vanished, leaving no disturbance in the air or trace of its having been there.

Zalia blinked and looked around, but nothing had changed.

"Soooo, what exactly is the price for what just happened? And also what just happened?"

"*Stand and stay strong, Zalia. I have given us a chance, it is up to you to guide others on the path that will lead to your success now.*"

Her concern grew.

"Up to me now? What about you?"

She had a sinking feeling she knew what the price had been.

"*I'll see you on the other side, young Druid.*"

The stars above them began to slowly fade, before disappearing entirely. The only source of light was the glowing starlight wolf beneath her, the darkness outside of which even her enhanced eyes could not penetrate.

"*Guide them. For me.*"

The light of the wolf blinked out.

For the . . . eighth time? . . . ninth time? . . . in recent months, Zalia woke up without full awareness of where exactly she was.

She lay on a small cot, blankets covering her. It was inside of a comfortable tent that had a large hide covering the floor. The flaps of the tent were secured by a series of small straps of leather that looped around hooks. Sun was shining against the sides of the hide tent, throwing shadows across the area and highlighting the central tent pole by the light streaming through a hole at the peak of the tent.

The only other source of light in the tent was the tiny wolf puppy made of starlight, glowing gently as it slept in her lap.

Zalia gently sat up and reached a hand forward, stroking the side of the puppy. It woke up and looked at her with curious eyes, head tilted to the side.

"What did you do?" she asked it.

It tilted its head to the other side as if trying to decipher her words yet not quite being able to.

A hand reached through the flaps of the tent and began unhooking the leather straps one by one. She was about to summon her sword and prepare to fight her way free if she had to—the memories of being woken by her captors to be tortured over the past month and a half were fresh in her mind.

Before she got the chance, though, she saw the jet black hair, then the head of Ember push through the flaps and into the tent, followed by the rest of her.

Not being able to fully form words, a burst of emotions ranging from misery all the way to happiness broke free from her in the form of a strangled-sounding cry.

Ember rushed over and knelt beside the cot, grabbing Zalia into a tight hug. The starlight puppy wriggled around, trying not to get crushed between the two of them.

"It's alright," Ember whispered, "I've got you. We've got you."

Zalia started crying, the stress and pain of her experience flowing away in one long, comfortable and *safe* hug. A hug powered by strong emotional healing magic.

"You've really got to stop being the reason my emotional healing levels so quickly."

Zalia sob-laughed at that.

"I'll try my best."

Her voice was rough and raw, but she felt a lot better. Ember tended to have that effect on her.

Zalia pulled back, holding one hand on the side of Ember's face.

"How are you? Are the others alright?"

Ember smiled, taking her hand and pulling her up, the starlight puppy rolling off onto the cot.

"Don't worry, they're alright. I just wanted you to myself for a moment."

Zalia scooped up the puppy under her arm as Ember pulled her out of the tent. She was immediately assaulted by both Boreal and Aylie latching on to her.

"Oh, I've missed you all so much."

A fresh wave of tears rolled down her face but was quickly overcome with happiness. She was with her family again, safe. The biggest issue that sat on her shoulders at that moment was what to do with the super cute starlight puppy wriggling in protest under her arm.

She handed it to Aylie.

"Here, hold this."

Aylie took the puppy awkwardly and quickly received some radiant licks to the chin.

"Where did you get the starlight puppy, if I may ask?" Ember asked.

Zalia inspected the little thing and knew, not just from the description she received, that it was indeed the new form of the starlight wolf.

Starlight Wolf Pup - Tin rank (Ascendant)

She wasn't exactly sure what "Ascendant Tin rank" meant, but it confirmed her suspicions.

"That is my dear friend, the starlight wolf. It made a bargain with something called Balance to help us. This is the sacrifice it made."

Aylie looked at the puppy with wider eyes, coming to the realisation that the wriggling starlight was the very same spirit that had blessed her.

"It's taken care of us from afar, sure, but has done so nonetheless. Now it's our turn to take care of it, I think."

"It made a bargain? What exactly did it bargain for?"

Zalia scratched her head.

"Well, I'm not exactly sure. I guess we'll find out?"

At that moment, a portal was ripped open in reality beside them, and her old friend Ro-ak, better known as Nateysta, tumbled out.

CHAPTER FORTY-NINE

Nature's Back

Zalia

Nateysta!? Ro!?"

Zalia stared at her godly friend. He looked in bad shape, the leaf-feathers covering his body going a yellow colour, patches already falling out dead.

The portal closed again, the brief look Zalia got into Cormaine sending shivers down her spine.

"Zalia, where am I? How did you bring me here?"

His voice was rough, whispery, and sounded as if he was in pain. She looked down at where he lay on the floor, still in shock. This is what the starlight wolf had bargained for.

As he painfully stood up, she rushed over and helped support him. Then, she grabbed the large nature crow into a hug.

"What are you doing?"

"I'm glad you're alive."

She pulled back and inspected him a little closer. The yellowed feathers were looking healthier by the second. Ro-ak was also beginning to look around as if just noticing the nature-covered surroundings.

"Where am I?"

"This is the kingdom of Endaria, on the planet of . . . uhhh, well, something. It's the sister world of Cormaine, the place I came from when I arrived on your world."

"Ah, of course. And.. . . . did you bring me here?"

Zalia stepped aside to where Aylie was still holding the wriggling starlight puppy.

"The starlight wolf, your old friend, made a bargain to bring you here."

The puppy finally broke free of Aylie and ran over to sniff about Ro's feet. It then looked up, tilting its head.

"What did you do, dear friend? How did you end up this way?"

He knelt back down, leaf-feathers now back to a healthy, mottled green.

The puppy yipped, taking a step back and getting down low, as if preparing to jump at Ro.

"It was part of the bargain. To keep the balance, I think."

Ro looked up sharply, dark, beady eyes glinting with light.

"Balance."

Zalia looked back at Ember, then realised she was waiting for her to introduce them.

"Oh! Ro, this is Ember and Aylie. You've met Boreal as well, of course. They're my family. Ember, Aylie, this is Nateysta, spirit of the forests and mysteries. God? Spirit or god, something like that. I also know him as Ro-ak, though that was before I knew he was a powerful spirit."

Ember stepped forward, while Aylie looked like she was staring right into Ro's soul. Remembering her powers, she might actually have been doing just that.

Boreal was looking onwards from beside Aylie, eyeing the starlight puppy with suspicion.

"Good to meet you, I've heard a thing or two about you from Zalia. Thank you for keeping her safe in Cormaine."

"Greetings, Ember, Aylie. Hello again, Boreal. Zalia must have not told the tale in its fullest, as she was the one to protect me, in a way. I was dormant when she arrived there, only revived thanks to her actions."

Ember turned to look directly at Zalia.

"Is that so? Maybe you should tell me your version of the story sometime."

"I'd be glad to."

"Actually, that's a good point! What did happen to you after you sent me and Boreal through the portal?" Zalia added, her attempt at deflecting the conversation defter than she usually managed.

"The fight was painful. There was not much I could do against the two thousand-eyed ones. I managed to tear the avatar of one of them apart, yet the other subdued me. It has been . . . attempting to put me back into dormancy ever since."

Zalia frowned.

"The avatar?"

"Like this form you see before you. It was not dead, simply put out of the fight for a long time. It reformed eventually. I survived this long thanks to you again, Zalia. I felt the faith you had in me, the rituals you dedicated to my name. The altars you built in my honour. I owe you once more."

"I didn't really know what I was doing, to be honest. I just wanted to make sure you weren't forgotten once more."

"Which you did. I sense a few others venerating my name. Who are they?"

Zalia looked at Ember, then scratched at the back of her head.

"Huh?"

He turned his head to look in what had to be the direction of the war camp.

"That way, you do not know who?"

She thought about it, trying to figure out who it could possibly be.

"Some farmers, maybe? I never told them about you, though, so I don't know how that could have happened."

"Some of them kneel at my altar, even now."

Oh.

"Ahh, shit, I didn't expect them to go in there. Well, I guess you have some devoted . . . again? You used to have a religion, right?"

Ro actually managed to look uncomfortable.

"Well . . . yes? I had those who made prayers to me. I did have temples, after all."

It was weird to consider. She had just thought of Ro as her superpowerful friend. It only really hit then that he was a god that people worshipped. Sure, she had been in the temples dedicated to him, she had even made prayers to him herself, but having other people who were actually *alive* that were praying to him? It nailed it home just a little bit more.

"Huh. Anyway, it's actually great you're here. We need your help."

She went over and sat down on a log seat that Ember had probably put there, considering the other two that formed a rough circle with it. Ro came over and settled in on the ground, wings folding around himself. He kind of looked like a bush.

"I figured as much. I see no other reason the starlight would have brought me here."

She didn't miss that Ro simply called them "the starlight." She thought it was probably due to him seeing the world differently. To her, she only knew the starlight wolf by that very form. Ro probably saw that form as an avatar only, the power behind it being the real person.

"The demons have invaded this world, just as I feared. I didn't succeed in stopping them."

Ro's head bobbed a little.

"I see. Can the people of this world not fight them off?"

"Well . . . they probably could, if that was all. Unfortunately, there are others in this world that are responsible for bringing them here. They aren't exactly *helping* the demons per se, but they are definitely a threat. Also, there is one of the thousand-eyed ones in the capital, and the nature spirits of this world will not act to remove it. I think that's why the starlight wolf brought you here."

"I see . . . it is very like the starlight to sacrifice their own power, their

memory and sense of self, to bring something here that may fight this creature, rather than doing so personally. I would love to help, Zalia, but I fear I may be too weak to defeat it."

Zalia sighed, looking down. No, that couldn't be right.

"What about with some time? There is so much nature here! Surely you can recover your strength quicker."

She gestured to Ro, indicating the already healthier looking leaf-feathers he now had.

"Yes, perhaps. I had not considered how much easier it is to recover my strength. It will also be much harder for the thousand-eyed one to maintain its own strength here. Yes, I might be able to defeat it with time."

Better.

Ember was still standing, looking between the two as conversation continued.

"How strong are these 'thousand-eyed ones' you two are speaking of? Can't you kill them with your aura at Silver now, Zalia?"

Ro's head stretched towards Zalia, piercing eyes inspecting her closely.

"So that is what I sensed here. I thought it was just the life around us. How did you get that skill to Silver so quickly? You became Bronze not so long ago."

"No, Ember, even with this, I couldn't kill one. I'll be able to survive in its aura, maybe even still be able to fight. These things are Ascendant, though, so no, killing it on my own is definitely off the table."

Aylie sat down right next to Ro, then started inspecting his leaf-feathers.

"What are you doing, child?"

The starlight puppy came up and started inspecting the leaf-feathers with Aylie as well. Ro looked to Zalia in confusion and she shrugged, indicating she didn't know either.

"You're . . . different. Your soul isn't on the inside like everything else."

Ro looked back down at Aylie and Zalia raised an eyebrow.

"What powers do you have, child?"

Aylie didn't answer, so Zalia did for her.

"A few, but she can see the souls of things and has the ability to know things from something called the astral?"

"Curious. How did she come by these classes?"

Zalia pointed at the starlight puppy.

"A blessing from our dear friend."

Ember perked up.

"What is the astral? Both Zalia and I have been trying to teach Aylie about her powers, but we don't really know what they do ourselves, some of them at least."

"The astral is . . . complicated. Most will not learn or have need of it until much higher ranks, as it is unusable to you without a certain level of power. To have access to it at the rank of Tin is a powerful ability indeed."

"Just . . . complicated? Is there anything at all you can tell us about it?" Ember pushed.

"I will try. The astral isn't really a place for most, rather a plane where thought exists. This isn't to say that anything that thinks is on the astral, so much as to say it is a plane where thought is free to travel. Your mental communication power uses the astral as a method of transferring thought from one creature to another, for instance. The bonds you share, both with people and with heirlooms make use of the astral as well."

Zalia remained silent, thinking over the information. It was certainly interesting, though not necessarily useful to her at that moment.

Ember wanted to know more though.

"Aylie's ability says that part of her soul walks the astral. What does that mean then?"

"Very interesting. She may be able to pick up on things through the astral, then. Thoughts, bonds, mental communication. All of these might become visible to her as she advances in rank, much as the trees and sky are visible to us."

That got Zalia's full attention.

"Really? That seems extremely powerful."

"It is, in certain circumstances. Depending how her abilities advance, she may be able to manipulate those things as well. That is a power that must be used very, very carefully."

In her mind, Zalia saw Starfall as Aylie's most powerful ability. On paper, it certainly was. Even just through the most recent demonstration of the ability during the fight with the shapechangers, it appeared to be so. That opinion shifted slightly after hearing what Ro had just said, however. The power to manipulate people's bonds, hear their thoughts, or even change them. A dozen questions rose to her mind. Would she be able to break someone's bond with their heirloom? What about bonds between people? What about putting thoughts into people's minds?

Even based on those things, she immediately agreed with Ro. They would have to be *really* careful.

"She is able to interact with people's souls as well. What does that mean?"

Ro turned back to Ember.

"She also has this ability? That is . . . quite something. She will be dangerous when she grows older. Very dangerous."

Zalia looked at Aylie, who was still inspecting Ro closely. The weight of raising her suddenly grew ten times heavier on her shoulders. Raising a kid normally was a hard enough task. There was so much you could get wrong, so many things you had to keep in mind. Adding in the fact that she would grow up to be extremely dangerous and powerful, well, that added a whole extra layer.

"Oh. Wonderful."

CHAPTER FIFTY

Ointment

Zalia

Aylie sat on the floor inspecting Ro-ak closely. Zalia watched her, digesting the information that Ro had just told her. If Aylie was listening, she showed no sign of surprise at the explanation of her abilities. She might have even known a few of those things, having picked up on thoughts, bonds, and mental communication through her abilities already.

"What did she mean by 'your soul is different'?" Ember asked Ro.

"If I'm correct, Aylie here has seen how I truly exist. When you become Ascendant, your soul is no longer confined to a mortal body. This has happened to me. My soul exists in many places now: my temples in Cormaine, here, my altar elsewhere in this world, partially around those who are my friends or venerate me. There is part of me with each of you. I am able to consolidate parts of that soul into one place to form an avatar, like you see before you now. I am also able to consolidate all of it to attain my full power, as I did during our final battle in Cormaine, Zalia. It is then that I'm most powerful, yet most vulnerable."

A thought occurred to Zalia.

"So, if someone who was able to interact with a soul were to somehow destroy it while it was all consolidated in one place, would that potentially be a way to kill an Ascendant being?"

Ro-ak said nothing, dark eyes glimmering. His silence answered her question.

It was perhaps not something that people of her rank were supposed to know, to even be thinking about. Still, it might be useful to know in their current situation, considering what they were up against.

"Well, thank you for the information. It has been pretty hard trying to help her figure out those abilities. I'm a little apprehensive about the Dreamweaver ability as well, though I understand that one perfectly well."

"The ability to influence dreams. That will definitely level up to have connections with the Astral Walker ability."

Thinking about it, Zalia saw the connection that Ro had seen immediately. She wasn't entirely sure what people's dreams were, whether they were subconscious thoughts or a result of the mind's nightly cleansing process, but she did know that they came from one's thoughts. Which just happened to be on the astral, or so Ro said.

Just like that, Ro had given her enough information to start predicting how Aylie's powers would advance. Damn, she had missed the big leafy guy.

"Thanks, Ro, I appreciate the information. This is going to help us more than you know."

"It is the least I can do for you, Zalia. Now, how do you wish to proceed?"

At that question, everything came crashing back down on her. Her torture, what was happening in Endaria, what they needed to get done and what had happened already.

"Nope, not today," she said.

She didn't push all those memories into her vault; she knew how bad of an idea that was. She did, however, push them to the back of her mind. Tomorrow.

Ember took one look at her, reading her emotions through their bond.

"We'll go over it tomorrow. For today, maybe just accustom yourself to this world and the nature here. I'm sure it is a little different than what you're used to," Ember supplied.

"A good idea, Ember. I will be back soon."

Ro took to the air, his smooth and casual flight a stark difference to his struggle to stand moments earlier.

Zalia turned to Ember, feeling *very* overwhelmed.

"It's a little much, at the moment."

Ember came and scooted onto the log seat next to her, squishing up close.

"I know, I've got you though, don't worry."

Zalia took one of Ember's hands in her own and rested her head on her shoulder.

"How did you find me before I woke up?"

Ember gave a little laugh.

"Oh, well, you kind of fell from the sky."

Zalia frowned.

"I what?"

"We were trying our best to catch up to Hildebrandt and you fell from the sky. Slowly, so you didn't hurt yourself. You and the little starlight puppy just floated down."

Zalia couldn't help but laugh gently as well. She could imagine the concern and fear that Ember would have had, only for her to float down as if from the heavens with a wolf pup made of stars.

"Was I out long?"

"Nah, you just slept the night."

"And what about Hildebrandt, has she come back yet?"

Aylie was still looking to where Ro had flown off; the starlight puppy was looking wistfully after him as well.

"She was a day or so ahead of us, she should be back by late tonight if she is going full speed to get back here."

There was a moment of silence before Ember spoke again.

"Do you want to talk about it?"

Zalia knew what she was asking about straight away. While she had told Ember and Boreal as much as she could through the bond, there was a lot they hadn't heard yet.

"Not . . . not yet. I will, and I won't lock the memory away just . . . not yet."

She felt Ember nod and she didn't ask any further. Zalia appreciated Ember for that, more than she could know. Well, maybe she could,.considering their bond.

It was an interesting thing to think about, the fact that their bond was something that was *real* on another plane. Part of the existence there, rather than something ethereal and inexplicable. She didn't like the idea that it was possible for something with the right powers to interfere with a bond. Even more, she disliked the idea that it was possible to read the emotions or words passed between them. It felt like an invasion of their privacy. She would have to make sure Aylie knew not to abuse her power in that regard.

Not that she expected Aylie to do so; she just knew from her years in the other world that power had a way of influencing people.

Resting comfortably beside Ember, Zalia decided to feel out the new limits of Healing Presence. The base healing was definitely increased, perhaps by half between Bronze nineteen and Silver one. Each level gave a little bit of a boost, but the jump across ranks was quite significant. All in all, while she couldn't measure accurately, she would say it had doubled in potency from Bronze one, while the increase in power from Iron one to Bronze one would have been half as much of an increase. If she were to assign a numerical value to its power at each level with Tin one being one, Iron one would have been three, Bronze one would be seven, and Silver one would be fifteen.

The bigger part of the power increase was the actual effect of the Silver ability. Stretching her senses, she couldn't reach the outer limits of what the ability affected. It could go for kilometres.

If her other abilities followed a similar curve in strength, it was no wonder the jump in power between Bronze and Silver was so great, and the difference between Silver and Gold even greater. That scale would go on until Ascendant, the rank at which things worked much differently. Hildebrandt was probably stronger than Nateysta in raw power, yet the fact that he was almost impossible to permanently kill changed things a lot. He also had an aura strength that Hildebrandt would not be able to match unless she reached Ascendant as well.

Thinking of Ascendants, she now had a little star puppy Ascendant to deal with. How the hell did she raise an Ascendant?

Did it . . . need to eat? Level up? Did it need daily prayer?

Maybe she should ask Ro about that as well, he might know.

"You know what I need to do?"

"What's that?" Ember whispered.

Zalia lifted her head and looked at her beautiful partner.

"Gardening."

"Gardening?"

"Yeah, come on."

She stood up and pulled Ember up along with her. Her vault door opened, and two vines covered in leaves and pastel-coloured flowers grew into a large oval doorway. Gentle light came through the portal that appeared in the arch and she pulled Ember into the vault with her.

At the back, Zalia kept a small collection of all her different herbs, at least one of each so she didn't lose any. The half circle space had a workbench lining the outer wall that was covered in various dried, crushed, cut, and whole herbs.

She walked to the little garden area with Ember and knelt down on the dirt. After a moment's hesitation, Ember sat down on the dirt with her too. Rather than use any of her many powers to easily harvest and prepare herbs, she simply started pruning with her hands. It was easy enough to snap off pieces of the herbs. She wasn't worried, since any damage to the plant was healed by the ever-present healing from the vault.

Ember looked a little uncertain, so Zalia started teaching her what she was doing. She had been somewhat of an herbalist before she had ever gotten magic, yet hadn't really done traditional gardening and herbing since then.

She started by teaching Ember which sprigs to take and which to leave. Some of the more woody old growth wouldn't do well, since it was the main piece of the plant. The newer green growths that were still soft and sprouting many leaves were the ones she took. She didn't take all of them, though, leaving some for each plant. That way the remaining new growth would benefit from the extra space and nutrients from the plant, leading to a healthier plant.

Once they had gathered a few good handfuls of herb sprigs, they went to a bench and worked together, taking the leaves off. Sometimes it was better to pull them off one by one, and other times it was better to run their hands down the length of the stem, opposite to its direction of growth. Once they had a pile of nicely sorted leaves, Zalia had to stop Ember from throwing away the remaining stems.

There were many uses for stems of herbs, and Zalia taught Ember a few of them. Some of the nicer-smelling herbs she wound together to form wreaths. Some of them she hung about the vault, their gentle, woody smell spreading further through the already earthy-smelling space. Others could still be used in her ritual magic, though they required additional refinement with the use of Preparation.

Usually, if she wanted to dry the leaves, it would be better to hang them up while on the stem in a sunny spot. With Preparation she didn't need to do that, and as they didn't have anywhere to hang them up that they'd be staying, she didn't bother. It made her want a home for them, so she could show Ember that step too.

She used her stone manipulation powers to create a mortar and pestle. With that, she was able to crush them.

Since the herbs hadn't been dried, many of them turned into a sort of paste. Surprisingly, they became something she hadn't actually created before using Preparation.

> **Snow-leaf Ointment (Potent) - Bronze rank.**
> **Will heal burns when applied.**

It wasn't really useful to her at all. It wasn't powerful and was entirely over-taken by Healing Presence. Somehow, though, the simple joy of creating something new with Ember brought her a calm, contented happiness.

CHAPTER FIFTY-ONE

Culmination

Zalia

Zalia stood looking at the array of poultices and ointments that she and Ember had made from the various herbs she had.

> **Bitterbalm Poultice (Potent) - Bronze rank.**
> Will cause necrosis to the applied wound along with an ever-present sense of dread.
> **Frozen Heart Poultice (Potent) - Bronze rank.**
> Will rapidly heal cuts, abrasions, and other surface wounds.
> **Flame-root Oil (Potent) - Bronze rank.**
> Extremely flammable.
> **Dodge-vine Oil (Potent) - Bronze rank.**
> Can be applied to armour to provide a slight enhancement to its protectiveness.
> **Manifest Paste (Potent) - Bronze rank.**
> Capable of solidifying incorporeal beings.
> **Zephyr Mist (Potent) - Bronze rank.**
> When breathed in, can replace the need for breathing for an extended time.
> **Water Lily Stem Juice (Potent) - Bronze rank.**
> Wonderfully tasty drink not much different in effect to eating the stem of the Water Lily.
> **Water Lily Petal Ointment (Potent) - Bronze rank.**
> Can drastically reduce fever and other side effects from sicknesses.
> **Cavern Fungus Shade (Potent) - Bronze rank.**
> When poured over an object, this will hide it from sight for an extended period of time.

> **Adastem Juice (Potent) - Bronze rank.**
> **A creature that drinks this will be able to adapt to their environment for a short time.**

It had been a fun experience experimenting with what kind of refined material the herbs would turn into. The poultices were kind of pasty with pieces of solid plants all through them, with the others turning into oils, paste, or even juice. The two that were most interesting to Zalia were Zephyr Mist and Cavern Fungus Shade. They sat in two separate bowls, the Zephyr being a white mist and the Cavern Fungus Shade looking like liquid darkness. She might have called it an oil, if not for the little box of information describing it as a shade instead.

Some of these, unlike the Snow-leaf Ointment, might actually be useful to her. Putting aside their usefulness as items she could give to people, they were also able to do some things that her rituals couldn't do easily, not without Preparation, at least.

She went to find Aylie, wanting to talk to her, and found her playing with the starlight puppy.

"Hey, Aylie, how are you doing?"

Aylie looked up as the puppy gnawed on her hand a little.

"Ok."

Zalia sat down next to her, lifting the puppy into her lap and patting it.

"I wanted to tell you I'm sorry for disappearing for all that time. Some very . . . insistent people wanted to talk to me. I hope you've been alright."

Aylie looked down, fiddling with her hands.

"At first I was very scared. It was such a long time, and I didn't know where you had gone. But then, I remembered that you came back last time and knew you would this time too!"

Zalia pulled her close for a hug, her heart feeling warm and fuzzy.

"Of course, Aylie, and I always will."

She felt a little bad for making the promise, not knowing if she would be able to keep it. Despite that, though, she felt good, better than she had days before, that was for sure. It was good to just do something simple, easy, and consequence-free for once. An evening with Ember messing around with plants followed by a heartwarming talk with Aylie was exactly what she had needed.

As it always did, however, reality soon came knocking.

Ro arrived back at the little campsite, seeming excited and invigorated. Zalia could immediately tell the difference in the spirit, a mixture of strength and joy practically visible all over his body.

"There is just _so_ much nature here! Alive, thriving, chaotic, beautiful nature."

His words brought a broad smile to her face. She had felt similar things when first arriving in Endaria. Compared to the world she had come from, it was basically a wild forest, untamed and untouched. She leaned against the inside of her vault portal, looking out at him.

"I'm glad you are feeling a little better."

He was practically *glowing*.

"Very much so. To be in a place so fresh and clean, free of the corruption. I had forgotten what it was to soar skies filled not with the dead but the songs of birds and breeze."

"Feeling eloquent, are we?"

"The beauty of nature requires more complex language to convey. You will understand when you are older."

She snorted a laugh, stepping fully out of the portal as Ember walked past to check on Aylie.

"You were just reborn, which basically makes you a child."

"Being reborn is a fact of life for an Ascendant. Perhaps you'll understand that one day too."

Zalia turned to look at the starlight puppy running around Boreal, nipping at her gently. Thankfully, Boreal had apparently grown the patience of a saint after being around both Aylie and now the puppy, and only gave half-hearted retaliatory swipes.

"Speaking of being reborn, what exactly do we do with them?"

Ro turned to follow her gaze, his beady dark eyes focusing on the pup.

"An excellent question. Much as the story told, when I was younger, Starlight guided me to become what I am today. I feel that I should do the same for them, yet I have a feeling that Aylie will be a better guide than I ever could."

She looked to where Aylie was still kneeling, also watching the pup.

"Aylie? Why?"

"For the reasons we spoke of earlier. At this time, she might be young and inexperienced. The lives of Ascendants are long, quite long indeed. I believe it will not take much time before Aylie is better at seeing hidden truths and divining the secrets of the world than I am. I may be a spirit of mysteries, yet Starlight is a spirit of the stars. Oftentimes, they could unveil things even I could not. Yes, I think that the blessing Starlight has given the child was for this very reason."

Something about that didn't quite play right to Zalia. She had urged Aylie to trust the starlight wolf, to accept the blessing and the class that had come with it. Had the wolf only done that so it would have a backup in case it needed to sacrifice its knowledge and life to Balance?

Thinking that, though, wasn't it fair for the wolf to want some way to regain what it needed to sacrifice, even if it might take a long, long time? It wasn't like the wolf had harmed Aylie in any way. It had given her a class that would end up beyond what any normal Endarian would ever expect to gain themselves.

"Well, first things first, then. We gotta give them a name. Or maybe we let Aylie give them a name."

"Starlight is a perfectly apt name for them."

"Look, I don't disagree with that. But, I think we should give them one anyway. I mean, I gave you Ro-ak, and you like that, don't you?"

Ro turned to look at her, his large head covered in vines.

"I will concede that point. A name, then."

Zalia walked over to where Aylie and Ember were chatting and sat down on the ground next to Aylie.

Ember was talking to Aylie about her powers, going over a few of the things that they had learned from Ro earlier that day. While Aylie had been there for the conversation, she had also been a little . . . in the clouds. She had been more interested in Ro's aura than the words he spoke.

Zalia only spoke up once Ember was done.

"Hey, I think we should give the starlight pup a name. I thought you should give a name to the rebirth of the creature that gave you your blessing."

"A name," Aylie said thoughtfully.

She was playing around with a few strands of grass using Plant Manipulation and they danced and twirled under her directions.

"Something to do with the stars, maybe."

Aylie nodded in agreement, still looking thoughtful, though her gaze had turned to where the puppy was chewing on Boreal's tail.

In the fading light of the day, the pup was beginning to glow gently. Light, blue light reflected off the crystal shards that grew from Boreal's back and shoulders.

"Luminescence."

Zalia considered it.

"It's a little long. How about Lumin for short?"

She looked to Ro, who seemed fine with the idea.

Aylie nodded and Zalia urged her to go teach the puppy their new name. For her own, somewhat selfish reasons, she wanted Aylie to grow a bond with the pup. If she did, then Aylie would grow up protected by an Ascendant being. Zalia wasn't her birth mother, but was starting to properly think of herself as that to the girl. And what mother wouldn't want an extremely powerful being protecting their child?

Zalia sighed, realising it might soon be time to get back to reality. Hildebrandt would no doubt be arriving soon, and then they'd have to go back to the war camp. From there, she didn't really see any path other than to use her new Silver rank Healing Presence and the aura of Ro to push into the capital. There, they could take down the thousand-eyed one. It would be a huge strike against the invasion, taking out their most powerful piece on the board. If she was right about the demons fighting out of fear rather than loyalty, it might even cause some of them to start fighting amongst themselves.

She settled in as Ember cuddled up next to her on the ground, intending to fully appreciate the last few moments of peace they might get for a while. The idea of taking Ember, Aylie, Boreal, and the newest member of their family, Lumin, away to some remote spot once the invasion was over grew more and more in her mind. Freeing Cormaine was still in the plans for her, but why not wait until Aylie was grown and stronger, until Ro had gathered more strength, until she herself had ranked up to Silver, maybe even Gold rank.

Zalia was right in her assumption, as Hildebrandt arrived in a flash of movement less than three hours later. She was covered in dust, dirt, and various pieces of destroyed plant matter. It was almost like she had forgone going *around* the plants and had just gone through them instead.

She looked at Zalia and Ember, looked at Aylie and Lumin, then at Ro. Then, she sat down on a log, dropped her tower shield to the ground, and Zalia watched in amazement as all the stiff, tense, ready-to-fight energy fled from her body.

In a moment, Hildebrandt went from dangerous almost-Emerald ranker, to relaxed woman who just so happened to be wearing plate armour.

Once she'd had a few minutes to settle in, Zalia began to explain who Lumin—previously the starlight wolf—was, who Ro was, what had happened with Balance, and how they had gotten here. She explained the significance of having Ro on their side now and what it meant for their plans going forward. The one thing she didn't reveal was Ro's explanation about Aylie's powers. That was something she wanted to keep secret.

Hildebrandt took it all in with near silence, then told Zalia that she had destroyed the entire keep that she'd found her in. Apparently, there hadn't been anything of importance there, though Zalia had no doubt the woman would have found the cell as well as the power-limiting bracelets.

Then, Ro repeated a question from much earlier.

"How do you want to proceed, Zalia?"

This time, she was quite a bit more ready for it.

"I think we should go back to the war camp and convince them that now is the time to strike at the capital. What has happened there since I've been gone?"

This wasn't something she'd considered yet, and Ember replied.

"A force to the south of the capital has slowly been making its way east and north to meet up with the main camp. They had just arrived when we left to find you, Zalia. Larel was with them, and she took over command of the Morning's Shade while Hildebrandt came to get you. That army is now as strong as it is going to get, and the camp is completely overflowing. We managed to get the Morning's Shade settled in to your Grove well enough, though. I think they might be of the same opinion that now is the time. We only lose out by waiting, we're as strong as we're going to get."

Hearing that only reinforced Zalia's idea.

"Right, then we go back and strike at the capital. I was thinking we take only the strongest people and strike quick and hard at the thousand-eyed one that lives there, but maybe a bigger attack is a better idea. Hildebrandt? You'd know better than me."

The woman looked up from where she was chewing on some type of hard ration, dried meat perhaps.

"Well, we certainly could try that. If we failed, it would be the end of any chance to take back the capital, though. I don't really know their numbers and how many high-rankers they have, do you?"

Zalia shook her head. She knew that there was one Ascendant, but what about Gold rankers? There had to be a few, at least. If she remembered correctly, the king was, and he was definitely on the enemy side.

"Ah, we should probably leave the tactical decisions to the generals. Either way though, now *is* the time."

Ro shifted from where he stood, head turning.

"I am in agreement. I am stronger now than I was in Cormaine. The sheer presence of nature here has revitalised me more than I thought possible, and I believe I can take down one of the thousand-eyed ones in a one-on-one fight. Are you sure there is only one there?"

She'd almost forgotten he was here, he stood so still. Like he was a part of the forest around them, which he was, in a way.

"I think there is only one, though it's hard to tell. What else can we do, though? None of the other nature spirits or gods will help us. Lumin has already tried to push them to action."

"If there are two, I might be able to hold them back long enough for you to do your work. This one might be strong enough to help me in destroying them, once your fight is over."

Ro turned his piercing dark eyes to Hildebrandt, who looked a little uncomfortable under the gaze. She wasn't as used to being around powerful gods and spirits as Zalia was, evidently.

"Alright, well not much more we can do without talking with the generals. Let's get a good night's rest and be off for the camp in the morning, then."

The others all nodded their assent and packed in for the night. Not Zalia, though, she stayed awake staring into the small, crackling fire as thoughts tumbled through her mind. Similarly, Ro stood there as a part of the forest around them, motionless.

All the mystery, pain, fear, desperation, and hard work that she and the others had put into figuring out the rituals and events surrounding them was coming down to this one final fight. Whether they freed the capital and took out the thousand-eyed one and the king, or not—it would decide the fate of Endaria for the years to come. Zalia just hoped they would come out on top.

CHAPTER FIFTY-TWO

Accidental Religion

Zalia

The travel from the campsite out in the wilderness to the army camp took almost two weeks. During that time, Lumin had grown closer and closer to Aylie as they began to spend every minute together. It must have been something about the blessing that connected them or just simple happenstance, yet good friends they became. During the time in which she spent the majority of the days teaching Aylie, her Teaching passive increased another five levels, bringing it to Iron seventeen. Low Light Vision also finally ticked over to Bronze.

Congratulations! Low Light Vision has reached Bronze 1.
Low Light Vision becomes Enhanced Vision.
Enhanced Vision - passive.
Tin - You see better in low light areas.
Iron - Your vision is able to pierce magical darkness of the same rank or lower of this ability.
Bronze - You are able to filter out too-bright light to a certain extent, and gain the ability to discern details at greater distances.

It was another nice addition to her multitude of visual abilities. Sure, it didn't allow her to see any better close-up, but she could now look up and into the sun without trouble. It was a wonderful thing to watch, the glowing orb of fire shifting and swirling in the sky. A star to guide by day, as true as any of the others that lit the night.

While they weren't doing anything other than travelling as long as they could each day, their waking hours were filled with anxiety and tension. They knew what they were moving towards, no matter how beautiful their surroundings always seemed to be. That was partially a result of Zalia's ability, which healed away any corruption in the landscape long before they ever saw it. She got a feeling that Ember missed seeing those wounds in nature heal before their eyes.

The trio of Aylie, Boreal, and Lumin managed to relieve their tension a little bit by the sheer amount of not only cuteness but lighthearted idiocy they displayed. Boreal had taken on a more sobered adult role, looking out for the other two as they travelled. Meanwhile, Aylie and Lumin worked together to be as great of a pain in the tail for the icy cat as they could. Zalia personally took a little bit of joy in it, seeing the same expression on Boreal's face now she must have had on a daily basis while raising her.

Hildebrandt stayed mostly silent on their journey, as did Ro. Zalia spent as much of her time with Ember as she could, while still putting aside as much time to teach Aylie about her powers as was possible. She didn't miss that Boreal started trying to teach Lumin how to hunt too.

When they finally arrived at the war camp, it was to a scene of chaos. The camp was overflowing with people, the push by Indis to try and expand the walls to fit more people obviously having failed. It looked like another small area near the main camp had been set up with a temporary enchanted dome, one that flickered and flashed, imperfections obvious in its form.

The people who were either lying about or wandering through that refugee camp looked lost, abandoned and hopeless.

There was another line of refugees with guards leaving for the south, and Zalia recognised the guard at the front as the one she had spoken to so long ago when she'd first come back to Endaria. Well, it wasn't that long ago, but it certainly felt like it. The actual interior of the camp was likewise packed with people, to the point that trying to walk through would be a mission indeed.

Instead of heading there, they went to Zalia's Grove.

Aylie and Lumin sprinted ahead, followed by an excited yet more sober Boreal.

Inside the Grove was a mix of different people and creatures. Farmer Mate's people were happily farming away, the fruit of their labour quickly evident as all the plants in the Grove grew at a quick and steady pace. The man's cows were wandering around free, apparently needing no pen or leash, as the magic of Zalia's Grove gave them the urge to help out much as the other animals inside.

Birds flittered about, and possums and other small critters ran around cleaning and packing up the belongings of the many people who lived there.

The Morning's Shade had moved in as well, as Hildebrandt had said. They looked to be at an absolute loss, standing around without anything to do as the animals of the Grove took care of everything for them. They even seemed to be delivering lunch to some people, Morning's Shade members accepting wooden plates filled with different fruits and berries from the little hands of a few squirrel-like creatures with antlers.

Many of those creatures swarmed about Zalia as she returned, making greetings in chatters, purrs, and bird songs. After greeting her, however, Ro-ak was nearly buried as the animals all wanted to take a turn inspecting the newcomer. Being a spirit of nature, Zalia wouldn't be surprised if Ro ended up with a few worshippers from amongst the Grove animals.

Hildebrandt immediately broke off and went to the group of lost-looking Morning's Shade, while the devious trio of Aylie, Lumin, and Boreal disappeared deeper into the Grove with shrieks, giggles, and yaps.

Zalia was happy to see a little bit of childhood innocence still making an appearance in Aylie.

She and Ember went and found old Farmer Mate.

"Hey, Mate, how is everything?" Zalia greeted, shaking the man's hand as he stood up from the dirt.

"Finally back then, 'ey? 'Bout time you came and sorted this lot out."

He gestured broadly to the entire Grove, as if the entire thing's existence annoyed him. She got the sense he was happier than he showed, though.

"Well, don't worry, I'll be sure to set everything straight as soon as I can. Wouldn't want my hardest working farmer getting anything but the best."

He scoffed and huffed a bit.

"Oh, off with it, I don't need your praise, young woman, leave it for the other youngins."

Despite the words, she could see the hint of a smile tugging at the corners of his mouth.

"How is everything, anyways? All well here?"

"Well, despite this lot"—he gestured around vaguely again—"this Grove you've got here is quite the thing. Ain't seen nothin' like it 'fore in my time, all these animals goin' 'round and cleaning up after us and whatnot."

It was wonderful to hear, and brought Zalia not a small amount of happiness.

"What about the refugees down the hill by the war camp?" Ember asked, stepping forward.

"Ahh, a sorry lot those are. We feed the ones what come up 'ere an' ask for food, but most of what we grow goes down to the smart ones in the army. They know a thing or two 'bout numbers an' all that, I tell ya."

Zalia was only a *tiny* bit surprised by his generosity.

"Did I see Ole Feral just wandering around somewhere as well?"

Mate turned back to her, trying to brush some of the dirt from his hands onto the equally filthy work pants he wore.

"Ah, yeah, she's takin' to wanderin' about. Loves the freedom, ya know?"

Zalia nodded, entirely in agreement with the cow's opinions of cages. Especially now.

"Well, I suppose there's no harm done, then. Do you th—"

Zalia cut off as Mate's gaze locked onto something behind her. She turned around, and it appeared he had finally spotted Ro.

"Is that the one that your altar back there talks about in the writin'?"

Zalia raised an eyebrow. She had known that some of the farmers were praying to Ro from what he had said, yet she hadn't expected Mate to be one of them. Dire times could turn even the most cynical religious, apparently.

"It is, yes. What exactly have you people been doing with that altar?"

For once, she saw an expression on the gruff man's face that wasn't reminiscent of a scowl. He looked a little sheepish.

"Well, a few of the lads found that altar behind the waterfall back there an' we figured the god it spoke of was the one what powered this whole Grove. One thing turned to another, an' now a few of us give daily thanks for what it gives us."

Zalia stared blankly at him.

She could feel such amusement building in Ember through their bond that she was surprised the woman didn't laugh out loud.

"Well, you should go meet him, then."

Mate looked a little worried.

"And don't worry, he's quite gentle and very understanding. Oh, and he loves shiny things."

Mate fished around in his pocket and brought out a silver coin, then trudged off towards Ro.

Trying not to laugh herself, Zalia sent a mental communication to Ro.

"Please be nice to Mate, and don't tell him the Grove is my ability, not yours."

She didn't see any harm in letting the farmers believe it was Ro who was the power behind the Grove. To be fair, it was quite an unusual power for a Bronze ranker to have. She hadn't seen anything like it in others of similar rank.

Linking her arm through Ember's, she walked through the Grove towards the crack in the rock far at the back. There, she went behind the waterfall to where Ro's altar was.

A farmer respectfully left the little cave when she entered, and Zalia finally burst out laughing as she saw the mound of coins, silverware, and other shiny objects in the space. When she'd left, Zalia had taken the little shiny pieces of metal from her vault that Ro had collected in Cormaine and put them on the altar. It looked like the farmers had continued that ritual.

"Oh god, I've revived a religion."

She put her hands on the sides of her head, half amused, half concerned.

"Honey, that's what happens when you build altars to your friends who also happen to be gods, then walk around the kingdom performing rituals dedicated to them."

Ember gave her a tight hug, also starting to laugh. It was ridiculous.

"Alright, sure, why not. All it can do is make Ro that little bit stronger. We can use all the help we can get."

CHAPTER FIFTY-THREE

Mobilisation

Zalia

As they sat in solitude, in a cave behind a waterfall, Zalia told Ember what she had been through. Everything that had happened from the moment she had been captured to the moment she had floated down from the sky with a starlight puppy.

Things got a little fuzzy for her around the constant torture. She had thoroughly lost track of time, having been there for much, much longer than she thought. Perhaps it was how often she passed out, for who knew how long each time. Maybe it was the fact she had been locked in a cell without windows, out of reach of the sun and stars. It could have been the torture itself, the pain enough to make her mind simply shut down until it stopped.

The reality was probably a mixture of all three, a horror she didn't quite manage to convey to Ember.

Learning about the demon being there led them down a path of discussion that resulted in Ember having many of the same thoughts Zalia had. Juniper was a piece on the board of the Astar, who were also responsible for the massive ritual. The king possibly was under their control somehow. Even the idea that Hidey was being controlled by them. Sure, Juniper had been in control of some of his actions, but from the conversation Zalia had with him, and after getting this new information, it was highly likely the Astar were as well.

It was all theory, as they had no solid proof other than the fact the demons *were* working with the Astar. At least, *a* demon was working with two Astar. They didn't know if there were any more of them involved.

They had to assume it was all of them. If it wasn't, then it would be a lot easier to deal with. If it *was* all of them, they would suffer from not being prepared for it.

Ro-ak came to find them before long, barely managing to fit through the entrance of the cave and into the small space.

"So this is my altar, you wouldn't believe what I just had to deal with. They all kept trying to give me shin—"

He didn't finish the word "shiny" as he observed the hoard of reflective metallic objects filling the cave.

"Zalia, what have you done?"

It was her turn to look sheepish.

"Well, I might have accidentally started a new religion dedicated to you, where they believe giving you shiny things is an important part of it?"

"Why would you . . . ?"

"Look! Remember when you were just a little crow following me around, collecting little shiny bits and pieces and giving them to me? Well, when I left, I put them on your altar here. The farmers found it and started doing the same."

Ro stared at her.

"I'm a spirit of forests and *mystery*, not forests and shiny things."

"Shiny things can be mysterious. Well, they can distract *from* mysteries. By being shiny," Ember put in.

Zalia and Ro turned to her, staring.

"We should go see Indis."

"Agreed."

They left the Grove, Ro taking flight soon after leaving the cave to avoid dealing with the farmers again. He seemed pretty distressed at the idea of having to talk to them. Maybe that was why gods didn't appear before or talk to their followers very much. They were just all introverted.

Zalia told Aylie through mental communication where they were going, and received on the vaguest confirmation of her words. It was a stark contrast to Aylie's previous behaviour of sticking to her like glue. Having her eyes open to a whole world that no one else could see was having an effect on the girl already.

She knew there were a few other "gods" that the people of Endaria . . . not necessarily followed or worshipped, but talked about. Zen had mentioned one a few times, though Zalia had forgotten the name. Either way, none of those ones had ever shown up here to help or participate. Only a select few of the nature spirits, or old gods, as they called themselves, were doing anything at all.

Ro rejoined them on the ground as they approached the war camp, the mass of people arrayed outside the walls beginning to become an obstruction to their passage. Zalia had been able to restrict the Silver rank effect of her aura enough that it didn't affect the war camp from her Grove, and pulled it even tighter to herself now.

She leaned over and whispered to Ro as they started pushing through the crowd.

"Hey, Ro, are you able to take other forms?"

"For what reason?"

Zalia looked around to the people beginning to whisper and watch with wide eyes.

"You're the spirit of mysteries, right? Well, right now you're being kinda really in the open and obvious."

"Hmm, perhaps I can alter this form? It is not something I've done in a very long time."

He went silent for a moment as they walked, concentrating.

Just as the gates to the war camp came into view past the crowded people, his form altered and shifted, reduced to a shorter figure covered by a hooded cloak, with only the gleam of light off his beady black eyes visible from within.

"Will this do?"

His voice was still the same, but the figure was a little less attention-drawing.

"It'll do. Just be quiet until we get an audience with Indis or the general."

Zalia was dressed in what looked like simple farmers' clothes didn't draw much attention. She just wished she still had the floppy, wide-brim hat Ember had bought for her. Maybe she could buy another one.

When they arrived at the gates, the nervous man whose task it was to inspect people greeted them. Usually he only came out when people arrived, but it seemed like they permanently had one gate open these days, with this man inspecting everyone who entered.

When he looked at Ro, the guy's eyes seemed to bug out of his head for a moment. Then panic flickered across his face, replaced soon by the most neutral face she had ever seen him maintain, all semblance of nervousness gone.

What the hell?

"You alright?"

"Mmm? Er, yes. Everything is fine, all good. You may enter, of course."

The Silver rank guard flanking the man looked at him, then at Zalia, equally confused.

She shrugged at him, then walked past into the camp.

They trudged through the masses of people, the massive increase in numbers not only due to more refugees but also an increased presence of soldiers. This must be because of the army group that had joined up with them from the far south of Endaria, further west.

It took a while to get past the people, but eventually, when they found themselves approaching the command building, Ro spoke up.

"Are you starting a religion to yourself as well, Zalia?"

She turned to him in confusion, then followed his gaze to where her statue still stood, now fixed so that Boreal was the right size.

"Oh, hell no. That is Indis's fault."

"Who is this Indis you keep mentioning?"

"Ah, well. That is a really long story. A friend? Kind of? Sort of maybe the leader of this country right now? But not really. Ex-noble, now kinda a semi-leader of the rebellion. Again, long story. We're going to go meet her and General Faian right now."

"I see."

He stared at the statue for a few moments longer before they moved on.

Without Boreal at her side, Zalia was able to blend in with the people a little bit. She, her partner, Ember, and their small edgy friend hidden in a cloak.

If she had thought the command building was busy last time she'd been there, it was nothing compared to the storm in front of the place now. It took them twenty minutes of pushing, shoving, and strong-arming before they managed to get into the building and past the clerks.

There, she finally had a bit of personal space as she left the busy entrance room behind. It was only a short distance to Faian's office, a noticeable increase in guards on duty standing by doors and hallways.

Some of the guards must have recognised her and Ember because they were let through without much trouble.

She knocked twice on Faian's door and opened it after a yelled "Come in!"

Poking her head through, she saw the general by herself at her desk, writing on some piece of paperwork.

"Zalia! You're alive, good. And who is that behind you, Ember and . . . ?"

"I am Nateysta, spirit of the forests. It is good to make your acquaintance, Indis," Ro introduced himself, his grating yet melodic voice filling the room.

Zalia smacked her hand into her forehead.

"Nateysta, this is General Faian, one of the commanders of this army."

She moved aside to let Ember and Ro come into the room.

Faian was looking at Zalia with a raised eyebrow and she just shrugged. She looked back to Ro as he spoke again.

"Apologies, General Faian. I come from your sister world, Cormaine, to aid in your fight here. The old god, Starlight, has sacrificed themself to bring me here to take part in your war."

Faian's one raised eyebrow turned to two as her gaze flicked back to Zalia once more.

"Straight to the point, then. Ro is an Ascendant being, a god basically. He can help us take the capital."

That piqued Faian's interest.

"Take the capital? Are you sure? Scouts we have sent there say that the aura surrounding the city only grows stronger and stronger the closer you get."

Ember poked Zalia.

"This one should be able to get us pretty damn close without having to worry about that corruption now. What Ro is here for is to fight the thing emitting that corrupting aura."

Faian stood up, excited.

"You can fight it? Really? Well, that is excellent news. You said he was Ascendant—if that is true, I don't doubt the power of your abilities." She grew somewhat sober. "But I must ask, what do you want in return for this?"

"In return? Nothing, as of yet. Partly, I do this to repay the life debt I owe to Zalia. However, I would ask that when the time comes, you help me free my world of these demons too."

Faian tapped her finger on the table repetitively, deep in thought.

"I would love to help you, but I must ask. Realistically, how helpful will we be in freeing your world? We can barely protect our own from this invasion."

A guttural croaking that Zalia realised was a laugh came from under the hooded cloak.

"Oh, young general, do not worry. The lives of Ascendants are long indeed. You might not be powerful now, but in ten, twenty, a hundred years from now, how many strong people will you have? A kingdom that is focused on building an army to destroy these demons would be one I would consider a most valuable ally, and I have a feeling that is where this kingdom will be going after this."

Faian's finger tapped a little faster.

"We are going to need you to win this, I feel. We have a good number of strong fighters amongst our ranks, but that corrupting aura and its source has been a big roadblock in launching an assault on the capital."

Then, Faian turned to Zalia.

"I'm trusting you on this one. If you say this Nateysta is the answer to our problem, then I'll take it. Is he the solution?"

Zalia didn't hesitate.

"I trust him with all of our lives, then more. Yes, he is the answer."

Faian nodded, her finger stopping its incessant tapping.

"Right, agreed then. We will begin preparations to mobilise immediately. The overpopulation of this camp is getting worse and worse, and we need to strike the capital to take back a bigger city soon or things are only going to get worse. Tell me, Nateysta, do the demons know you are in this world? What are the limits of your powers?"

Zalia and Ember took the back seat as Ro was basically interrogated for information on what he could do and what his powers were. In the end, Faian decided that it would be best for Zalia to hold back the corruption as long as she could manage, and only when they had to reveal Ro's presence would he unleash his power. If they made it look like they were making a desperate final attack on the capital, then having Ro as a surprise against their enemies might turn a tactical advantage. This was all pending agreement from the other generals, of course.

Partway through, Zalia realised she and Ember were no longer needed in the conversation. She interrupted to ask to be excused to talk to the Hidden, telling

Ro to communicate with her mentally if needed. Faian agreed, calling in her advisor, Ryn, to assist them with getting into the prison cell holding him.

They had theories about the Astar, and she hoped that a conversation with Hidey could prove a few of them.

CHAPTER FIFTY-FOUR

Astar Involvement

Zalia

Zalia and Ember stood before the cube that contained Hidey, silent. Hidey did not speak either, and Advisor Ryn waited off to the side politely.

"It is good to see you once more."

Zalia chewed on her lip, thinking.

"And it is good to . . . hear you again Hidey. I've discovered . . . something recently that I wanted to talk to you about."

"Is that so? I'm always open to talk to you, Zalia, though I do suggest that you always be careful to whom you speak."

Zalia tapped her foot on the ground, considering her words carefully. She would have to make sure she didn't give away anything important to Hidey. Especially about Ro.

"The Astar, what do you know about them?"

"Hmm, the Astar, a curious subject. Not many people know of them, with even fewer ever having met them. Why do you ask?"

Ember gave her a warning look, but Zalia took her hand and gave it a squeeze, comforting her.

If it was the Astar who were controlling Hidey, then they would already know of her escape considering it was from *them* that she had escaped.

"I was recently captured by the Astar, and there was a demon with them who tortured me. They are working together. I think it is the Astar who are behind the ritual that brought the demons here in the first place."

There was a long period of silence, and for a moment, Zalia thought Hidey wouldn't respond.

"It has been noted by one of the few people who have met the Astar that they appeared to be good at spatial magic."

It wasn't a confirmation, she knew he couldn't give her that. It was as close as he could get, though, the words mimicking the thoughts she'd had not so long ago when learning about the Astar's involvement in the first place.

"I understand."

She considered her next words carefully. It would be great to get confirmation of it being the Astar who otherwise controlled Hidey, but inquiring about that would reveal that she knew he was being controlled in the first place.

They stood in silence, the only sound the tapping of her boots on the cold, stone floor.

"You're a good friend, Hidey. I only wish that Juniper hadn't made you do the things you did. We're going to help you somehow, hang in there."

A whispered "*thank you*" followed her out of the room.

She walked briskly up the stairs, hearing Advisor Ryn lock up the door behind her as Ember strode to catch up.

"You alright?"

Zalia gave a small, quick nod, wiping a single tear from her cheek. It wasn't fair, what Hidey had been through.

"We should help the army get ready to leave," she murmured.

She could feel Ember's concern pulsing through their bond.

"Are you sure?"

Zalia hesitated only a moment before taking a deep, stabilising breath and nodding again.

"Yes. I'm sure. There's something I want to talk to you about, though."

They emerged from the stairs and Zalia took them into a side room, the same one that Indis had gone off at her in some months ago.

"Alright, what is it?"

Zalia fiddled a little bit, then started speaking.

"Obviously, Aylie can't come on this assault. It wouldn't be fair on her to take her, nor would it be safe."

Ember nodded slowly, as if trying to figure out where this was going.

"She should stay in the Grove, it's probably the safest place for her. I assume some of the soldiers will stay behind at the camp to protect the remaining refugees."

Ember nodded again.

"I agree, where are you going with this?"

Zalia swallowed, anxiety battling her will to continue the conversation.

"And, I think you should stay with her."

She felt the anger and shock that Ember experienced at the words, yet her beautiful, wonderful partner held it back before replying.

"I don't like it, but I'm willing to hear you out. Why?"

She started with the obvious, which she was sure Ember had already thought of.

"One of us should stay with Aylie to get her out of here if things go wrong. After what she's been through with her family . . . I couldn't leave her alone again. I have the ability that holds back the corruption for the army and so . . . well, it makes sense that you stay behind."

What she didn't say was that she didn't want Ember to be part of the assault because she didn't want anything to happen to her. She wanted Ember to be safe and out of harm's way. She wanted Ember to live her life without experiencing the horror that was a thousand-eyed one. It was most likely selfish, and definitely bad of her to let those fears control her actions, but it was how she felt all the same.

Ember pursed her lips and tapped her finger to them a few times in thought before replying.

"I see. And did you consider that Ro could protect the army with his aura all the way into the capital by himself? That it isn't necessary for you to go either?"

Zalia opened her mouth to answer, but Ember wasn't done, obviously having heard the unspoken part despite her silence.

"And, did you consider how worried and scared we would all be waiting for you to come home? I won't be there to have your back. You'll be going into a city with who knows how many strong enemies, of which we know one is a gods-damned *Ascendant being*!?"

Everything Ember said was true. She knew. Zalia knew it. There was no point in arguing those facts. They both knew that keeping Ro a secret longer might help their chances as well, however. Faian had just said it some minutes earlier.

"I did consider all of that. I know. It sucks. I don't want it to be this way, but I think it's for the best."

Tears formed in the corners of Ember's eyes.

"Oh damn it, Zalia," she whispered.

Zalia stepped forward and wrapped her arms around the slightly smaller woman.

"I know."

They stayed that way for a little while, Zalia trying to comfort Ember and being comforted in return.

After a short time, they were both settled again.

"Alright, I'll do it, Zalia but . . . you'll take Boreal with you, at least?"

She squeezed Ember's hand.

"Of course, I don't think I could get *her* to stay behind if I tried."

"I hate this," Ember murmured.

Zalia took Ember's other hand and held them both tightly.

"I do too. We are going to win this fight, though. We're going to win it, and I'm going to come back and you, me, Aylie, Boreal, and Lumin are going to go live somewhere nice. Somewhere out of the cities, but close enough that we can still go to them if we want. Somewhere with a nice, big garden. Somewhere that Aylie can grow up in peace."

Ember smiled warmly at her.

"I'd like that very much."

Then she stood up, pulling Zalia to her feet as well.

"You ready?"

"Yeah, I'm ready. Let's get out there and get this done."

"Kick their asses for me, would you?" Ember asked.

"Of course, honey, all in a good day's work."

After their conversation, they had gone to General Faian, who had asked them to bring the Morning's Shade down to the war camp in preparation for departure.

It seemed like the army soldiers would be first in the column, having had significantly more training than the Morning's Shade when it came to moving and fighting as a single unit.

The Morning's Shade however, were all individually stronger than most of the soldiers simply due to their class choices. Where the soldiers had classes that usually pointed towards better teamwork and fighting as a unit, due to their evolutions and ability upgrades moving in that direction as they ranked up, the Morning's Shade had the very opposite.

The point of the organisation was to send off small groups or individuals to take care of more complex or mysterious situations facing the kingdom, or any-one who could afford to hire the group. As such, they would be a powerful rear guard, not only due to their significant strength but because of their individual ability to adapt to situations better.

It was also partly to ensure their disorderly conduct didn't get in the soldiers' way.

On their way back to the Grove, Ro joined back up with them.

"I have been looking around at your people and find myself shocked at how few high-ranking members of your race there are. Hildebrandt is amongst the most powerful of your race, why is this?"

Zalia frowned, stepping around a low bush.

"You know, I've asked that a few times before myself. Nobody has ever had an answer for me."

They both turned to Ember.

"Hey, I don't know either. I always thought that the kind of people who reach those ranks are also usually the people who like to explore. At a certain point they wander outside the borders of the kingdom and never really come back. Maybe things outside the borders are much more dangerous than inside them. The north is definitely more dangerous, that's for sure."

Zalia chewed her lip, thinking.

"Why are the Astar doing this? If they wanted to just wipe us out, I'm sure they could. What if they're doing it simply to keep the human race weak?"

Ember looked at her.

"What are you saying?"

"If you were somewhat cold and calculating and had a neighbouring kingdom you wanted to keep from getting too powerful, as well as extremely well-developed spatial magic powers, what would *you* do? Think about what the Astar *just* did to me. I got annoying, then they decided to take me out of the equation."

"Zalia, are you saying you think the Astar have been kidnapping and . . . what, killing any high-ranked humans who get too powerful?"

Zalia sighed.

"I don't know, Ro, it's just a thought. It's a possible explanation. It has always struck me as odd that there are no higher-ranked people in this kingdom. Originally I just thought that they remained hidden most of the time, but if there was a time for them to show themselves . . ."

Ember swore under her breath.

"Shit, Zals, that's horrible to think about. Like they've been . . . culling us. If that were happening, how could we not have seen it? Surely the king . . ."

Zalia gave a grim smile.

"The king. The king, who, according to Indis, had a very, very sudden change of personality soon after his father died. Hidey, who was in charge of the Morning's Shade intelligence. Who knows how long this has been going on? If we're correct, that is. The more I think about it, the more I believe it must be the answer."

Then she remembered Hildebrandt saying that Matthias had disappeared. She had a sinking feeling that he hadn't gone willingly.

It really brought home to her that she'd been extremely lucky that the starlight wolf was her friend. Without them, she might have ended up as just another dead powerful human that got too big for their own boots.

"Fucking Astar. Maybe this is all just completely wrong, but if it's right, they have a lot to answer for."

CHAPTER FIFTY-FIVE

To War

Zalia

Getting the Morning's Shade to leave the Grove in an orderly manner was akin to herding cats. Luckily, Zalia had plenty of experience in that regard, and with the help of Hildebrandt, had them up and moving in short order.

Ember, Aylie, and Lumin all came with Zalia and Ro as they trailed the Morning's Shade on the way to the camp.

When they arrived at the front of the army camp, it was to a scene of somehow orderly chaos.

The soldiers' departure was orderly, lines and units neatly forming up. Carts hooked up to beasts of labour were slowly trundling into one single line leading towards the capital. Units of soldiers were slowly splitting off and flanking carts that were moving away from the camp.

Faian had only vaguely explained the plan to her, the way the troops would be ordered and managed. They would take a small town about halfway to the capital to use as a midpoint for their supply train. Some soldiers would need to be left behind to guard it, as well as a small contingent to guard the carts that would go back and forth.

All in all, it sounded like a managerial nightmare, but from the looks of it, the generals had it well under control. She was once again surprised at the pure competency of not only Faian but the other generals and the soldiers under their command as well.

The chaos in the scene came from the desperate refugees and civilians who were outside the walls of the camp. Seeing that so much room was being vacated, quite a few people had decided it was time for them to move in and were pushing to be let into the camp. This created a nightmare for the gate guards, as they had to let out soldiers and make sure to filter the refugees at the same time.

Hildebrandt slowly led the Morning's Shade into the chaos, quickly being intercepted by an advisor to one of the other generals. Luckily, the members of the organisation decided grouping closely together was better than being split up, though many of the civilians kept their distance from the well-armed and armoured group.

Prior to the invasion, the Morning's Shade was a well-known organisation that not much was known about. People often feared them a little, simply due to the mystery surrounding their members and the not-so-truthful stories that tended to pop up around them.

A lot of that was forgotten now, it seemed. Many of the refugees didn't give them a second glance other than to keep out of their way, simply wanting to get within the enchanted walls of the camp.

Zalia was a little surprised at the speed with which things were advancing, but recalled Faian saying that the only thing they were waiting on was a solution to the possible Ascendant being in the capital. They had evidently been preparing for this attack since the camp was set up, the soldiers aware of what they needed to do and supplies already stockpiled for the event.

The Morning's Shade was led to one side to wait for the last of the soldiers, and Zalia and her group stood near them. It would be time to say goodbye soon.

Zalia watched Aylie, looking for any hint of what she was thinking.

"Aylie, you, Ember, and Lumin won't be coming with me and Ro to the capital. I want you to stay here and be safe in the Grove."

Fear and concern reared its head from within Aylie, her face dropping and arms wrapping around herself.

"Why? You told me that I had power now, that I would be able to fight back. I can come with you! Didn't you see how strong my ability is? I can help!"

Her voice was quiet as usual, yet grew louder. And she wasn't entirely wrong. Zalia had said those things.

"I know, but this is not like Ostoss. This is going to be a much bigger, longer, and more dangerous fight. It wouldn't be fair to take you into that. You have power now, but not on the level of the things we're going to be encountering there."

Her reply was only a whisper.

"If it is so dangerous, why are you going there?"

Zalia had been thinking about the same thing a bit recently. When she had first come to Endaria, she might well have not gone. Hell, even a few months earlier when she was Iron rank, they had decided to only pass off some information to Hidey and then leave the conflict for good, letting the army deal with it.

She was a changed woman from who she had been then, though.

"All of these people here," she started, gesturing widely around them, "need someone to stand up for them, to take back their home. Sure, I'm not as powerful as quite a few others here. I definitely don't have the kind of logistical or tactical skills that the generals have. What I do have are powers almost built to fight these things and knowledge of our enemy that the generals might need. You have those kinds of powers too, but now isn't the time for you to fight. When you are older, we can talk about you joining in on this kind of fight, but for now, you just need to stay safe. Alright?"

Aylie opened her arms wide and Zalia took her into a deep hug.

"Boreal will be with me, and we'll take care of each other. I want you to do something for me though ok? I'll only sleep every few days, but I want you to try to send me dreams. Talk to me through them, alright? You'll know I'm safe that way, and I'll know you're safe too."

She felt Aylie nod vigorously, and only hoped that she would be able to send the dreams over that distance.

They hadn't experimented much with the dreamweaving; Zalia was sleeping too little to really make good use of it. It was something that Zalia definitely wanted to get into once this was all over, though. Its potential for long-distance communication or even information gathering was quite unique. After all, who expected someone to try divine your secrets by manipulating your dreams?

"Be strong for me. I'll come back."

"Please be careful, mum, I don't want to lose you too."

She squeezed Aylie even tighter, tears in her eyes. Her voice sounded so small.

"Don't worry, darling, I *will* come back."

She pulled away and initiated a little ritual magic using Water Lily Petals to clean up Aylie's face while she neatened up her hair.

"Take care of Lumin as well, alright? The little one will need your guidance while I'm away."

Aylie nodded and tried to put on a strong face, a good effort despite the few new tears and slight wobble in her lips.

Boreal came up to pepper Aylie with soft body checks and hugs in her own manner while Zalia stood and hugged Ember.

"Keep her safe, keep yourself safe."

"Don't worry about us, you just keep yourselves safe. I want *both* of you to return safe and sound."

Then Ember pulled away and turned to Ro.

"I don't know if you're some kind of god or what, but you damn well better bring them both back to me ok? You hear me?"

Zalia restrained a laugh at the *very* confused-looking Ro. She doubted he had people talk to him that way very often, if ever.

"I will try my best . . . Ember of the flames."

Zalia made a choking, coughing sound, holding back the laugh, and Ember looked at her quizzically.

"Just . . . breathed in too much."

The members of the Morning's Shade started to walk off, following behind the final unit of soldiers on the way to the capital. Time to go.

Ember took her hands one last time, holding them tight.

"Come back."

Zalia nodded.

"I will."

Ember gave her a long, deep kiss, then pulled away. Zalia reluctantly let go of her hands and turned away, following the Morning's Shade.

Each step away was harder than the last, her body telling her that she should turn back and stay with them. The strength of emotions bouncing between her and Ember's bond made it all the worse, the urge to change their plans almost overwhelming.

A minute of walking later, it slowly became easier. The decision was made, to war she went.

Another half an hour later, Advisor Ryn came to get her. Faian wanted her closer to the centre of the column, so that her aura could stretch out across the entire army. She didn't bother to mention that it would either way, following the man and allowing her aura to finally flow back out again now that they were far enough from the city.

At the centre of the column was the army's food stock. Mostly cured and salted meats as well as various dried fruits and nuts. She even spotted the chef, whom she hadn't seen since the original war camp further north, surprised that he would be coming with them.

At the very, very front were the army scouts, a few staying close while others roamed far ahead of the column. To the forefront of the column stood Hildebrandt. She wasn't a part of the army, but being a tanky class and arguably the highest ranked member amongst them, she would be invaluable if attacked from there.

Behind her were a few squads of heavily armoured soldiers, followed by a squad of earth mages who flattened out the terrain for the armies passing through. All of the generals and their advisors, clerks, and other logistical teams were seated just behind the vanguard, the most protected part of the column. The bulk of the army came after that, dozens of squads of lighter-armoured soldiers, armed with spears, bows, or nothing at all.

The largest organised force she had seen was during the clash between two squads all the way back in the first weeks she had entered Endaria, when it had seemed like a simple rebellion fighting the kingdom.

This was something on an entirely different scale. A proper army, thousands of people strong.

The sheer power flowing through the air made her skin tingle, and her vision through Aura Perception was a confusing mess of thousands of overlapping auras and powers.

Her other forms of sight weren't much better either. Her vision of both heat and vibration was overwhelmed by the mass of sound and bodies that was the army column. It was hard to feel anything other than confident in their chances of victory with so much strength gathered in one place.

Her own aura spread out over the whole group, further adding the organised chaos.

Both Boreal and Ro were still with her, the latter disguised as a cloaked figure. She wasn't sure what the soldiers had been told about him, though suspected it was close to, if not, nothing.

Once more, Advisor Ryn came to collect her and bring her slightly forward in the column to where General Faian and General Ballast were. She passed a squad of cavalry on the way, admiring the varied mounts they had. Most were horses, though a few rode on other similarly shaped creatures that were not. She guessed that they had to be at least the same size as to fit together as a unit.

She was brought into the protected spot between the vanguard and soldiers where a flurry of movement signalled their location. As usual, there were various ministerial types making notes and writing things down, using mobile desks they had tied around their midsections.

After a few moments, she was brought up to the generals.

"Yes? What did you need?"

Ballast looked over at her.

"Ah! Zalia, welcome. Boreal, good to see you. And this must be our guest! Wonderful to have you with us."

He followed up the welcome with a heavy but friendly thump to the back, which seemed to confuse Ro even further. Poor thing, he was *not* used to people.

Faian took over before Ballast confused him even more.

"We need to know if there is anything more. You have told us about the high likelihood that the population of the capital is now undead, along with details on the Ascendant being. Please, any and all information might be helpful, even if you don't believe so."

Zalia collated her thoughts, ordering what she knew about every demon and the Astar, then began talking.

CHAPTER FIFTY-SIX

Defender

Zalia

The journey from the war camp to the town at the midway point they planned on capturing might have taken Zalia only a few days. That was if she had been by herself, though. The army column moved along like a slow-plodding beast; the time required for the earth mages to flatten out the land ahead and the slow-trundling carriages to keep up made it almost boring for her. Almost.

Zalia felt like she was crawling, the pace so much slower than her normal movement. That gave her a lot of time to think, though.

Thoughts of her time in prison being tortured, of the implications of their recent discoveries, and of what she and the army were heading towards battled to be at the forefront of her mind. The thoughts of Ember, Aylie, and Lumin outstripped them all, though. She felt both concern and appreciation for them, worried that something would happen to them while the army was out at war, and happy that they were somewhere other than going towards that war.

The first conflict happened on the second day of travel, as they were attacked by a group of a few hundred crazed soldiers. Scouts came running, yelling about an attack.

General Faian quickly began calling out orders.

"Vanguard, shields up! Administrative staff back! Earthen unit, defences!"

Like a well-oiled machine, the army reacted.

The vanguard, in the face of hundreds on hundreds of crazed soldiers that were foaming at the mouth as they charged, set up a shield wall. They allowed the scouts through, the soldiers still some distance away. Then, the first row dropped low on their knees, the second row standing between, with the third holding shields high. This formed a three-layer-high wall of shields held by the weight and strength of a powerful unit of people.

The earth mages just behind them built stone walls with stairs to their tops on either side of the vanguard as the administrative staff pulled back, led by a unit of lighter-armoured soldiers.

"Archer and area units, take your positions!"

As two units from behind the administrative group split to allow them through, they ran up the sides of the column and onto the stone wall. Half the earth mages followed the administrators, building the wall further and further down the column.

General Faian gave the order and hell rained from above.

"Fire!"

The mages and archers on the wall activated various abilities and Zalia activated her Flight to get a better view of the fight. The crazed soldiers seemed to be struggling a little bit and she soon realised why. Her aura, now expanding over a massive distance, was hurting them. It wasn't enough to kill them, or even harm them seriously, but it *was* enough to put them in pain and slow them a little. She hadn't considered that by allowing her aura to spread out as far as it could, she might also attract the attention of any corrupt being in that area.

Waves of fire rolled over the enemy soldiers even as they still charged. Arrows rained down, some exploding with various elements or just sheer force. The ground underneath them roiled and rolled, slowing their charge almost to a standstill, even knocking some over. A slick ice formed over the still-shifting ground, further disrupting the enemy's charge.

As cooldowns were used, and the rain of attacks slowed, the enemy continued their charge. They managed to recover some of their momentum, the sheer rage and mindlessness of the soldiers allowing them to ignore wounds and their dead and dying comrades. In addition, while they didn't have an inkling of tactics, it wasn't so easy to kill Bronze and Silver rankers.

A single figure stood out from the vanguard with armour, mace, and tower shield at the ready. Zalia watched as Hildebrandt settled her feet and stood her ground. A fiery aura permeated the air around her, slowly spreading across the battlefield. The rest of the vanguard seemed to stand firmer, stronger.

The aura that normally came from Hildebrandt was one of something solid, more . . . permanent than everything else. The aura that came out of her when she was in battle was something more like a promise. A promise of protection and of retaliation should any harm come to those under that protection.

It reminded Zalia of Ember just a little, though Ember protected through healing, while Hildebrandt protected by being the wall between her enemies and her friends.

As she watched, the slowly expanding fiery aura reached the approaching soldiers and they began to scream in pain. The lower-ranked ones further back disintegrated, anything of Tin or Iron rank lasting no longer than a few moments.

The Bronze ranked enemies managed to push through the pain, the combination of Hildebrandt and her own auras enough to start injuring them. The Silver rank ones struggled a bit less, though still looking pained in their rage-filled charge.

A huge explosion rocked the battlefield, originating in the centre of a mass of enemy soldiers. What must have been the torn-apart bodies of fifty of the crazed soldiers rained down across the field, spraying blood and gore.

Hildebrandt had done that, it was the same ability she had used to blow up the wall of the fort Zalia had been kept prisoner in.

Once the few remaining crazed soldiers that didn't die in the continuous onslaught of various spells and arrows got within twenty metres of Hildebrandt, she started swinging her mace. Zalia was confused for only a moment as bolts of fiery energy left the mace and impacted enemy soldiers with explosive force. A Silver ranker was blown away, torn into pieces.

A few of them reached Hildebrandt but she didn't even bother blocking. The moment they struck, two bolts similar to what her mace swings created flashed out and struck the attackers. They were blown away into a fine mist, their remains burning into smoke.

It wasn't very long before nothing remained of the enemy other than a few body parts strewn across the battlefield. Many of the soldiers had simply stopped and watched as Hildebrandt single-handedly destroyed the enemy. It was a terrifying sight. If that power were turned on them, there wasn't much that their organised, orderly, and tactically sound army could do. That is why both Ro-ak and Hildebrandt were there.

Of course, there was also Larel back with the Morning's Shade. She was their only other Gold ranker, though not nearly as strong as Hildebrandt, considering she was at the tip of Gold, only a rank or two from reaching Emerald. Zalia wouldn't be surprised if a few of the woman's abilities were Emerald already.

Now that the fight was done, it didn't take long before the walls were torn down and they were back on their way. As they moved past the corpses of the fallen, all the remains were buried by the earth mages until there was no sign that the fight had taken place at all. Even the undergrowth was regrown by Zalia's aura.

She went and found Hildebrandt and Faian after the fight.

"Thank you for your help," Faian was saying.

Hildebrandt gave a salute.

"Happy to help, we're here to help the kingdom, aren't we?"

Given the crispness of the salute, Zalia wondered if the woman had been a soldier once. She could see on Faian's face that she was thinking the same.

"General, Hildebrandt. I believe my aura was what pulled those crazed soldiers to us. It hurts them, though not enough to properly harm or kill them. Should I retract it to just cover the army?"

Zalia could feel the corrupting aura more and more, its power slowly pushing against her own so that it didn't reach as far as it might have. She had a feeling it wouldn't be long before all she could do was cover the army anyway.

Faian thought for a moment before replying.

"No. Leave it for now. It might not be a bad idea to drag out as many of the enemy as we can before reaching the capital. Having them behind us and near to where the caravan will run could end up being disastrous. Scouts are searching the lands for them as we speak, and we'll take any fight we have to as it is. Might as well let them come to us."

Zalia only gave a simple nod as confirmation, gesturing to Hildebrandt that she wanted to talk for a moment.

General Faian returned to the constant organisation she had to deal with as the two of them stepped away for a moment.

"That's the third time I've seen you fight now and I have to say, I'm a little awed by your powers."

Hildebrandt gave her a wide smile.

"Aw, thanks. Look, both times you've seen me fight properly, I have been completely in my element. Mindless hordes attacking us? Now, that I excel at. All my abilities are based around standing my ground and getting hit."

Zalia tapped her foot a little, considering. She wanted to ask to see Hildebrandt's abilities.

"I don't know if this is something rude to ask, but I want to see what your abilities do. Is that ok? It might help with what we're going up against to know what your limitations are."

Hildebrandt hummed in thought.

"Hmm, I have shown General Faian already, which is why I ended up in the vanguard. If it was anyone else I'd tell them no, but I want to see yours as well Zalia. I'm quite intrigued by the uniqueness of your abilities, as well as the fact you have three classes. Willing to trade?"

Zalia nodded, showing her abilities to the woman and receiving a host of information in return.

Class - Warrior - Gold
Linked Attributes - Strength, Dexterity
Active Skills
Godly Strike (Previously Strike) - Gold
Tin - You can strike your enemy harder.
This now allows you to hit ethereal beings.
Iron - In addition to hitting harder, you also hit faster.
This now has significantly increased impact.
**Bronze - When this hits an enemy, the damage they take from Backlash
is significantly increased.**
This now also slows the affected enemy.

Silver - You can now strike enemies without being near them. Strikes made with this ability become ranged, out to a distance of ten metres. This is now increased to twenty metres.

Gold - Your strikes are infused with godly power, impacting them with a burning force that ignores most armour.

Stand Your Ground (Previously Speed Maneouvre) - Emerald

Tin - You may now "Stand Your Ground." When standing your ground, you are less affected by all knockback.

Iron - When standing your ground, allies near you are also less affected by knockback.

Bronze - When standing your ground, you and your allies are no longer affected by knockback at all.

Silver - When standing your ground, Backlash deals significantly more damage.

Gold - When standing your ground, you emit an aura that burns your enemies and protects your allies against damage.

Emerald - When standing your ground, enemies have a significantly harder time moving around you to attack anyone else. You are the wall that stands between them and what stands behind you.

Explosive Force - Emerald

Tin - You may make a single stronger attack with a longer cooldown.

Iron - This attack now creates an explosive force that is extremely strong against structures and elementals.

Bronze - After the explosive force goes off, a concussive wave flows after it.

Silver - The area affected by this attack is greatly increased, as well as no longer needing to be directed by an attack. You can apply this ability anywhere up to twenty metres from you.

Gold - This range for this ability is now a hundred metres. Additionally, when standing your ground, this ability becomes significantly stronger.

Emerald - The area of this ability is increased. The range increases to one kilometre. Enemies that survive the explosion are affected by one instance of Backlash.

Passive Skills

Soldier's Endurance (Previously Endurance) - Emerald

Tin - You have increased stamina.

This now also increases your resilience.

Iron - You have increased resistance to the effects of lost sleep and exhaustion.

This now also gives you the Physical Resistance passive which is the same level as this ability.

Bronze - You can ignore a great variety of lesser wounds.

Silver - You can ignore one major wound and function as normal.

Gold - While your body is still intact, you can ignore the effects of most wounds. Age ceases to affect you.

Emerald - As long as your soul holds, you can ignore any damage done to your body. This also gives you the Mental Resistance passive at the same level of this ability.

Recovery - Gold

Tin - You recover stamina and mana quicker.

Iron - You recover health slowly over time, closing wounds and eliminating disease.

Bronze - All recovery is increased significantly.

Silver - When you trigger Backlash, the effects of this ability are increased. Additionally, your armour and shield are affected by this ability.

Gold - Allies protected by Stand Your Ground are affected by the Tin, Iron, and Bronze rank effects of this ability.

Specialisation - Defender - Emerald

Linked Attributes - Vitality, Resilience

Active Skills

Defend the Kingdom (Previously Protective Shield) - Emerald

Tin - You can summon a small floating shield. This shield can be directed to block attacks.

This now allows you to create a second one to defend an ally.

Iron - Strikes blocked by this shield trigger Backlash.

This now triggers twice if the shield is defending an ally.

Bronze - You may now create a small, short-lived dome instead. All instances of this ability are also stronger. This now allows you to make a bigger dome as long as it is used to defend allies or buildings under your protection.

Silver - You may make a long wall with this ability.

Gold - After an extremely long cooldown, this ability can now be used to cover a large area in a dome. This dome lasts for a day and does not allow anything or anyone in or out.

Emerald - When using the large area dome, it now allows allies to enter and leave as they wish. Additionally, this ability becomes virtually indestructible.

Backlash - Emerald

Tin - When you block an attack, the source of the attack is struck as if you hit them.

Iron - This retaliatory damage is now empowered by Godly Strike (Previously Strike).

Bronze - Enemies affected by Backlash are thrown backwards. Additionally, they are slowed.

Silver - When Backlash triggers, nearby enemies are hit with a much weaker version of this ability.
Gold - Backlash no longer only triggers if an attack is blocked, but now also triggers if an attack hits at all.
Emerald - Backlash now triggers twice.
Passive Skills
Enduring Aura - Emerald
Tin - You and allies in your aura have increased resilience.
Iron - This now increases stamina.
Bronze - When Backlash triggers, resilience and stamina are now further increased for a short time.
Silver - Magical constructs created by you and your allies have an increased lifespan and durability.
Gold - Your soul is now as resilient as your body. Allies have a slight increase to the strength of their own souls.
Emerald - You give off a sense of permanence, seeming more solid than everything else around you. Allies are strengthened by your presence, able to ignore minor wounds and mental strain. Additionally, you can ignore a variety of effects that are targeted at the body. This includes any physical or mental traumas.

"Wow, that is a lot. I guess it really starts to add up at your rank."

Hildebrandt nodded, still reading.

"You're going to have it worse than most. Not only do you have three classes but from the looks of it, they're all quite complex. Mine are simple for the most part, easy to use and with very distinct use cases. What you have here is . . . yeah."

"Tell me about it. Healing Presence alone has a ridiculously long description."

Zalia read over Soldier's Endurance again.

"Sorry, age ceases to affect you?"

Hildebrandt shushed her.

"Don't say it out loud like that, but yes. Most people get abilities that affect how they age at about Gold rank. At least, the few Gold rankers I know have. Matthias has one, as does Larel."

Zalia thought about how that Gold rank brewer, Harrick, had a special brew that slowed age.

"Will I get one too?"

Hildebrandt chuckled.

"Well, if you reach Gold, yes. I'd say Survivalist is the one most likely to have it, out of them all."

Reading through Hildebrandt's abilities once more, Zalia kind of understood what she had said. Her abilities were all focused around being hit, with most of them having effects that changed, triggered, or were triggered by Backlash.

The other major theme was protecting allies while standing her ground. Walls, shields, an ability literally called Stand Your Ground.

"Well, I'm glad to have you with us. I have a feeling we are going to be fighting a lot of mindless hordes. In fact, I know we will."

Hildebrandt grimaced.

"Yeah, I heard. I'm not looking forward to being the one to have to destroy the majority of them. They were the kingdom's people, once."

Zalia mimicked her expression, realising fully what that meant. They would have to destroy the undead bodies of the entire capital city's population. Her own Healing Presence would play a large part in that as well.

"I know what you mean. It's going to be traumatic, to say the least."

It certainly would be for Zalia. She hadn't missed the part of Hildebrandt's abilities where she was immune to physical and mental trauma, as well as pretty much every wound possible. It looked like the only way to actually kill her was to destroy her soul, however that was possible. It might explain why she was one of, if not *the* only person in the kingdom to be close to reaching Emerald rank.

Her thoughts turned again to the Astar and their involvement. She felt bad for Matthias. It wasn't a sure thing that they were the ones to have taken him and even possibly killed him, yet it was likely. He hadn't deserved that, however cold he had been as a person.

Those thoughts haunted her as they continued marching towards a city filled with the undead. It would be a long, long time before Endaria recovered from this war.

CHAPTER FIFTY-SEVEN

The Fields of War

Zalia

A few days later, Zalia stood with the leaders of the army overlooking a large town. They were in the flatlands now, out of the hilly area where the army had set up their war camp. She had been told that the town was known as Et's Way. It was a crossroads for the road leading from the north of Endaria to the south, with another road travelling west to the capital. Being relatively close to the town, she had her aura suppressed to only cover the army, so it didn't draw any attention.

Faian had explained how Et's Way had been a major mercantile town, with most business and imports for the capital needing to travel through it to get there. That was apart from a few smaller towns closer to the capital, though those were more like town halls for farming communities than they were proper towns. Indis had added to that explanation, going into mind-numbing detail about the financial significance of the town before Ballast cut her off.

The aura of the thousand-eyed one was stronger now, significant enough for her to feel the strain of holding it back day and night. When they set up to sleep, the army enchanters had taken to putting up shoddy temporary wards that were able to block at least some of the corrupting aura. That way she could rest herself, ready for the next day's travel.

Her job was to get the army safely to the capital without needing to expose Ro's presence. Once they were there, she would just be another soldier on the field. Most of the major fighting would be done by Ro and Hildebrandt, with Larel as backup for wherever needed it.

Looking down at the town, a few things were obvious. One, the population of the town were definitely no longer human. They shambled through streets, banging against walls and doors without much thought in their heads. Perhaps a few higher-ranked members had time to get out, but without healing or some sort of protection against the corruption, she knew they wouldn't have lasted long. Without her own Healing Presence, it would be a matter of hours before she succumbed to the aura at its current strength. Craftsmen, farmers, and the like wouldn't have much of a chance.

What was obvious, other than that, was the demonic presence in the town. It wasn't *immediately* obvious like the undead population was, but looking closely, there was a focused red haze over the town that gave away their presence. It was like Cormaine, even having the slight scent of sulphur coming across the breeze. Of course, it could be caused by the undead, but Zalia thought it was the demons. It felt more like a heavy concentration of the corrupting aura rather than the undead's presence.

Everyone looked to Generals Faian and Ballast.

"Two major threats. The undead are the biggest one, with possibly tens of thousands of them in there. Hildebrandt should be able to take care of those herself, with the vanguard unit as backup. Those we'll have an easier time drawing out of the town, making as much sound as we can," Faian started.

Ballast scratched at the stubble on his neck.

"Agreed, though we should send the earth mage unit and an area archer unit to cover their retreat if needed. If I'm not mistaken, that red haze means demons?"

Zalia nodded confirmation.

"I believe so. I think it's the corrupting aura that causes that. Much like you see over the capital."

Everyone looked out over the plains towards the capital, the air above it a red haze that marked their destination.

"Wonderful. I'd like to see how the Morning's Shade fare in taking them out. The narrow streets and close quarters are going to be a lot easier for small groups to navigate through."

Hildebrandt frowned, not looking happy about it.

"Wouldn't it be better to draw them out as well? I don't like the idea of sending teams in there where they can get overwhelmed."

Advisor Ryn stepped forward.

"Based on previous encounters, I do not believe the demons will fall for that. They are against retreat from what we have seen, but neither are they stupid. If they see or sense someone of Hildebrandt's rank, I believe it is most likely that they will send for reinforcements of a high enough rank, if they have any."

He then stepped back, looking to Faian.

"Perhaps instead of sending them into the town, we can have them position themselves around the perimeter. That way they can take out any fleeing demons. In the case that Zalia is wrong and there are none, no harm done. If there are, though, we don't want them escaping to bring back any more high-ranked enemies."

Hildebrandt seemed more in tune with that idea, nodding approval.

"Good. Zalia, you will go with Hildebrandt and the vanguard to draw the undead's attention with your aura. I assume that will work on them the same as it does on the crazed soldiers?"

Zalia rubbed lightly at her chest, remembering the sword that had gone through it, courtesy of a Silver rank undead.

"Yeah, it works a lot better on them, actually. It's able to kill some of them, though with the larger aura being much weaker, I'm sure it will take quite some time."

Faian tapped her chin.

"Good. That sounds like the best plan, as long as everyone agrees. We'll send some of the lighter-armoured units to back up the Morning's Shade as well. Perhaps some of the focused ranged units?"

Ballast nodded agreement, looking intently down at the town. Zalia wasn't sure, but it seemed like he was visualing the battle even as they made the plans for it.

"Yes, though I think it's best to split them in half to ensure they don't bring too much attention. With Larel down there to back any up that need it they should be relatively safe. I'd like to have a medical unit near the side of town opposite the vanguard, along with a legionnaire unit to keep them safe."

The legionnaire units were lighter-armoured than the vanguard, utilising javelins, spears, and abilities focused more around high movement combat. From what Zalia had seen, the medical units were quite quick on their feet as well, more like combat medics than doctors.

Zalia kind of got distracted at that point, idly scratching Boreal's head as Hildebrandt, the generals, and the advisors spoke.

In the end, nothing about the plan really changed, though there was a lot of organising around what would happen with the main army body. They also set up fallback points, places earth mages would fortify and where reinforcements would wait.

Larel was put to be with the legionnaire and medical units, as a front liner to make room for the medical units to do their job. Split into small groups evenly along the perimeter of the town were various groups of Morning's Shade members and focused target units, each group containing at least one Silver ranker.

As prepared as they would get, and wanting to strike as soon as possible, Faian only waited long enough for the scouts to search the nearby area around the town before orders began flowing. Messengers using mental communication powers stood next to Ballast and Faian, sending out orders to various leaders amongst units, while Hildebrandt went and told her people what was happening.

It seemed that all at once, the still and relatively silent army column began to move. Structures were built by earth mages, with walls going up and a fort appearing out of the dirt and stone around them. Lightly armoured groups of four of five began to depart, finding their way down the hill and around the town edges.

Zalia still had her aura suppressed and waited with the vanguard as the flurry of motion began to slow. General Faian stayed at the vantage point that looked over the town with the messengers next to her. General Ballast took up his huge two-handed mace and joined the vanguard, standing in their midst. She didn't really know what kind of powers the man had as a general, but she assumed they were focused heavily on leading and morale.

Tension began to build as everyone got ready for the fight ahead of them. This wasn't a fight against an enemy army, however, as much as it was a fight against an entire town's population. It was to be a smaller version of the fight that would take place at the capital, a taster of what was to come.

Zalia knew it, the soldiers all knew it. If they had the time, resources, or means to figure out if bringing back these people was possible, they would have done so. Unfortunately, it simply wasn't possible.

Before long, the orders came and the vanguard began to move out.

The vanguard approached Et's Way, beginning to chant in unison. It wasn't any type of magic or power, simply the deep, throaty chant of soldiers moving into war. The sound reverberated through her bones and as they got louder, she saw the first undead begin to charge out of the town.

They stopped, the chant continuing. Hildebrandt planted her feet firmly and the fiery aura began to expand from her. Zalia released her own aura, the power streaming out across the town, even going to far as to reach the other side and the units waiting there. It had been risky for them to go out of her protection, but was a needed risk all the same.

The one silent undead became two, then three, and before she knew it, hundreds, then thousands were streaming from Et's Way.

The vanguard continued their chant as charging undead began to disintegrate under the power of both Hildebrandt and Zalia's powers.

Soon, the sheer mass of bodies began to somehow physically push back Hildebrandt's aura and the undead came closer.

They came close enough for most of the vanguard to properly see their opponents. They looked . . . like people.

Glowing bodies turned to ash before Hildebrandt's power, yet the undead pushed ever onwards.

The first of them reached the vanguard, exploding into mist as Hildebrandt's Backlash triggered.

As before, one became two, and then the numbers kept growing as the majority of the vanguard in their shield-wall formation needed to fight back the undead hordes.

Zalia cast rituals, setting off small explosions that were a poor mimicry of Hildebrandt's massive ones. Cursed fire spread amongst their ranks, even as her original, more focused aura tore apart the low-ranked undead. Boreal stood by her side, protecting her while she worked.

Slowly, the still human faces of the undead turned to rotten ones, strips of flesh hanging off their bodies as Zalia's larger aura began to affect them.

Cries and screams of battle came from the vanguard. Step by step, they moved back, making room for the next wave of undead so they couldn't climb on the bodies of their fallen before them. Blades impacted flesh, bare hands impacted shield.

Only Hildebrandt didn't move, her power creating a radiant ring around her, and any undead that dared approach were blown away into a fine mist or disintegrated by the power of her aura. Another huge explosion rocked the battlefield, body parts mixed with dirt thrown everywhere.

Zalia felt tears on her face, the horror of the slaughter not lost on her in the moment. These had been people, *the* people of Endaria. Turned to mindless monsters by the demons that were invading. Hatred filled her heart then, the incomprehensible horror finally becoming real at the sight of thousands dead. It had been one thing seeing the reanimated skeletons of long-dead Bathar, it was another to see the almost lifelike bodies of recently dead civilians. Something about the fact that they still had faces made it so much more *real.*

She cast Nature's Wrath, and for a moment, her power became that of a god's. Stone smashed, wind tore, and fire cleansed. A whirling storm of elements shredded droves of undead to pieces. Two fire elementals burned through swaths more. She almost used all her mana, yet when she came down the undead still pushed forward.

Still, Hildebrandt stood her ground, explosions of power sent forth, each attack against her met with death, twin bolts of energy vaporising each attacker.

Zalia didn't know how long had passed when a mind spoke to her.

"A Morning's Shade squad is running your way, they need help."

Zalia immediately cast the ritual of flight, floating upwards and away from Boreal to see across the battlefield.

Just as the voice had said, a small trio were sprinting their way, hundreds of undead on their heels. The Silver ranker of the group was running a fighting retreat, cutting down as many foes as they could, each only replaced by another. Some of the undead from the seemingly endless swarm approaching the vanguard noticed them and began to split toward the running team. They would be pincered.

Zalia flew quick, as fast as she could. One of the Bronze rankers went down under two undead.

She hit, the force enough to smash the two undead into gory remains across the battlefield. With the use of Fight or Flight, time slowed and she picked up the Bronze ranker, casting the flight ritual on the other two members.

Just moments before the undead smashed them from two sides, they took flight.

CHAPTER FIFTY-EIGHT

The Price of War

Zalia

Zalia walked solemnly across the battlefield, looking at the faces of the dead. What remained of them at least.

The sheer number of corpses painted a horrific, blood-soaked picture that showed the slow step-by-step retreat the vanguard had taken, with a single circular spot near the beginning of the bodies that was knee-deep in ash. It was the place Hildebrandt had stood her ground, holding no bodies at all. Everything that had attacked her had been burnt away or turned into a fine mist by her power.

Many of the vanguard behind and around her held similar solemn expressions, others with tear-streaked faces or fear evident in their eyes. Despite how many had been burnt away, the number of dead that remained was nothing other than horrific.

Zalia felt numb, like she was an outside observer watching her own body step across the field. She didn't know what to say, what to do. Boreal, for her part, was not so much horrified at what had happened as much as she was concerned for Zalia.

There were just so many.

She looked at the face of a young boy, no older than Aylie, his body below the chest missing entirely. This had been someone's child, perhaps one of the other thousands of people strewn across the battlefield.

What had once been a road surrounded by a grassy field was now a mass grave.

Her aura was still flowing across the entire thing, growing back the grass that had been trampled down. It slowly grew long enough to start hiding some of the horror.

She walked up to Hildebrandt, not properly processing that the ash around her had once been people. Hildebrandt still stood firm, a beacon of light, solidarity, and strength on the battlefield. They had lost a few good men during the fight. Zalia had seen one of the vanguard torn from the front line and slowly clawed, beaten, and torn apart under the mass of undead. She knew there were others, too.

Without Hildebrandt, there would have been a lot more.

"How are you holding up?"

Zalia looked blankly up at her.

"This . . ."

Hildebrandt nodded.

"Yeah."

They stood in silence, looking around them. As everything settled into Zalia's mind, a realisation dawned on the edges of her consciousness. They would have to do this again, possibly more than once, as their destination was the capital of the kingdom. What had its population been?

"I've had word that there were demons in the town after all. They tried escaping and took out one of my teams before being caught by Larel and a couple of the adjacent teams. There was only one other team that went down while Larel was busy, making a total of seven dead. The majority of the vanguard lives as well, though they're still counting. All in all, it's minimal losses for what we were up against."

Zalia nodded. It was a small comfort.

"A fresh unit of legionnaires has been sent to scour the rest of the town for any possibly hiding."

Zalia nodded again. Boreal rubbed against her leg.

She was glad for her heirloom armour and how easy it was to clean with Heat Resistance. The soldiers that would have to clean the remains of this battle off their own armour . . . well, she didn't envy them.

"What now?"

Hildebrandt put a comforting hand on her shoulder.

"Go and rest. Faian and the army can take care of everything else."

Zalia could feel her hands shaking and looked down. Why were her hands shaking?

"Ok."

She opened her vault right there, stepped in, and walked to the back of the room where she passed out.

When Zalia woke up, she was momentarily confused as to where she was. Then the memories of the previous day flooded back through her mind and she shuddered.

Her breathing came jaggedly as panic tried to set in, but the calm, warm lights and comforting aura of her vault helped her fend off a breakdown. She dreaded having to go through that again.

Boreal was snuggled up beside her, purring gently. Zalia hugged her close, burying her face into Boreal's thick fur and blocking out the outside world for a few more minutes.

Soon though, the world came calling and she had to get up. Her aura would have been somewhat weaker while she slept and the army was relying on that to survive. They were able to see past the far edge of Healing Presence, where the grass was dead, the ground dry and cracked, and the odd tree here or there warped and twisted, much as they had been in Cormaine. That was what awaited them if she was unable to hold up.

Well, Ro would take over at that point, but they wanted to keep him secret as long as possible.

When she stepped out of the vault, Hildebrandt was still planted firmly before it. Everything else outside of that had changed though.

The battlefield had been made clean. Earth mages must have been working hard, because the bodies were gone, the wild grass having overtaken entirely. The nearby town had been fortified, enchanted stone walls built and the army having moved in. She wouldn't have thought they had only been there for a few hours with how settled it all was.

"They've been hard at work."

Hildebrandt turned to her, looking her up and down.

"Yes, they are quite quick at what they do. I'm impressed."

The way Hildebrandt stood, the feeling of sturdiness she gave off, made it hard not to be comforted by her presence. It was as if she was a solid boulder standing tall in the current of a rushing river.

"Have you . . . ever done something like this?"

Zalia personally had, in Cormaine. That had felt different, though, the people so long dead and disconnected from anything she knew. They were almost entirely skeletons at that point, no flesh remaining on them. These undead, on the other hand, had faces still.

"No. And I hope I never have to do something like it again."

The memories of the battle were seared into her mind. Shambling people blasted into mist or burned to ash by the cursed fires she spread. Screaming vanguard soldiers dragged away and slaughtered by the ever-silent undead. Swords and spears slashing and piercing. Blood, despite being undead, so much blood.

"Where is Faian?"

Hildebrandt pointed out a large state house taller than the rest of the town's structures, and Zalia headed off towards it. She ran her hand through the long grass as it brushed past her, trying to get her mind into a space where it could rationalise everything they had done. It *was* for a good cause, it *was* for a good reason and it *was* necessary. So why did it feel so wrong? Maybe wrong wasn't the right word. It was just . . . it was just horrible.

She was allowed through the gates and she could see in the expressions of the soldiers a haunted look that mirrored her own emotions. Many of them had puffy eyes, evidence of tears. It hadn't occurred to her until then, but many of these soldiers probably had people they knew, family or friends, that had lived in this city. This city, or the capital. They had been part of a rebellion, sure, but not all of them would have had time to get families and friends out. Some of them were definitely more affected than others, though. A few of the soldiers were stoic, looking less sad from loss and more disturbed by what they had seen.

The rituals had happened so suddenly, without much time to even stop it, let alone evacuate people from affected areas. Now these soldiers were killing undead that might be people they had known. It was bad enough for Zalia, but it was nothing compared to what a lot of them must be going through.

The town was near silent, no boasting or cheering, no shouted stories of kills made. No, this was a solemn and quiet place, filled with the grieving. This hadn't been a fight against an enemy nation, or even against the demon invasion. This had been a violent burial.

All through the camp were similar sights. Horror-stricken faces, traumatised soldiers, men and women trying to hold themselves together. Many didn't seem to want to take houses for themselves to sleep, simply curling up on porches or benches. She didn't blame them. Some of the soldiers looked as if they were doing better than others, though. They comforted the rest of the group, helping them clean up or organise themselves.

Zalia's thoughts strayed to what would happen if they did win. She didn't know what would happen if they managed to kill the thousand-eyed one, whether the undead would die without the power of the creature, or if they would need to clear out every single town within a hundred or so kilometres of the capital.

She hoped, for the sake of the soldiers, that it was the former.

It took a short walk through the town before she reached the state house, even the usual whirlwind of administrative types that accompanied Faian somewhat subdued.

She found Ro still with the generals in a room with a long table, obviously being kept close in case they needed to make a snap decision to show their hand.

"Zalia, come in."

Their advisors were there too, along with a few other people unknown to Zalia.

Zalia could see that Faian was much like many of her soldiers, horrified by what had happened. Yet she still maintained a posture of strength, shoulders squared and eyes focused. She was ever the stoic general, even in a time like this.

General Ballast was missing his usual joviality, but somehow looked less affected by everything than Faian was.

Zalia looked awkwardly at everyone in the room, then back to Faian.

"General . . . what's the plan?"

Faian watched her closely, then nodded.

"We'll rest here for a day, then leave behind a small contingent to protect the town. It's . . . hard to say how long it will take us to get to the capital from here. There are unknown numbers of . . . of undead and demons."

She heard something unspoken in Faian's words. Those who were left behind would be those who couldn't, or shouldn't, go on. Not all of the soldiers would be able to handle it. Zalia didn't know if she could herself.

"Understood."

Unfortunately, in her case, it wasn't a choice.

CHAPTER FIFTY-NINE

To the Capital

Zalia

Having the rest of the day to rest was a godsend. With the army enchanters able to work together to protect against the corruption, life for Zalia was just a little easier. She didn't have anything to do, however, so the time was entirely spent thinking.

There wasn't much that thinking could accomplish either. There was simply one path forward. They knew what they were doing and why. All they had to do was do it.

The one thing she did have that she could do during that day was look through her messages from the fight.

> **Congratulations! Hunter's Mark has gained two levels, reaching Bronze 7.**
> **Congratulations! Survivalist and associated skills have reached Bronze 10.**
> **Congratulations! Herbal Magic has gained three levels, reaching Bronze 10.**
> **Congratulations! Nature's Wrath has reached Bronze 7.**
> **Congratulations! Protection of the Wilds has reached Bronze 7.**
> **Congratulations! Druid class has reached Bronze 7.**

The next day came slowly, the sun rising as sluggishly as the usually quick and orderly army. It seemed that even Faian didn't want to leave. Once they did, there wouldn't be much of an opportunity to turn back.

The plan set by the generals was to punch straight through to the capital, where they would either capture it or die trying. They didn't know how many demons there were in the capital or surrounding towns, but the army was as strong as it was ever going to get, while the demons could only get stronger. Zalia already knew that they had some way of bringing more of them from Cormaine, as the obsidian-skin demon hadn't come over during the initial ritual.

That was the main source of motivation for the seemingly reckless plan. It was now or never.

The army gathered, down about five hundred soldiers—those who were staying behind, to protect this centre point. Another large caravan would have left the army camp further back west not long after the main army contingent had. This would be protected by similar enchantments, a strange oval contraption carried by beasts of burden, with a unit of healers to ensure the people survived whatever remaining corruption leaked in. It wouldn't have worked for the main army; the size of the contraption needed to accommodate the number of soldiers was just unrealistic. For smaller caravans though, it would do just fine.

With Boreal by her side, Zalia moved to the protected section behind the vanguard, where Faian and Ballast were.

They left Et's Way, Zalia peripherally curious about who exactly Et was, and headed again for the capital.

Without much to do, Zalia began practising her wood manipulation. She hadn't had to watch where she was stepping for quite some time now, her subconscious more than capable of managing that for her. If she continued growing the mental attributes, would there be many more things that she didn't actively have to do?

In a way, that theory somewhat held up when considering Ascendant beings. The way they acted was very much in tune with their nature, as far as she had seen. The starlight wolf had acted like the stars, guiding, showing the way in darkness, giving hope. What if it had just been doing all of that subconsciously, not actively? It was interesting to consider.

She made a little wooden sculpture of Delphi, separating it from the main chunk of wood and storing that away. It wasn't the best, but after a little bit of work, it was passable. She showed it to Boreal, who sniffed at it, nuzzled it, then continued walking.

With slightly lower numbers, Zalia had a little easier time maintaining the wider aura of Healing Presence. She had to be careful with it, she found, as it could be a strain on her to allow it to act on its own. When it was at the limit of its distance, which it reached if she wasn't paying attention, it exhausted her much quicker than when she actively kept it restrained. It felt like it should be the opposite, but she put it down to her theory about the subconscious. Perhaps she was pushing it to its maximum distance subconsciously, causing that greater strain unintentionally.

Either way, it was manageable at a distance of a few hundred metres, enough to cover the length of the army. She wanted to play around with shaping it some time, to make it into an oval or square, rather than the circle it was now.

It was a few hours before a small commotion drew Zalia's attention from her thoughts. Towards the front of the vanguard, Hildebrandt blasted an undead into mist. It seemed to be alone, just a single undead out in the wilderness. Nevertheless, Faian stopped the army and sent scouts out all around them, looking for the source of it. According to their maps, there wasn't any town close to this place.

When the scouts found nothing, they put it down to the undead wandering this far from Et's Way.

A short half an hour later, they found another. Perhaps forty minutes after that, two more. It happened once more twenty minutes after that. At this point, Faian didn't stop the army for the disturbances anymore.

Very soon, it just became a normal occurrence to them. Every now and then, they would come across one or two undead that were just wandering about the wilderness. Often, they were blown into a fine mist by Hildebrandt before anyone else could react.

One day of travel turned to two, then three. The undead wandering about the wilderness became more common and more numerous. Groups of four or five began appearing, often within ten to twenty minutes' walk from each other.

The capital was looming over them now, half a day's walk away across flat plains. There was no doubt in any of their minds that they had been seen at this point, the tension and worry amongst the army building ever higher.

Everyone was preparing themselves for a large-scale battle similar to how Et's Way had been. Most were silent, though a select few turned to constant joking about to relieve their tension. Zalia had to focus everything she had on holding back the aura. Even this far out, it was strong enough that she almost couldn't handle it. It wouldn't be long before they would have to reveal their secret, before Ro would have to use his own aura to hold back the corruption.

They didn't know what would happen to the undead if Ro was able to neutralise the thousand-eyed one's aura, but Zalia suspected they would react to Endaria's normal air much as they reacted to her own aura.

Today was the day they began their assault on the capital. Faian and Ballast were constantly in one conversation or another, making plans.

She hadn't been told everything yet, but Zalia did know that her role in it all was to stand amongst the army, using her aura to heal and protect them as much as she could. Ro would fight the thousand-eyed one, and assuming everything went well, would then help eradicate the demons after that. If he struggled to take it down, Hildebrandt would need to leave the army to help destroy it. They would just have to defend themselves from the undead as well as they could while that happened.

Unlike in Et's Way, the entire army would be in a single group. They should be able to last against the undead for longer than just the vanguard by themselves were able to. They were strong, for sure, but just simply didn't have the killing power that the area specialist units did. Mages and archers with abilities focused on area attacks would be invaluable in this fight.

Zalia wasn't quite sure why the generals didn't use them to help the vanguard during the fight. Maybe they felt it wasn't worth exposing the entire army to the horror directly, or wanted them as rested as possible for the attack on the capital.

While Et's Way, a relatively large town by the scale of this world, had a population of just over thirty thousand at last count, the capital greatly outscaled that with a population of upwards of two hundred and fifty thousand. Two hundred and fifty thousand against perhaps five thousand soldiers. They weren't the worst odds in the world, when you thought about the considerable difference in power between the undead and the soldiers in the army. These were Bronze and Silver rank trained soldiers, while their opponents were mostly Tin and Iron rank mindless undead without any abilities at all.

There was, however, also the rest of the army that had fought for the king.

During the early days, when the Morning's Shade had gotten involved, the king had run a recruitment drive for the army, conscripting many of the young men and women from around the lands. Those had just been farmers and other non-combatant types for the most part, yet there had been quite a few of them.

Those soldiers, if they were even still alive and not undead by now, would be armed and armoured. That would make them a considerable threat.

There were also the city's walls to take into consideration.

Ro had promised that he would be able to break a hole in the wall for them to begin the battle, which would create a choke point they could use against the undead. Then, he would go off to fight the thousand-eyed one and they would hold that point as long as they needed to clear out the city.

There had been an argument amongst the leaders that sending in Ro-ak alone to take out the thousand-eyed one first would be a better idea, yet in the end, they agreed that being as close as possible to provide backup if needed was the better way to go about it.

That was what Zalia had picked up by standing there, listening as much as she could manage. There were a million more specific details she just couldn't keep straight. Troop placements, how to react to various situations that could arise and all other sorts.

They stopped for a rest about two hours' march from the city. There was still no reaction from the demons, no countering force sent out to attack or intercept them. Just the odd undead here or there, wandering the plains.

Zalia was struggling. She was struggling a lot.

Holding back the corruption had become so hard that she lay on Boreal's back, too concentrated on her task to even walk anymore. She had to hold out, just a bit longer. When they reached the city, then she could let go of her aura and focus on the fighting.

The army enchanters, now much smaller in number than before, rushed about trying to get the protection against the corruption up and running. Zalia waited impatiently, panting, sweating and in a weird kind of pain as they worked.

It felt like her soul was on fire, like the mental or . . . magical strain of what she was doing caused a different kind of damage. It was like what had happened when she spent almost a week consecutively running. A not-quite-there pain that wasn't in her body.

It took the enchanters half an hour, but they got the protection up. Zalia was able to breathe properly and even relax slightly under the significantly lessened pressure.

Faian began sending out messages to unit leaders, explaining their battle plans in detail, going over exactly what each unit would need to do and what their role in the coming battle would be.

Ro-ak stood nearby, silent as ever, but watching the capital intently.

The red haze over the top of the wall was moving ever so slowly like it had finally sensed them and was waking from its slumber. Or perhaps they had only just gotten close enough for it to care about them.

It was only ten more short minutes before they packed up the barrier and Zalia had to strain against the aura once more. Pain wracked her as it smashed down like a physical force, but she held on.

Ro looked at her in concern, but she waved him off. She *could* hold it, she *would*, as long as she needed to.

They began marching towards the capital.

The time to retake Endaria had come.

CHAPTER SIXTY

Fight for the Capital

Zalia

Zalia managed to hold back the corruption for another hour before it became too much. Her own power shuddered, then collapsed under its oppressive power. The entire army came to a stop, some falling to their knees, others still standing, all in pain as their inner beings were attacked.

It only took a few seconds before Ro-ak's power was released, a warm, earthy blanket spreading across the land. Soldiers all around her slowly recovered, yet many of them looked shaken. She had been holding back the power, using Hildebrandt's presence as a post to hold herself up against. The rock-in-a-river aura that she emitted was the only reason Zalia had been able to hold out as long as she had.

Faian had the army back up and moving in short order, but stared towards the capital with concern. They were still an hour's walk away, and there was yet to be a response.

Zalia managed to push herself to a sitting position, quickly recovering now that she didn't have to hold back the power of an Ascendant being any longer. She wished she could have gotten them all the way to the city wall, but hadn't expected to.

Turning to Ro-ak, she could tell he was doing much better than she had.

"Ro, what's happening? Can you feel what they're doing in there?"

The release of his power had turned him back to his natural form, that of a crow with leaves for feathers and a hood made of vines. His legs were that of tree trunks, feet made from roots.

"I can feel the panic in the thousand-eyed one's aura. It did not know I was here. It has blocked me from seeing within the city, yet I feel it is preparing to react."

That got the attention of both generals, and Faian began immediately sending out orders. They would be able to send out scouts with the possibility of discovering something now that Ro's aura was protecting such a larger area of space. His aura felt somehow similar to Zalia's own, not the same, but like it was a relative.

A few groups of people split off from the army, running towards the city. They looked scared, yet as they watched, a few undead wandering nearby died under Ro's power. They fell apart in strips before collapsing to the dirt. Various plants grew from their bodies, sped up by Zalia's now unhindered aura.

"Preparing to react how?" Faian asked.

Ro's power-filled gaze turned to Faian, and she flinched despite herself. It was one thing to talk to Ro in the form he had been holding to attract less attention, it was another to see him with his power out on display. He was yet to release it fully, something he would only do when in combat with the thousand-eyed one. Zalia still remembered her first contact with an Ascendant, the starlight wolf. She had come out of that shaking.

"I cannot tell the exact details. I only know that it means to act, somehow. To an Ascendant, their aura is their being. Some creatures like this one never learned to hide away their intentions from their aura, rather using it as a means of intimidation. It means to scare us."

Faian nodded, then turned back to their march.

As they got closer to the dark, looming walls of the capital, the tension in the army could be felt like a bowstring ready to snap. Soldiers put worry, fear, and anxiety behind stoic, determined expressions. More undead bunched around the base of the wall, some turning to move towards the army. Many of the undead from all around the fields were beginning to approach them now, though they fell to Ro's power soon enough.

Ten minutes from the wall, they saw the large metal gates of the city swing outwards.

Faian immediately called a stop, waiting to see what would come through. They had planned to break through the city wall, but it didn't look like they would get the opportunity now.

A flood of undead burst out of the city, some tripping and the others rolling over them like a tide. They started filling the plains, so great in number that it was hard to stand their ground.

Ballast gave the order, and the army reacted.

The whole army rotated as one to face the incoming wave. The vanguard put down shields, building the wall of steel that would be their first line of defence.

Earth mages began excavating deep ditches in front of the vanguard as well as to the sides and behind the army. Walls were soon added to those, units of lighter-armoured mages and archers rushing to fill up the tops.

Two units of soldiers took flight, wielding bows and air magic.

Zalia joined them, while Boreal went to join a group of legionnaires, the soldiers there looking a little emboldened to have a fearsome fighter like her by their side.

The few administrative people still with them, the ones Faian couldn't do without, went to the very centre of their fortification, with a stone structure built around them. This had been one of the alternate outcomes that they had planned for, evident by the quick and orderly way they reacted.

The majority of the army had to stay within the walls, out of sight. Each wall had small gaps for the soldiers to sling spells and arrows out of, with the legionnaire units on both flanks.

A fiery and vengeful, yet protective presence spread across the battlefield as Hildebrandt took her stance at the very front of the vanguard, activating Stand Your Ground.

Then, they waited.

Zalia realised she wasn't breathing at all and forced herself to take a deep, steeling breath as she watched the endless flow of undead spilling from the gate.

The few enchanters they had with them were rushing about the edges of the army, inscribing quick and imperfect runes into the walls.

From over the city walls came a horde of flying demons.

Ro flew high above her and the archers she was with, growing in size. He doubled, then tripled his previous form, his aura similarly growing in strength.

In the distance, up the hill that the capital was built upon and at its peak, the thousand-eyed one lifted up from the castle there.

It flew at speed on demonic bat wings lit with a dark flame towards Ro, who held his ground above the army.

The horde of undead began melting away from the combined powers of Ro, Hildebrandt, and Zalia. Still, they came, the aura of corruption around them building as their numbers increased, protecting them more and more.

The auras of the two Ascendant beings intermixed and overlapped, warring with each other before they clashed. While the earth and air around the army were still, it felt as if the very world was being shaken and torn apart to their magical senses.

Spells and arrows flew from the walls. Large chunks of earth ripped themselves from the ground and crushed chunks of undead. Swaths of flame followed, chased by a storm of various other elemental spells and abilities.

Zalia released her own arrows, quick sharp lines of brilliant light showing their path as they punched through countless undead each. She need not even aim, as the mass of undead was such a big target that the arrows' tracking abilities found their own marks. Instead, she focused on releasing arrows as quickly as she was able.

The horde filled the pits made by the earth mages, slowing their charge, before smashing into the vanguard with the sounds of groaning metal, grunts of straining people, and weapons stabbing. Hildebrandt swung at blurring speeds, her mace sending out bolts of energy that tore apart entire sections of the undead. A huge explosion rocked the field as she let off Explosive Force.

Zalia and her unit had to turn their attention to the swarm of flying demons, the small ones of Tin and Iron rank. They shot down as many of the approaching swarm as they could, many of the ranged soldiers down in the square below turning their spells to the new threat as well.

Above it all, the thousand-eyed one let out a terrible screech as it clashed with Nateysta. Deep, resonant, booming sounds echoed down from the battling titans, the physical fight a shadow to the deeper fight that could be seen only with magical senses. The sheer force of the clashing Ascendants sent many of the flying demons tumbling, allowing Zalia and the other flying units a little more room. Soon though, the demons were upon them.

Zalia had to focus her attention entirely on her own battle as the flying soldiers switched to long, thin swords. They performed expert aerial maneuvers as they fought the demons, cutting them down with precise strikes.

The demons scratched and tore at her armour as she flew and dodged, never stopping, constantly swinging. Each strike cut one or two of the demons in half, yet there were always more to replace them. Some started latching on to her, but she quickly disposed of each of them. They were pushed lower and lower in the air, trying to keep close to each other. Zalia cut a demon off one of her allies' backs, and another of the flying soldiers cut down a demon that had been going for her head. A few of the flying soldiers were taken down by swarms of the demons, though were quickly rescued as they fell into the army below.

The earth mages opened a hole in the flanks as two legionnaire units rushed out of each side. One was led by Larel, each punch an explosive force sending undead tumbling through the air, the other led by Boreal, who pounced with precision, ripping apart several undead in a few short moments. Her icy magic spread through the enemy, slowing them down and freezing them to the ground.

The legionnaires threw javelins with incredible strength, the rain of weapons sending the entire front of undead sprawling. They followed up Boreal and Larel with their spears, stabbing in quick and precise movements. They were fast, each of the soldiers' abilities focused on their physical strength and speed. The undead barely had time to react to the strike.

Zalia dropped lower and started using Hunter's Mark to spread her cursed flame through the flying demons. The high-pitched screeching that ensued was loud enough to cause her pain, the flaming demons knocking into others and setting each other aflame.

Soon, there were dead and dying bodies dropping from the air like tiny flaming meteors.

Not a moment too soon, the enchanters finished their work and a weak shuddering energy formed a dome above the army. Zalia thought the falling demons would shatter it, but the dome grew stronger by the moment, the enchanters down below working hard to fix the flaws in their design.

As quickly as they had left, the flanking strike units retreated back within the walls, quickly shored up by the earth mages waiting. They had done their job, taking some pressure off the vanguard for a moment.

The battlefield stopped as a vine that must have been twenty metres wide grew from the ground in an instant. It smashed through the undead, reaching upwards and impaling the side of the thousand-eyed one. Zalia looked upwards as the thousand-eyed one summoned a dark, roiling flame that burnt down the vine, the scorch mark down the vine reflecting on Nateysta's own body. His wide wings beat heavily, blowing the thousand-eyed one back as their struggle continued.

It was in that brief pause that Zalia saw a bunch of demons grouping up further away from the army. There must have been a few hundred of them, of the type that Zalia was all too familiar with. With her bettered eyesight, thanks to many different enhancing effects, she was able to see the obsidian-skinned demon at their fore.

CHAPTER SIXTY-ONE

Reclaimed by Nature

Zalia

Zalia stared wide-eyed at the demon, flashes of memory passing through her mind. Torture as her body was decayed and healed in a constant cycle, their fights, the loss of hope she had felt. The death of Delphi. Now that creature was here to stop them from freeing the capital.

The smaller flying demons pulled back for a moment to stop the spread of her cursed flame.

She initiated mental communication with General Faian below.

"There is a group of higher-ranked demons gathering. We might need to pull Hildebrandt to respond to them once they get here."

All she got was a simple acknowledgement before the lower-ranked Tin and Iron demons began their attack again.

Bow in hand, she shot several arrows in quick succession. Each shot cut down three or four of the low-ranked demons, piercing with enough power to continue onwards. It wasn't long before she had to switch to her sword once more, the sheer number of demons overwhelming them.

They got low enough that Hildebrandt's aura began to burn away at the demons' flesh, giving Zalia and the two flying units a little room to breathe. At the city walls, the obsidian-skinned demon began to fly towards the army. Zalia hoped Faian would have some response to it.

Far overhead, Nateysta bit onto one of the thousand-eyed one's wings with his beak and ripped it off. The large flaming wing scorched his face before Nateysta whipped his head around, throwing it into the air. Their fight became a spiralling descent as the thousand-eyed one dropped. One of its spiked limbs pierced through one of Nateysta's tree-trunk legs, dragging him down with it.

Another explosion rocked the field below them as Hildebrandt continued her devastating attacks, dirt, stone, and flesh raining down across the battlefield.

Zalia didn't want to use Nature's Wrath just yet, but had no choice as they began to get overwhelmed by the flying demons. She activated it, and two wind elementals formed by her sides. Down below, a large chunk of the undead stopped as they were grasped by barbed roots growing from the ground. Moving above the rest of the flying soldiers, she summoned a whirlwind of air, slowly filling it with fire until a firestorm raged above, pulling in the low-ranked demons and scorching them to ash. It grew stronger as Zalia funnelled power into it, and she only stopped once her mana began to drop low.

The horde of Tin and Iron ranked flying demons were now thinned out, and the remainder of the creatures began to flee as the effects of Hildebrandt's aura and Zalia's wrath became too much for them.

Unfortunately, the group of higher-ranked ones had arrived.

"Watch out!" she screamed.

But it was too late as they teleported amongst the flying soldiers all at once, many of the men and women not responding quickly enough as swords, daggers, and claws found spines, throats, and heads. Many of the soldiers died immediately.

Zalia found herself face-to-face with a Bronze demon as she spun about and attacked. She was used to this strategy, having faced it many times.

She parried a strike, using the burst of speed to strike back immediately. Her attack, filled with the power of the stars, struck and slashed through the demon's arm, then continued halfway through its torso. It flailed at her with its other arm, flying backwards to pull itself off her blade, but she continued the attack. With a flap of her wispy air wings, she lunged forward and skewered it through the throat.

It made a gurgling sound as she drew the blade out, letting it drop from the sky.

A quick check on the rest of the flying soldiers found them in chaos. Any sense of formation had been lost as everyone engaged in one-on-one or one-on-two fights. Arrows and magic flew up from the army below, evening the odds for the outnumbered soldiers.

Without a second to waste, Zalia pushed into the fray. She saved a soldier by stabbing the demon he was fighting in the back, just as it was about to rip out his throat. He died a moment later to a dagger straight through to his heart. There was no chance to save him, the anti-death measure of Healing Presence having been used long ago at the start of the battle.

The dagger the demon wielded left it at a disadvantage to Zalia, and she avenged the man, cutting down his killer with three quick, brutal strikes.

Looking for her next opponent, one found her as the obsidian-skin demon dropped down at her from above. She managed to swerve out of the way at the last moment, deflecting its clawed hand and striking back, scoring a thin line down its shoulder.

It made a hissing sound at her, and she hissed back.

Obsidian grew from its shoulders and ripped off, forming four floating jagged spikes. She watched them warily, then flew backwards as quickly as she could. They sped after her, controlled by the demon.

She flew past a few battling duos before grabbing a demon from behind and spinning it around to face the oncoming spikes. One of them impaled the demon, getting stuck halfway through its body.

Zalia teleported away in the same instant, watching for the spikes. She saw them, three still chasing her as they dodged around other fights. With a quick check to her mana, she could see that she was almost out. She would need to drop down to the ground to allow it to recharge; the constant drain of Flight was quickly depleting it.

Without any other choice, she was about to fly down to the ground when a power radiated across the field, originating from Faian. It wasn't warm and comforting like her own healing, rather, it felt like pure energy. Resolve filled her body and her mana recharged. She felt fresh again, as if the fight had just begun.

It wasn't a moment too soon as the three obsidian spikes found her again. Rather than dodge them, she activated Protection of the Wilds. She chose Zephyr as the enhancing effect to the shields, and every member of the army was covered in an ethereal shield enhanced with the power of wind. It felt as if a whirlwind had whipped up around the army, yet none of their members were affected.

She used the moment to launch her own attack on the obsidian-skin demon. Ignoring the spikes that left three deep grooves in her new shield, she sped up to it and struck. Each of her blows were blocked easily but she didn't give up.

Nearby, Nateysta and the thousand-eyed one crashed to the ground with a deafening boom, crushing thousands of undead beneath them. Their struggle for supremacy continued, wings beating, spiked limbs stabbing, and bodies rolling about over the earth, crushing even more undead. Zalia only hoped the colossal fight didn't roll over the army.

In short moments, her shield was broken by the Silver ranked demon. It grabbed her arm and kicked her in the chest, ripping the arm from its socket as she tumbled away through the air, screaming in pain.

She could see the fervor and excitement on its face. It had enjoyed torturing her before but wasn't going to let her live this time.

The smirk vanished as the demon was blasted into mist by a bolt of power sent from below.

There Hildebrandt stood, facing upwards as she sent bolts smashing through the demons above. She ignored the undead for a short time as Zalia's protective shield kept each member of the vanguard safe from the undead.

Zalia felt a morbid sense of satisfaction at seeing the obsidian-skinned demon vanish like that.

A pained screech resounded across the battlefield as Nateysta summoned more vines that stabbed through the thousand-eyed one's body. Dark flames rolled across the battlefield, scorching Nateysta and the undead alike, but he didn't let go, summoning more vines as his beak closed on one of the creature's legs. He tore that off too, clawing at the demon's body with his large, jagged, root claws.

The thousand-eyed one screamed, struggling in pain as it did whatever it could to survive. The battlefield was set alight, the army thankfully just out of reach, as its three remaining legs stabbed at Nateysta. Its one wing flapped in desperation trying to get it off the floor beneath the stronger nature spirit.

Despite the flame and sharp legs of the thousand-eyed one, Nateysta didn't let up. He tore at it with vine, claw, and beak until its mad scramble for survival finally stopped.

The corrupting aura that was laid across the land slowly faded away, replaced by Nateysta's own.

Nature had reclaimed its rightful place in this world.

Across the battlefield, all the undead streaming out of the city dropped to the ground, finally dead, as the power that had kept them animated was no longer present. The rest of the demons tried to flee, but were quickly blasted away by Hildebrandt as she threw bolts of power from the ground.

Just like that, the battle was over.

Zalia dropped from the air and found her way to Boreal. It looked like the flanking units had left the walls to fight the undead once more when she had activated Protection of the Wilds, and Boreal had a long gash down her side. Zalia focused all of her healing on Boreal and herself, as the gash healed over and her own arm regrew.

She dropped down and hugged Boreal tightly. They had survived the battle. There was a lot to do still, to help Endaria rebuild, to take the fight to the Astar and Cormaine, but for now, they had survived.

As tempted as she was to just open up her vault and go pass out, Zalia felt surprisingly fresh. Whatever ability Faian had used was quite powerful, something she should have expected from a general.

Soon enough, Faian had the army mobilised once more.

They marched their way past the countless bodies and to the city gates. They had to spend a while clearing out a passage there, as the number of undead that had been squashed up against the walls trying to get through the gates could be described as nothing other than horrific. It was a pile, tens of thousands crushed into one large mass of bodies.

They managed to get through and into the city eventually, greeted by the sight of more undead, the smell of rot and disease filling the air. Despite all that, it was silent.

The silence was somehow more disturbing than the undead. This was the capital of a kingdom, and as such, it should have been noisy, filled with the sounds and smells of life. Only death and its accomplices waited for them here.

They advanced cautiously through the city, the vanguard at the fore and scouts roaming through the buildings and streets nearby. Faian called a halt as they heard a scream of fear and pain from the direction one of the scouts went. She quickly gestured for a unit of legionnaires to investigate, and they ran towards the screams.

Sounds of battle quickly followed before the legionnaires came back, dragging the body of a feline-like demon, the same type that had killed Aylie's family.

General Ballast got one of the army's telepaths to inform the other scouts of the danger, but it was too late, as they started hearing other sounds of battle amongst the narrow streets and tall buildings. Zalia poked Boreal to get her attention and told Faian she was going out there, then the two of them sprinted off amongst the maze-like city. It didn't take long for them to find some of the demons.

They ambushed one together, Boreal jumping it from behind and grabbing its neck in her powerful jaws. Zalia shot it in the head just as Boreal twisted, a savage *snap* resounding in the alleyway. They continued onward quickly, finding more and more of the creatures.

They battled through the city, almost always finding the demons roaming by themselves like solitary hunters.

They ran across a group of legionnaires who were doing the same thing and both went their separate ways after killing two of the demons that attacked them. Unfortunately, one of the legionnaires went down in the attack.

Zalia and Boreal found fewer and fewer demons and eventually decided to go back. They sped up again when they got close enough to hear the sounds of battle coming from the army's location. They arrived to chaos.

The army had found the human garrison of the city: the maddened soldiers. They were fighting in the main road with skirmishes happening throughout the adjacent alleys and streets. The bulk of the army was under constant attack from the feline demons as they ambushed them from house doors, windows, roofs, streets, and alleys. No avenue of entry was safe.

On the rooftops near the enemy army were archers raining chaos down amongst Faian's people who were desperately trying to erect any kind of barriers they could.

Zalia cast her flight ritual and then ran through a wall using her armour's incorporeal ability. She flew straight up through the roof and unleashed three arrows in quick succession, dropping three enemy archers. Each shot gave her invisibility and a boost in speed as she flickered in and out through the air, sending off more arrows towards more archers. Most of them turned their attention to her, and she was soon having to dodge more than she could shoot. A quick ritual using Zephyr major and Dodge-vine minor gave her a powerful shield against ranged attacks. The arrows shot in her direction were pushed away from her body, though some still hit. A few of the arrows simply passed through her due to her incorporeal nature when wearing the armour, but some of them were obviously magically imbued as they were deflected by her armour.

She twisted in the air, dropping another two archers with arrows to the head, an arrow from return fire striking her shoulderplate and shattering.

Boreal jumped from the shadows and ripped that archer from the rooftops.

The battle down below was going better now, the earth mages amongst the army having managed to close off a lot of the entry points the feline demons were using.

As the flying units in the army realised Zalia was taking down a lot of the archers, they flew up to join her in finishing the job. It wasn't long before they now had the high ground, pelting the enemy army with arrows and spells from above.

The army began to advance, pushing the enemy up the hill with earth mages blocking side entries as they advanced. A few of the enemy soldiers began to flee, and soon the rest of them broke. Only a few stayed to the last, dying with sword in hand.

They marched up to the castle at the top of the hill. There, the large gardens outside the front of the castle had been crushed beneath the weight of the thousand-eyed one. As Nateysta joined Zalia there, though, the land began to thrive once more. A wilder garden grew from the remains of the old.

They left most of the army there as they began constructing hasty fortifications. There were still enemies in the city, even if they had been severely cut in number. A few of them went inside the castle—the smaller Nateysta, still scorched and covered in wounds, Zalia, Boreal, Hildebrandt, Larel, the generals, and some advisors, including Indis.

They went to the throne room, where the skeleton of the king, crown upon his head, sat on his throne. There was no undeath in the body, only the peaceful rest of the dead. Nearby, Zalia found the body of Darren, Juniper's son. She didn't know if he had any part in the events leading up to this, but thought he deserved a better fate. Juniper had been lost in her own grief and had done things others would not have because of it. Darren had still been young, though, without much experience of life.

But what was done was done. Now they had to look to the future.

Zalia stood up from where his body lay and moved over to where Indis knelt on the floor, tears streaming down her face as she looked at the body of the king. The man she had done so much for, the man she should have married, had the demons not invaded.

Zalia shook her head, then went back outside. Looking over the horizon, she could feel where Ember, and Aylie, who was with her, were waiting.

She had her own family that needed her.

About the Author

Leif Roder is the author of the Hunting and Herbalism series, originally released on Royal Road. They studied both aeronautics and software engineering before quitting university and moving abroad, where they began writing books on their phone while on the bus on the way to work. This eventually turned into a full-time career as an author. Now, they write all kinds of fiction, from fantasy to sci-fi with a sprinkling of magic to short stories about cats. They also enjoy a little wall climbing and archery as a treat. Roder lives in New Zealand.